The Regency

LORDS & LADIES
COLLECTION

*Two Glittering Regency
Love Affairs*

A Poor Relation
by Joanna Maitland
&
The Silver Squire
by Mary Brendan

The *Regency*

LORDS & LADIES
COLLECTION

The *Regency*

LORDS & LADIES
COLLECTION

Joanna Maitland &
Mary Brendan

MILLS & BOON®

All the characters in this book have no existence outside the imagination of the author, and have no relation whatsoever to anyone bearing the same name or names. They are not even distantly inspired by any individual known or unknown to the author, and all the incidents are pure invention.

First published in Great Britain 2005 by
Harlequin Mills & Boon Limited,
Eton House, 18-24 Paradise Road, Richmond, Surrey TW9 1SR

THE REGENCY LORDS & LADIES COLLECTION
© Harlequin Books S.A. 2005

The publisher acknowledges the copyright holders of the individual works as follows:

A Poor Relation © Joanna Maitland 2001
The Silver Squire © Mary Brendan 2000

ISBN 0 263 84574 5

138-1105

Printed and bound in Spain
by Litografia Rosés S.A., Barcelona

A Poor Relation
by
Joanna Maitland

Joanna Maitland was born and educated in Scotland though she has spent most of her adult life in England or abroad. She has been a systems analyst, an accountant, a civil servant, and director of a charity. Now that her two children have left home, she and her husband have moved from Hampshire to the Welsh Marches, where she is revelling in the more rugged country and the wealth of medieval locations. When she is not writing or climbing through ruined castles, she devotes her time to trying to tame her new house and garden, both of which are determined to resist any suggestion of order.

Readers are invited to visit Joanna's website at www.joannamaitland.com

Chapter One

'Carriage stopped up ahead, m'lord.'

Lord Amburley did not spare a single sideways glance as he took his curricle past the stationary vehicle at the gallop and raced towards the bend in the wooded road.

'M'lord—' The groom made a move to look back.

'Keep your eyes on the road ahead, Brennan,' said the Baron sharply.

Brennan gave a grunt of surprise and turned to stare at his master, but Lord Amburley clenched his jaw grimly, ignoring the unspoken question. A moment later, they had rounded the curve and the groom was grabbing wildly for the side of the curricle, as the team was brought from headlong gallop to steaming halt in the space of a few yards.

'M'lord—' began the groom, sounding agitated.

'Keep your voice down. If he realises we've stopped, we'll never take him by surprise.' Lord Amburley reached under the seat with his free hand as he spoke. 'What are you waiting for?' he added in an exasperated whisper. 'Go to their heads, man. I've got my hands full as it is.' Extracting a pistol from its hiding place, he jumped down and started to make his way cautiously into the trees that now hid the curricle from the carriage.

Just before he disappeared into the thick cover, Lord Amburley threw a final instruction over his shoulder. 'Get the other pistol, Brennan. That ruffian may well be armed—and he may have accomplices, too. If you hear any shots, bring the curricle back up the road—at the double. And don't be afraid to shoot if you have to.' He did not wait for a reply. He knew his groom would obey his orders to the letter, whatever the risk.

It was probably no more than a few hundred yards to the stationary vehicle, but it took Amburley an infuriatingly long time to pick his way through the neglected woodland. The snap of the smallest twig among the dense leaf litter might betray his presence. And he was determined to retain the advantage of surprise. He had seen only one assailant raising his hand to attack the woman by the carriage, but the man was unlikely to be alone. Since the end of the war, the roads were full of bands of starving, desperate men, preying on unwary travellers, especially women. Nothing could excuse such crimes, in Amburley's view, even though many of the robbers were ex-soldiers, thrown on the scrap-heap by a wickedly ungrateful country.

He crept forward, silently cursing his failure to remove the white driving coat that might so easily betray his presence. He would need to use all the available cover, just as he had learnt to do when he was a soldier in Spain. Pity he had no troop of men at his back, this time.

At last he could see the outline of the carriage through the trees. Taking refuge behind a gnarled oak, he strained his ears. Only one low voice—a woman's—sounding neither distressed nor anxious. Remarkable, in the circumstances. In Amburley's experience, gentlewomen usually had a fit of the vapours at the first hint of danger. Perhaps she was only a servant, after all.

However much he tried, he could not quite make out what the woman was saying. Then he heard a second voice—male, deep, a little hesitant.

Amburley risked a quick glance from his hiding place. There was no one else among the trees. The assailant must be alone. Strange—but certainly welcome. It stacked the odds in his own favour.

Levelling his pistol, he walked slowly towards the stationary vehicle.

As he emerged from the trees, the woman started and gave an audible gasp. Everyone else turned, saw, and froze—the coachman on the box, the groom mounted behind, at least one other female cowering in the dark recesses of the carriage—and the woman's assailant.

Confronted by this petrified tableau, Amburley had

time to wonder why neither coachman nor groom had made any move to overpower a single attacker who—he could now see—was neither young nor strong. The two servants appeared to have left the woman—a plain, worn-looking person of indeterminate age, her face hidden by the poke of her faded bonnet—to fend for herself. Odd, unless—

'Pray, what *are* you about, sir?'

On hearing her educated voice, Amburley's first thought was that this woman must be much younger than he had supposed. And fully in command of herself.

'Would you be so good as to put up that pistol, sir?' A slight edge of annoyance had crept into the shabby young woman's voice. This was surely no mere servant.

Keeping his pistol steady, Amburley half turned from the would-be assailant, who was looking increasingly shifty, as though he might take to his heels at any moment.

'Certainly, madam,' Amburley said evenly, not taking his eyes off the man. 'Just as soon as I have an explanation as to why this man was assaulting you.' He raised his pistol a fraction, so that the man would be in no doubt of his willingness to use it, if he attempted to escape.

The accused man took two steps back, eyes suddenly wide with fear at the sight of the gun's menacing little black muzzle. He made to speak, but no words came out.

The woman moved smartly between Amburley and his target, turning her back on the pistol and putting her hands reassuringly on the older man's arms. 'Don't worry, Jonah,' she said gently. 'I'll deal with this. Nothing will happen to you, I promise.'

She turned sharply then, shielding Jonah with her body. Fixing her gaze on the pistol, she said, in a voice that had lost all trace of gentleness, 'By your speech and your dress, sir, you are a gentleman. So I ask you again to put up your pistol. I have not been assaulted. And I have no need of your assistance.' She glanced up at his face for a second—without meeting his eyes—and then resolutely returned to staring at the pistol. 'Whatever you thought you had seen, sir, you were mistaken. Thank you for attempting to rescue me—but there really was no need.'

With that, she turned her back once more and began to reassure Jonah, who had not yet fully recovered from his fright.

Amburley stood for a moment before letting his pistol hand drop. By gad, she sounded anything but grateful for his attempted knight-errantry. Indeed, she reminded him of his mother's companion—sharp and shrewish, as most poor relations became, given half a chance. What a farce he had blundered into. He had been so sure the man Jonah was about to strike her— but it seemed he had been totally wrong. If his old comrades could see Major Amburley now... For a second or two, annoyance warred with amusement. Then he smiled to himself and shook his head resignedly. Heaven help him if this story ever got about. He would never live it down.

The woman had continued to busy herself with the man Jonah. She seemed to be intent on avoiding any further discussion. 'My apologies, madam,' Amburley said. 'Obviously, you do not stand in need of my assistance. I shall not trouble you further.' Still, she did not face him.

Amburley concluded wryly that he had attempted to rescue a mannerless harpy. Next time he saw a lady under attack, he would do well to drive past, if this was the thanks he could expect. He started back towards the trees but could not resist adding, with exquisite politeness, 'I wish you a safe onward journey. Good day, madam.'

'He's gone, ma'am.' Jonah's voice was a half-strangled whisper.

Isabella Winstanley forced herself to straighten her shoulders. There had never been any danger—so why was her stomach still turning like a frightened child's? And why had she been insufferably rude to a man who was trying to help her? Had she even thanked him? She could not remember. She realised that she had barely looked at him. Would she recognise him if she met him again? He was tall, certainly, and she fancied his hair had been quite dark—but she could not be sure. In the shadow of the trees, the light could play tricks.

'Miss Isabella.' Isabella's abigail, Mitchell, was

pushing open the door of the carriage and sounding agitated. 'Miss Isabella, it's Miss Sophia…'

Isabella took in the situation at a glance. Sophia Winstanley, her pretty but penniless young cousin, had taken one look at the man with the gun and fainted clean away. How ironic. Only two days earlier, Sophia had been rhapsodising about romantic adventures—handsome strangers lurking in shrubberies, or ghosts and hauntings to send shivers down the spine. Sophia had fancied it would be quite agreeable to meet a ghostly apparition—provided, of course, that it drove her into the arms of an eligible gentleman who just happened to be nearby. Poor Sophia. She would never forgive herself, for this gentleman had certainly been eligible.

Heavens, how can I tell that, Isabella wondered, when I hardly know what he looks like? Was there something—?

At that moment, Sophia stirred, groaning. Her eyelids fluttered, and then snapped wide open. Obviously she was remembering the sight of the gun that had terrified her.

'He has gone, Sophia. There is nothing to be afraid of now.' Isabella's voice was gentle and reassuring once again. She reached into her reticule and offered her vinaigrette. 'Try this. It will make you feel better.'

Sophia took a cautious sniff. 'What happened? I don't understand…'

'Neither do I,' said Isabella. 'I can only surmise that, when the gentleman with the pistol saw Jonah hailing the carriage for me, he somehow assumed that I was being assaulted, and so he rushed gallantly to my rescue—terrifying you, and everyone else, in the process. However, he has gone now. And we, too, must be on our way, or we shall be late arriving at the posting house.'

'But, Winny—' began Sophia.

'I must just say my farewells to Jonah,' said Isabella matter-of-factly, ignoring the nickname she had repeatedly asked Sophia not to use. The last thing she wanted at present was a dispute about names—or a host of questions about her would-be rescuer.

'Thank you for your company today, Jonah. I could not have visited such a remote village without your escort—nor achieved half as much with the children without your help. I am only sorry that your kindness should have led to such a scene. It was my fault. I should not have chosen such an isolated spot to meet the carriage, however convenient it might have seemed.' She pressed some coins into his palm and he smiled, revealing a gap in his front teeth. 'You'll take care of those little ones, won't you?'

'Don't you worry, ma'am. No harm will come to 'em, I promise. And a blessing on ye for the help you've given to our poor orphans. Ye're a saint, that's what ye are, and—'

'Jonah,' began Isabella, blushing, 'I am nothing of the sort, as you know very well.' She put one worn black boot on the step of the carriage before the groom could climb down to assist her. 'But thank you, all the same, and God bless you. Goodbye, Jonah.'

Silence reigned in the carriage at last. It had taken Isabella more than half an hour to answer enough of Sophia's questions to pacify her. In the end, Isabella had forbidden all further discussion of it. The gentleman would certainly wish to forget their absurd encounter had ever happened. He was probably mortified by it.

And so was she.

She settled back in her seat once more, trying to focus her attention on the Yorkshire scenery. It was no use. She could not stop worrying about what had happened. She had always taken such care not to be seen in her 'poor relation' guise by anyone from her own station in life—it was the only way of being sure she could keep her philanthropy a secret—and now she had been caught out. Admittedly, the gentleman in question had been a complete stranger, but that could not guarantee her anonymity. If the gentleman came to London for the Season, he was bound to meet her somewhere.

And Isabella would have to be there. Flight was impossible. For she had agreed to chaperon pretty, portionless Sophia for this one London Season so that the child might have a chance of making a good match. Such a promise could not be broken. If they encountered the unknown in London, Isabella would just have to brazen it out, relying on the fact that her usual elegant appearance was a world away from the part she was playing today.

Sophia interrupted Isabella's painful reverie. 'How long will it take us to reach London, Winny dear? I am so looking forward to being at Hill Street again, especially as, this time, I shall be *out*. How many balls do you think we shall attend? Shall I have many partners, do you think? What about—?'

Isabella found herself smiling at Sophia's infectious enthusiasm. 'Sophia, please do stop to draw breath,' Isabella said. 'If you keep asking so many questions all at once, people will think that you are not at all interested in what *they* might say in reply.'

'You mean I talk too much. That's what Mama says,' replied Sophia, without much evidence of remorse. 'I am much more circumspect with people of consequence, I promise. Oh, and Winny—'

Isabella felt she dare not let that pass again. 'Sophia dear, *must* you call me ''Winny''? It's such a very odd name for a lady.'

'But you said that your brother uses it quite often,' Sophia protested. 'You do not really mind, do you?'

'I concede you are merely copying from my quite incorrigible brother—so, yes, I give you leave to continue. But pray,' she added with a laugh, 'not in company. I should not like to be widely known as ''Miss Winny Winstanley''.'

'I shall try to remember,' said Sophia in a small voice, looking down at her clasped hands. After only a moment's silence, she began again, on the subject that Isabella had been hoping to avoid. 'Who do you think he was? The man with the pistol, I mean. Do you think that he—'

'That encounter is not to be discussed,' said Isabella flatly. 'Not with anyone. Do you understand, Sophia?' She waited for the girl's nod of agreement before continuing, 'You must see that it could be disastrous for my reputation—and yours—if it were known that I went about the countryside alone, visiting destitute soldiers and orphans.'

'But you are helping them,' protested Sophia hotly. 'How can that destroy your reputation?'

'My motives would be of no account, I'm afraid. Ladies of the *ton* do not consort with the lower classes—not for any reason. You will learn that they never go anywhere without a servant in attendance, either. And they certainly do not dress like servants.' She glanced down at her drab brown dress and fraying shawl. 'If I were discovered, I would never be admitted to Society again. You must never betray, by so much as a look, that you have seen me like this. Promise me, Sophia!'

'I promise. At least, I promise to try,' said Sophia.

Isabella felt the tension relax in her shoulders. 'I shall be satisfied with that. And now, let us talk of something else.'

'Yes, let's,' said Sophia more eagerly. 'Tell me about your first Season—er—Isabella. Did you have many offers?'

Isabella smiled resignedly. 'I only ever had one

Season, I'm afraid, and no offers, so there is little to tell.'

'But why?'

Isabella shrugged. Although she had avoided telling the story until now—over the years, she had learnt to be content with her single state, but it still hurt too much to discuss the deaths of her parents—she knew that Sophia would pester her until she gave in. 'My Season was cut short because my papa became ill and had to return home,' she said quietly.

'But surely there was no need to pack you all off back to the country?'

'I was only too happy to go, Sophia, I assure you. Mama needed my help to nurse Papa.'

'Oh.' Sophia seemed to have realised, at last, where the story was leading. She sat for a moment, thinking. 'Could you not have had another Season? Later, I mean, when…' Her voice trailed off.

'It suited me to remain on the family estate with my brother, Sophia. He could not run it alone.'

'But surely he runs it alone now,' protested Sophia.

'He is a grown man now—and married. He does not need an older sister looking over his shoulder.'

'Is that why you went to live with Lady Wycham?'

'Partly.' Goodness, the child was certainly persistent. Isabella knew she was going to have to embroider the truth from now on. To the outside world, it was Lady Wycham who had the money and Isabella who was the poor relation. It was a fiction both worked hard to maintain.

'I don't understand,' said Sophia.

Isabella sighed. 'Great-aunt Jemima invited me to join her in Hill Street last year. She would have been alone, otherwise, so it suited us both. I can enjoy as much as I wish of London Society—and she has company about the place. Even more, now that you are joining us,' she added, with a gentle laugh.

'And I shall be as good as gold, I promise,' said Sophia. 'It is so very generous of Lady Wycham to frank my come-out—' Isabella hoped she was not blushing '—and I intend to make her proud of me. Wait and see!'

'I'm sure you will. Aunt Jemima is looking forward to taking you to our French modiste for your new gowns. Your dark colouring is all the crack these days, you know. Fair hair is sadly passé, I'm afraid,' she added with a mischievous glance across at the abigail who spent so many hours arranging Isabella's honey-gold curls. 'Should I cover it with a turban, do you think?'

A moment later, they were engulfed in laughter.

In the late afternoon, the carriage arrived at the Bell in Barnby Moor where they were to spend the night. Isabella alighted first to see that all was in order for her party, leaving Sophia, chaperoned by Mitchell, to make a more leisurely descent. Sophia was just remarking on the unusual degree of bustle in the inn-yard, when Isabella returned, grim-faced.

'It is too vexing,' she declared. 'The rooms that

were bespoke for us are not available, it seems. The inn is full of gentlemen, here for some sporting event about which I did *not* enquire. The landlord appears to have preferred the immediate custom of these *gentlemen* to the prior written instructions of a lady. You will please return to the carriage, Sophia, while I try to resolve matters.'

With firm tread, Isabella returned to the inn to do battle with the landlord for the promised rooms. By the time he eventually appeared, looking hot and flustered, she had been kept waiting for more than ten minutes and her patience had worn extremely thin. Her eyes had lost their usual grey-green calm to become very stormy indeed; her foot was tapping in a rhythm of irritation; and, with her threadbare clothes enhancing the effect, she knew she must appear a veritable harridan. She fully intended to make the most of it in this encounter.

The landlord, however, seemed to be in no mood to acknowledge the justice of her claim. He stated flatly that no rooms were to be had, either in his inn or for several miles around and, furthermore, that the locality was no place for ladies at present, with so large a gathering of sporting gentlemen in residence.

Isabella would have none of it.

Their heated discussion was beginning to attract the attention of the gentlemen assembled in the coffee-room behind her. Isabella could not help but notice that the level of their conversation had become muted as they listened avidly to hers but, driven by the justice of her cause, she would not be deterred. 'Two chambers and a private parlour were bespoke for Miss Winstanley, besides accommodation for the servants. I insist they be provided immediately. If you have been so lax in your duty as to let them to some of these gentlemen, you must simply require them to move elsewhere. I shall wait here until you have made the arrangements.'

By this time, the coffee-room was almost silent. Isabella coloured a little but stood her ground, wondering whether the men now staring at her defenceless back would have been so reluctant to come to her aid if she had appeared in her normal elegant guise.

The landlord was in a quandary. 'I'll ask among the gen'lemen, if you wishes, ma'am, but I don't see as 'ow I can do what you says. T'wouldn't be right.'

'Nor is it right to fail to undertake your commitment to two ladies,' flashed Isabella.

The landlord shrank a little before her fiery look. His hesitant response was forestalled by the arrival of a young gentleman from the inn-yard who immediately said, 'Landlord, you have wronged these ladies. I insist that you look to their needs—immediately!'

Isabella's stormy gaze softened a little at the sight of the young man. His intentions were good, certainly, though they were of little practical help. And the landlord was looking thoroughly mutinous.

The landlord's response was interrupted by movement from the coffee-room—one of the gentlemen there strode out to join the little group in the hallway.

Isabella swallowed a gasp at the sight of that tall dark figure. She recognised it at a glance. Somehow—impossibly—his powerful outline had become deeply etched in her mind.

It was her would-be rescuer—again!

Chapter Two

Isabella found herself confronting an imposing figure, dressed now in immaculate riding dress and top-boots. She was struck by a sternly handsome face, dark eyes of unfathomable depths, and curling black hair that seemed to invite a woman's fingers to touch it. This time, she found she could not drag her gaze from his face. Suddenly, she forgot to breathe.

The newcomer paused for a moment alongside Isabella's frozen figure, raking her from top to toe with a long, appraising glance that seemed to search out every shabby, demeaning aspect of her appearance. She felt as if he had stripped her naked. Then, with a tiny shake of his head, he simply turned away without a word.

Isabella remained motionless, though her heart was pounding now at the extent of the man's disdain. He was dismissing her publicly. But what else could she expect? In the light of her behaviour earlier, it was hardly surprising that he would not even acknowledge her. She wanted to sink.

Isabella thought she saw the merest hint of a condescending smile on his lips when he turned away from her. In a trice, mounting fury had overcome her embarrassment. How dare he treat her so? First, he pretended to be a knight in shining armour, and then he treated her like a...like a common doxy. This was no gentleman. For no gentleman would look at a woman as he had looked at her. The man must be a libertine. A man of his stamp would doubtless prefer to gaze on women with more opulent, and visible, charms. Isabella told herself she was glad of her dowdy appearance if it protected her from a handsome ladykiller. Isabella Winstanley would never have truck with such a man.

She forced herself to assume her normal outward calm, but her wayward thoughts continued to whirl. Her heart was still racing. And the strangest feelings assailed her.

She was still trying to recover her inner composure when the tall gentleman began addressing his friend. 'I had not pictured you in the role of knight errant, Lewiston, I must admit—but I am sure *your* offer will be appreciated.'

Isabella felt the colour rising in her cheeks at the slight but unmistakable emphasis in his words. Her would-be rescuer was clearly determined to make her feel thoroughly ashamed of her earlier behaviour. And he was succeeding.

He did not so much as glance in her direction as he continued, 'I imagine you were about to offer the ladies one of our chambers and our private parlour. And without so much as a "by-your-leave", either,' he added wryly. 'If I were introduced to this lady, I might be more amenable on that subject, you know.'

Isabella was hard put to hide her astonishment. The man now spoke as if he had never set eyes on her before.

Mr Lewiston's relative youth was evident in his response, for he coloured and stammered a little, before admitting that he himself had not yet been introduced to this particular lady.

The tall gentleman immediately took charge of the discussion, turning a sudden and devastating smile on Isabella that did the strangest things to her knees, much as she steeled herself to resist. 'I hope you will forgive my friend's shocking want of manners, ma'am. I gather he very much desires to be of service to your party in your present difficulties…though I do not fully understand what they might be. Perhaps you could explain a little more, Miss…?'

A number of unflattering descriptions arose in Isabella's mind, of which 'dissembler' was probably the least insulting. Unable to voice her opinion of him without lapsing into impropriety, she swallowed her wrath before explaining, in her best poor-relation manner, that she was Miss Winstanley, en route for London with her young cousin, Miss Sophia Winstanley. But she could not resist adding, with a touch

of asperity, 'You are, I fancy, already well acquainted
with the details of our predicament, sir. The landlord's views on our arrival must have been heard by
every one of the gentlemen in the coffee-room.'

She knew she was yielding to her worst impulses
by saying such a thing, but she felt so strange in the
presence of this man. Somehow, she felt impelled to
provoke a reaction from him.

It did not come, because the landlord could no
longer contain himself. He burst into vehement self-
justification. 'My lord,' he began, 'you knows that
this b'aint no place for ladies just now, with so many
sporting gen'lemen staying here. I only—'

Isabella cringed inwardly. Good God—not merely
a libertine, but a peer as well. It was worse and worse.

The landlord's excuses were cut short by the un-
named lord. 'However well-meant your concern,
landlord, the fact remains that rooms were bespoke
for this lady and you have let them elsewhere. Furthermore, it is already too late for any of your guests,
male *or* female, to journey on in search of accommodation elsewhere.' With a sidelong glance at Isabella which confirmed that he had indeed heard all of
her discussions with the landlord, he concluded,
'Since this lady's instructions predate those of the
sporting gentlemen, it is clear that the gentlemen must
make way for the ladies. So, what do you propose,
landlord?'

In truth, the landlord had nothing much to offer,
since all his rooms were taken and it was not in his

interest to offend the free-spending sporting guests. At length he ventured, 'If some of the gen'lemen might be willing to share, summat might be done, p'rhaps. But I don't know…'

'We have already offered the ladies the use of our sitting room and one of our bedchambers.' He looked blandly across at his friend. 'And since Lewiston would not really enjoy sleeping in the stables, he may share my room. That leaves, I think, only one more chamber to find. You can do that, surely, landlord?'

Isabella's senses were reeling. Why should a rake put himself to so much trouble for someone he obviously considered beneath his touch? And someone who had spurned his help once already that day. Perhaps… But no. Doubtless he had caught sight of Sophia—who looked, for all the world, like a pretty young heiress. Just the sort of prey that such a man would seek to fasten on. Pity the hapless female who was unwise enough to fall into his clutches. He was charming, too, no doubt about that. She would not easily forget that devastating smile and its effect on her. She was feeling it still.

Isabella straightened her spine, waiting until she felt sufficiently in control of her emotions to speak. 'You are most kind, gentlemen,' she said, carefully addressing her remarks to the space between the tall unknown and Mr Lewiston. 'I am sure my cousin will agree that she and I share a chamber also. There will be no need for further inconvenience to the guests on that score. I take it the landlord can find accommodation for the servants?'

The landlord readily agreed that he could. Then he fled from the scene, ostensibly to see to the readying of the rooms.

Isabella, now relieved of the immediate worry, felt some sympathy for him. It could not be easy dealing with a forceful lady and an arrogant lord at one and the same time. Arrogant? No, it would be unjust to call him so, however much she might detest his libertine ways. He was simply very firm about what was to be done. His manner was certainly daunting, but he was self-assured rather than arrogant, a man who was used to issuing commands and who expected them to be obeyed. It would probably be unwise to cross him, too, for there was something in his demeanour that suggested ruthlessness as well as strength. He… Enough! What on earth was she about, letting her mind wander so in the hallway of a posting house?

Isabella's tumbling thoughts were interrupted by the arrival of Sophia in her usual tempestuous fashion. 'Winny, dear,' she began, and Isabella's heart sank as she recognised a gleam of sardonic amusement in the tall gentleman's eye, 'Mr Lewiston has so kindly offered to resolve all our problems for us. I have—'

Clearly, Sophia must be stopped before Isabella was even further embarrassed. Her predicament was already wretched enough. 'Yes, I know, Sophia. Thanks to the kind offices of these two gentlemen, we have somewhere to sleep tonight, even if we are constrained to share a bedchamber. My lord,' she added pointedly, 'you must let me make you known to my cousin, Miss Sophia Winstanley. Sophia, this is Lord…'

'Amburley, at your service, Miss Sophia Winstanley,' he continued coolly, as if Isabella had known the name all along. He favoured Sophia with a brief, hard smile and bowed over her hand. Then, turning to Isabella, he took her hand also, adding, with another bow, 'And at yours, Miss Winstanley, of course. The burdens of a companion on a journey such as this are not lightly borne. I hope I may have helped to relieve them in some small way. If there is any other service you require of me, ma'am, please do not hesitate to ask. And now we will leave you. I am sure you will wish to assure yourselves that your accommodation is adequate.' With a further bow, he released Isabella's hand and left them to return to the coffee-room, followed by a rather reluctant Mr Lewiston.

Isabella looked dazedly at her hand. It felt as if it were burning, yet there was no outward sign of heat. Her face, too, felt as if it were on fire. Was this an example of how a rake's practised charm was exercised? She shook her head, vainly trying to clear her disordered thoughts. She longed for solitude so that she might attempt to make sense of what had happened. But, of course, sharing a room with the effervescent Sophia would prevent any opportunity for calm reflection. It was hopeless.

Isabella now wished with all her heart that she had never succumbed to the urge to visit that rural orphanage. It had led her into two encounters with a man who affected her composure as no other had ever done. Not that it mattered, for he clearly regarded her as a poor, used, spinster companion, put upon by all and an object to be pitied. She felt deeply embarrassed and somehow shamed. Her only refuge was in the hope—earnestly felt—that she would never set eyes on Lord Amburley again. She did not see how her injured self-esteem could survive a third meeting.

'You carried that off perfectly, Winny,' said Sophia. 'But for you, we should be sleeping in the stables.'

Isabella smiled weakly in response. At least Sophia had not recognised Lord Amburley.

'Shall we retire to our parlour now?' continued Sophia. 'I so much want to tell you about my conversation with Mr Lewiston.'

Isabella nodded agreement. It would certainly not do to learn Sophia's views about the perfection of Mr Lewiston's figure and address in the hearing of the coffee-room gentlemen. That would be the final humiliation of an absolutely dreadful day. Fortunately, the landlord returned at that moment, and so they were soon ensconced in a comfortable parlour with easy chairs and a welcome blaze in the hearth. With a sigh of relief, Isabella removed her all-concealing bonnet and sank into a chair. Privacy, at last.

'I must tell you, Winny, about my encounter with Mr Lewiston. He must have witnessed our arrival, for he was seeing to his horses in the yard. They are very fine, by the bye, so I collect he must be a rich young man.'

'That need not be so,' interposed Isabella. 'Many a young gentleman of address is deeply in debt and hanging out for a rich wife to solve his problems.'

'I do not believe Mr Lewiston is such a one. How can you possibly suggest such a motive for the young man who helped to rescue us?' Sophia stopped short as the full import of Isabella's words struck home. 'Besides, I am not rich.'

'No, Sophia, you are not rich but, just for the moment, you have every appearance of it. You ride in a fine carriage with an abigail and servants in attendance. Your shabbily dressed cousin is naturally assumed to be your companion, while you yourself are dressed in the latest fashion. No one would guess it is thanks to your own nimble fingers, you know. No, indeed, you seem to have all the outward trappings of an heiress.'

'Oh!' Sophia blushed to the roots of her hair. 'Oh, dear! What shall we do?'

'Nothing. Tomorrow we shall wait until the gentlemen have left before we emerge as ourselves. And even then, I shall ensure that there is not so much difference in my own appearance as to cause comment. Then we can forget all about this unfortunate occurrence…and start preparing for your London Season. We must have you do justice to the Winstanley looks.' Her mischievous smile lit up her eyes.

That final sally was not enough to restore Sophia's spirits. 'But what if we should meet Mr Lewiston or Lord What's-his-name in London? I should die of mortification.'

'If you should meet either Mr Lewiston or Lord Amburley, you will behave as if nothing had happened, my dear. After all, *you* have done nothing, except to be your true self. The imposture, such as it is, has been mine, and *I* shall have to deal with the consequences if we should meet either gentleman again. However,' she added consolingly, 'I do not believe we shall. Although I do not go into Society very much, I have lived in London for almost a year now, and I have not heard of either of them. No doubt they are northern gentlemen who do not come to London for the Season.'

In a bedchamber further along the corridor, Lord Amburley was changing his coat, musing abstractedly on his two encounters with the elder Miss Winstanley. She was remarkably sharp-tongued—but perhaps that was not surprising, considering how shamefully she was treated by her young employer. It was not a fate he would wish on any woman, however poverty-stricken.

His valet's voice intruded insistently. Peveridge

was clearly determined to indulge his irrepressible taste for gossip, now that he had an audience of two. 'Miss Winstanley is a real lady, m'lord, and a considerable heiress to boot, by all accounts.'

'Is she, begad?' said Mr Lewiston, who was reclining at his ease in a chair and nursing a glass in his hand. 'Well, well.'

'Pray do not encourage him, George,' said his lordship. 'I have been trying for years to persuade him out of his reprehensible tendency to gossip, and now you are like to undo all my hard work with a careless sentence or two.'

The valet grinned at Mr Lewiston, as if to say that no amount of effort on the part of Lord Amburley would ever cure that particular malady.

'Come, Leigh, I will have the truth out of you. Are you not at all curious about the circumstances of the lovely Miss Winstanley?'

'I know all I wish to know about that young lady,' countered his lordship. 'She is young and quite pretty, I grant you. If you listen to Peveridge, she is also rich. You could have concluded that yourself from her mode of travelling, without recourse to Peveridge's sources.' Peveridge cleared his throat at this point as if preparing to intervene, but subsided at a warning glance from his master. With barely a pause, his lordship continued evenly, 'Peveridge can no doubt give you detailed information on her family, her financial circumstances and her marital ambitions. I know nothing of those, nor do I desire to. The rich Miss

Winstanley is empty-headed, frivolous and spoilt. No doubt she has been indulged from birth.'

'How can you suggest such a thing, Amburley?' growled Mr Lewiston. 'You yourself admitted you know nothing about her.'

'I know her kind very well. Did you compare the poverty of the poor relation's dress with the expense of the young lady's? The cost of that single fashionable outfit was probably more than the companion receives in a year. And to address her as "Winny"… If there had been the least doubt as to her lowly station in life, that would certainly have settled it.'

'It could be her name, you know. Winifred, perhaps?'

'I take leave to doubt that, George. Did you not notice how she blushed? I believe she was quite put out.' Until the words were spoken, he had not been aware that her reactions had registered with him at all.

'She did seem a little strained, I admit, but I put it down to the difficulties of the situation. However, you went out of your way to be kind to her, I noticed. Indeed, you were much more solicitous to the poor companion than to the lady.'

'Since the lady had you to defend her, my friend, she clearly had no need of me. The companion, by contrast, had no one, not even her charge. She is—' He stopped in mid-sentence. For some reason, he did not feel able to share his assessment of the poor companion, even with his friend. Deliberately, he pushed her shabby image to the back of his mind, before continuing, 'I sought only to allow her to recover her composure a little. If I succeeded, I am glad.'

'You are very much your mother's son,' said Lewiston, after a thoughtful pause, 'with your concern for the poor and disadvantaged. Perhaps you should set up a foundation for impoverished spinsters?'

Lord Amburley smiled enigmatically. 'I have not the means, George, as you know very well—and, in any case, one philanthropist in the Stansfield family is quite enough. My mother does my share, I think—though only among the orphans.' His eyes narrowed suddenly. 'You, by contrast, could certainly afford to support such a worthy cause. Why not adopt your own suggestion?'

'I have not the taste for it,' came the prompt reply. 'I fear I fall into your category of empty-headed, frivolous and spoilt.'

The following morning was wet, which dampened everyone's spirits. Isabella waited anxiously in her chamber for the gentlemen to leave the inn. She had exchanged the hideous brown dress for a simple but modish travelling gown of deep green, which she planned to hide beneath a plain dark pelisse when she emerged. There was also a matching hat, but Isabella would not dare to put it on until she was safely in the carriage and miles from this unfortunate inn. For the present, she would continue to hide her hair completely under the battered brown poke bonnet.

Her main concern now was to avoid any further meeting with Lord Amburley. Until she was sure he had left, she dared not even venture into the parlour, lest he call to see how they did.

She had suffered mortification enough, she told herself. She was resolved to leave without meeting him again, even if she had to resort to ill-manners to achieve it.

Isabella returned to the window to check again on the departure of the gentlemen. To her relief, she saw that the curricle Sophia had described was standing ready in the yard. In spite of her preoccupation, she could not help noticing that the horses were quite as fine as Sophia had supposed. Mr Lewiston had a good eye, then, and might be wealthy after all. What a pity Isabella's actions had ruined everything for Sophia.

The sound of voices in the parlour next door distracted her from this depressing train of thought. Sophia's voice, conversing with a man. Thank goodness Mitchell was present as chaperon, so that Isabella need not join them.

She drew near the connecting door and, without *quite* putting her ear against it, found a position from which she could overhear all that was said. She told herself sternly that it was her duty to listen. Was she not, after all, the guardian of Sophia's virtue?

The voice proved to be Mr Lewiston's. Isabella breathed again.

Mr Lewiston was advising the ladies to delay their

journey until the rain eased. He feared Miss Sophia might catch cold if she travelled in such weather.

'But what of you, sir?' responded Sophia. 'Are you not about to set out for your prize-fight, or whatever it is you are all here to see? I thought I saw your horses standing in the yard?'

'They are Amburley's horses, I am sorry to say,' admitted Mr Lewiston ruefully. 'I should give much to own them.'

'But they are not for sale,' put in a deeper voice.

Behind the door, Isabella smothered a gasp. A shiver ran down her body and she swayed on her feet. Amburley was there, just a few feet beyond the door. And it was all his—horses, wealth, everything. Surely a titled man of means would be bound to appear in London at some stage, whatever reasons had kept him away in the past?

Light suddenly dawned. What a fool she had been! Of course, he must have been with Wellington's army. How could she have missed something so obvious? His bearing, his air of authority, everything about him betrayed the soldier. He would be recently returned from the wars. There must be estates somewhere, she supposed. Oh, she prayed they were a long way from London and in need of his constant supervision. She could not *bear* the thought of meeting him again. A rake—and a hero too, no doubt. There could not be a more dangerous combination.

Chapter Three

Sophia looked around with glowing eyes. 'Oh, Isabella,' she breathed, 'I have never seen such beautiful fabrics. It's…it's like Aladdin's cave.'

'Just wait until you have seen Madame's designs.' Isabella smiled.

Sophia's dark eyes opened even wider, as Madame Florette's elegant black-clad figure re-entered the room, followed by a bevy of attendants carrying yet more bolts of splendid silks. Madame waved them into the background, before inviting the ladies to seat themselves on her delicate spindle-legged chairs.

'*Bien*, mademoiselle.' Madame was beaming at Isabella, no doubt in anticipation of a very large order. 'I am at your service.'

'Come, Sophia, let us make a start by choosing some simple morning dresses.' Isabella smiled encouragingly. 'Madame Florette has impeccable taste. You may trust her judgement.'

'Mademoiselle Winstanley is most generous,' re-

sponded the modiste with a self-satisfied smirk. 'Mademoiselle Sophia will be a pleasure to dress. Such
colouring, such a figure.'

Over the course of the morning, a bewildering collection of gowns was selected for Sophia. Isabella was
glad she had taken pains to ensure that there was no
mention whatever of price, for it was vital that Sophia's feckless parents should not find out how much
was being spent on their eldest daughter. What little
they had was devoted to educating their five sons—
and paying their debts. They did not seem to care that
Sophia and her sisters were destined to become penniless old maids. As a spinster herself, Isabella had
determined that Sophia, at least, should have the best
possible chance of making a good match. And she
was quite prepared to conceal the expense of the Season from Sophia's stiff-necked parents, knowing that
they would welcome a wealthy suitor with open arms.

'And for you, Miss Winstanley,' urged Madame, 'I
have just received the most beautiful jade-green silk
shot with gold. With your colouring, it would make
an exquisite ball-gown.' With an imperious wave of
the hand, she dispatched a hovering attendant to fetch
the bolt of cloth.

The jade and gold silk was irresistible. 'With a
lighter green underdress, mademoiselle, in this aquamarine satin, to bring out the colour of the silk…and
then a gold gauze scarf for your arms.' Madame was
sketching rapidly. 'We will fashion a special orna-
ment for your hair too, I think, to pick up the greens

of the gown and of your eyes. It will look ravishing, I assure you.'

'Isabella, it is too beautiful for words. You must have it, truly.'

Isabella yielded. She knew just how well the gown would become her. Partly as a result of Madame's beautiful creations, Isabella Winstanley could hold her own among the best-dressed women in London. She was now wearing a carriage dress of emerald green, with a jaunty little hat of the same colour perched on top of her honey-gold curls. Even though Sophia's dark colouring was the prevailing fashion, it was Isabella's striking looks that had drawn every eye since their arrival in London.

Isabella was laughing gently with Sophia as they emerged to return to their carriage. Sophia, concentrating on their conversation, failed to notice a gentleman in her path and almost collided with him.

'Oh, I do beg your pardon, sir,' she began. 'Why, it is Mr Lewiston! Oh!' Her face was suffused with the deepest blush, and she began to stammer uncertainly, 'I...I had not thought...to see you in London. I...' Her voice trailed off; she was unable to utter another word.

Mr Lewiston saved her, at least for the moment. 'Miss Winstanley, how delightful to meet you again. I cannot think how I was so remiss as to fail to ask you for your direction in London. I hope you will permit me to call?'

Sophia had no choice but to acquiesce. 'I am staying in Hill Street with my godmother, Lady Wycham,' she said. 'I am sure she would be delighted to meet you.'

'And would you do me the honour of making me known to your companion?' asked Mr Lewiston, casting an appreciative glance at Isabella.

'Com…companion?' stuttered Sophia, suddenly ashen.

'I do not think I have been introduced to this lady,' said Mr Lewiston patiently, ignoring Sophia's apparent want of wits.

Isabella intervened to save the situation. She extended her hand, noting with satisfaction how steady it was. 'I am Isabella Winstanley, Mr Lewiston, a distant cousin of Sophia's. Lady Wycham would welcome a chance to meet you, I am sure. We have heard about your chivalrous rescue of Sophia in the north.'

It was Mr Lewiston's turn to stammer as they shook hands. 'Indeed, ma'am, I…I did nothing more than any gentleman would have done for a lady in distress, I assure you.' Recovering his composure, he continued gamely, addressing Sophia once more, 'I shall call tomorrow, if I may?'

Sophia answered with a smile and a slight nod. She was still incapable of speech. With an elegant bow, Mr Lewiston handed them into the carriage and stood watching as they drove off.

Sophia sank into the cushions, as far as possible from the window. She had turned extremely pale. She sank her head into her hands, pushing her modish new bonnet askew in the process, and began to sob weakly.

Isabella, too, was a little pale, but she despised such missish behaviour. Her keen intellect was busy searching for a solution to their dilemma. Mr Lewiston had not recognised her, she was certain. If she was careful both in her appearance and her behaviour, she could continue to dupe him. She could not afford to fail.

'Do not distress yourself, Sophia,' she said firmly, grasping Sophia's shoulder and giving her a tiny shake. 'He did not know me. Nor will he, if we are careful. I shall continue to act as though he and I had just met, and so shall you. If he should ask after your "companion"—though I dare swear he will not so lower himself—you will say that she is with her family.'

'Oh, I could not,' protested Sophia, trying to dry her tears with a scrap of lace. 'I have not your talent for acting a part. Pray do not ask me to, Winny.' Her voice was quavering; the tears threatened once more.

'But I require you to,' replied Isabella resolutely, giving Sophia a stern look, which stopped the gathering tears immediately. 'Remember, Sophia—what I am asking you to say is no more than the exact truth. "Winny" *is* with her family.' Isabella softened her gaze with a slight smile as she continued. 'However, you *must* now cease to call me by that name. It would certainly betray us.'

* * *

They did not have much time to reflect on the possible horrors of the forthcoming visit from Mr Lewiston, because they were preoccupied with the preparations for Sophia's first party—Lady Bridge's
soirée—that very evening. Although London was as
yet quite thin of company, Isabella had judged it wise
to allow Sophia to make some acquaintances at a few
small gatherings, before launching her into her first
grand occasion.

For this first party, Sophia chose the prettiest of the
evening gowns she had brought from Yorkshire. None
of Madame Florette's creations could arrive for some
days yet, however many seamstresses she might set
to work on them. But Sophia's home-made gown
would by no means disgrace her, since she possessed
real skill both in cutting and in stitching.

'Thank you so much for lending me your pearls,'
said Sophia, as soon as she joined Isabella in the hall.

'You look lovely,' replied Isabella warmly. 'Pink
does indeed become you.'

'While you look quite beautiful,' responded Sophia
promptly, casting admiring glances at Isabella's classical gown of old-gold silk, and the necklace and ear-
rings of intricate gold filigree. 'You look like a princess from a fairy-tale.'

Secretly pleased, Isabella thanked her cousin demurely. 'But you should not say such things, you
know. At my age, I am more likely to be the wicked
witch than the good fairy.'

'Nonsense,' chimed in an older voice. 'You do

yourself an injustice, as ever, Isabella. You look very well indeed, my dear.'

'Oh, Aunt,' protested Isabella. 'How can I retain my countenance, if both of you put me to the blush?'

Lady Wycham ignored that protest completely. 'Come, my dears, the carriage is waiting.' The elderly lady, clad in imposing purple and leaning lightly on an ebony cane, led the way to the steps.

Barely ten minutes after their arrival, Sophia was chattering gaily with their host's two nieces, while the hostess herself was seated by Lady Wycham, enjoying a comfortable coze.

'Will you favour us with some music, my dear?' asked Sir Thomas. 'It is always a delight to hear you sing.'

Isabella inclined her head towards her host and moved to open the pianoforte. First she played a German minuet, its demure rhythm making little impact on the hum of conversation in the salon. Then she turned to a book of Italian songs, accompanying her low, rich singing voice with soft arpeggios. Almost as soon as she started to sing, the level of noise in the room fell, as the guests stopped to appreciate her beautiful voice. Sir Thomas watched her with a beatific smile on his face. Hardly anyone moved.

At the end of three songs, she made to leave the instrument but was met with a chorus of requests for an encore. She felt the warmth of a flush on her cheeks as she nodded her acquiescence. 'Very well,' she smiled, 'but just one more.' Her choice this time was completely different, a sad Italian ballad, which she sang very quietly, but with great expressiveness. The room remained totally hushed until the last note had died away, and then there was a burst of enthusiastic applause.

Isabella felt pleased; she knew she had performed well. She raised her eyes from her music to acknowledge the applause—and looked straight into the hard, dark eyes of Lord Amburley.

For a moment she sat immobile, stunned. How could this be happening? She felt her flush return and deepen under his gaze, while she strove both to regain her composure and to find an escape route from this nightmarish encounter. What could she do? It was so terribly difficult to order her thoughts with his penetrating gaze resting on her face. Had he recognised her, perhaps? Heavens, he was coming over to the pianoforte. She rose hurriedly in an attempt to avoid him, but it was too late. Sir Thomas was before her.

'I think you cannot have met Amburley,' began her affable host. 'He has not been in town for some years. The wars, you know. He arrived a little late this evening but, luckily, in time to hear you sing. May I make him known to you?'

Isabella nodded dumbly, trying to recover control of her decidedly wobbly limbs. Her mind was still in a whirl. Foremost among her thoughts was the awful certainty that he could not possibly be the libertine she had earlier judged him to be. Rakes were not received by the upright Lady Bridge.

'Miss Winstanley,' continued Sir Thomas formally, turning slightly to be sure of including his lordship, 'may I present Lord Amburley?'

'Your servant, ma'am.' His lordship had stopped by the far end of the instrument, Isabella noted, just near enough to avoid being impolite. He now bowed distantly to her, without moving forward to shake hands. 'My compliments on your performance. You have a most…unusual voice.' His voice was cool and expressionless, his manner stiff.

Curtsying politely, Isabella contrived a slight smile which did not reach her eyes. Inwardly, she was suddenly seething, her anger forcibly expelling her earlier weakness. She had been much too generous in her previous assessment of this man. Not a rake, perhaps, but both arrogant and overbearing in the extreme. She had received many compliments on her singing in the past, but a cold and patronising 'unusual' was certainly not one she would cherish. Better that he had refrained from voicing his evident disdain. Hateful, hateful man!

She would not allow him to overset her. Let him begin the polite conversation, if he dared. The spark of challenge was unmistakable as she raised her head proudly to look him in the eye.

If Lord Amburley observed that fiery spark, he gave no outward sign of recognition as far as Isabella could tell. Indeed, he seemed to be completely devoid of any human feeling—he just stood motionless by the pianoforte, surveying Isabella through half-closed lids.

Isabella refused to be cowed. Clearly his lordship did not desire to prolong their conversation. *She* certainly had no wish to do so. 'If you will excuse me, gentlemen, I must rejoin Lady Wycham,' she said politely, turning to leave. Sir Thomas nodded genially. Lord Amburley responded with only the slightest bow, keeping his hard eyes fixed on Isabella throughout. She could feel his gaze boring into her back, as she moved away to join her great-aunt once more, keeping her pace measured and deliberate. She might feel like running from him, but nothing—nothing—would be allowed to betray her inner weakness to such a man.

'Why, Isabella,' exclaimed Lady Wycham, 'whatever is the matter? You look quite ill. Have you the headache, my dear? You really should not have agreed to perform for so long.'

'I am quite well, truly. It is just a little warm with so many people in the room. I shall be recovered in a moment, I assure you.' Taking a deep breath, Isabella raised her eyes to survey the company and discovered, with a sigh of relief, that Lord Amburley was no longer anywhere to be seen. A little of her colour returned.

But she had forgotten about Sophia, who was signalling urgently from across the room. Isabella swallowed a moment of panic. What should she tell Sophia? She reminded herself sternly that he had shown no sign of recognition—with luck he had completely forgotten his encounters with 'Winny'.

Sophia drew Isabella into a shadowy alcove, desperate to know what had happened. 'What did he say? Did he recognise you, do you think? Oh, what are we going to do?'

'Be calm, Sophia,' answered Isabella, doing her utmost to appear so herself. 'There is no reason to be agitated, I am sure. Lord Amburley did not know me. We were introduced by Sir Thomas, that is all.' She cut Sophia's protest short, lest the child fret herself into an attack of the vapours. 'He will, of course, recognise you when you meet, and you must acknowledge him, as you would any other gentleman. Remember that your ''companion''—''Winny''—has gone to stay with her family. You may say, quite truthfully, that you are staying with your godmother and your distant cousin *Isabella*. Can you do that, do you think?' She laid a gloved hand gently on Sophia's arm.

'I shall try,' promised Sophia, looking pale and strained.

The inevitable meeting with Lord Amburley took place at supper, towards midnight, just when Isabella had begun to hope that he might have left. Isabella and Sophia were seated in the midst of the same group of young people they had joined earlier, and all were enjoying Lady Bridge's generous hospitality.

Isabella felt, rather than saw, Lord Amburley's entrance. Turning her head fractionally so that she could observe the doorway out of the corner of her eye, she saw that he was lounging near the door, apparently engrossed in discussion. She clenched her hands together in her lap to stop them from shaking.

Let him not notice us, she prayed silently, and if he does, I will *not* blush. Heavens, why cannot I have more self-control? What can it be about that man that oversets me so? He may be used to intimidating others, but I refuse to let him do so to me.

Trying to hide her confusion, she sipped gingerly at her champagne flute.

'Miss Winstanley,' said the well-remembered voice immediately behind her, 'how delightful to meet you again—' Isabella started and turned, only to find that he was clearly addressing Sophia, not herself '—I beg your pardon,' he corrected himself, 'I should have noticed that both Misses Winstanley were present. Miss Sophia, I hope you are well after your ordeal on the North Road? Are you fixed in London for the Season?'

Sophia answered with commendable self-possession that she was. A short, polite exchange ensued, after which Lord Amburley quickly withdrew. Sophia visibly relaxed.

Isabella noted that his lordship had not enquired after 'Winny', nor had he favoured her with any further conversation at all. She concluded that he had not given her another thought. Unaccountably, she felt piqued.

'Lord Amburley is not much given to light conversation, it seems,' she said softly to Sophia. 'Perhaps that is just as well, in the circumstances.'

'I am glad he is gone,' confided Sophia. 'There is something about his eyes that frightens me. I felt as if he could read my very thoughts.'

Isabella's eyes widened in sudden recognition—for that was exactly how she had felt earlier, at the pianoforte. Then, she had not been able to put it into words. Now…now she had to admit that Lord Amburley would be a very dangerous man to cross.

Chapter Four

While society ladies were sleeping away the exertions of their late night, Lord Amburley was much occupied. He had never lost the soldier's habit of rising early, though nowadays he used the time to exercise his horses rather than to inspect his troops. He revelled in the solitary beauty of the park and the freedom he enjoyed there in the early morning. Later in the day, there were always too many prying eyes for his comfort—the rigid etiquette of the *ton* sat very uneasily on the shoulders of the man of action that he had been.

It was a beautiful, late spring morning, but Amburley barely noticed the birdsong or the budding trees. The huge grey he rode seemed to be itching to gallop across the fresh, dewy grass but was held to a sedate walk by an iron hand. The horse tossed his head in protest.

Lord Amburley was still in Sir Thomas's drawing-room, listening to a heart-stoppingly beautiful voice—and worrying at the riddle of the woman behind it. He had observed her closely while she sang. She was remarkably handsome—her glorious golden hair and her glowing complexion were a revelation to him. Only those unforgettable grey-green eyes confirmed her double identity—and her duplicity. She had been totally in control, too, until she caught sight of him. From then on, her agitation—and Miss Sophia's—had been apparent, though she had masked it well in the supper room. A good actress, he supposed.

But what—in truth—was she? On the road, he had met a poor relation with a sharp tongue and more concern for poor Jonah than for polite behaviour. Now, she was transformed into a lady of the *ton*. One guise must be false, of course—and, remembering her guilty reactions of the previous evening, he knew which it must be.

None the less, he found he could not help admiring her. She had more than beauty—she had spirit. No shrinking violet she, in spite of what she was. And yet, her inexcusable behaviour must surely be condemned by any right-thinking man?

The grey shook his head again, more forcefully. 'All right, old fellow. You've made your point. You think I'm good for nothing this morning, don't you? Well, we'll see about that.' He let the horse have his head. The grey needed to shake the fidgets out of his legs. If only Amburley's own concerns could be so simply resolved.

* * *

Around ten o'clock, while Lord Amburley was partaking of a light breakfast in his rented house in Jermyn Street, Mr Lewiston was announced. 'Good God, George, you are up betimes,' exclaimed his lordship, waving his friend to a chair. 'I have not known you to emerge before noon, unless there was a prize-fight to attend. What brings you here at this hour?'

'I have some news,' replied Lewiston. 'I must tell you that I encountered Miss Winstanley yesterday, quite by chance. You recall the young lady we rescued on the North Road? Well, it was she. And I have discovered her direction in London. Quite wonderful luck! I mean to call on her today. Will you accompany me?'

Lord Amburley did not immediately reply. 'Did you, indeed? And was she still in looks?'

'Indeed she was. She looked quite lovely. And so animated, more so than before, I fancy. I think that that dowdy companion we met up north had a malign influence on her. Miss Winstanley seemed in much brighter spirits without her louring presence.'

'Miss Winstanley was alone?' asked Lord Amburley sharply.

'Of course not,' snapped Mr Lewiston. 'She was accompanied by a distant relation—a Miss Isabella Winstanley. She is much older than Miss Sophia and a perfectly proper chaperon. Though I should perhaps warn you that she is a most elegant female herself, not beautiful exactly, but certainly striking.'

Lord Amburley raised an eyebrow. Isabella Winstanley was much more than striking, surely? But that was not a subject for discussion with Lewiston. 'And what has become of the poor companion? ''Winny'', was it not?'

'I have not the least notion. In any case, what has she to say to anything? You are not about to have another attack of philanthropy, are you, Leigh?'

'No. Merely curious.' Lord Amburley busied himself with the coffee-pot as he spoke. 'Tell me about your encounter, including the distant cousin.'

'There is little more to tell. Miss Winstanley—Miss Sophia Winstanley, I mean—almost collided with me outside Florette's. We exchanged a few words. Miss Sophia introduced me to her companion, and then she told me she was staying with Lady Wycham in Hill Street. Lady Wycham is her godmother, you know.'

'Well, no—in fact, I don't know her ladyship, I'm afraid,' responded his lordship flippantly.

'Sometimes, Leigh, you are quite exasperating. I did not expect you to *know* Lady Wycham, dammit; I was simply explaining how things are. If you'd just let me finish…'

'Oh. Is there more?' His lordship sat back, calmly drinking his coffee.

Lewiston continued doggedly. 'Kenley has told me all about the Misses Winstanley. Your man Peveridge was right about her being an heiress. Apparently Lady Wycham is very well-to-do, and Miss Winstanley is her nearest relative. She is expected to inherit everything. I dare say she will be the catch of the Season—beauty, breeding and a fortune into the bargain.'

'With Kenley involved, she will certainly become the centre of attraction—he is a gossip-monger of the first order. I have never understood why he spoils his own chances of winning heiresses by spreading the news all over London. After all, everyone knows he's mortgaged to the hilt. But you mean to be first in line yourself, I collect?'

Lewiston glowered in response. 'I have no need of her fortune, as you know perfectly well. I mean only to further my acquaintance with her and, perhaps, to warn her about some of those who may have mercenary motives.'

This was serious, Amburley realised. And there was an edge in Lewiston's tone that suggested... 'I trust you do not include me in that category, do you, George?'

Lewiston laughed. 'Why, no, of course not. I know you are not hanging out after an heiress for a wife...or indeed any wife at all, as far as I can see. And even if you were, I doubt you would choose someone of Miss Winstanley's tender years. The cousin, now, might be more to your liking. I'd say she is past five-and-twenty, but she is very well-looking, none the less. I gather she is a poor relation of some kind, though, and totally dependent on Lady Wycham's generosity, so you couldn't really afford to—' Lewiston broke off at Amburley's dark frown. 'What is the matter, Leigh?'

'I will thank you not to interfere in my private affairs, George. I know you mean well... However, what is important at present is that I prevent you from making a complete ass of yourself in this case.' Lewiston gave an audible gasp. 'As I said, an ass,' repeated his lordship. 'You clearly did not look closely at Miss Isabella Winstanley. If you had, you would have recognised the "malign" companion of our earlier encounter.' Lewiston now looked as if he had received a blow in the solar plexus.

'I chanced to meet both ladies at Lady Bridge's soirée last night,' continued Lord Amburley evenly. 'Miss "Winny" is attempting to pass herself off as a lady of fortune, no doubt in the hope of catching a husband. Your Miss Sophia, probably abetted by Lady Wycham, has clearly put quite some investment into her companion's appearance, for she appeared as a very fine lady indeed. Miss "Winny's" manners are irreproachable, of course, but then that is often the last resort of the impoverished. It's a pity she is indulging in such a shameful masquerade. She would have been better to take honest employment as a governess. She is certainly well qualified for that. She plays and sings delightfully.'

Lewiston put his cup down with a clatter. 'I don't believe it,' he gasped.

'What other explanation can you offer?' countered his lordship grimly. 'We both met Miss "Winny". There can be no doubt of her lowly station in life. Unless I am mistaken in my identification of her as

Miss Isabella—and I assure you I am not—there can be no other explanation. Your Miss Sophia is not only rich, frivolous and spoilt, she is also prepared to perpetrate a disreputable fraud upon you and other unsuspecting gentlemen of the *ton*. I have to say I am not surprised. Heiresses tend to have little regard for morality.'

He rose from the table and strode to the window, frowning out on to the busy street. 'I see that you doubt me. It is understandable, perhaps, that you think my judgement has been swayed by my own experience of society ladies. However, once you have paid your respects in Hill Street and looked upon Miss Isabella Winstanley with new eyes, you will doubt no longer, I promise you.'

'I am sure you are wrong, Amburley,' said Lewiston coldly, making to rise from his chair, 'and I shall take pleasure in telling you so, as soon as I may. Such a delightful and well-bred girl as Miss Sophia would never be party to so base a deception. It is not possible.'

'As you wish,' replied Amburley calmly. 'But since my opinion cannot be put to the test for some hours yet, let us turn to happier pursuits. I was intending to take a turn in the ring at Jackson's parlour this morning. Will you join me? It might improve your temper to plant me a facer.'

'No doubt it would, if I could do it,' admitted Lewiston, forced into unwilling laughter, 'but I know very well that I cannot. You are much too skilled for me, and I prefer not to suffer your left again, thank you. I will gladly accompany you, though.'

Good humour temporarily restored, they left for Gentleman Jackson's boxing parlour.

Although Mr Lewiston's dress was the height of fashion and his coat owed its immaculate fit to the artistry of Weston, he nevertheless looked nothing out of the common way by comparison with the tall and imposing figure of Lord Amburley at his side. Mr Lewiston kept fingering his cravat—a mathematical that he had laboured over for nearly two hours. It felt too tight. 'I think, perhaps, we should not go in, Leigh,' he suggested, tugging at it yet again.

'Do you tell me you do not care to catch Miss Sophia in her outrageous behaviour, George?'

'What? Oh, heavens, no! This cravat of mine. It's not, I fear, quite what I should like. Perhaps I should—' At that moment, the great door swung open to reveal the uncompromising stare of Lady Wycham's butler. Retreat became impossible.

Lady Wycham greeted them amicably from her place on the sofa in the blue drawing-room. 'Sophia has told me all about your gallant rescue, Mr Lewiston. Believe me, we are most grateful to you both.'

'It was nothing out of the ordinary, ma'am, I assure you.' Mr Lewiston blushed. 'I was glad to be of service,' he added with a smile for Sophia, sitting beside Lady Wycham.

The elder Miss Winstanley was seated on the other

side of the room, entertaining another guest. Mr Lewiston could hear her voice fairly clearly, but was unable to study her face without turning round. Surely this voice was different—lighter, younger?

After a few minutes, Lady Wycham asked Sophia to present Mr Lewiston to those other callers with whom he was unacquainted. 'Forgive me if I do not rise to make the introductions myself, sir. I am afraid I am no longer as spry as I once was.' While Lord Amburley, looking faintly amused, remained in conversation with Lady Wycham, Mr Lewiston accompanied Sophia to the window where Sophia performed the introductions, first to Miss Isabella Winstanley, with the reminder that they were 'distant cousins, you will recall', and then to the Earl of Gradely, who bowed and left.

Mr Lewiston appraised Miss Winstanley with some care. She was the same height, pretty much, he admitted, but 'Winny' had been thin, while this lady, though slim, was elegantly formed. No. Amburley *must* be wrong.

'Is this your first visit to London, Mr Lewiston?' enquired Isabella, looking into his face and determined to maintain the bright, youthful character that had successfully deceived him so far.

He did not immediately reply. For a moment, Isabella fancied his mind was elsewhere. She hastened to fill the silence. 'Have you visited Westminster Abbey since you arrived in London, sir?' she said quickly. 'I assure you it is a magnificent edifice and repays a journey. Sophia and I attended divine service there on Sunday last. It was truly moving. The music in particular was most beautiful.'

Mr Lewiston looked suddenly nonplussed. He stammered a little as he made to answer Isabella. Then he paused for a moment, as if trying to collect his wits, before finally responding to Isabella's inconsequential conversation in much the same vein. When Lord Amburley strolled over to join them, some minutes later, the conversation was still centred on such delights of London as might properly be discussed before ladies.

Mr Lewiston tried to bring his friend into the discussion. 'You must have seen all the sights, of course, Leigh?'

'Too many years ago,' agreed Lord Amburley, making no attempt to include Isabella in his remarks. 'I am more familiar now with the great churches of Madrid than of London, I fear. I shall be forced to reacquaint myself with them, now the war is finally over.'

Isabella was incensed. She determined that she would no longer be ignored by this arrogant man. She would force him to acknowledge her. 'Were you many years in the Peninsula, my lord?' she asked innocently.

'I joined Wellesley in eighteen ten, ma'am,' he replied tersely, directing a stern gaze at Isabella.

She swallowed, refusing to be intimidated. 'And your family was content for you to go? I fancied it was more usual for the heir to kick his heels at home, and that only younger sons joined the colours. I collect your parents did not share the received opinion?'

'No, ma'am, you are mistaken,' he rejoined sharply. 'The heir did indeed remain at home. I was the younger son merely, and required to make my own way in life. I inherited the title only in eighteen twelve, on the death of my elder brother.'

Isabella paled with anger at his condescending manner. How dare he? He had purposely made her simple question sound impertinent. 'Did you leave the army then, sir?' she continued calmly, refusing to be daunted by his hard eyes.

'No, ma'am. I remained until Boney was sent to Elba.'

'Even then, he was afire to be off again when Boney escaped,' interposed Mr Lewiston, ingenuously, 'and would have gone, had it not been for Lady Amburley's entreaties.'

'You allow yourself too much latitude in interpreting my motives, George,' returned his lordship, with a generous smile that softened his features markedly. In that moment, he seemed to Isabella to reveal a character totally different from the hard, taciturn man she had judged him to be. 'My mother's wishes happened to coincide with my duty. I was not in a position to quit the estates again, however much I might have been tempted.'

'But you have yielded to temptation now, my lord, have you not, in coming to London?' Without pause for thought, Isabella had decided that, if he would condemn her for impertinence, she would give him cause. She fixed an innocent smile on her lips.

Lord Amburley turned back to Isabella and surveyed her slowly. It was exactly the same calculating look he had given to 'Winny' on their encounter at the Bell inn. Then suddenly, he laughed. '*Touché*, ma'am. I have indeed yielded to the delights of the London Season. Though, before you reproach me further—' Isabella lowered her eyes, suddenly conscious of the impropriety of her outburst '—I should reassure you that my estates are now in good enough order to be able to survive without my ministrations for a month or two.'

Isabella raised her gaze again to discover that he was now laughing at her. Infamous! Her earlier embarrassment was replaced by righteous anger. She must—and would—find the means of repaying him in his own coin…and soon.

The door had hardly shut behind the two men, when Lewiston launched into a slightly incoherent recital of the stages of his enlightenment. 'What the devil do they mean by entertaining Gradely? He's the worst sort of fortune-hunter. Puts me in mind of some ravening beast, waiting to prey on the innocent and helpless. If *he* should make her an offer…'

Amburley waited patiently for the tirade to end before gently steering his friend back to the question of Isabella's identity.

'I would not have believed that they were one and the same, but for her eyes. They are a most unusual colour. I noticed that at the inn. But she did not guess that I had rumbled her, I'd swear to that,' Lewiston added, with obvious self-satisfaction, 'so we still hold all the cards.' He paused. 'It's a devilish tricky situation, though, Leigh,' he added uncertainly. 'You are quite justified in saying they have practised a disreputable deception on us, yet I cannot readily believe Miss Sophia is truly guilty. She is such an innocent… In the circumstances,' he continued, after a moment, 'I thought it best to say nothing, at least for the present. To be honest, I wanted time to think.'

'Very wise, George,' agreed Amburley. 'Revenge is a dish best eaten cold.'

'What the devil do you mean, "revenge"?' exclaimed Lewiston. 'What need have I, or you for that matter, to wreak vengeance on that poor girl?'

'Easy, George. Remember that they set out, quite deliberately, to dupe us. Let us consider the situation dispassionately, before we pronounce upon the appropriate retribution. The facts are simple. Miss Sophia Winstanley, the heiress, has a distant cousin, Isabella, also called "Winny". Said cousin is only a poor companion, but has now been dressed to the nines in order to appear as an equal. We do not know why, nor who is responsible for this disreputable scheme, though I must say that it is much more likely to have originated with the rich Miss Winstanley than with the poor relation.' He cut short his companion's attempted defence of Sophia. 'However, I attach the largest part of the blame to the elder Miss Winstanley. A lady of her years and experience should never have consented to such a bird-witted escapade, however tempting the bait. It was always bound to fail.

'By the way, George,' he added, 'I think you owe me an apology, for doubting my ability to detect a fraud.'

Lewiston's jaw dropped momentarily.

'Do not bother to beg my pardon, old fellow,' Amburley said, with a sardonic smile. 'I understand that you are much more concerned about Miss Sophia's feelings than mine.'

'Leigh, you are quite outrageous,' returned his friend. 'Yes, of course you were right. But what are we to do?'

'For the moment, I think, we shall simply wait and observe developments. We could *easily* spread the tale now, of course. Nothing simpler. But I think— not yet. I confess to being intrigued by this potentially disastrous make-believe of theirs. I should like very much to know what occasioned it. Indeed, I intend to find out. Then I shall decide what is best to be done.' He paused. 'I beg your pardon. *You*, of course, will take whatever action you think is right. It is not my place to make decisions on your behalf.'

Lewiston shook his head. 'I have no present intention of betraying them, Leigh. Indeed, I rather think we should not unmask them at all, unless it is clear that mischief is afoot. To be honest with you, I cannot believe it is more than a silly prank.'

'Ladies of Miss ''Winny's'' age and background should not become involved in pranks,' declared Lord Amburley flatly. 'I may yet bring her to rue it, I dare say. However, I agree that, for the present at least, we should simply watch and wait.'

They turned the corner and approached his lordship's door. 'Are you bidden to the Duchess of Newcombe's ball tomorrow, George?' Lewiston nodded. 'Doubtless *both* the Misses Winstanley will be there. We shall have ample opportunity for spectator sport. It promises to be better than a prize-fight.'

Chapter Five

Sophia awoke early next day, the day of her first ever ball. She made no attempt to go back to sleep, scrambling out of bed and into her dressing-gown without ringing for her new maid. Then, eyes shining with excitement, she hurried along the corridor to Isabella's room, where she knocked briefly and entered, without waiting for an invitation.

'Isabella, forgive me for…' Her words trailed off, and she looked at her cousin in astonishment. 'Good God,' she exclaimed, 'whatever are you doing, dressed like that at this hour?'

Isabella was not best pleased at the interruption to her plans, nor was she prepared to indulge Sophia's curiosity. With a stern look, reminiscent of Lady Wycham at her most haughty, she replied sharply that her private business was of no interest to her young cousin.

'But those are the clothes you wore to visit the orphans,' protested Sophia, refusing to be silenced.

'If anyone were to see you, there would be a scandal. Surely—'

'Sophia,' interrupted Isabella sharply, 'I shall thank you to allow me to be the judge of what I may or may not do. And where I go is of no interest to anyone but myself.' She turned to her maid. 'Have you my gloves, Mitchell? Thank you.' Drawing them on, she spoke more gently to Sophia. 'Now go back to bed, my dear. It is much too early for you to be about. Even on the day of your first ball,' she added, with a slight smile. 'Say nothing to anyone about what has happened here, even to me. And ask no questions. They will not be answered.' With a quick nod, Isabella opened the door and was gone.

It was still quite early when Sophia entered the breakfast room. Even so, Isabella was before her, now dressed in a light morning dress of cream cambric trimmed with green velvet ribbons and calmly pouring coffee. Sophia's mouth formed an *O*, but no sound came out.

'Good morning, Sophia dear,' beamed Isabella. 'I hope you slept well, for it will be a long night, I fancy. Will you have some coffee? Or shall I ring for chocolate?' Isabella was quite determined that no allusion to their earlier encounter would be permitted, but Sophia surrendered with only token resistance.

As the day wore on, Sophia's excitement visibly increased, until Isabella at last managed to persuade her to rest in the late afternoon. Relaxing on her own chaise-longue, Isabella abandoned herself to thoughts of her own attempted début, nearly ten years before. Then, with her father still alive, she had been viewed as a potential heiress, but it had not brought happiness, merely a train of grasping fortune-hunters. She shuddered at the memory. She and her brother had been wise to pretend that everything had been left to him. Better to be an old maid than to be pursued for money alone. Isabella had no regrets, now, about pretending to be dependent on Aunt Jemima. Her life was her own, and she could live it in comfort, even though she would die a spinster.

She smiled with sad irony at the memory of her come-out. White and pastels were all very well for brunettes like Sophia, but pale-complexioned blondes tended to look merely insipid. And gentlemen were unlikely to be enamoured of a lady who looked them straight in the eye, or worse, overtopped them when she rose from her seat. Lord Amburley, now, was a much better partner for a tall lady. She would not even reach his shoulder. Dancing with such a tall gentleman—waltzing, perhaps?—might be delightful. She would put her hand on his shoulder, where the warmth of his body could be felt through the fine cloth of his coat. His gloved hand would rest in the middle of her back—perhaps even against her bare skin—while he guided her firmly through the throng of dancers. She would feel his warm breath on her face as he complimented her on the lightness of her dancing. His dark eyes would…

Isabella checked herself severely before her musings advanced even further into the realm of daydreams. A man should not become the subject of missish fancies just because he happened to be rather taller than the ordinary. He certainly had little, other than height, to recommend him. Unless, perhaps, that underlying sense of humour which had betrayed itself when she taunted him? Resolutely, Isabella put his lordship from her thoughts and rose to begin her preparations for the ball.

Madame Florette's jade creation was a wonder of expensive simplicity, allowing the beautiful shot-silk overdress to fall in graceful folds from a high waistline below a deeply scooped *décolletage*. The neckline and the tiny sleeves were edged with the aquamarine satin of the underdress. The open edges of the overdress were similarly trimmed and finished with tiny aquamarine satin buttons and loops.

Isabella was more pleased than she was prepared to admit. She had almost persuaded herself that she was now past the age when a lady hoped to be admired, and that she should settle quietly into spinsterhood. But faced with the fairy-tale gown, she knew a moment of youthful excitement ill-suited to an 'ageing spinster'. Let us see whether he can ignore me now, came the unprompted thought.

Soon Isabella was standing in front of the pier glass, critically assessing her reflection. Mitchell's new way with her hair was most becoming, she decided. The rather looser knot of curls on top made her look very young. And Mitchell's suggestion of aquamarines was right too, mere trumpery though they might be.

Answering a light tap at the door, Mitchell admitted Lady Wycham's maid. 'Can you come to my lady, please, miss? She's took bad.'

Isabella immediately hurried to Lady Wycham's apartments. She found her great-aunt lying on her bed, partly dressed for the ball, but with a silk dressing-gown over all. She was very pale, and a hand was pressed to her throat.

'Oh, Aunt,' gasped Isabella, 'is it one of your spasms? Shall I send for Dr Ridley?'

'I shall be well again in a moment. Parsons should not have fetched you.' She looked severely at her faithful maid, but it had no visible effect. 'Only I fear I may not be able to accompany you tonight.'

'But we shall stay here with you,' exclaimed Isabella. 'We cannot possibly go when you are unwell.'

'Nonsense, Isabella. I am quite recovered now.' She attempted, unsuccessfully, to sit up. 'Perhaps not quite enough to accompany you, but certainly enough to be left in Parsons' care. I *insist* that you take Sophia to the ball. You must simply make my excuses to the Duchess.'

Isabella was torn between her duty to her aunt and her desire not to disappoint Sophia. Her indecision must have been apparent.

'Isabella,' said Lady Wycham curtly, 'what *is* the matter with you? Have you windmills in your head, child? I take it you will do as I ask?'

'Dear Aunt, I should rather stay here to see to your comfort—' Lady Wycham drew breath sharply, as a preliminary to another biting retort '—but I know that you will not tolerate it. So, if you insist, I shall chaperon Sophia to the Duchess's ball.'

'I do wish it, my dear. Thank you. I know I can trust you to ensure she behaves as she ought.' A sudden look of concern shadowed her face. 'You will make sure she does not waltz?'

Isabella smiled reassuringly. 'Have no fear, Aunt. I have been drilling Sophia for weeks on the subject of the waltz. She knows she may not dance it until she has received permission at Almack's. And that is one rule she will not dare to break.'

Lady Wycham gave a sigh of relief and smiled lovingly at Isabella. 'You look quite beautiful in that gown, my dear child. Do not waste your looks among the chaperons tonight. Promise me that you, too, will dance.'

Isabella knew that, if she was to be Sophia's chaperon, it would hardly be proper for her to dance. Chaperons did not do so. A small voice whispered that chaperons did not dress in gowns of shot silk either, but she pushed that thought to the back of her mind, while she grappled with Lady Wycham's request. She could not refuse without upsetting the old lady, so she agreed, consoling herself with the thought that, at her age, she was unlikely to be asked to dance at all.

Having made her curtsy and Lady Wycham's excuses to the Duchess, Isabella led the way into the huge ballroom, where thousands of brightly coloured flowers were already beginning to wilt in the heat of the banks of candles. The ballroom was full to overflowing with beautiful ladies and elegant gentlemen, some in scarlet regimentals, and the noise of their conversation was so loud that it was barely possible to hear the orchestra. Sophia was soon laughing and chattering in the midst of a gathering of young people. Isabella watched contentedly for a few moments, prior to joining the chaperons at the side of the ballroom.

She was startled out of her reverie by a voice in her ear. 'Miss Winstanley, do you tell me you are become a chaperon? And do you plan to assume the turban too?'

'Why, Lady Sefton,' laughed Isabella, 'how you have found me out. I am guilty, I fear, though not yet of the turban. My aunt, you must know, is rather poorly this evening, and we could not deny Sophia her first ball.'

'I see. You are both very generous. Which is she?'

'The dark girl in white, with the pink roses and the lace shawl.'

Lady Sefton's sharp gaze assessed Sophia. 'Hmm.

Yes. I dare say she will do very well. What is her background?'

Isabella felt the need to dissemble a little here, in front of one of the influential patronesses of Almack's. Lady Sefton believed Isabella to be Lady Wycham's pensioner. It would not do for her to suspect that Sophia was penniless, too—especially as, in Sophia's case, it was true. 'We are distant cousins, ma'am. She is from the Yorkshire branch of the Winstanleys. Her father's seat is Locke House, near York.' Isabella hoped she had said enough to divert Lady Sefton from the uncomfortable subject of Sophia's expectations.

'A pretty chit, indeed. I like her style. Shall I send vouchers for Almack's for you?' Lady Sefton smiled, clearly conscious of the prize she was offering. 'We never did have the pleasure of seeing you grace the floor there, my dear, which is a pity.'

'You are very kind, ma'am. Thank you, on behalf of Sophia. I know she will be delighted. And if my dear aunt is well enough to accompany us,' she added with a twinkle, 'I may yet avoid the turban.'

'But you must not await a visit to Almack's to dance. Why, you look radiant tonight, my dear Miss Winstanley, and such looks must not be wasted on the dowagers.' She made an unmistakable signal to someone out of Isabella's line of vision and, hardly a heartbeat later, Lord Amburley stood before them, bowing to Lady Sefton with a quizzical smile on his face.

'Miss Winstanley,' announced Lady Sefton, 'may I present to you Lord Amburley as a suitable partner for this dance?'

Isabella knew a moment of indescribable panic. Dear God, why did she have to choose *him*? She forced herself to curtsy to his lordship, while racking her brains for a suitable means of refusing him. She could not possibly dance with him—touch him... 'You are most kind, ma'am,' she stammered eventually, 'but I am truly unable to dance this evening, since I am here as chaperon to my young cousin.' With growing embarrassment, she noted how Amburley's jaw tightened at her rebuff, while he raised his glass to survey her slowly from head to foot. His incredulity was obvious. Some chaperon she!

Lady Sefton, however, was not so easily diverted from her object. 'Nonsense,' she protested. 'Your aunt's indisposition should not prevent your enjoyment of the evening. I insist you dance. And if it sets your mind at rest, I will keep an eye on that chit of yours. You will oblige me in this, Amburley?'

Lord Amburley bowed his acquiescence and offered his hand to lead Isabella into the set that was just forming. Isabella stared at his gloved fingers. Her stomach turned molten, generating a wave of heat in her lower body. For a moment, they stood in embarrassed silence. Then Isabella forced herself to put her hand in his, praying he would not notice the slight quivering of her fingers. He guided her to her place with a light, firm grip. She detected the faintest hint of a tangy cologne when he moved away to stand opposite her. The warmth from his hand seemed to have invaded her whole arm, which tingled strangely.

She knew she should speak, but she could not even look at him.

Lord Amburley's good manners prevailed. 'Miss Sophia looks charmingly this evening, ma'am. She does you credit.'

His routine politeness broke the spell that had gripped her. She was mistress of herself once more—and horrified at her momentary loss of control. 'Thank you, sir.' She paused uncertainly, searching for a safe topic, for it was clearly her turn. 'Is Mr Lewiston here this evening, perhaps? Sophia would be glad to meet him again, I think.'

'He is before you, ma'am,' said his lordship. 'Look towards the group around Miss Sophia when you come down the set. He is already among her bevy of admirers, begging for her hand for this dance.'

A moment later, she saw that this was true. A host of young men was flocking around Sophia. Isabella wondered idly how it was that Sophia had become quite so successful, quite so quickly. But she could not pursue that puzzling thought while engaged on the dance floor—especially not when partnered by Lord Amburley.

Above all, she must not lose control again.

His voice broke into her thoughts. 'And may I add, ma'am, that Miss Sophia is not the only Winstanley lady to attract admiring looks tonight?'

Isabella was surprised to find that his words did not overset her. She was blushing a little, she was sure, but she was still in control. For the first time that evening, she dared to look into his face. The disdain he had shown before did not seem to be there. His dark eyes—the colour of rich chocolate, she decided—seemed to have lost the hardness she had flinched from on every one of their previous encounters. Obviously, he could be absolutely charming when he chose. But why should he be? Not simply to oblige Lady Sefton, surely? No. It was more than charm. There was something indefinable in his look, too. Humour, perhaps? Or was it pity for an old maid? Please, no. That would be too much. She knew well enough that she was destined to end her days as a spinster, but no one—no one at all—would be allowed to pity her for it. She could feel the anger rising in her throat at the very thought.

The movements of the dance parted them then, for which she was thankful. It gave her time to bring her tumbling thoughts into some kind of order. For the next twenty minutes, nothing more was said, and Isabella took care to avoid his eyes. She breathed a silent sigh of relief when, at last, the dance was over.

'Thank you, ma'am,' he bowed. 'It is quite delightful to dance with a lady who has such stimulating conversation.'

Oh, how dare he? Now, he was roasting her in tones of studied politeness. 'You are too kind, sir,' she replied quickly, mimicking his manner. 'One has little chance to exercise one's wit in country dances when one is so often parted from one's partner. It is important to save one's breath for the exertions of the figures, lest one fail to do them justice. Do you not agree?'

Lord Amburley smiled dangerously. 'A veritable hit, ma'am. I collect I should not fence with you, for I am like to be bested. However—' he raised the dance card at her wrist '—I fancy there may be an opportunity later for a lengthier interchange. I shall look forward to it.' He scribbled on her card, bowed again, and left her.

Before Isabella could check to see what he had done, Sophia returned, pink and a little breathless, but glowing with animation. No wonder all the young men had been milling round her. It had clearly been right not to deny her this ball.

'You were dancing with Lord Amburley.' Sophia seized Isabella's dance card before she could reply. 'And he has taken the waltz for his second,' she exclaimed. 'I am not at all surprised, for you look truly beautiful tonight. Now that they know you will dance, all the other gentlemen will be queuing to fill your card. It is strange that Mr Lewiston should be so wrong, however. He told me Lord Amburley does not dance.' She lowered her voice to a conspiratorial whisper as she scanned the ballroom. 'His lordship has disappeared,' she said. 'He is most often to be found in the card-room, I believe.'

'Sophia, that is the worst kind of gossip,' bit out

Isabella, in a sharp undertone. 'You must not repeat such things.' There was no opportunity to pursue the matter, however, for Sophia was soon led off to the floor by another young cavalier.

Sophia's predictions proved right. Isabella's dance card was soon so full that she felt a pang of conscience at neglecting her duties as chaperon. However, she reassured herself that she could still keep a wary eye on Sophia from the floor and, since she was in no way troubled by the cut of the young men who partnered her charge, there was unlikely to be any cause for concern.

Just before supper, Lord Amburley reappeared to lead Isabella into the waltz. This time she was ready for him. 'You did not give me a moment to tell you, sir,' she said quickly, 'that I do not dance the waltz.'

He quirked an eyebrow but said nothing, fixing his direct gaze on her face.

'Forgive me. It is…you see…'

He continued to stare.

Isabella's embarrassment was finally converted to anger by his steadfast refusal to make the polite response that any reasonable man would have offered. 'I cannot dance the waltz, my lord, because I am here as chaperon to my cousin and *she* is not yet permitted to do so. If you had asked my permission before writing on my card, I should have told you so at the time.' She knew that her sharp tone had betrayed her annoyance. Damn the man! Why could she not keep her temper under control where he was concerned?

Lord Amburley still said nothing, but raised her dance card to peruse it. 'And what a pity that your card is now full, so that there are no others for which I may ask the favour of your hand. I am quite at a stand.' His piercing glance suggested he was nothing of the kind. His next words proved it. 'But you will, I am sure, favour me with your company, if I invite you to sit here while the others waltz? May I procure you a glass of champagne?'

Chapter Six

Isabella perched rather uncomfortably towards one end of the sofa. His lordship lounged at the other, apparently quite at his ease, watching her. He had removed his gloves and stretched his free arm nonchalantly along the back of the sofa so that his fingers were within inches of her bare shoulder. She could almost feel the heat of his skin. She wrenched her eyes away. She appeared—she hoped—much calmer than she felt. Inside, she was a turmoil of conflicting emotions—though anger, indignation and embarrassment were the only ones she was prepared to put a name to. She had been adroitly manoeuvred by Lord Amburley into a distinctly improper speech and then into an awkward, though mercifully public, tête-à-tête. She had much rather have been almost anywhere than sitting so close to him, wondering what his next move would be—for she still found it impossible to predict his actions, or to gauge his motives.

Steeling herself, she resolved not to help him to

begin a conversation. Since he had desired her company, he must make the first move.

'I am sorry to learn that Lady Wycham is indisposed. A sudden turn, I collect?' He was regarding her ball-gown pointedly.

Isabella refused to lose control of her temper again. 'Lady Wycham suffers from spasms, sir, which come on without warning,' she responded stiffly. That should surely be enough for any gentleman to acknowledge the need to change the subject.

Apparently unabashed at her words, he bent his quizzical gaze on her. Clearly he was wondering why she had come to the ball at all. What kind of hard-hearted woman did he consider her to be? Isabella could feel her anger rising again, like bile in her throat. She would not demean herself to make excuses for her behaviour. Let him judge her as he chose. She deliberately returned his frank gaze.

For several moments, neither moved. Then, since he was clearly not going to speak, Isabella was forced, in common politeness, to turn the conversation herself. 'I did not see you dance again, my lord. Indeed, I concluded that you had been so *stimulated* by my conversation that you had left to seek stimulation elsewhere.' She permitted herself a slight smile.

He quirked that infernal eyebrow again, surveying her coolly. 'You are right, but only in part, ma'am. I certainly had no intention of missing this *waltz* with you. But, in the meantime, I did retire to the card-room. It is not my habit to dance with young and foolish girls.'

Isabella bridled. How dared he? 'It is true that I cut my wisdoms years ago, sir, though it is unhandsome of you to remind me of it. Am I also to take it that you do not class me as foolish?'

'There can be only one polite answer to that question, ma'am. And yet I hesitate to give it. Your having asked it at all does suggest a certain…shall we say, lack of forethought?'

However indignant she might be at his high-handed behaviour—and she was—Isabella had to admit the justice of that rebuke. An involuntary gurgle of laughter escaped her, as she realised the absurdity of her position.

'That's better,' he said, with a sudden smile that made her heart begin to race. 'Anger makes your eyes sparkle magnificently, but I think I prefer the twinkle of laughter. You should laugh more often.'

'Oh, how dare you say so! You are outrageous!' But, in spite of herself, she smiled still.

'Indeed I am, ma'am. But it was worth it to see that radiant smile. It outshines even the golden radiance of your gown.'

Now *that* really was too much, even for him. 'Come, my lord, let us speak of other things. I am neither young enough nor foolish enough to listen to such flummery. Tell me—' she clasped her hands demurely in her lap '—what do they play in the cardroom?'

'Piquet. And whist, I believe. Do you play?' He seemed genuinely interested.

'A little. Especially piquet. My late father enjoyed it very much, particularly towards the end of his life, when more active pursuits were denied him. We were used to play almost every day. Lady Wycham enjoys a game too, although she is not as skilled as my father was.' She caught herself up then. Now, why had she volunteered so much information to him about her private life? Something to do with his quiet way of listening, perhaps? But dangerous, and to be avoided. She must take more care. She had not the least idea of what his object might be, but she was sure that he had singled her out for some purpose of his own.

'It sounds as if you are a practised player, ma'am. Do you care to enter the lists against me?' He favoured her with a half-smile and that quirked eyebrow again.

Every line of that sternly handsome face challenged her to accept. Every instinct of her own urged her to run. In her heart, she could admit she was afraid to meet his challenge—but her pride would not allow her to let him see her weakness. She refused to let him triumph over her, even in such a small thing as a game of cards.

'By all means,' she replied smoothly, determined not to lose the advantage to him this time. 'And the stakes?'

Her prompt response had clearly surprised him. After a moment, he said, 'The usual stakes would not be right for such an encounter. May I suggest—?'

'Indeed, sir, I have no wish to offer you less than any other opponent. And I play to win, I assure you. Why do we not play for the same stakes as you were playing for earlier, in the card-room here?'

'Do you know what they were, ma'am?'

'No. But I feel sure they would be equally appropriate for a match between your lordship and myself. May we agree on that?' She was perversely pleased to see that he was frowning now. No doubt, he was more used to dealing with demure damsels who hung on his every word.

'First I must tell you, Miss Winstanley, that Gradely and I were playing for a guinea a point. I believe that we—'

Isabella stretched out a hand to stop him in mid-sentence. 'Forgive my interrupting you, sir. I collect you were about to propose some lesser stake for our game. Pray do not embarrass me by suggesting any such thing.' She was further gratified to see him flush slightly at that. 'I should like to play for the stakes you mentioned. Are we agreed?'

That hard, calculating look had returned to his eyes. 'I do not pretend to understand you, ma'am, but at your insistence I will agree. I warn you that there will be no quarter given.'

'No, sir, none. Nor is any expected.'

'If you will favour me with your company at supper, ma'am, we can agree the time and place for this contest of Titans.'

'You are too kind.' She threw him a look that suggested she thought him quite otherwise, but he did not react at all to her veiled sarcasm. 'Unfortunately, I already have a supper partner for this evening. As to the venue...' she paused, mentally reviewing her calendar '...I believe Lady Morrissey's soirée on Friday would serve very well. Provided, of course, that we allow any onlookers to believe we are playing for chicken-stakes.'

'As I would be more than happy to do,' he countered hotly. 'Why do you insist on such stakes?'

'It must be in the blood, do you not think? Excuse me, here is my supper partner.' She rose and, with the slightest bow to his lordship, turned to take the arm of an elderly gentleman who led her off towards the supper room.

It was some moments before his lordship could gather his scattered thoughts. She had surprised him again. And his admiration had grown, in spite of his best efforts to condemn her. There was something... He shook his head in vexation. He did not understand her at all. But he could not but be impressed by her cool poise in the face of such enormous financial risks. She must feel very sure of herself—and yet he knew that there was not the least possibility of her matching his skill with the cards, since he was widely acknowledged as one of the finest players in London. What's more, she could easily lose a fortune.

He explained as much to his friend Lewiston who, frustrated in his desire to escort Sophia to supper, had come to join him on the sofa. 'I challenged her to piquet and she insisted, positively insisted, on playing for a guinea a point. She must feel very certain of winning. Even on a single rubber she could lose several years' salary.'

'Perhaps she fuzzes the cards,' suggested Lewiston.

'A female Captain Sharp?'

'Why not? She is trying to foist herself on Society as something she is not. If she cheats in that, may she not also cheat at cards?'

'No, I think not,' responded Lord Amburley immediately, 'not a lady of her breeding. Besides, there is no man alive—or woman—who can cheat me at cards and remain undetected. And if you should prove to be right in your suspicions, believe me, I should expose her on the spot.' As he spoke, he felt absolutely certain that he would not be called upon to honour that promise. He did not seek to wonder how he knew.

Lewiston, well aware of his friend's remarkable skill at the table, did not pursue the matter further. He turned the subject instead to something that was obviously much nearer his heart. 'I could not obtain more than one dance with Miss Sophia, no matter how I tried. The news of her expectations seems to have travelled fast. Kenley's doing, probably. Every gazetted fortune-hunter in London is after her. She is such an innocent that she is like to be taken in at every turn.'

'Do not tax yourself about that, my friend. With a duenna as *sharp* as Miss "Winny" to protect her, she will come to no harm. More likely that you impressionable young men will need protection from her.'

'What? That's gammon, Leigh. I am in no danger from Miss Sophia.'

'No, of course not. Young ladies of her stamp look for a title as well as a fortune. You fail to qualify on the first count, even if not on the second.'

'Leigh, I fail to understand you,' Lewiston said tetchily. He seemed to be in no mood for such banter. 'Why is it you can never see any good in females?'

Amburley refused to be ruffled. 'You exaggerate, George,' he drawled. 'I see much good in females who are useful according to their station. It is just the simpering, empty-headed ones I cannot abide.'

'Now it is you who exaggerate. I have seen many an empty-headed piece on your arm over these last months. You seem to have both time and tolerance for *them*.'

'I referred to *ladies*, George, not members of the muslin company. They, however empty-headed, fulfil a role in life. They make no secret, either, of their designs on a man's pocket-book. If the blunt is not forthcoming, then—' he made a gesture as of blowing away a feather '—such *ladies* will be gone too. It is better so, I believe.'

Lewiston looked quite horrified at his friend's bleak verdict on womankind, but he was too well-mannered to prolong such a discussion, especially at a ball. Raising his champagne glass, he gave a short, forced laugh and said, 'Come, Leigh. Let us drink a toast to your success against Miss "Winny" on Friday.'

Silently they drank. Then, arm in arm, they descended the stairs.

Although it was early morning when the Winstanley ladies returned to Hill Street, Isabella visited her great-aunt before retiring. She found her sleeping peacefully, watched by the faithful Parsons.

'She agreed to take a few drops of laudanum, miss, and she fell asleep around midnight. You'll visit in the morning? She will be agog for news of the ball. Would have stayed awake for your return, if I'd let her.'

Isabella smiled. 'Then I shall not ask you how you *persuaded* her to take the laudanum. You were quite right, of course, but I had better be here early to give her the news. Goodnight, Parsons, and thank you.'

Isabella returned to her own room. Her body was tired—she was not accustomed to dancing so much—but her brain was on fire. Every time she tried to focus her thoughts on Sophia's astonishing success, a hard and handsome male face intruded.

Why on earth had she done it? If he should prove to be the better player, she could easily lose several hundred guineas. Not that the money mattered a jot, of course, to someone in her position. But to lead him to believe she was an inveterate gambler…she must have been out of her mind. Or was it, perhaps, an unconscious desire to demonstrate, by a highly circuitous route, that she was neither poor nor a companion after all? She shook her head. It was impossible to straighten her ravelled thoughts. Why was her peace of mind so affected by what one rather haughty lord thought of her? Why this ungovernable desire to outface him?

I am *not* developing a *tendre* for him, she told herself firmly. He is the last sort of man to attract me. He is far from truly handsome—and his want of address is lamentable. He hardly ever speaks and, when he does, it is usually to say something outrageous. How could I even begin to like such a man?

Memories of their encounter at the inn crowded in on her. There, he had been equally strange in his manners, but she could now admit that he had proved generous in assisting a poor, plain companion. Truly, the man was a riddle.

Isabella tossed and turned for some hours, unable to exclude Lord Amburley from her thoughts or to resolve her own feelings. Clearly, sleep was impossible so, giving in to the inevitable, she rose and donned her comfortable old riding-habit.

'A brisk ride in the park will blow the cobwebs away,' she replied to Mitchell's suggestion that she return to bed. 'And I promised to visit my dear aunt as soon as she wakes this morning. I cannot be a slug-a-bed today, Mitchell.' Seeing the abigail's concern, she added, 'But if it will please you, I will rest this afternoon. Now, where are my riding gloves?'

Some twenty minutes later, Isabella was trotting off in the direction of Hyde Park, accompanied by her groom. She felt strangely exhilarated. She told herself it was the combination of early morning air and sunshine on her skin. As she neared the park, the raucous sounds of awakening London receded and the fresh scent of young leaves surrounded her. On such a morning, it was good to be alive.

'I have neglected you shamefully these past two days, Princess,' whispered Isabella, stroking the neck of her big bay mare. Princess twitched her ears in response. 'If every morning is as glorious as this, we shall certainly ride out together, I promise you.' Turning to the groom behind her, Isabella said, 'I am going to give Princess a good gallop this morning. She is much in want of exercise.'

'Are you sure that's wise, Miss Isabella? It's all very well in the country, but ladies don't go galloping in Hyde Park.' He spoke with the familiarity of one who had known her when she sat her first pony.

Isabella smiled generously at him. 'Come, Tom, you have no need to be concerned today. You can see for yourself that there is no one about. It is much too early. Anyone who might recognise me is at home sleeping off the effects of last night's ball. Shall we race?' She was as animated as a mischievous child enjoying a forbidden treat.

With a sigh of resignation, Tom nodded. 'It'll be no race though, miss, not my old nag against the Princess.'

Recognising the justice of that, Isabella gave the groom a good start, then touched her heel to the mare. The big bay changed almost instantly from gentle amble to powerful gallop. Her long raking strides covered the ground easily and she gained steadily on the groom in front, with Isabella bent low over her neck, urging her on. Isabella was quite unconcerned when her hat slipped and part of her hair came down. There was no time to stop for such trivial matters. Winning was all-important.

Isabella reached the winning post, a large tree, fractionally before Tom. She turned to him, half-dishevelled, her eyes sparkling with laughter and her bosom heaving. 'You were quite right, Tom,' she gasped. 'Princess is not to be bested. But, ah, what a splendid run. We must do this every morning.' She leant forward in the saddle, clapping her mare's neck. 'Well done, my Princess. I knew you could do it,' she cooed.

Absorbed as she was in communion with her beloved mare, Isabella did not at first see the gentleman on horseback sitting quietly among the trees watching them. At length he stirred his mount to a walk and the movement caught her eye.

Amburley again! Devil the man! He appeared everywhere, especially when she was least prepared for him. Well, on this occasion, she simply did not care. She had been behaving like a hoyden and looked it. Let him take her as she was.

Isabella lifted her chin a little as she turned towards him. Still somewhat short of breath from the race, she hailed him gaily. 'Why, good morning, my lord. I had not thought to meet any of last night's guests so early. You are about betimes.'

Lord Amburley walked his horse forward to join her, surveying her carefully all the while. Isabella tried to look unconcerned, but was very conscious of her rather shabby green habit and her unkempt appearance. She knew her hair was half-tumbled down her back, but she did not realise how beautiful it looked, glinting like guinea-gold where it caught the early morning sunshine. Nor did she realise that, with her jaunty hat askew and her green eyes sparkling, she had an endearing look of impish youthfulness.

'Well met, Miss Winstanley,' he replied politely, touching his crop to his hat. 'I might say the same of you, might I not?'

'Why, yes, sir. I suppose you might. But I have no intention of pulling caps with you over which of us has the right to be more surprised by this encounter. Such a wonderful morning is not to be so squandered.' Smiling to herself, she rose slightly in her saddle to look round at the beauties of the almost empty park. She felt so wonderfully free this morning. Nothing—and no one—would be allowed to spoil her pleasure.

'I should always give way to a lady in such a discussion,' he returned with a slight bow.

'Thank you, sir. I had not thought to win that bout so easily.' She half-bowed in acknowledgement, looking up at him through her dark lashes.

'There is, however, a small impediment to your complete victory, I fear, ma'am.'

Isabella raised her head and looked him full in the face. His rich chocolate eyes were glinting strangely, but—yet again—she found his expression impossible to read.

'You do not ask about the impediment, ma'am. Very wise, but I shall tell you, none the less. Since I returned from the wars, I have been unable to revert to my lazy old ways. I cannot break the habit of rising with the dawn and, since there is little else to entertain me at such an hour, I exercise my horses in the park.' His expression remained resolutely impassive while he delivered this master-stroke. There might have been a fleeting glimmer of humour in his eyes, but it vanished so quickly that it was impossible to be sure it had ever been there.

Isabella was baffled. The man was a riddle. She could not begin to divine his motives, even in a mere battle of words. But she was determined not to be bested, even in so trivial an encounter. 'I yield, my lord, immediately,' she said quickly. 'I do hate to see a man struggle so to hide his triumph.'

Lord Amburley's lips twitched a little ruefully at her sharp wit. Then, recovering himself, he commented, 'That is a very fine mare you are riding, Miss Winstanley. Many a gentleman would envy you such a mount.'

'Lady Wycham keeps an excellent stable,' lied Isabella. 'But I doubt Princess is up to your weight,' she added, casting an ironic eye over his tall person and the huge grey he rode. 'She may be fast, but she is a lady's mount.'

'I did not think to ride her myself, ma'am,' he said ruefully. 'I recognise the difficulties of mounting a man of my size.' He ran his gloved hand down the grey's neck. 'Did you enjoy the ball last night?'

Isabella was not one to resort to the usual comments about 'a shocking squeeze'. 'Yes, sir, I did,' she said frankly, 'though I have not danced so much for a very long time.' Behind her, Tom's horse was growing restless. 'Forgive me, I am neglecting the horses. After such a mad gallop, we must walk them.' With a slight bow, she started away.

Lord Amburley urged his grey into a walk also. 'Will you not permit me to ride with you for a space, ma'am? There can be nothing to concern you, surely, accompanied as you are by your groom?'

'I fear that is not quite how some would choose to view the matter, sir,' she said with mock severity. 'It is not usual for single ladies to ride with gentlemen when the park is thus deserted. It would have the appearance of an assignation.'

His lordship continued to walk the grey at her side. 'I promise to keep my distance, lest prying eyes observe and make improper deductions. Would you have me search the bushes?' he added, with a slightly quizzical look.

Isabella burst out laughing. 'I fancy you are trying to roast me again, sir,' she gasped.

'Yes, it is quite outrageous of me, as you have said before. I plead the same defence. You look splendid when you laugh.' He favoured her with a long, admiring look, which brought so much colour to her cheeks that he immediately offered an apology. 'Forgive me, ma'am, for speaking out of turn. It was not my intention to embarrass you in any way.'

Isabella reddened even more. Heavens, what was she about? Determined to prevent this dangerous conversation from continuing, she swallowed hard and challenged him to a gallop. He agreed, apparently with relief. He did, however, insist on giving her an advantage, to allow for her mare's shorter stride and earlier exertions. For once, Isabella did not attempt to argue.

On this occasion, Princess did not win. The big grey overhauled her easily. Lord Amburley was not even breathing hard by the time Isabella reached the winning post, looking rather more tousled than before.

Pulling off her precariously perched hat and letting the last of her hair tumble down her back, she admitted defeat. 'Even when she is fresh, the Princess could not outpace your grey, sir. We were quite out-classed.'

'You were defeated but not, I think, outclassed, Miss Winstanley,' he conceded. 'You and your mare make a fine pairing.'

Isabella felt herself blushing yet again and quickly made to turn her mount towards the park gates. 'I think I must now be returning to Hill Street, sir, before I am cried a hoyden all over London.' With no little difficulty, she pinned up most of her hair and replaced her hat. She refused to consider how disreputable she must look.

He raised his hat in polite farewell. 'It would be my pleasure, ma'am, if you should again choose to ride in the park unreasonably early.'

Was that an invitation? Isabella was not at all sure what to make of him in this strange mood, but she did know that she would risk her reputation by meeting him again in such a way. Whatever she had earlier suggested to Tom, it must now be forgotten—no matter how tempting the thought...

'It is not my habit to ride quite so early, I fear, but thank you for your company, none the less. And now, if you will excuse me, sir?' With a genuine smile, she bade him farewell and trotted towards the exit, closely followed by the groom.

His lordship sat motionless astride the big grey, watching her receding back. His dark eyes narrowed as they followed her passage, and a thoughtful frown creased his forehead.

This was a completely different woman from the poor relation—or the enigmatic lady of the *ton*. This Miss Winstanley was utterly captivating, with her frank, open ways and her manifest joy at simply being alive on a beautiful spring day. He found himself wishing that he had not met her at all before today, that he knew nothing of her deceit. The glorious creature who had laughingly raced him across the park was the kind of woman who could haunt a man's dreams.

Chapter Seven

Although still early, it was later than she had planned when Isabella arrived back in Hill Street.

Mitchell took one look at her and briskly set about bringing some order to her hair, muttering darkly as she combed out the tangles. 'Her ladyship is already awake. She has been asking for you,' she chided.

'Oh, dear. I had hoped to be there when she awoke. Make haste with my hair, Mitchell. And I shall have to change out of this habit.'

'I should think so, indeed. I cannot imagine why you chose to go riding in that shabby old thing, when you have two others hanging in the clothes press. Her ladyship would be shocked to know you had worn it in Hyde Park.'

'But her ladyship will not know, Mitchell, will she?' said Isabella with emphasis. 'I wore the old habit because it is comfortable. The newer ones are designed for displaying oneself at a gentle amble. They are not suitable for taking real exercise.'

'I just hope nobody saw you dressed like that, miss.' Mitchell pursed her lips in disapproval. 'I would never live it down.'

Isabella fervently hoped that Tom would not betray her in this. 'You surely did not expect me to meet anyone so early, did you?' she asked innocently.

Mitchell merely grunted and began to unbutton the offending garment.

Barely five minutes later, properly attired in a simple morning gown, Isabella was by Lady Wycham's bedside. 'Dear Aunt, are you recovered this morning?'

'Much better, thank you, my dear, though no thanks to Parsons, who will insist that laudanum is the cure for everything.'

'It did allow you to sleep, however. And I fancy it will have eased the pain?'

'Well, yes,' admitted the old lady grudgingly. 'But tell me about the ball. Was Sophia a success?'

'Much more than I dared to hope, though she did look lovely. She was surrounded by admirers, almost from the moment we arrived. She may yet become a toast.'

'Sophia? I beg leave to doubt it. You, rather—especially looking as you did last evening.'

'Oh, Aunt, how can you? At my age?'

'Nonsense, child. You are only twenty-six—still young enough, I'd say. Did you keep your promise?'

Isabella plunged into a vivid description of how often she had danced and with whom, casually mentioning Lord Amburley's name among her list of partners.

'Amburley is the only personable one among them,' pronounced Lady Wycham. 'An interesting gentleman, I would say.'

'I know very little about him,' volunteered Isabella, trying to tempt her great-aunt into continuing, 'except that he was with the Duke in Spain and inherited on the death of an elder brother.'

Lady Wycham closed her eyes, frowning in concentration. 'There was a scandal some years ago, I seem to remember. He would have been about twenty-five, then. Ah, yes.' She nodded to herself. 'You were in mourning at the time, I think. Amburley's fiancée jilted him. He was forced to leave England.'

'Why? Was there a duel?' Isabella had paled.

'Hardly. The lady jilted him for his brother, the heir. The two brothers were at daggers drawn, as you can imagine. The old lord sided with the heir, of course—he was bound to, I suppose—and shipped young Stansfield out of the country. He eventually made his way to the Peninsula and joined the army. And he never saw his father—or his brother—again.' She gave a short, mirthless laugh and opened her eyes once more. 'The irony of it is that—as it turned out—the lady married the wrong brother. I understand she is left with almost nothing now, except her title and her very small jointure. It would have been different if she had produced a son, of course.' Lady Wycham was overcome by a fit of coughing, and Isabella hurriedly fetched a glass of water.

Isabella knew she should not tax her aunt's strength, but she found she was longing for more. 'I collect it is not a rich estate, then? Yet Lord Amburley does not seem to lack for funds.'

'A façade, I suspect. It could be a good estate, I believe, with some investment, but it is still heavily mortgaged. And, besides the widow, there is the Dowager—the present Baron's mother. She is much given to good works, which must be a further drain.' Lowering her voice even more, she added, 'I had heard that he finances her from his winnings at cards.'

Isabella choked.

'Good heavens, Isabella, are you all right?' cried Lady Wycham.

'Yes, Aunt,' coughed Isabella weakly, 'perfectly, I assure you. I cannot think what came over me.'

'Too much dancing and not enough sleep,' concluded Lady Wycham sagely. 'You look very pale, my dear. Are you sure—'

'Yes, dear Aunt, truly I am quite well. But I *am* a little tired. Perhaps I should lie down for a while.' That was not really true—but Isabella knew that it was the best way of avoiding Lady Wycham's increasingly difficult questions.

It was early afternoon when Isabella awoke. She lay on her back, gazing sightlessly at the window through the open bed-curtains. Amburley's face was not to be banished from her mind. Heavens, she had even been dreaming about him. Her body felt somehow different—soft and fluid, and aching for something that seemed to have been snatched away. She had been warm and melting in his embrace, thirstily drinking in the subtle male scent of him, twining her fingers in this thick black hair. And then he had—

No. He had not. He had been about to kiss her, but somehow it had not happened. Her practical side intervened to point out that it was not at all surprising. A woman who had never been kissed was bound to find it rather difficult to imagine how it felt, even in a dream.

However much she tried, Isabella was unable to drive thoughts of Lord Amburley completely from her mind. She found him unfathomable but—she had to admit, to herself at least—immensely attractive in his enigmatic way.

And Lady Wycham's intriguing description of his early disappointment... How on earth was it that an old lady who went about so little could be always so well-informed? Isabella smiled to herself. Her great-aunt never revealed her sources, but they were certainly reliable. It might even be possible to find out more about Amburley's past by that route. The tale of the rift between the brothers had been tantalisingly brief.

Relaxing back on her pillows, Isabella allowed her normally practical mind to muse on what little information she had. Jilted! And for his own brother! What a terrible blow to his pride, and doubly so when he was rejected by his father too. No wonder he seemed so unbending in his dealings with women. He had every reason to despise them all for causing him so much humiliation. And, if he had been nursing a broken heart all these years…

Isabella's common sense reasserted itself. Sophia might fondly imagine a man sighing for years for his lost love, but she did not. Such a man would have made a pretty poor soldier. Besides, Aunt Jemima had implied—and her information was to be trusted—that the widowed Lady Amburley was living in straitened circumstances. If Amburley had any feelings for her still, he would surely have seen to her comfort? Or had she been too proud to accept his 'charity'?

Enough! There was no way in which she could divine his feelings by indulging in idle speculation. And she was quite as foolish as Sophia, even to begin to allow her thoughts to wander in his direction.

Flinging back the covers, Isabella jumped out of bed and pulled the bell for Mitchell, silently vowing that she would keep herself so busy over the next few days that she would have no time to think about anything, especially not about Lord Amburley.

Isabella remained true to her word until Friday morning, when Lord Amburley was forced back into her thoughts by an innocent enquiry from Mitchell as to what she would wear to Lady Morrissey's soirée.

Isabella turned quickly and walked to the window,

taking several deep breaths as she did so. Then, in a passable imitation of her normal voice, she said, 'I am not sure. What do you suggest?'

Mitchell seemed to have noticed nothing. 'It will be quite a large affair, Miss Isabella, so you'll need to look your best. What about the blue crepe? I finished the new trimmings yesterday. Nobody would recognise it now.'

'That sounds splendid, Mitchell,' said Isabella, turning from the window. 'Would you fetch it so that I may see?'

The blue crepe gown had been transformed. The rather old-fashioned blonde lace trim had been removed and replaced by ruched ribbons in shades of blue darker than the dress itself. And instead of the old underdress to match the lace, Mitchell proffered a silk slip of deepest ultramarine that picked up the shade of the darker ribbons. The ensemble was exquisite.

'Shall you wear your mother's diamond collar, Miss Isabella?'

'No, I think not. You know I never wear it. The stones are too fine for a poor relation. No, I think the aquamarines again. They are such a pretty colour...and will look interesting against the deep blue, do you not agree?'

'The necklace certainly becomes you, but surely you wore it just a few days ago? What about the sapphires instead?'

'I do not care to flaunt the contents of my jewel

case, Mitchell. Too many questions would arise. The sapphire pendant would suit, I admit, but I prefer the more unusual colour combination, I think.'

Mitchell dutifully fetched the aquamarines to set against the dress. The combination was striking—so the discussion of jewellery ended there.

When they arrived at the soirée, Lady Morrissey greeted Lady Wycham with real concern, enquiring after her health. Isabella felt a twinge of guilt. She would not for the world have wished ill on Lady Wycham, but the old lady's presence tonight deprived Isabella of the excuse of chaperoning Sophia. Clearly, the meeting with Lord Amburley was fated. Isabella felt as if a dark cloud were looming over her. Even if she tried to escape, it would follow.

Hardly had their party established itself in a corner of the saloon than Lord Amburley himself was bowing over Lady Wycham's hand.

'I am delighted to hear of your recovery, ma'am,' he smiled. 'It is a pity you were not able to attend the Duchess's ball to witness the success of Miss Winstanley and Miss Sophia. I'd wager that neither of them lacked a partner the whole evening,' he added, looking pointedly at Isabella, who groaned inwardly. He seemed to have the old lady eating out of his hand. How was it that a man who was so cold and forbidding at one moment, could be so charming the next?

Lord Amburley was now devoting all his attention

to Lady Wycham. 'I must tell you, ma'am, that I learned at the ball that Miss Winstanley is a fine piquet player. I have never pitted my skill against a lady, and I confess I am intrigued to try her mettle. If you permit, I should like to challenge her to a rubber or two.'

Lady Wycham looked inquiringly into his lordship's face, but his expression was inscrutable. He had made it seem as if this invitation were the most natural thing in the world.

Isabella knew her great-aunt would find some means of turning the challenge aside if she showed the slightest hint of reluctance. But it was now a matter of honour. She nodded bleakly.

'Well, sir,' said Lady Wycham a little uncertainly, 'if Isabella wishes to accept, I can see no reason to gainsay you.' She continued to look a little concerned as she added a hurried afterthought. 'I take it you will not play for high stakes?'

'I shall happily play for any stakes Miss Winstanley cares to name,' responded his lordship with an innocent smile. Lady Wycham visibly relaxed. 'Are you ready, ma'am?' He rose, still smiling, and offered his arm to Isabella.

'You make it very difficult to refuse you, sir,' she returned instantly, then immediately regretted her words. She must give her great-aunt no cause for anxiety. But Lady Wycham had already turned away.

Isabella rose gracefully. Placing the tips of her fingers on his arm, she discovered that the cloth of his immaculate black evening coat was infinitely smooth and soft to the touch. She could feel the warmth of his body through the layers of material, almost as if she were touching his skin. And that faint hint of his citrus cologne assailed her senses. Yet again, she found she was more aware of this man than of any other she had ever met. And from the merest touch!

Leading her towards the card-room, Lord Amburley lowered his voice to a conspiratorial whisper. 'There is no need to go through with this if you have changed your mind, Miss Winstanley. Indeed, I pray that you have.'

'Do you, my lord?' She prickled visibly. 'But I am not so craven, nor so lost to a sense of honour that I would cry off, I assure you.'

Lord Amburley's expression hardened. Again, he bestowed that cold, calculating look on her, making her shiver inwardly. Again, she recognised the streak of ruthlessness that she had discovered in him during their first encounters.

In cool, correct tones, his lordship then informed her that he had at no time desired to question her honour or her courage. He would play, as he had promised, for any stakes she cared to name.

Isabella despaired of her own impulsive tongue. How could they be so easily at daggers drawing? Why had she set them at odds by bristling so, in response to his simple offer to let her withdraw? Her response had been purely instinctive. She barely understood her own motives, except that she had fancied

she detected a note of pity in his offer. To be pitied—
especially by Amburley—was intolerable. She would
let him see she was a woman to be reckoned with.

'We agreed, as I recall, sir, to play for a guinea a
point. Three rubbers?'

He nodded, drawing out her chair.

'And shall we say twenty guineas the game, besides?'

Lord Amburley barely suppressed a gasp. Isabella
was not surprised—after all, she was insisting upon
extraordinarily high stakes. He threw a penetrating
look at her, holding her gaze. For a moment, she
thought he was about to round on her. Then he
seemed to take a renewed grip of himself, forcing
calm back into his features as he took his seat opposite her. He dropped his gaze to the cards.

Watching his strong fingers expertly shuffling the
pack he had just broken, Isabella became increasingly
conscious of his skill with the cards. Everything she
had heard about him—and her own common sense—
told her she was likely to lose. Her instinct told her
his lordship was now sufficiently piqued by her inexplicable conduct to give no quarter. Yet her irrepressible sense of humour whispered that, however
much she lost, it was all in a good cause. After all, it
would go to fund his mother's good works! The un-
bidden thought that losing would be an act of pious
generosity brought a greener gleam to her eyes and a
chuckle to her throat. She attempted to disguise it as
a cough.

'May I fetch you a glass of wine, ma'am?' offered his lordship, with exquisite politeness. 'I should not want any dryness of the throat to disturb your concentration.'

The chuckle could no longer be contained, especially as a little of his hostility seemed to have disappeared. She allowed herself to laugh softly, hoping to dispel yet more. 'I shall certainly want for concentration if you roast me so, sir. I declare it is wicked of you.'

'I could not resist, I fear. And I meant to punish you for the joke you did not share. Will you tell me what it was?' He was gazing down at her now, invitingly.

Isabella could not tear her eyes away from his. 'I...' She searched for an acceptable half-truth. 'You will now think me a sad creature, since I alone am responsible for the situation we are in. On a sudden, I saw how ridiculous my actions have been.' She continued quickly, as he made to speak. 'Forgive me, sir, but, in spite of what I have just said, I am still determined to proceed as we have agreed. I beg you will simply accept that, however strange it may seem.' She might concede that her actions seemed inexplicable, but she would never withdraw. Isabella Winstanley was no coward.

Lord Amburley frowned. A hard shadow passed across his face and was as quickly gone. He looked into Isabella's limpid eyes. What did he see there? Isabella had no way of knowing. Her motives were impenetrable, even to herself. She thought he gave a little shrug, as if accepting that he had no choice but to continue.

'As you wish, Miss Winstanley. Will you cut for deal?'

Chapter Eight

The first hand was remarkably even. Both players
lingered over their discards and over their play, feeling for the opponent's weaknesses. Eventually, Isabella won by a handful of points, but neither scored
well.

'Well played, ma'am,' said Lord Amburley generously.

'I had the slightly better cards only, I think,' she
admitted, dealing the second hand. To her surprise,
he made only three of the five permitted discards. He
must have very good cards, she supposed, though his
expression revealed nothing at all. The remaining
cards improved Isabella's hand markedly. This would
be a real test. She waited expectantly for his first declaration.

'A point of six, ma'am?'

'That depends on its value,' she responded quickly,
reckoning the total of her six hearts.

'Fifty-five?'

'I have fifty-eight.'

'I concede your point, ma'am. Do you concede my quint?'

Isabella's own sequence of five hearts to the ace could only be equalled, not beaten. His lordship conceded her fifteen points.

'I offer besides a quartet of aces,' she added quickly, since that too was unbeatable. 'Repique, I believe.' She then proceeded to take Lord Amburley's opening lead and to lay down her remaining eleven winning cards. 'And capote, also.'

His lordship threw down his cards. 'A splendid hand, ma'am. Unusual for the dealer to score so well against the major hand.'

Isabella raised her eyes from the task of recording her score, but there was nothing to be read into his expression. 'Even the dealer may have a share of luck sometimes, my lord,' she responded a little tartly, gathering up the cards to hand to him. 'Shall you see if you may do as well?'

With a slight nod he began to shuffle the cards. Luck did not favour either player, however. The four remaining hands of the first game were evenly matched and low-scoring. Isabella's first deal had given her enough points to win this game by a size-able margin.

'I have exactly one hundred points, ma'am,' announced Lord Amburley, with some evidence of relief. No doubt the thought of being rubiconned by a female—especially this one—was singularly unpleasant.

In the second game, they won three hands apiece. But Lord Amburley scored well in his, while Isabella's scores were pitifully low: only ninety points.

'My game, I believe, this time,' he said, quickly leading his last winning card.

Isabella threw down her last card with a laugh. 'And as I have failed to reach the rubicon, you will be several hundred guineas to the good. Still, we are all square on games won.' She threw him such a rueful glance with this last remark that he was forced into an unwilling laugh. He summoned a footman with a tray of champagne.

'For my cough, sir?' she asked archly.

'No, ma'am, for your concentration. I won that game on the luck of the cards only. And the luck may always change.'

'You mean you would prefer an opponent who was less sharp?'

He seemed startled by her choice of words and paused a moment to search her face. 'I think I have met a redoubtable opponent, Miss Winstanley. I may need all the help I can get.' He placed a glass of champagne by her hand.

She raised it to her smiling lips. 'As do I,' she said, and sipped. 'It is your deal, sir.'

Isabella eventually pipped him to the deciding game and the first rubber. A quick reckoning, however, showed that, for all her efforts, the rubber had netted her only thirty-five guineas.

'An excellent rubber, ma'am. Clearly the champagne improves your play,' he observed with the merest hint of a smile. 'Another glass?'

'Thank you, no. I think I shall need a clear head if I am to win a second rubber. I should prefer lemonade, if you please.'

He nodded and rose to fetch it himself, leaving Isabella watching his retreating back as he strode out of the card-room. Abstractedly shuffling the cards, she found herself admiring the set of his broad shoulders and the easy grace of his long stride. He returned almost immediately to place lemonade by her, with champagne for himself. When she won the cut, he sat back, drinking his champagne and watching her deal.

Isabella felt his keen gaze and willed her hands to behave normally. She refused to consider why he paid such close attention to her movements, for that would undermine her confidence completely. Better to concentrate simply on one hand at a time.

The play proceeded in silence for several hands. At the end of the next game, Isabella breathed a sigh of relief as she recorded her winning score. With one rubber and one game under her belt, she now needed only one more game to win both the second rubber and the match. And she was nearly two hundred guineas ahead, to boot.

As Isabella shuffled the cards to begin dealing, Mr Lewiston came into the card-room, looking about him. Seeing the seated pair, he came across to join them, though he knew better than to disturb the players by speaking to them. He simply eyed Amburley's score-pad and grimaced.

'You may speak, if you are so minded, George,' invited his lordship curtly, 'provided it is not simply to remind me of how badly I am losing. I am already well enough aware of that.'

Isabella glanced up from her shuffling but said nothing. She smiled tentatively at Mr Lewiston.

'Forgive me, ma'am. I should not disturb your play. If you permit, however, I should like to watch for a space. It will be instructive to see Amburley beaten.'

'George—'

'Mr Lewiston—'

Their protests came in unison—his exasperated, hers embarrassed. But Mr Lewiston showed no sign of chagrin over his outrageous remark.

'Mr Lewiston,' repeated Isabella, in the patient accents of a governess to an irritating child, 'you must know very well that nothing is certain until the last card is played. There may yet be a very long way to go. I pray you will not embarrass me—or indeed his lordship—by suggesting that victory is certain to be mine.'

Mr Lewiston had the grace to flush, a very little. 'Apologies, ma'am,' he muttered in a low voice. 'I had no intention… I apologise—'

'Oh, for goodness' sake, George, do hold your

tongue,' said his lordship testily. 'You are interrupting our game. Stay if you must, but, I beg of you, stop your chatter and let us concentrate!'

Mr Lewiston flushed hotly under this rebuke but seemed to take it to heart. He stationed himself silently behind Lord Amburley.

Isabella returned to the business of dealing, wishing that Mr Lewiston had not remained. She found his presence disconcerting. She should be grateful, she supposed, that he had not chosen to stand behind her and watch her every move. That would be even worse.

Isabella dealt for the opening hand of the next game feeling very tense. Although she tried hard to concentrate on nothing but the cards, her thoughts insisted on straying to Lord Amburley and his friend. What were they thinking? It was impossible to deduce anything from Lord Amburley's face for, in spite of the impatience and irritation he had just shown his friend, he appeared relaxed and unconcerned. A good actor, she concluded, as any fine card player must be. But I am sure he does not relish the thought of losing to me, especially in front of an audience.

As the game proceeded, neither player made any mistakes, but the cards rather favoured his lordship—with only one more hand to be played, he was nearly fifty points ahead of Isabella. She fancied his lack of concern had become less of a pose. No wonder. She would need very good cards indeed to win the game on this last hand.

Isabella picked up the cards he had dealt her, offering a silent prayer for good luck. She found she really did want this victory, even though she was still at something of a loss to explain why.

Her hand was fair, but by no means outstanding. She was unlikely to win with such cards. Instead, she consoled herself with the thought that she might still win the rubber by two games to one.

As Isabella led out the cards of her point suit, she realised that her hand was much stronger than she had thought—there was a real possibility that she might be able to take all twelve tricks. Such a clean sweep would give her the second rubber—and victory.

She won the first ten tricks quickly and paused to reconsider her last two cards: the queen of hearts and the eight of spades. The queen was a certain winner; the spade less so. Lord Amburley certainly held the ace of clubs; it was possible that his other card was a spade, though it was more likely to be a second club. She had planned to take the eleventh trick by leading her queen. Provided he retained his ace—as was to be expected—she would win the last trick with her spade.

She hesitated.

Raising her eyes to his face, she detected a tightness around his mouth that had not been there before. He must know that the odds were stacked against him. Perhaps he was even imagining how his friends would roast him when the knowledge of his defeat became public? No doubt he would be in some degree humiliated—yet another blow for a man who had already suffered so many blows.

She looked again at her cards. The players at the neighbouring tables were all watching them now. The atmosphere around the table had become tense and expectant. She felt again that it was somehow doom-laden, even as she recognised that she was ascribing momentous importance to a mere card-game.

And then she knew. Her decision was made. She could not do it—at least, not like this.

Before she could change her mind, Isabella led the eight of spades, giving him a clear opportunity to deny her the rubber.

Lord Amburley looked up with a start to stare into her face. After a moment, he took the trick with the nine of spades and led his ace of clubs to win the last. He smiled oddly as she dropped the queen of hearts on to it.

'My game, ma'am, I believe,' he said softly, 'though it was a close-run thing.' His matter-of-fact words did not match the scorching intensity of his eyes, searching her face. Mr Lewiston's presence was apparently forgotten.

Tearing her eyes from his, Isabella busied herself with her score-pad and responded that there was still much to play for; she hoped to emerge the winner from the next game.

But she did not. Lord Amburley won it comfortably to square the match at one rubber apiece. Then, to

Isabella's vexation, he ran out the deciding rubber in two quick and very profitable games.

'Allowing for the additional points for games won, I make that a lead of 537 points, Miss Winstanley. Do you agree my figures?'

In Mr Lewiston's presence, Isabella contrived to remain light-hearted about her losses. After all, he did not know the level of the stakes. He would probably assume they were playing for pennies.

'My figures exactly, sir. A splendid win, I admit, particularly in the last rubber. And now,' she continued with apparent unconcern, 'I feel I ought to return to the drawing-room. I have neglected Lady Wycham for a very long time.'

To her relief, Mr Lewiston took that as a hint to leave them. She faced Lord Amburley across the card table, where the cards remained scattered as they had been at the end of the last hand.

'I shall need a little time—' she began, but was allowed to get no further.

'Miss Winstanley, I have no desire to press you for payment. I beg you will settle this matter when you are ready.' He was pushing the cards around as he spoke, without looking at her directly. Then he picked up one card and held it in his fingers, studying it intently. 'May I add, without any desire to indulge in idle flattery, that you are without doubt one of the finest players I have encountered? I have rarely met an opponent who judged the game so nicely. Or one who made so few mistakes.'

He let the card fall face-up on to the table. It was the queen of hearts!

For a long moment, Isabella's heart seemed to stop beating altogether, then it began to pound furiously. Good God! He knew! She gazed, mesmerised, at the card on the table. Then, with a supreme effort of will, she raised her eyes to his face, to meet the mockery there.

She did not find it.

'You are pale, ma'am,' he murmured, with obvious concern. 'I have kept you much too long in this hot and stuffy card-room. Let me escort you to where the air is fresher.' He rose, politely offering her his arm once more.

Isabella was numb. Without a word—for she was incapable of speech—she allowed him to lead her into the drawing-room. But he did not immediately seek out Lady Wycham, as Isabella had expected.

'I am sure you would welcome a turn about the room now, after sitting for so long.' It was a statement, not a question, and he moved her away from her party as he spoke.

After a moment's silence, he broke into Isabella's disordered thoughts once more. 'Would you do me the honour of driving in the park with me tomorrow, ma'am?'

Now *that* was the last thing Isabella had expected him to say.

'Or on another day, if tomorrow is not convenient,' he added smoothly.

What choice did she have? She could think of no reasonable excuse for denying him. 'Thank you, sir, I should like that,' she answered simply. 'Tomorrow will be quite convenient.'

'I shall call for you at four, then.'

Lewiston rejoined Amburley as he returned to the card-room. 'Well?' he asked cryptically.

His lordship raised an eyebrow. In truth, the last thing he wanted was a discussion now. But it could not be avoided, even though he was not at all sure of his own conclusions. She must have known something of his reputation as a card player, and yet she had persisted, poor though she was, in naming those astonishing stakes. And then losing.

Lewiston lowered his voice. 'I suppose you saw nothing... What we discussed, you remember? Did she...?'

'I saw nothing, George, nothing at all. And I do not believe there was anything to see. To be sure, I did wonder at the start, because of her luck as dealer. But I had the same odd luck myself, later on. No. There was nothing to see.' He paused to catch up another glass of champagne and take a long swallow. 'Besides—I won, and handsomely.' He grinned at his friend.

'You could have lost the whole bout in that second rubber.'

Lord Amburley clapped his friend on the shoulder. 'You mean, *you* would have done so in my place.

Believe me, I knew pretty well which cards she held. I had every intention of winning that hand, even if she…even if she had not made that mistake.'

'Will she pay up, do you think?'

'She has asked for time. She intends to pay, I believe. It remains to be seen whether she can, and also why she…' He found he had no desire to discuss Miss Winstanley's play with anyone. It seemed unfathomable. If she had deliberately thrown that hand, as he suspected, her motives were obscure indeed. Better simply to accept that her excellent card-playing skills had deserted her for a second. There were still puzzles enough, deciding between the parts she played. Lord Amburley frowned into the middle distance, recalling the many riddles she posed.

His friend was looking inquiringly at him. 'Just what are you planning, Leigh? I've seen that look before. And the last time, I recall, no good came of it. No good at all.'

His lordship surveyed his friend with suddenly narrowed eyes and a half-smile. 'Do you care to take a small wager on that, George?'

Chapter Nine

Well before the gentlefolk were out of bed, Isabella was to be seen quietly making her way out through the mews at the back of Hill Street. Shrouded in a dark shawl and her battered brown bonnet, she climbed unaided into a hackney carriage that seemed to be waiting for her.

'Let us be on our way quickly,' she whispered urgently. The jarvey set the horses forward at a brisk trot.

The mews was almost deserted as the cab pulled away. Only a solitary street urchin seemed to be about. He was small, dirty and ill clad. He was huddled in one of the corners as if he were half-asleep and dreaming of better times, and he paid no attention to the cab and its occupant when it moved past him, starting to gather speed.

Then, all at once, the sleepy figure came alive. No sooner had the hackney passed beyond the spot where he stood, than he was no longer on it. In the blink of an eye, he had swung himself up on to the back of the cab and concealed himself there beneath the tarpaulin.

The cab and its passengers, the acknowledged and the stowaway, turned the corner and disappeared from view.

'There is a young varmint, my lord, asking after you most particular.' The butler's lofty disdain pervaded every syllable of the description. He seemed disappointed to find that Lord Amburley did not respond immediately in the same vein.

'Does he have a name, this young person?'

'Sam, my lord, I believe. Shall I send him about his business?'

'No, thank you, Wilson. Will you show him into the book-room?'

The butler's mouth opened and then shut again at the sight of his master's expression. With a bow, he left the room.

The 'young varmint' was shown in. He appeared little abashed by his elegant surroundings and started across the turkey carpet.

'Did you wipe your feet downstairs, Sam?'

'Course I did, yer honour. Yon whey-faced cove wouldn't let me in the door 'til I wiped everyfink in sight: feet, 'ands—'

'Yes, thank you, Sam,' interrupted his lordship, with a grimace. 'I take your meaning.' He sat down

behind the mahogany desk. 'Now, I take it you have
learned something already?'

Sam took a deep breath and launched into his narrative. 'Ever so early this mornin', it were. Weren't
nobody about, or nearly. So I sat meself round the
back, out o' the wind. Then this jarvey drives up an'
stops outside the back entrance o' the gentry ken, the
one what you told me t' keep me glims on. So, I
ups and says to meself, "Them's strange doings."
Didn't give no sign, o' course. The jarvey, 'e didn't
even notice I were there, I reckon.'

His lordship sighed. 'Might you just tell me what
happened, Sam? I have no doubt you carried out your
role to perfection, so let's not waste time on describ-
ing how good you are. The fact that you're here, and
in one piece, speaks for itself.'

The urchin grinned, exposing a mouthful of broken
and missing teeth. 'Right y'are, yer honour. As I were
saying, the jarvey, 'e just sat there. Then, about ten
minutes after, the gate opens and out comes the gentry-mort, all wrapped in a black shawl, climbs into
the cab and they're off at the gallop.'

'Is that all? Describe this lady in the shawl. Was
she alone?'

'She were uncommon tall, guv'nor, just like you
said.' His lordship allowed himself a slight smile.
'Couldn't see 'er 'air, though. Wore a brown bonnet,
pulled down around her phiz. Didn't 'ave nobody wiv
'er, neither.' He paused.

'You look remarkably pleased with yourself, young Sam. I take it there's more?'

'Aye, yer honour. I 'itched meself up on the cab as it passed and settled meself down, all right and tight, ter go wiv 'em. And so I did.'

His lordship burst out laughing. 'Well done, Sam. Believe me, I have never doubted you. Now, tell me, where did she go?'

'You'll not believe it, guv'nor, but it's the truth, swelp me it is.'

'Sam…' Lord Amburley allowed the rising note in his voice to sound more than a little menacing.

'The Fleet.'

'What?'

'Honest to God, guv'nor, she went to the Fleet.'

In a calmer voice, Lord Amburley asked, 'Did she go *into* the Fleet?'

'Aye, yer honour, that she did. I see'd her. Stayed above an hour, I'd say.'

'What did the jarvey do? Did he wait? And where were you?'

'I weren't going to 'ang around there, not more'n I could 'elp. Not the jug, o' course, but stands t' reason, a man don't—'

'What did the jarvey do?' repeated Lord Amburley.

'He drove off, o' course. Came back again, though, just afore the gentry-mort come out again. So it must 'a been fixed 'tween 'em. She got back in and they was off. Didn't 'ave no chance ter go wiv 'em, that time. Sorry, yer honour.'

His lordship leaned back in his chair and allowed himself to smile. 'Sam, you've done well. Here.' He handed some coins to the boy, who beamed. 'There's more where that came from, if you keep at it. I want to know if she goes anywhere else, particularly dressed in that way. And I want to know whom she visits in the Fleet.'

'Could go yerself, guv'nor, an' ask,' suggested Sam cheekily. 'Mite difficult fer me ter go in there.'

'Do your best, Sam. There's a guinea in it for you, if you get me a name. No doubt you have contacts?'

Sam nodded. 'Best be off, yer honour.' He paused, a mischievous light in his eyes. ''Ere, guv'nor, what's yer lay with this 'ere gentry-mort?'

'That, Sam,' responded his lordship coldly, tapping a finger along his nose, 'is not your business. And if I were to find you had been doing a little enquiring on that subject, I should be very displeased—very displeased indeed.'

Sam backed towards the door. 'Honest, guv'nor, I didn't mean nuffink. I'll do me best, like you said.'

'Good,' said Lord Amburley. 'Come back the minute you have anything. I promise it will be worth your while.'

With those encouraging words ringing in his ears, Sam made his way out.

Lord Amburley continued to sit at his desk, gazing unseeingly in the general direction of the moroccobound copies of Latin classics on the book-shelves opposite and resting his chin on his steepled fingers.

He could not understand this latest intelligence. Or, at least, the only conceivable circumstances which would fit were particularly unflattering to Miss Winstanley.

Why on earth had she gone into the Fleet? To be sure, it was less dreadful than the prisons for the common felons, like Newgate, or worse, the convict hulks moored offshore. They were feared by even the most hardened criminals. But the Fleet was still a terrible place where no gentlewoman—or gentleman for that matter—would ever willingly set foot. Some gentlemen had no choice, of course, if their debts caught up with them before they could vanish abroad.

Could she have a relative in the Fleet? She had said something about gambling being in the blood. A brother, perhaps? Or a lover? Somehow, that last idea was singularly unpalatable to his lordship, and he dismissed it instantly. She had gone to the prison unchaperoned, which no lady would do, except perhaps to visit her family. Miss Winstanley was unquestionably a lady, and so—

A discreet knock on the book-room door was followed by the entrance of the butler. 'Mr Lewiston has called, my lord. Shall I show him into the—'

'No need for all that formality, man,' said the gentleman in question, breezing past the butler. 'I can announce myself. Mornin', Leigh.'

For the second time that morning, the deflated butler was forced to retreat.

'You're not busy, are you, old man? Because we've got to do a bit of knight-errant work, and sharpish.'

Rising from his chair, Lord Amburley smiled at his enthusiastic young friend. 'A damsel in distress, I take it, George. May I ask who it is this time?'

'The heiress, Sophia Winstanley, of course. It's Gradely. He is planning to call in Hill Street to ask permission to pay his addresses to her. He must be stopped.'

Lord Amburley raised an eyebrow. George Lewiston was impetuous and unpredictable, but this behaviour was unusual, even for him. 'Must? You may want her for yourself, George, but you'll just have to enter the lists with everyone else, including Gradely. I dare say his title will count in his favour, though.' He narrowed his eyes. 'On the other hand, you're rich while he, by all accounts, is practically cleaned out. He needs a rich wife.'

'But he will not have Sophia,' Lewiston burst out. 'You don't understand, Leigh. It's not that I want her for myself—though I'll admit she's a taking little thing. No, it's Gradely. He's a gambler, a hell-hound, a… Leigh, you and I don't really know him, but Kenley does, and he says Gradely has strange habits. He says…he says Gradely likes to hurt people, especially women.'

His lordship frowned. 'Do you believe Kenley? He may simply want the heiress for himself, you know, and be using you for his dirty work.'

'I've thought of that. He's promised to produce evidence, if necessary. One of the opera dancers, last year, still has the scars. And in any case, Kenley's no longer after Sophia. He's pursuing another interest now.'

'I see,' said his lordship slowly. He had never known Lewiston so serious about a woman before. 'What are you proposing to do?'

'I thought that I...that we might warn him off, let him know we know about his little "habits" and will make them public if he persists in this.'

Serious Lewiston might be, but his judgement had not improved one jot. 'Really?' said Lord Amburley witheringly. 'George, you are letting your enthusiasm overcome your reason. It's impossible to "warn him off", as you put it, without proof. And the word of an opera dancer won't do for this, not a year after it happened. No doubt he bought her off at the time, but he'd always deny it. He'd simply swear she was lying and you had paid her to testify. And, what's more, Gradely would be bound to call out his accuser. He's a crack shot, I believe.'

'So are you,' protested Lewiston.

His lordship laughed mirthlessly. 'I thought it might be coming to that. No, George, it won't wash. We can't warn him off. And I have no intention of meeting Gradely at dawn, in order to save your precious Sophia's pampered hide.'

'But we can't just—'

'However,' continued his lordship meditatively, 'there may be a subtler way. I have promised to take

Miss Winstanley driving this afternoon. I shall somehow contrive to warn her about Gradely's ''predilections''. She is a sensible woman, too sensible to dismiss such an allegation out of hand. She will be bound to take steps to ensure Gradely's suit is turned away.'

'But you can't talk to a single lady about such things. She could have the vapours—or worse.'

'Miss Winstanley? I doubt it. I should be most surprised to find that *anything* would undermine that lady's composure.'

'Does that include losing a small fortune to you last evening?'

'Yes. Nobody would have known it from her face. She was totally in control throughout. And she is a very fine player indeed.'

'You said that before.'

'Well, it is none the less true. Don't play against her, George. She would fleece you shamefully.'

'Perhaps I should, though,' said the younger man with a sudden grin. 'Then she could use those winnings to pay her debts to you.'

'Don't you dare! I don't want her let off that particular hook. I shall find out what her game is eventually—and keeping her under pressure to find so much money will *encourage* her to make mistakes sooner.'

'You could have her watched.'

Amburley prevaricated. 'Do you think that would serve? She is a lady, after all.'

'Perhaps not. She probably never goes anywhere without a maid or a groom.'

Lord Amburley smiled slightly but said nothing.

'Perhaps she will let something drop when you take her out later?'

'I shall try to ensure that she does,' promised his lordship.

Promptly at four, Lord Amburley reined in his greys in Hill Street and jumped down from his phaeton, throwing an instruction to Brennan to walk the horses while he waited. There was no telling how long he would be.

But Isabella Winstanley was not a lady in the ordinary style. When he was shown into the drawing-room, she rose to greet him dressed in a jade-green walking dress with matching hat and pelisse. The colour suited her wonderfully well. Lord Amburley was reminded of how enchantingly dishevelled she had looked at the end of that ride in Hyde Park. He determined to set a light note for today's encounter. It was just possible that she could be charmed into dropping her guard.

'Miss Winstanley,' he exclaimed in mock contrition, pointedly scrutinising her apparel, 'forgive me. I must have mistaken the hour. I had no intention of being late for our appointment.'

She was clearly not deceived. 'You are here precisely to the appointed hour, sir, as you know very well. Is it *so* unusual not to be kept waiting by a lady?'

Her quick wits had beaten him. It was quite impossible to make a reply that was both proper and truthful, so he simply bowed and offered his arm. 'If you are ready, shall we go?'

He noticed with approval that she was in no way daunted by his high-perch phaeton, which he had chosen to drive on this occasion, at least in part, to test her mettle. She settled herself calmly, while he spread a rug over her knees and gave his horses the office.

'Do you drive, Miss Winstanley?'

'I was used to, once, when we lived in the country. My father taught me.'

'If you drive as well as you ride, ma'am, I should like to witness it.'

'Oh, no,' she responded, then coloured in obvious embarrassment. 'I did not mean… My lord, you go out of your way to put me to the blush.' She swallowed and continued stiffly, 'Thank you for the pretty words about my riding. And as to driving—no, I do not pretend to be a whip.'

He raised an eyebrow and glanced sideways at her. 'What a pity. I had thought you might like to try my greys.'

She tried unsuccessfully to suppress a chuckle. It was a mannerism he found oddly attractive. 'Must you always roast me every time we meet, sir?'

'Yes,' he answered simply. 'Unless, of course, you

were to learn to control your habit of rising to my bait. Then, I fear, the pleasure would wane.'

He could tell that she was refusing to allow herself to smile.

'There must be a better word than "outrageous",' she mused aloud, watching his hands as he deftly guided his greys through the crowded street. 'What about "abominable"? Or "unpardonable"? Yes, I rather like "unpardonable". What do you think, sir?'

'I think, ma'am, that you are roasting *me* unpardonably when you know I am too preoccupied with the traffic at present to give you full measure in return.'

'Oh!' She laughed aloud at this palpable hit. 'If that is the quality of your wit when you are preoccupied, sir, I shall take care not to cross swords with you when you are at leisure.'

They drove on in silence until they had completed a circuit of the park. Then Amburley halted his team.

'Would you like to take the reins for a spell now, Miss Winstanley?' he invited. 'They are no longer quite so fresh.'

'Are you sure, sir? After all, you have no reason to believe I am to be trusted with them.' She was smiling up at him in the most disconcerting way.

'No? I have seen both your courage and your composure, ma'am, and I value your good sense. If you were not sure you could drive them, you would not make the attempt. Will you?'

She nodded, taking the reins and the whip he offered her in her gloved hands. He looked on approvingly as she felt the horses' mouths and started them into a walk. He was pleased to see that his judgement of her abilities was amply borne out.

'You have been well schooled, ma'am,' he said, as she completed the circuit and pulled up. 'I hope you noticed the looks of envy in all the carriages we passed.'

'No, sir, I did not,' she responded promptly, returning the reins to him. 'I was much too busy minding my team.'

'Well, no doubt the prime topic of conversation after divine service tomorrow will be how Miss Winstanley drove Amburley's greys in the park.' Immediately, he wished the words unsaid. They made him sound insufferably conceited.

But Miss Winstanley seemed to have missed the point completely. Her reply took him by surprise. 'I would hope to hear a more Christian subject aired on such an occasion,' she protested quickly. 'A little concern for our fellow-beings, perhaps, especially those less comfortably circumstanced than ourselves.'

'You speak with passion, ma'am. Not many ladies of the *ton* think as you do.' He started the phaeton into motion once more.

'No. I wish they did. There are so many poor souls who could be helped—orphan children, women fallen on hard times, families deep in debt, old soldiers with no means of support. The list is endless.' She seemed genuinely distressed at the thought of their plight.

What an extraordinary woman she was—full of contradictions. Still, she had given him a chance to probe just a little.

'There are many who suffer through no fault of their own, I grant you, and we should help where we can. But, equally, there are many who have brought punishment on themselves, by running up enormous debts, for example.'

If he thought to provoke a reaction from her by that statement, he was disappointed. She said nothing at all. But he was heartened to note the figure of Lord Gradely, on horseback, coming towards them.

'And good families are affected quite as much as the poor,' he continued, with barely a pause. 'Indeed, they have further to fall. I can think of many of my acquaintance who are but one step in front of the tipstaff. One in particular who is like to be pursued both for the Fleet and for Newgate, unless he is very lucky.'

Miss Winstanley turned to stare at her companion.

'Why, speak of the dev—' Amburley said. 'Gradely, how d'ye do?'

The three exchanged pleasantries for a few moments before the phaeton drove on, its occupants bowing and smiling to their acquaintances. It was not long before they were on their way back to Hill Street.

Lord Amburley was delighted to note that his companion seemed suddenly preoccupied. Thinking about what he had 'accidentally' let slip about Gradely, he hoped. But what if she failed to take the hint?

Chapter Ten

Isabella lost no time in visiting her great-aunt to ask about Lord Gradely and to wonder aloud why Lord Amburley should have taken such pains to give her a hint against him. Strange, strange man.

Lady Wycham was somewhat reticent on the subject of Gradely. He was an inveterate gambler, to be sure, and practically penniless, but she would not be drawn on any other vices, forbidding Isabella to press her further. 'It is of no account, in any case,' she concluded. 'He cannot be interested in Sophia, for she is not well-endowed enough for him. You are, of course, but there is no reason to believe he knows of your fortune. Besides, you are much too sensible to contemplate an attachment to such a man. It is a puzzle why Amburley should go to such lengths.'

Isabella agreed readily. She had felt not the slightest liking for Lord Gradely and, since her great-aunt clearly knew something to his detriment, Isabella would willingly avoid him as much as possible.

＊　　＊　　＊

The Gradely puzzle deepened a few days later,
however, when he called on Lady Wycham, just as
Mr Lewiston had predicted. But Lady Wycham was
more than a match for him. Lord Gradely had barely
got as far as the fateful words about asking her permission to pay his addresses, when the old lady cut
him short, with acid politeness. She regretted, of
course, but she could not grant him the leave he
sought. And, without actually being rude, she gave
him to understand that further visits to Hill Street
would not be welcome.

Lord Gradely left in something of a hurry, looking
rather less collected than when he had arrived.

Lady Wycham immediately confronted Isabella.
'My dear, what have you done to make Gradely think
you might welcome his addresses?'

'Why, nothing, Aunt. I have barely spoken to him.'
She was blushing fiercely. 'Surely there must be some
mistake?'

'I do not see that it could have been Sophia who
interested him—though I admit he was in the middle
of asking permission when I stopped him. I felt it was
wiser not to hear him out—one of those interminable
rehearsed periods about his feelings. Nonsense, all of
it. No—somehow he must have found out about your
money, Isabella. You *must* be more careful.'

Isabella acquiesced weakly, though she was certain
that she had given Gradely no encouragement whatsoever. Yet Amburley—somehow, Amburley had
known what Gradely planned. What on earth was

happening to her? Since she had met Lord Amburley, her life seemed to be spinning out of control.

However much she racked her brains, she could not imagine how Gradely might have thought an offer might be welcome. Never had she shown even the slightest partiality for him. Of course, if Gradely were barely one step ahead of his creditors, marriage might be his only hope. Perhaps he believed that she was Lady Wycham's heir. Perhaps he thought that, at her age, she would be so desperate for a husband that she would accept any offer, even from a…even from a what?

Lord Amburley had hinted at Newgate gaol— something worse than debt, then. And Isabella had instinctively believed him.

I'm sure he deliberately went out of his way to warn me, she thought, smiling softly as Amburley's face rose in her mind. Why on earth should he do that? And how did he learn of Gradely's plans?

With a shudder, she realised that all the gentlemen of the *ton* might know. They might even be taking wagers on the outcome. And a wager could account for Amburley's behaviour too. After all, he was known to be a gambler.

Isabella gave herself a mental shake. She refused to believe it could be so. Surely Amburley was too honourable to do any such thing? He must have been trying to warn her, to save her lest she might be tempted. But why?

Lord Gradely's astonishing visit had thoroughly

disrupted Isabella's plans for the morning. She had intended to pay a call on her banker's, in order to arrange to settle her debts to Lord Amburley, and then to go riding in the park, perhaps with Sophia. She now felt incapable of either. Nor could she continue to struggle with the impossible Gradely puzzle. Isabella decided to turn her attention instead to reassuring practical matters—the final arrangements for Sophia's coming-out ball.

She and Sophia settled down to spend the rest of the morning poring over designs for the decoration of the ballroom and discussing colours and accessories. It was well past noon when they were interrupted by a message that Lord Amburley had called.

'Did he ask for me?' Isabella demanded a little crossly, not having the least desire to be interrupted at that moment—especially by the man she was trying so hard to banish from her thoughts.

'He asked for Lady Wycham or yourself, miss,' came the reply, 'but her ladyship is resting and is not to be disturbed.'

There was no help for it. After his warning about Gradely, it would be churlish to refuse to receive him. 'Tell his lordship that I will be with him directly. And have some madeira sent in.'

As she checked her appearance in the glass, Isabella considered what might lie behind this visit.

He must want to know if his warning about Gradely was taken to heart, she concluded, deliberately allowing her irritation to grow. And if he did make a wager, he may even want to know if he can collect on it. Well, he is doomed to disappointment, for I shall certainly not tell him. With a stubborn tilt to her chin, she made her way to the drawing-room to meet his lordship.

He was standing by the window, looking out on to the street. The madeira tray stood untouched on the side table. As the door opened, he turned quickly and bowed. His eyes did not leave her face, and a slight smile played around his firm mouth.

Isabella did not return it. She merely dropped a polite curtsy. There was no need to advance to shake hands after that. Her 'Good day, my lord,' had a hint of sharpness in it.

Lord Amburley frowned slightly at her unaccustomed reserve. She could feel his eyes assessing her in that calculating way of his. Yet his voice sounded quite normal. 'I dare say you will not believe me, ma'am, but I have taken your strictures to heart.'

Isabella's eyes widened in surprise. What could he be talking about? 'Indeed, sir?'

'Mindful of your words, I have determined to visit some of the London monuments which I have so neglected.' He smiled—but his eyes were still hard. 'I wondered whether you might care to accompany me this afternoon?'

Isabella refused to believe for one moment that this invitation had an innocent motive. All of his lordship's actions seemed to be carefully planned—even a drive in the park. 'Alas,' she responded smoothly, 'that is not possible. Much as I would like to help you to make up for your earlier deficiencies—' in spite of the sharp look these words provoked, she managed to remain a picture of demure innocence '—I am not free this afternoon.' In response to his impertinently raised eyebrow, she added calmly, 'I am engaged to visit my banker's in the City. However, I—'

'I hope you are not visiting your banker's on my account, ma'am,' interrupted his lordship, with unwonted vehemence. 'You will recall that we agreed there was nothing pressing in the matter of our game last week.'

'You mistake matters,' replied Isabella hotly, feeling the colour rushing into her cheeks. '*I* agreed no such thing. Debts of honour have to be paid promptly—even by women.'

'Miss Winstanley…' Perhaps it was the stubborn set of her chin and the martial glint in her eye that gave him pause. Whatever the reason, he began again on a marginally softer tack. 'As it happens, ma'am, it was my intention to make my first pilgrimage to St Paul's. It would be my pleasure if you would accept my escort to the City. Perhaps you would enjoy a visit to the cathedral before you transact your business?'

Isabella pondered this suggestion for a moment, forcing herself to ignore his possible motives and to focus solely on the rational aspects of his unexpected invitation. By rights, a gentleman should not take a lady driving into the City, even in an open carriage, but a visit to St Paul's would allow her the satisfaction of paying every guinea of her debt to his lordship in person. She consoled herself with the thought that, after all, she was now of an age when the rules for single ladies did not need to be applied quite so strictly.

'You are most kind. I accept.'

'I shall call for you at three, if that is convenient?'

'Perfectly, thank you,' she responded with cool politeness.

He arrived promptly at three. Barely five minutes later, he was handing her into his curricle and spreading a light rug over her knees.

'You do not drive your phaeton today, sir?'

'No, ma'am. I thought you might like to try your skill with my curricle. It is better adapted for the city streets.'

Isabella threw him a frankly quizzical look. 'Have you something particular in mind, sir?'

'Quite so, ma'am,' came the enigmatic reply. He took his eyes from the greys for a brief moment to look down at her, apparently daring her to quiz him further.

She tried unsuccessfully to look outraged but, faced with that challenging gaze, she was quite unable to revert to her earlier coolness. After a moment, she collected herself enough to say, 'My lord, you will allow me to say that I have the strongest suspicions of your motives today. I believe they go beyond a desire to admire Sir Christopher's great work. I take it you do not propose to tell me your plans?'

'No, Miss Winstanley,' he responded curtly, but with the slightest twitch of his handsome mouth. He was concentrating on threading his team through the narrow streets.

Isabella was torn between indignation and laughter. And she knew that he was observing her inner conflict from the corner of his eye.

'Outrageous, ma'am?' he suggested coolly.

Her laughter bubbled forth. No doubt, just as he had expected.

'No, indeed. Abominable! Quite abominable!'

After some minutes, he said evenly, 'I have a proposition to put to you, ma'am.'

Isabella surveyed him quickly. Perhaps she should not have come. He would not, surely, make any improper proposal to a lady?

'I see I have roused your interest,' he continued. 'It concerns our earlier wager.' He pointedly ignored the darkling look she cast at him. 'I offer you a second challenge, ma'am. A curricle race—between us two. If you win, your debt is cancelled. If I win, you pay me double.'

Isabella was incensed. How dare he propose anything so improper? It was a moment before she was sufficiently in control to speak. 'You do not, surely, expect a lady to take part in such a scheme?' she asked witheringly.

'Few ladies would have the courage, I own…but I

had thought that you, ma'am, were of that intrepid number.'

'Intrepid? Or foolhardy? Certainly not. I do not care to risk my reputation in a public race for such a stake.' The words were out before she understood their full import. He would think she was an out-and-out coward. She groaned inwardly, recognising—too late—how much his good opinion mattered to her.

After a moment's pause, he said, tantalisingly, 'Of course, it need not be a *public* event. It could be known only to ourselves.'

Isabella was now truly intrigued. Was he looking for an opportunity of losing to her, so that he would not have to collect on their earlier wager? She wondered how he had intended to manage the affair, however, and her inner devil prompted her to provoke him a little more. 'I do not see how that could be done, sir.'

He smiled knowingly, clearly believing he had hooked his fish. 'Trust me, ma'am, it can be done. A town race might serve, for example.'

Isabella did not understand him and allowed it to show on her face.

'Permit me to explain,' he said. 'We agree a course through the town from, say, St Paul's to Westminster Abbey. Then one of us drives it against the clock. The other does the same, and the better time wins.'

'But it would be bound to attract attention with two curricles—'

'Ah, no, ma'am. Not two. One. That is the beauty

of it. Just one curricle, driven along the same course, but at different times.'

'It could not possibly be a fair contest, my lord,' she protested, forgetting altogether that it would be quite improper to participate in any kind of race at all. 'The traffic, the weather…oh, anything could happen.'

'Indeed so. And that makes the challenge all the more interesting. Let me tell you the rules. The first whip can choose both day and time as he—or she— thinks best. The second can also choose as he thinks best, provided only that he completes the course within the agreed time span. Two or three weeks is usual. Do you dare to test your skills, Miss Winstanley?'

'I have no curricle to race against you, sir. You must find another opponent.'

'Ah, but that is easily remedied. You may drive this curricle and this team.'

'Good God! You must think I have windmills in my head. *Your* curricle and *your* team?' She began to laugh at the absurdity of it all. How on earth had she allowed the discussion to come this far? Surely, no lady would ever agree to such a proposition?

'You would be able to get to know my team before the event, of course,' he added silkily, as her mirth subsided. 'And there would be an appropriate handicap to take account of my greater experience. You would not need to better my time to win. Shall we say…anything less than double? With odds like those, Miss Winstanley, do you dare to refuse?'

Isabella was torn between a strong desire to accept his challenge and best him, and the inner promptings of her better self against such unladylike behaviour. The challenge seemed truly unavoidable if she were not to lose face completely. Yet, were her behaviour to become public knowledge…

He is sure, she thought, that I will accept. And he thinks he is totally in control. Well…

Looking full into his face—which seemed to show a degree of satisfaction already—she smiled sweetly. Then, with wide-eyed innocence, she agreed to the wager. 'However,' she added smoothly, 'I do not agree to the proposed stakes. Double or nothing? Paltry, my lord, paltry!' She was gratified, then, to see his jaw muscles tighten. 'If we are to race, sir, the stakes must be worth the candle, especially for a poor female against whom the odds will be very long indeed. If I should win, the prize shall be… Do you dare to hazard your matched greys?'

Lord Amburley's hands tightened involuntarily on the reins and his precious greys shied slightly in protest. 'I believe I have underestimated you, ma'am,' he said after a moment, in a strained voice. 'But as I issued the challenge, I cannot now refuse the stakes you suggest.'

'While if you should win—'

'Those stakes shall remain unchanged,' he stated

flatly. 'Twice the original debt. I would not accept more.'

It was now much too late for Isabella to draw back.

Isabella tried to bring some order to her thoughts, pushing the promptings of her conscience as far as possible to the back of her mind. Simpler to concentrate on practical matters. In the circumstances, her visit to the City need not take place that day. Instead of St Paul's, they turned aside to visit Westminster Abbey, which would provide splendid cover for the necessary discussions about how the race was to be run without attracting the attentions of the *ton*.

'It cannot take place for some weeks,' said Lord Amburley, as they walked together down the great nave. 'You must have time to become accustomed to my team, and frequent excursions are out of the question, of course. That would excite all sorts of gossip.'

Isabella flushed slightly. She was beginning to appreciate the enormity of what she had agreed to. Heaven help her! She could not draw back now.

'I suggest we drive out about once a week for the next two or three weeks and decide on the course and the timing after that. Would that meet with your approval, ma'am?'

She nodded helplessly. Devil take the man. He had it all too pat. And she was caught like a bird in lime.

'And since I shall be driving out with other ladies in the interim, the *ton* will conclude that Amburley has at last been converted to the pleasures of female company in his carriage. Do you think that will serve, ma'am?'

'That will depend on the ladies you invite, I fancy,' she replied acidly.

'Yes, you are right. I shall think carefully about that. I should not want to raise the hopes of any fond mamas... A ticklish problem, indeed.'

Isabella refused to consider what might be the implications of that.

He turned her away from the stained glass they had been admiring. 'And now, ma'am, will you be so good as to instruct me about the inhabitants of the Poets' Corner?'

By the time they were ready to return to Hill Street, Isabella's good humour was almost restored. She knew that he was deliberately exercising his charm on her, but she found herself quite unable to resist. He had gone out of his way to be entertaining during the remainder of their visit to the Abbey, and he had even encouraged her to drive the curricle for part of its return journey.

She thanked him prettily as she handed back the reins. 'Shall we see you at Lady Sefton's this evening, sir?'

'I am otherwise engaged, I fear. Such a pity. Musical evenings can be so...' He paused, clearly searching for a suitably ambiguous epithet.

'Soporific, sir?' She looked archly at him through her lashes.

'Viper!' he exclaimed with mock horror, stirring the greys into motion once more. 'I should not dare apply such a term to an evening arranged by one of our foremost hostesses. No single gentleman would risk his entrée to Almack's by such language.'

Isabella's silvery laughter burst forth.

'That's better,' commended his lordship. 'In point of fact, I am sorry to miss Lady Sefton's soirée. At least, I am, if I shall miss hearing you sing.'

Isabella blushed rosily, not only because of her companion's pretty compliment, but also because it gave the lie to her earlier conclusion that he did not like her voice. How many other times had she misjudged him?

Lord Amburley must have noticed her confusion, for he politely turned the conversation. 'Has Lady Sefton sent you vouchers for Almack's, Miss Winstanley?'

'I fear so.'

'Fear, ma'am? Why, surely it is the ambition of every young lady?'

'It is certainly Sophia's, and it will be gratified on Wednesday next. For myself…I shall go as chaperon to Sophia, nothing more.'

'Truly? Surely not. I count on your dancing, ma'am. I particularly hoped to waltz with you there.'

'You are roasting me yet again, my lord,' protested Isabella, remembering how uncomfortable their last 'waltz' had been. 'Do you truly mean to attend the assembly at Almack's? I had thought you would certainly have a prior engagement then.'

'No, that would never do. Besides, I must seek out suitable ladies to drive behind my team for the next few weeks. And where better than Almack's?'

Lord Amburley dined alone after his return from the excursion to Westminster Abbey. He felt much in need of a period of calm reflection to consider what he had learned of the Misses Winstanley and—more pressing—to apply his keen intellect to the many puzzles which remained.

The two women could not have been more unlike—not only in age and appearance, but also in temperament and tone of mind. He had instantly characterised the younger Miss Winstanley as 'empty-headed, frivolous and spoilt', not out of malice, but as a reflection of his experience of young and wealthy débutantes. He still believed he was right. He had never yet known one who was otherwise.

Amburley had paid little enough attention to Miss Sophia at the time—why should he?—but that was before George Lewiston had begun to take an interest in the chit. Lewiston *said* he wanted only to preserve her from Gradely. Well, that was done. For, if Sam's latest observations were to be trusted, Gradely had left Lady Wycham's house with his tail between his legs. But it still left Lewiston himself. Amburley was loath to see his friend leg-shackled to a woman of Sophia Winstanley's cut. He would regret it in a month.

It was too much to hope that Miss Sophia would prefer one of her other suitors, for none of them was as rich as Lewiston. Even heiresses—or rather, their parents—preferred wealthy suitors. Lewiston would have been the catch of the Season, had it not been for his lack of a title.

Might the chit be hankering after a title? Since she had wealth of her own, perhaps she could be lured away by a coronet? Amburley considered the possible field. Now that Gradely had fled the lists, there was only one unmarried peer available—himself. If Miss Sophia were to be tempted by a title, it would have to be his. It was only a barony, of course, but an ancient one, none the less. It would have to serve. Yes, he would have to test Miss Sophia, court her a little, prove that his assessment of her was a fair one. It was the least he could do for such a friend as Lewiston.

Lord Amburley wondered idly how Miss Winstanley would react, if he were seen to be aspiring to her younger cousin. As a loyal companion, she should be delighted at the prospect of a titled suitor, even a relatively impecunious one, for her wealthy charge. But her reactions were impossible to predict, just as they had been again today, on the question of the stakes for the curricle race. His proposal had been precisely and cold-bloodedly calculated to prolong his hold over her, and to provide a means of honourably cancelling her debt—if he should choose to use it. He had been quite sure she would accept his challenge, for she had too much spirit to hide behind the cloak of propriety. Indeed, he had counted on that, when devising his little scheme. But he had to admit he had underestimated his opponent's mettle—he had been too clever by half. Had she guessed his intention? She had certainly outmanoeuvred him very neatly. And with his prize greys now at stake, he could not afford to lose—so Miss Winstanley's debt would be doubled. God, what a coil!

He sipped meditatively at his port. It didn't really help. She was an enigma. Furthermore, he had yet to fathom out the secret of her double life and of her visits to the Fleet prison. On that subject, Sam was being remarkably slow.

He was still ruminating when Lewiston was announced. Lord Amburley realised, with a start, that he had forgotten their engagement to play cards at their club. He had allowed himself to become much too preoccupied with the Winstanley puzzle.

Rising, he greeted his friend affably, making no mention of his lapse of memory. 'Come and sit down, George. Will you take port or brandy?'

Lewiston, though keen to be off, allowed himself to be persuaded to a glass of port. 'Any news?' he said, as soon as the butler had closed the door.

'News?' Lord Amburley lounged back in his chair, still sipping his port.

'About Gradely.' Lewiston sounded anxious.

'Mmm. I think he called this morning and was rebuffed.'

'How do you know? Are you sure?'

'Pretty sure, yes. Your Sophia is safe from danger, from that quarter at least.' Lord Amburley could see the relief in his friend's face. He also noticed that Lewiston did not object to his use of the term 'your Sophia'. That seemed ominous, indeed.

'Shall we go?' said Lewiston, setting down his glass.

'A moment, George. There is something I need to discuss with you—here, in private.'

Lewiston looked surprised.

'It concerns Miss Sophia.'

Lewiston looked displeased. 'I do not wish to discuss her, not even with you, Leigh,' he said sharply.

Amburley hesitated. He had not prepared for this moment as well as he should have done. In all honour, he needed to give some kind of warning to his friend about what he had in mind to do. But how? He could say he planned to try his luck with the heiress, whose wealth would help him restore his estates; or he could say he planned to tempt her with his title, to demonstrate the faults of her character. In either case, he would be cutting Lewiston out, which could easily lead to a breach between them. And Lewiston would take little consolation from learning that his goddess had feet of clay, especially if that fact were publicly demonstrated by his closest friend.

His lordship resolved to try to find a middle way. He adopted his most nonchalant pose. 'I have no intention of saying a word against Miss Sophia, George. Who would dare, when she has you to defend her?'

Lewiston laughed rather unconvincingly.

'I have been thinking about her,' Amburley continued. 'It may be that I was too hasty in my judgement. After all, I hardly know her. I think, perhaps, I should make some effort to further my acquaintance with Miss Sophia. Why not, after all? She is young, pretty and rich; and—so far as I am aware—she has not yet indicated a preference for any of her many suitors.' Amburley cast a shrewd glance at Lewiston, to gauge his reaction, but he appeared to be studying the polished table-top.

Lewiston did not look up. 'Do I take it you intend to become one of them?' His voice sounded a little forced.

Lord Amburley did his best to sound light-hearted. 'I have no idea. Perhaps. It will depend on Miss Sophia. Of course, if your intentions are serious, I should not dream—'

Lewiston raised his head. 'I admire her, of course. And I am prepared to defend her against the likes of Gradely, as any man of honour must. But I do not believe she means to make her choice in her first Season. I think she is enjoying everything too much to form an attachment so soon. She is very young, after all. Being an heiress, she will always be surrounded by admirers. She can afford to take her time.'

Lord Amburley nodded sagely. How like Lewiston to underestimate his own chances with the heiress. He was too diffident by half. 'No doubt you are right. I shall become just one more of her bevy of admirers, I expect. I wonder, though—do you think the title might make a difference?'

Lewiston swallowed hard. 'It did not help Gradely,' he said stiffly, 'and he is an earl.'

'That puts me in my place, does it not?' Lord Amburley had been surprised into a laugh. 'Still, I am glad we are not at odds over this.' He rose quickly before Lewiston could decide to prolong the discussion. 'Shall we go now, George? I must say I have been looking forward to this evening. I feel lucky tonight.'

Lewiston groaned good-humouredly as they left the room. 'Heaven help the opposition then,' he said. 'It could be a very expensive experience.'

Chapter Eleven

The following Wednesday brought the all-important visit to Almack's.

Isabella had carefully instructed Sophia in everything she needed to know about the sacred portals of the Marriage Mart. Most important of all, Isabella stressed repeatedly, was the absolute injunction not to dance the waltz until Sophia had received express permission from one of the patronesses.

Sophia quaked visibly at any mention of those formidable ladies. She was obviously quite terrified at the thought that she might say or do something wrong in front of them.

Almack's was already fairly crowded when the party arrived. Luckily for Sophia's self-control, none of the patronesses she most dreaded was in view near the entrance. Having paid their compliments to Lady Sefton, Isabella and Sophia were able to move into the relative safety of the ballroom, leaving Lady Wycham in conversation with their hostess.

When she looked around at the frankly rather modest surroundings, Sophia's spirits lifted visibly. 'I really did not believe you, Isabella, when you said—'

'Hush. We can discuss that later, at home.'

Sophia nodded imperceptibly. 'Do you know everyone here, Isabella?' She was looking around, with interest, at the multi-coloured throng of young ladies and mammas, interspersed here and there with sober-suited gentlemen and scarlet regimentals. As yet, few of the gentlemen had arrived.

'No, dear, only a few of the older ones. I have been out of Society for a very long time. This is my first visit to Almack's too, remember.'

'But I thought that you and Lady Wycham—'

'You forget that I have not lived in London all that long, Sophia. And Aunt Jemima has not been well enough to allow of much entertaining. You saw that for yourself, when you visited last autumn.'

'It is such a shame,' protested Sophia. 'You wasted your youth nursing your parents, and now you are doing it all over again when you're—' She stopped, blushing fierily.

'An ape-leader?' finished Isabella tartly. She was gratified to see Sophia's blush deepen. Looking round to ensure they were not overheard, Isabella allowed herself to give vent to what she felt was righteous indignation. 'Whether or not I may be an old maid is of no moment,' she hissed. 'But understand that you are quite wrong about Aunt Jemima. I *chose* to come to London, to live a life of my own rather than being beholden to my brother and his wife, who were killing me with kindness. Aunt Jemima has given me a home and respectability—and a freedom which I could never have elsewhere. She owes me nothing—but I owe her a very great deal. You misjudge her shamefully.'

Sophia's contrition was clear to see. She mumbled the beginnings of an apology, which was cut short.

'There is no need to say any more,' said Isabella, rather more gently. It was important not to undermine the girl's precarious confidence. 'Now, I wonder who will be the first to invite you to dance?'

That was not difficult to guess, since Mr Lewiston could be seen making his way towards them. Sophia visibly brightened at the approach of his familiar figure.

'Good evening, Miss Winstanley, Miss Sophia,' he bowed, smiling warmly at both ladies. 'With your permission, Miss Winstanley, may I ask for the honour of Miss Sophia's hand for this dance?'

Isabella smiled her assent and watched them join the set which was forming. They did make an attractive couple, he so fair and she so dark. She wondered whether Mr Lewiston might come up to scratch—and whether he was sufficiently wealthy to take on Sophia and all her impecunious family. She must make it her business to find out. It would take both wealth *and* strength of character to cope with the feckless Yorkshire Winstanleys.

The first part of the evening passed quickly, and

the ballroom rapidly filled. Neither Sophia nor Isabella wanted for partners, though some of Isabella's were rather shorter than she could have wished. She consoled herself with the thought that, in the country dances at least, the difference in height was not very noticeable. If one of the shorter gentlemen asked for the waltz, however, she was determined to make her excuses. For the waltz, it was imperative that a lady have a partner who overtopped her. She caught herself wishing again for a chance to waltz in Amburley's strong arms but quickly pushed it out of her mind. Whatever he might have said, it was stupid to think of it now, since he was not even present.

But in that, she was wrong.

Lord Amburley had arrived late, just before eleven, when the doors were shut against all comers, however august. He had chosen to stand impassively in a dark corner of the crowded ballroom, his hooded eyes taking in every detail of the brilliant scene. He knew he could not expect any enjoyment from this evening's excursion but, none the less, he had decided it had to be done. He frowned darkly as he surveyed the dancers.

Presently, he was spied and joined by his friend Lewiston.

'Leigh! I had given you up. To be honest, I did not really believe you, when you said you would come. Do you dance this evening?'

'But of course. Why else does a man come to Almack's? Not for the quality of the wine, that's certain,' he added, with a grimace.

His friend laughed. 'You surprise me, I admit. Tell me, which of these beauties has found favour with your discerning eye?'

Lord Amburley gave his friend a hard look. 'I thought to try my luck with Miss Sophia.' Ignoring his friend's sharply drawn breath, he continued, 'I told you I should. I am minded to tempt her with a title. It's only a barony, of course, but it may serve to show her in her true colours.' Looking at his friend's expression, he wondered whether he should have avoided such directness. The answer came almost immediately.

'Amburley, that is monstrous!' exclaimed Lewiston, in outrage. 'You propose to trifle with Sophia, just to prove your warped theories about rich débutantes. Why, you—'

'Nothing of the kind, George,' countered his lordship evenly, determined to keep control of his own temper in the face of his friend's anger. 'If my theory, as you term it, is misplaced, then Miss Sophia will not respond to me at all, and no "trifling" will occur. If she chooses to respond, it is because she is as I have described her.'

'Nonsense! Have you considered that the poor girl might fall in love with you? Leigh, what you propose is not honourable.'

Without uttering a word, Amburley simply stared at Lewiston until the younger man coloured and looked away. 'I apologise, Leigh,' he said at last, rather stiffly. 'That was unjustified.'

Amburley's frosty stare melted immediately. He put his hand on his friend's shoulder. 'I promise you that there will be no question of love—on either side. Believe me, my intentions *are* honourable. I wish only to—' He stopped short. He had been about to admit that he was trying to save his friend from becoming attached to an unsuitable lady. 'I only wish to get to know the lady rather better,' he finished, lamely. He determined to say nothing more.

Amburley noted that Lewiston had now clamped his jaws tight together. Probably he was trying to prevent another outburst, since it could have led to a rift between them. Then, with the briefest of nods, Lewiston turned on his heel and strode back into the main part of the ballroom. Lord Amburley, apparently at his ease, lounged back against the wall, smiling grimly as he watched his friend approach Miss Sophia and lead her into the dance.

He had to admit they made a handsome couple. Miss Sophia might be spoilt, but she presented a very attractive picture. She seemed most animated, too. Every time the movements of the dance brought the pair together, they exchanged laughing remarks. And his lordship was not the only man watching her progress. He counted at least four more potential suitors watching avidly.

Half an hour later, Mr Lewiston returned Sophia to where Isabella stood in conversation with one of the chaperons, and a spirited discussion ensued about the respective merits of the various country dances. Isabella was pleased to see that all Sophia's earlier misgivings seemed finally to have disappeared. Two dances with Mr Lewiston and, no doubt, a raft of compliments, had set everything to rights again.

The musicians were just striking up for the next dance, when Isabella saw Lord Amburley approaching. Where on earth had he sprung from? She had been so sure that he was not present. She felt her heart begin to race and her colour rise slightly as he reached them. She told herself sternly to stop reacting like a green girl. His lordship was merely an acquaintance. It would be very…pleasant to dance with him again, even though it was not to be the waltz.

His lordship bowed with casual grace. 'Your servant, Mrs Ramsey. And yours, Miss Winstanley, Miss Sophia.' He smiled at them all. Isabella felt his manifest charm envelop them. Out of the corner of her eye, she saw that Mrs Ramsey was looking round anxiously to summon her daughter for an introduction to this most eligible gentleman. Isabella smiled warmly, anticipating his invitation.

'May I have the pleasure of this dance,' began his lordship, 'Miss Sophia?'

If Isabella lost a little of her colour when Lord Amburley led Sophia into the set, she gave no other sign of her inner turmoil. She concentrated with grim determination on pursuing her earlier conversation with

Mrs Ramsey and Mr Lewiston whose smile, she noticed, now looked a little strained.

Mr Lewiston does not welcome his friend's attentions to Sophia, she concluded, forcing herself not to think about her own feelings. Mayhap he is more taken with her than I had thought. But Amburley! He is the last man I should have expected to be attracted to a girl of Sophia's age and sophistication. She will not know what to say to him, even if he is merely being kind by distinguishing her in this way.

A tiny doubt intruded. What if he were not 'being kind'?

She was perversely grateful when Mr Lewiston interrupted her wayward thoughts. 'Miss Winstanley, would you honour me for this dance?'

'Why, thank you, sir. That would be delightful.' She placed her hand on his proffered arm, and they made their way into the set.

It was easier to watch Lord Amburley and Sophia from the centre of the dance floor. They seemed to be enjoying an amusing conversation, except when parted by the movements of the dance. Isabella could not help but remember her own dance with his lordship—she had hardly said a word to him. Was it any wonder he preferred the gayer company of a younger girl?

The end of the dance brought the two couples back together, as Lord Amburley returned Sophia to Isabella's side. Isabella fancied she detected a degree of coolness between the two gentlemen. Sophia, however, was all laughter and animation, blossoming in response to Amburley's subtle encouragement. Clearly Isabella had underestimated her young charge—and the effect of his lordship's ready charm.

Mr Lewiston said very little. His expression grew blacker and blacker until, eventually, he excused himself. Isabella did not miss the look that passed between the two gentlemen as he left.

Something has happened between them, she thought. And it concerns Sophia.

She pulled her thoughts back to the present, just in time to hear Lord Amburley offer to take Sophia in to supper. With a sideways glance towards Isabella, Sophia accepted with a smile. Isabella did her best to return it.

'Will you join us, Miss Winstanley?'

'Thank you, sir, but no. I must look to Lady Wycham. If you will excuse me?' Without waiting for his response, she dropped a slight curtsy, turned and made her way to the card-room, where she knew Lady Wycham was to be found. There she spent a slightly uncomfortable half-hour, chatting to Lady Wycham between hands and trying not to think about Amburley and what his motives might be. What was it he had said to her? That he did not dance with 'young and foolish girls'. Had he changed his tune in so short a space of time? Or was there something special about Sophia that had caused him to break his rule? Isabella had no way of knowing, but she thought—nay, feared—that perhaps Lord Amburley might be succumbing to Sophia's youthful charms. Many other gentlemen were pursuing Sophia—why not Amburley, too?

Isabella soon decided that, if Amburley was pursuing Sophia, he was making sure that no one else should suspect it. Following the supper interval, he danced almost every dance and rarely with the same lady. Isabella noticed that most of them barely reached his chest, though they all strained to gaze up into his eyes.

How distasteful, she thought uncharitably. At least, I am tall enough to look at him without making a spectacle of myself.

The next dance was the waltz. Sophia, sitting by Isabella's side, was putting up a brave pretence that she was quite unconcerned about being unable to dance it. She must know she would not be alone, for a great many of the young ladies present had not yet received permission.

A gentleman approached to invite Isabella to dance. Inwardly she groaned. He was much too short. They would look perfectly ridiculous.

'I thank you, sir, but I do not dance the waltz this evening. Pray excuse me.'

As the young man bowed and left, a well-known voice intruded from the other side. 'That is indeed a pity, Miss Winstanley, for I had hoped to have the pleasure myself. However, my good friend Lady Sefton has given permission for Miss Sophia to waltz this evening. Perhaps she will do me the honour?'

An awe-struck Sophia looked up to see that Lady Sefton was smiling encouragingly at her. Without so much as a word to Isabella, Sophia rose, curtsied to the patroness and departed happily on Lord Amburley's arm.

For a moment, Isabella felt totally isolated among the crowds in Almack's ballroom. It was as if an icy hand had clutched at her heart and were slowly crushing it. She sat completely still, watching the couple make their way into the dance, her eyes riveted to his broad back and the shining black hair curling above his collar.

Eventually, with an effort, she dragged her eyes away. What was the matter with her? She was behaving like a love-sick schoolgirl. Love-sick? Oh, God, no! Surely she could not have fallen in love with him? Please, no!

But in her heart she knew it was too late for such prayers. Her heart was given, even though the man of her choice could have no notion of it. She, who had remained immune for so many years, had fallen in love with a man who was clearly courting a girl of little more than half her age.

She glanced again towards the floor. She could see them whirling round, apparently totally attuned to one another. Then, thankfully, they were no longer in view. She let out the breath she had been holding, seemingly for ever, and turned away to seek out Lady Wycham once more.

No one shall ever suspect my feelings, she promised herself as she walked briskly back towards the card-room, least of all he. I may have lost my heart to a man who will never return my regard, but at least I shall salvage my self-respect.

A further shaft of the light of self-knowledge fell on her.

And this time, she vowed, I shall *not* allow my emotions to overcome my judgement. This time, there shall be no quarter given. This time, I shall win.

Chapter Twelve

It was noted by members of the *ton*, during the days that followed, that Lord Amburley was now playing an active part in every possible event of the Season and honouring a large number of hopeful young damsels in the process. It was soon rumoured that he was actively looking for a wife—the tabbies were agreed that he was of an age when he needed to be setting up his nursery. There was less of a consensus, however, on where his choice would fall, for he seemed to have no preferences among the many young ladies with whom he danced and flirted. It seemed to Isabella, sitting disconsolately among the chaperons, that only she noticed how often he was to be found with Sophia.

One afternoon, some time after that first evening at Almack's, Lord Amburley called in Hill Street, by appointment, to take Sophia driving in Hyde Park. She was certainly flattered by his invitation but, unlike Isabella, she was not ready when he arrived. He was left to cool his heels in the book-room, where Isabella heard him pacing up and down for fully twenty minutes.

When Sophia eventually emerged, she took one look at Amburley's high-perch phaeton, a vehicle with seats some five feet off the ground, and stopped dead in the open doorway. Isabella thought Sophia was about to turn and run. But good manners had been drummed into her since she came to London. She swallowed hard and made her way across the flagway. Lord Amburley helped her in, not without difficulty, and spread a warm rug over her knees. Isabella was sure he must have noticed how pale Sophia had become, but he showed no sign of concern.

When they drove off, Isabella could see that Sophia was gripping her hands tightly together in her lap, as if determined not to grab for the side of the phaeton. Isabella sighed. She doubted that even Amburley's charm could overcome so much terror.

The phaeton returned to Hill Street much sooner than Isabella had expected. She took one look at Sophia's ashen face and whisked her upstairs to her room and the ministrations of her abigail.

'I am afraid Miss Sophia is not used to riding in a high-perch phaeton, ma'am,' Lord Amburley confided when Isabella returned. 'She found it somewhat unnerving. I do apologise. I should have warned her that I planned to take my phaeton to the park.'

Isabella was far from convinced by his apology, but

she felt she must not let the full extent of her annoyance show. 'Indeed, you should, my lord,' she said. 'Very few young ladies are comfortable driving in such a vehicle. You must have known from the outset that she was ill at ease. You should not have gone.'

'I have already apologised to Miss Sophia, and to you, ma'am. My excuse, such as it is, is that I am not yet in the habit of driving ladies. I had no idea she might react in such a way. The only other lady who has driven in my phaeton certainly did not do so, after all.'

He looked at her for a split second in a way she could not fathom. Then he was all politeness again. 'Will you allow me to take you on that visit to St Paul's soon? On Saturday, if you are free?'

He did not need to mention the wager—it hung between them like a drawn sword. Forcing herself to assume a polite smile, Isabella accepted.

She had no choice.

Lord Amburley drove easily back to Jermyn Street, feeling quite pleased with his progress so far. He was dancing attention on so many women at once, that the tabbies would not know where to turn. No reputations were at risk, he was sure of that.

He had now completed his assessment of Sophia Winstanley. She was just as empty-headed and frivolous as he had supposed. Her entire conversation seemed to consist of second-hand wisdom—from her nurse, he supposed—and naïve gossip about the Season. He found himself feeling rather sorry for her. After all, it was not her fault that she had been brought up in rich idleness or that she had never had an original thought in her life. She was neither well read nor well informed. No doubt her mama had warned her that no gentleman would ever be attracted by such qualities. Such women had much to answer for—in failed and failing marriages—in Amburley's opinion.

But Sophia was not wholly without redeeming features, he admitted dispassionately. She had clearly been terrified from the very start of their drive today, but she had refused to cry off. She had certainly shown courage. And he had noticed during their recent conversations that she showed a degree of concern for Winny, the companion, that he had not expected. A mixed verdict, then—which he must, in all conscience, soon share with Lewiston, if they were to remain friends.

'I admit I was wrong about Miss Sophia,' he told Lewiston at White's the following day. 'I have conversed with her, danced with her, and supped with her. I have even taken her driving, though that was *not* a success, as I told you. She is conversable, provided you do not stray beyond the commonplace. She is not pretentious, as so many rich young ladies are, so I was probably wrong to call her "spoilt". Frivolous? Well, yes, but they mostly are at that age. She may well improve. As to the title, I doubt if she would have it, not if the price is driving in a high-perch phaeton.'

Lewiston had been as outraged as Isabella about the drive in the park and began to upbraid his friend roundly.

'I beg of you, George, no more! I have already had all of this and more from Miss Winstanley, who clucks over her charge like a mother hen. I do hope the family are paying her well, for she performs her role admirably.'

Lewiston ignored his diversion. 'Do I take it then, Leigh, that you will not be pursuing Miss Sophia any longer?'

'The odd dance for appearances' sake, nothing more. I must find some other ladies to take out driving.'

'What about Miss Winstanley? She may be only a companion, but she's a remarkably fine-looking woman and unquestionably a lady. Well read too, I should guess, so you would not be limited to frivolous conversation.'

'Miss Winstanley is an enigma,' pronounced his lordship, with a sudden frown. 'She is highly accomplished, rides and drives as well as most men, and yet she stoops to this infamous deception, in spite of her manifest sense of honour. Extraordinary!'

'You avoided my question again, Leigh.'

'Did I?'

Lewiston refused to be diverted again. Eventually, following further prompting, Lord Amburley admitted that he would drive out with Miss Winstanley, from time to time. 'But I have no intention of giving the tabbies food for thought in *that* direction, George. It *would* be dishonourable, were I to make a woman of her station the object of their scandal-mongering.'

That afternoon, it was noted that his lordship was driving in the park with yet another hopeful young lady at his side, but he disappointed them all by failing to appear in the evening at one of the grandest balls of the Season. Instead, he went to his club, to play piquet. When he rose from the table, many hours later, his winnings amounted to over two thousand pounds.

His lordship had not been long abed when a loud knocking was heard at the servants' entrance. The butler, struggling into his coat, stomped down the passage to open it.

'What d'you mean by making that infernal row at this time of the morning, you little runt?'

'Got ter see 'is lordship, quick,' gasped Sam, trying to push past the butler to get into the house.

'Oh, no, you don't,' cried the butler, gripping him by the collar. 'What's your business, eh?'

'I got ter see 'im, urgent,' repeated Sam. ''E told me 'isself, ter come at once, 'owever late it were.'

Still gripping Sam's collar, the butler pulled the boy inside and shut the door. 'Now, then. Just what did his lordship tell you *precisely*?'

Sam merely repeated, yet again, that he had to see Lord Amburley urgently, adding that his lordship would be very angry to learn that his orders had been disobeyed. The butler, clearly preferring to avoid sole responsibility where his master's wrath might be incurred, sent for Peveridge. If anyone knew what his lordship wanted, it would be the valet.

Peveridge took one look at the dirty visitor and pulled him into the pantry, shutting the door on his inquisitive colleague. Barely two minutes later, he came out again, almost colliding with the hovering butler.

'Keep him here, Mr Wilson. I'll fetch his lordship.'

His lordship was not best pleased to be shaken awake by Peveridge in the early hours of the morning. He sat up, cursing both his valet and the considerable amount of brandy he had consumed at the piquet table.

'If this is a joke, Peveridge, I'll wring your neck with my bare hands.'

'Now, m'lord, would I dare? You know I—'

'Peveridge!' thundered his lordship, momentarily forgetting his fragile head and immediately regretting it. 'Peveridge,' he began again, more moderately, 'what the devil is going on?'

The valet, for once, came quickly to the point, explaining about their young visitor.

'Right,' exclaimed Lord Amburley, now fully awake. 'Get me some hot water and bring the boy up here, while I dress. I need to talk to him myself.'

Peveridge's protests were cut short. 'Don't argue, Peveridge. Just do it! Now!' Peveridge made for the door. 'Oh, wash off some of his dirt if you must, but be quick about it. And with my shaving water, too.'

Downstairs, the fire was already lit and water put to boil. The canny old butler had already set about removing the boy's dirt, using the coldest water he could find. Peveridge was greeted by the boy's complaints before he was halfway down the stairs to the kitchen.

Five minutes later, having taken Sam up to his lordship, Peveridge was back again. 'Send round to the stables for the curricle, sharpish. His lordship wants it at the door in fifteen minutes, with the bays.'

Normally, Lord Amburley expected to spend some considerable time over his morning toilet, especially if he were planning to make calls. This morning, he almost reverted to his old military ways, but not quite. In battle, the set of a coat or the turn of a cravat had been immaterial. Now, he felt a need to look his best.

Sam watched as, with amazing speed, Lord Amburley set the immaculate folds of his neckcloth and donned a stylish blue coat. ''Tis well enough,' he said to his reflection, 'especially for the early morning light. Let's be off, Sam.' Leaving Peveridge gaping, his lordship ran lightly down the stairs, his leather hessians clicking on the polished wood. Sam followed barefoot at his heels.

By the front door stood the old butler carrying a

tray with a cup and saucer on it. 'Coffee, m'lord?' he asked, as if it were all an everyday occurrence.

His lordship caught up the cup and downed the hot liquid in a single draught. 'Splendid, Wilson. Just what I needed. What a wonder you are.'

Then the door was opened, and he was down the steps in a trice.

'I shan't need you, Brennan,' he said to the waiting groom. 'Go and have your breakfast.' The groom nodded knowingly but said nothing, still holding the restive bays with both hands. 'Up with you, Sam. Right, Brennan. Let 'em go!'

In seconds, the curricle was round the corner and out of sight, leaving much of his lordship's household open-mouthed on the flagway.

It took some time for the curricle to reach its destination for, in spite of the early hour, the City streets were thronged with workmen and tradespeople. At length, Lord Amburley spoke. 'Are you sure it was the same jarvey, Sam?'

'Aye, yer honour.'

'No doubt she has an arrangement of some sort with him. That makes matters rather more complicated.' He thought for a moment. 'You can recognise him, I take it?'

'Aye, yer honour,' said Sam again.

'Good. Then you must ensure he is not there to meet her when she comes out.' He continued, noting Sam's incredulous expression, 'It's up to you how you do it. Interfere with the horse, foul the traces—it doesn't matter, as long as it works. Are you game, Sam?' He opened his gloved hand in which a guinea was resting.

Sam gulped. 'Aye, yer honour,' he said a third time.

Amburley had to wait some twenty minutes before Miss Winstanley appeared. For some moments she stood, looking round for the hackney. It was nowhere in sight. Amburley fancied that, since the market outside the prison was very crowded, Miss Winstanley was assuming the cab had been held up by the traffic. It was obvious that she had decided to wait.

She drew her dark shawl more closely round her shoulders and seemed to be trying to shrink into her shabby poke bonnet. Since it had no veil, it provided little concealment. Passers-by were beginning to look enquiringly at the lone woman huddled in her shawl. Once or twice, a man made to speak to her, but one sharp look from those grey-green eyes sent them on their way. She began to walk a little, for there was a sharp wind blowing up from the river.

'May I be of assistance, ma'am?'

He spoke from above and behind her. She made no sign of recognition or acknowledgement and continued to walk.

'Miss Winstanley, may I not take you up from this place?'

At the sound of her name, she turned. Amburley,

now alone in his curricle, bent towards her and reached out his hand to help her to mount.

She looked mortified with embarrassment. She hesitated visibly.

Amburley reached lower. 'Forgive me, ma'am—I may not alight to help you. As you see, I am without my groom this morning.'

She put her hand into his and stepped lightly into the curricle. Then she sat silently, drawing her shawl more tightly still with her gloved hands.

Amburley sat silently too, thinking. In his haste to arrange this meeting, he had not had time to plan how he would handle it, once she was in his carriage. But he was not surprised, on reflection, to note that she had taken refuge in silence. She was a wise, calm woman.

He turned to look more closely at her. The terrible clothes did nothing to enhance her face and figure, of course, but she seemed to him beautiful, in a serene, distant way. Her complexion glowed with a rosy blush at his scrutiny. Still she did not speak.

'I hope I may be of service to you, ma'am,' he said seriously. 'I am sure your aunt would wish me to convey you back to Hill Street. Shall I do so?'

She swallowed hard and gripped her fingers together. 'You are very good, my lord. I am in your debt.'

The rest of the journey was completed in total silence. Miss Winstanley offered no explanation, and Amburley could not bring himself to embarrass her further by asking for one. It seemed that, once she realised he would not press her, she relaxed a little. At least, she unclenched her hands. She did not raise her head, however, as if she were relying on the poke of her bonnet to conceal her identity from any acquaintance they might pass.

As they neared Berkeley Square, Amburley broke the silence. 'Where shall I set you down, ma'am?' He wondered whether she had yet considered the effect of being delivered to her front door in such extraordinary circumstances.

'I...' she faltered.

'If you would prefer to approach your house on foot, I could set you down before we reach Hill Street.'

At her grateful nod, he quickly halted his team. She sprang down nimbly, without any pause for assistance, turning back towards the curricle to thank him briefly. Then she hurried away.

Amburley took his time with his team, all the while covertly watching her retreating back. Avoiding the main part of Hill Street, she turned into a street that must lead, he supposed, to the back of the house. Truly, she seemed to be two completely different women—a poor companion skulking out by the back door, and a fine lady stepping into her carriage from the front.

Driving away, he continued to puzzle over her actions. The image which stayed with him was of her slim form standing for a moment on the flagway, as she bade him farewell. She had been flushed with embarrassment. Her smile had been forced. And her eyes had seemed to be pleading.

Chapter Thirteen

None of the household saw Isabella slip in through the mews entrance and up the backstairs to the safety of her own room. She closed the door and leaned back against it, momentarily closing her eyes and letting out a long, anguished sigh. Dear God, what was she to do now? All the detail of their first meetings flashed through her mind, yet again, as it had done when she first heard his voice outside the Fleet. If he had harboured any doubts about the identity of 'Winny the companion', they had certainly now been dispelled. Her only consolation was the fact that he had been alone. A groom would have spread such a scandal all over London in a trice.

But how could she ever face him again? How could she ever explain?

Mitchell came in from the dressing-room. 'Whatever is the matter, miss? You look as if you've seen a ghost.'

'I suppose, in a way, I have, Mitchell.' She moved

away from the support of the doorway, tugging at the strings of her bonnet, which seemed to have knotted themselves to vex her. 'Oh, devil take the thing!' she cried, ripping the knot in exasperation. She threw the bonnet on to the floor and sank, half-collapsing, into a chair. She did not know whether she should rage or weep. In the end, she did neither, but sat staring fixedly in front of her.

'Miss Isabella! What on earth has happened? Miss Isabella! Please!' Mitchell stood uncertainly for a moment, seemingly transfixed by the strange state her mistress was in. 'I'll fetch her ladyship,' she said at length, turning to make for the door.

Isabella came to herself again at the abigail's words. 'Do not concern yourself, Mitchell. I am quite well, I assure you. I had an unfortunate encounter outside the prison while I was waiting for Tom, that is all.'

'I warned you it wasn't safe to go alone, miss,' Mitchell began, but her scolding was cut short.

'Oh, I was quite safe,' Isabella said, with an ironic smile. 'Whatever else he may be, Lord Amburley is a perfect gentleman.' She looked up just in time to see both shock and concern crossing Mitchell's face. 'He took me up in his curricle and brought me home.' She was still smiling the same twisted smile.

'Dear God!' exclaimed Mitchell fervently. 'Whatever did you say to him? How did you explain what you were about?'

'He did not ask for an explanation and, coward that

I am, I did not give him one. I shudder to think what his opinion of me now may be. And my disguise on the North Road is certainly uncovered.' She sighed again. 'Lord Amburley is an honourable man, but I doubt I shall escape the strictures of the *ton* over this escapade.' She buried her face in her hands.

'Don't cry, Miss Isabella, please don't. You've done nothing to be ashamed of, nothing to bring censure on yourself. You should have told him the truth.'

'The truth?' cried Isabella, raising her head. She was very pale, but her eyes were dry. 'Already he knows of my deception in the north. That is enough to make such a man despise me. God knows he thinks little enough of women as it is. Would you have me give him more reasons for his disgust?' She would not let Mitchell say a word but continued her tirade. 'No, no! I shall tell him nothing. Let him think what he will. And say what he will of me to all the world.' She buried her face in her hands once more and, this time, her shoulders shook with silent sobs.

Mitchell stood silently for several minutes, considering. She started towards her mistress, but then seemed to think better of it. The abigail's face showed deep concern as she said, 'Why are you so sure he will start the gossip? Surely he has never betrayed the detail of your first encounter?'

Isabella sniffed and reached for her handkerchief. 'What do you mean? There is no reason to suppose he had recognised Sophia's ''poor relation'' until today, when he met me dressed like this.' She blew her nose defiantly.

'That's as may be. His lordship has all his wits about him, though, and I fancy he already knew. And, what is more, I do not believe he'll betray you.'

'What makes you say so?'

Mitchell seemed to be screwing up her courage. She took a deep breath, waiting until her mistress was looking her squarely in the face. 'Because I know his lordship is a truly honourable man. You could not love him if he were otherwise.'

Isabella let out a long 'Oh!' and turned away. For fully five minutes she did not speak. At length, she rose and began to pace back and forth across the room, wringing her hands. 'What am I to do? Oh, God, what am I to do?' She had never in her life felt so at a loss. Mitchell might be only an abigail, but there was no one else to whom Isabella could turn.

Taking her mistress's hands in her own and forcibly stopping the frenzied pacing, Mitchell looked into the troubled grey-green eyes. 'Forgive my bluntness, Miss Isabella. There are two things you can do. You can brazen it out and carry on as if nothing had happened. Or you can trust him enough to tell him the truth. It is for you to choose.'

'Dear God, might it not be better simply to leave London for a while? I do not think I can face him again.'

'Miss Isabella, you have never run from trouble in your life. I do not believe you will do so now.' She started to the door once more. 'Let me fetch you a glass of wine to restore your spirits. Once you are rested, you will be able to think more clearly.'

As so often, Mitchell was right. Within the hour, Isabella was berating herself for her foolish and emotional behaviour. Thank God it was only her faithful Mitchell who had seen her momentary weakness. She would certainly not flee London, though she could not quite make up her mind about whether to take Lord Amburley into her confidence. It seemed such a fearful risk to take.

'You must decide soon, miss,' chided Mitchell. 'Have you forgotten that you are engaged to visit St Paul's with his lordship this afternoon?'

That reminder almost brought about a further bout of foolish emotion. With an effort, Isabella succeeded in controlling herself, partly consoled by the thought that a peer of the realm would not wish to be associated with a woman who behaved in such an irregular fashion. He was bound to send round some excuse for breaking their appointment. And she would not blame him for doing so.

By two o'clock, there was still no message from Lord Amburley. However unlikely it might appear to Isabella, his lordship did not seem to wish to cry off.

She dressed mechanically for their outing, not noticing what she wore. Only Mitchell's care ensured that Isabella still looked well enough, in spite of her unwonted pallor. Mitchell pinned the jaunty green

velvet hat on to Isabella's honey curls, allowing the
long feather to curl down to her ear.

'That colour does become you, miss,' she said,
with a degree of lightness much at variance with her
look of concern.

Isabella came to herself enough to notice what she
was wearing. 'Oh, dear. This is the very gown I wore
when I first drove out with his lordship.'

'And none the worse for that, miss. Do not say you
wish to change it, for there is not time. His lordship
will be here in a matter of minutes, and you know
you never keep a gentleman waiting. Go along now,
do.' Faced with Isabella's passive melancholy, Mitchell seemed to be reverting to the role of nurse.

Isabella had barely descended to the drawing-room
when his lordship was shown in, punctual to the minute, as ever. She flushed scarlet as she rose to receive
him, stretching out her hand, but quite unable to raise
her eyes to his face.

'Miss Winstanley, how do you do?' He took her
hand and held it for several moments, further increasing her confusion. 'May I say how splendid you look,
ma'am? That is a very fetching hat.'

The unexpected warmth in his voice penetrated
where the words themselves did not. She looked up
to find that he was smiling down at her, without any
hint of ridicule or disdain. She dared to hope that the
afternoon might not become the ordeal she had
feared. With a weak attempt at a smile, she allowed
him to lead her out and help her into the curricle.

* * *

Settling the rug around his passenger, Lord Amburley was well aware of the tension in her. It was no more than he had foreseen, when considering his tactics for this excursion. On this occasion, he had taken the time to plan carefully, as a good military man should. He knew he had made a poor fist of their meeting that morning. Indeed, he would not have been surprised if she had cried off from this one, on some pretext or other. Any other woman would have done so. But this one…? This one had a special quality that was beyond definition. Not for the first time, he found himself considering Isabella Winstanley with a degree of warmth that he had rarely bestowed on any member of the fair sex.

His lordship had determined to conduct this excursion as though their earlier meeting had never taken place. Any hint of a reference to it would be bound to drive her into a shell from which she would never re-emerge in his presence. She had certainly been mortified by their encounter that morning. No doubt, she was expecting at every moment to be exposed as a cheat and a hoyden all over London. He had not stopped to ponder over why he was protecting her reputation—he had simply decided on the spot that he, as a gentleman, must do so. He must show her, by polite concern and assumed normality, that her secret was safe with him. It would be difficult, for he could in no wise allude to what had happened, but he believed that she would come to understand his intentions by the end of a light-hearted and enjoyable afternoon.

'Will you drive on the outward or the return journey, ma'am?'

'I beg your pardon?' Miss Winstanley was visibly startled. 'Oh, I see. I fear I had forgot, my lord.'

Amburley forbore to quiz her about her lapse. Her wounds were as yet too raw. Later perhaps, when she had become a little more comfortable in his company. He set the greys in motion. 'They are, in any case, a little fresh still,' he commented, controlling them with practised skill. 'On our return, you will find them less of a handful, if you are minded to try them.'

She summoned up a nod. 'I should like that, my lord.'

Amburley relaxed a little. Now that she had begun to respond more normally to him, progress could be made. He embarked on a totally innocuous conversation about the events of the previous week, noting how her replies became gradually longer and easier. After half an hour of careful work, he reckoned that their rapport was as much restored as it was going to be on this occasion. He was silently congratulating himself on his success, by the time they walked up the steps into St Paul's.

'How long have you known the truth about me, Lord Amburley?' she asked in a low, quiet voice, her eyes fixed on the steps.

For once, his lordship was almost at a loss. He had

underestimated her courage yet again, it seemed. 'How long, ma'am?' he repeated, playing for time.

It appeared that, having begun on this perilous tack, she was not about to desist. 'Aye, my lord. When did you discover the truth? For my own peace of mind, I beg you will tell me.'

'When I first met you again in London, Miss Winstanley,' he responded simply. 'You were singing, most beautifully, at Lady Bridge's soirée.'

She blushed and fell silent.

Amburley could not tell if the blush was a result of his compliment on her singing, or of her shame at being thus unmasked. In an attempt to divert her thoughts, he began to talk randomly about the beauties of the cathedral they were entering. Now was surely not the time to ask about her excursions to the Fleet.

She seemed determined not to be diverted. 'Lord Amburley, I must ask you—how is it that the story of my outrageous behaviour is not the talk of London Society?'

'Why should it be so? Only Lewiston and myself are aware of it. I admit that we have been intrigued, but we have spoken of it to no one else. It is not my way to make sport of ladies, whatever they may do.'

She turned away quickly, without a word.

Amburley feared that he had embarrassed her yet again. Although he could no longer see her face, he fancied there was a tinge of a blush on her exposed neck. He should not press her further. And yet…she herself seemed to be intent on confessing her faults. He had assured her he was to be trusted. Perhaps she would confide in him about her visit to the prison? After a moment's deliberation, Amburley ventured a question, knowing that by doing so, he risked all their new-found rapport. 'Forgive me, Miss Winstanley, but I am still puzzled by our...encounter. Will you tell me why you—?'

'Pride, my lord,' she whispered, before he could finish. 'My stupid, stubborn pride.' There was a catch in her throat as she repeated the word. She straightened her back and lifted her chin, but she did not look at him. 'You will have concluded by now, my lord, that I have allowed it to rule my actions, even when my judgement tells me that I should not succumb. You must think me very wrong-headed.'

So she was too proud to admit to having relatives in the Fleet. At that moment, Amburley was in no mood to blame her. All the blame should fall on the person—whoever he, or she, might be—who had persuaded her to visit the prison thus unaccompanied. She should not have agreed, of course, but the principal fault did not lie with her. When she was less agitated, he would endeavour to discover the identity of the culprit, but there had been confessions enough for the moment.

'Who am I to sit in judgement?' he asked calmly, drawing her hand through his arm. 'Come, let us look at the stained glass. Do you wish to mount to the whispering gallery? I have never done so, but I am told it is worth the exercise.'

Then, placing his hand lightly over hers, he added, 'Do you dare, Miss Winstanley?'

Although the Isabella who drove back to Hill Street was a considerable improvement on the one who had left in mid-afternoon, she was yet finding the encounter uncomfortable, because she could not put aside her feelings for him. She had found it difficult enough to hide them earlier, especially at the moment when she realised how generously he was dealing with her. She had not dared to look at him then, lest he see her love writ boldly in her eyes. It seemed that he was, after all, everything that Mitchell had described—but she must not think of that.

She forced herself to remain practical, to make a dispassionate assessment of what had taken place. Lord Amburley had gone out of his way to restore her shattered spirits, and with a fair degree of success. She had admitted to him that her 'poor relation' pose had resulted from her stubborn pride. Of course, she had not explained why she was so determined to preserve her anonymity—that would have revealed her hidden wealth—but he had accepted her flimsy explanation calmly and had not badgered her for further details. Best of all, he had done nothing, by word or gesture, to allude to their meeting outside the Fleet prison.

Brennan hurried to the horses' heads as Isabella

halted the team outside Lady Wycham's house. Lord Amburley sprang down to help her out and escort her to the door.

Isabella felt a desperate need to end their encounter on a conventional note. 'Shall we see you at the opera tonight, my lord?' she asked.

'I have not yet decided,' he admitted frankly. 'Do you all go?'

'Sophia and I are joining Mrs Ramsey's party. Lady Wycham finds the opera rather too taxing for her strength.'

'I see.'

Isabella thought that he looked somewhat distant, for a moment.

'The opera it shall be, then,' he said, with a nod. 'I look forward to paying my respects in the course of the evening. Until then—your servant, ma'am.' With a swift bow, he returned to his curricle.

Isabella went slowly up the stairs to her room. The faithful Mitchell began to help her to remove her velvet gown but did not speak, for which Isabella was grateful. Mitchell always seemed to know when her mistress needed time to collect her thoughts. Isabella sat at her dressing table so that Mitchell could begin to unpin her hair.

'You do not ask any questions, Mitchell?'

Mitchell looked hard at her mistress in the glass, but said nothing. There was a smile of understanding in her eyes.

Isabella turned round to look squarely at the abigail

who was probably closer to her than any other person in the world. 'How did you know I loved him?' she asked simply. It was a day for honest questions and straight answers, she had decided.

'Because I know you, miss,' replied Mitchell, equally simply. 'Lots of little things…they just added up.'

'Does *everyone* know?' Isabella had become even paler at the thought of being the subject of gossip in her household and beyond.

'I have said nothing to anyone, miss, nor would I. How can you think so?'

'Oh, Mitchell, I did not mean that. You know I did not. I trust you above all others. No, I meant…if I have betrayed myself to you, others may have guessed also. Tom, for example. He was with me when I encountered Lord Amburley in the park, the morning after the Duchess's ball.'

Mitchell's lips tightened a little at the reference to the meeting in the park. She had probably suspected something of the sort.

'You need have no fears about Tom, Miss Isabella. He's not one to gossip, even if he did suspect, which I doubt. Unless…what did you tell him about this morning? He may well start to wonder, if he knows his lordship took you up.'

'I did not tell him. I said I was forced to hail a hackney to bring me back when he failed to meet me. He was so intent on making me his apologies—a problem with a broken trace or something of the kind—that he asked no questions at all.'

'And his lordship?'

'You have proved a better judge than I. He would have passed the whole afternoon without a single reference to our first meeting or to this morning's, but I could not let it be so. I had to know whether I was to become the butt of the Season. It was as you suspected: he recognised me at Lady Bridge's musical evening—and he has spoken of it to no one, save Mr Lewiston.'

Mitchell gave a small sigh of relief. 'Did you tell him about the Fleet, too?'

'No. In fact, I told him nothing at all. He simply said he had known all along, and it was not his place to judge me. Then he turned the subject. I could not bring myself to a further confession.'

'Even though it might have redeemed you in his estimation?'

'How so? He would not approve of such unladylike behaviour.'

'You cannot know that, Miss Isabella. After all, he finances his mother's good works.'

Isabella did not stop to consider how Mitchell might have come by that snippet of information. 'It is of no moment, in any case, Mitchell.' She took a deep breath. 'I believe he is developing a *tendre* for Sophia. It would be a good match for her. He is strong enough to resist the unreasonable demands of her family, yet able to keep her in relative comfort. I only hope she values him as she ought.'

'I don't believe it, Miss Isabella.' Mitchell sounded outraged. 'What on earth makes you think that?'

'He has been paying a great deal of attention to her of late and seems to be intent on pursuing her. And he was undecided about attending the opera tonight, until I told him Sophia would be there as well as I. It is not so wonderful after all. She is young, pretty and biddable. They seemed very gay in each other's company.'

Mitchell looked unconvinced.

Isabella turned back to the mirror. 'I should warn Lady Wycham, I think. She will need to be ready to tell him of Sophia's prospects when he calls. I doubt that her lack of dowry will weigh much against her other attractions.'

Chapter Fourteen

Preparing for the visit to the opera, Isabella did her best to put Lord Amburley and his feelings out of her mind. Nothing was left to her now except that stubborn pride of hers, and so she resolved to maintain her dignity, at least. She therefore chose to appear very much the *grande dame* for this meeting, in a gown of garnet red silk of expensive simplicity. Its severe lines and complete lack of ornamentation flattered her tall, slim figure but emphasised that she was no longer in the first flush of youth. She further enhanced the effect by filling the deeply cut neckline with her splendid diamond collar and adding matching ear-studs and bracelet. A diamond aigret sparkled in her honey-gold curls. The woman who stared back at her from the mirror looked magnificent, but cold and unattainable, rather in the style of a classical statue.

'My goodness, Isabella,' exclaimed Lady Wycham, when her great-niece came to her room to take her leave, 'you do look splendid. I had not seen you wear your mother's diamonds before. I thought you…' The thought trailed off, unvoiced.

Isabella felt a need to defend her apparent change of style. 'This gown is rather too plain without something striking by way of jewellery. The diamonds are all I have that can be worn with this shade of red.' Even to her own ears, it sounded rather lame.

The younger ladies took a fond leave of Lady Wycham and descended to the hall, where the butler placed Isabella's dark red velvet opera cloak round her shoulders. Sophia donned a white taffeta cape that had once been Isabella's. The contrast between the two could not have been more marked. Sophia looked young, pretty and innocent. Isabella was clearly a woman of the world, sternly handsome, daunting.

Isabella chose a seat at the front of the Ramsey box, as far to the side as possible. From there, she could enjoy a clear view of the stage and also, she hoped, an opportunity to listen uninterrupted to the music.

The first two acts passed all too soon. When the curtain fell, Isabella was recalled to a sense of the present and to the uncomfortable prospect of a meeting with Lord Amburley.

But he did not appear.

The great Neroni was soon producing more exquisite sound from the stage, but Isabella could not succeed in concentrating on the third act. What a hypocrite I am, she thought bleakly. I distance myself from the others so that I may lose myself in the music, but I cannot devote even half my attention to it. The greater part is occupied in wondering why he has not come, even when I know that it is Sophia he comes to meet. A hypocrite, and a fool besides!

Lord Amburley was not among the visitors to the Ramsey box in the second interval, either. Several of Sophia's cavaliers presented themselves, however, and set about making themselves agreeable. Sophia's laughter carried easily to the nearby boxes.

'Good evening, Miss Winstanley.' Mr Lewiston's familiar voice shook Isabella out of her reverie. 'You are a great lover of the opera, I collect?'

Isabella rose and extended her hand politely. 'Why, yes, sir, I am. Neroni was wonderful, did you not think?'

'I am afraid I have seen too little of the performance to dare to pass judgement, ma'am. My arrival was much delayed.'

'Oh, I am sorry to hear that. You missed a rare treat, I assure you.'

Isabella was searching for something else to say, when Sophia joined them. 'Why, Mr Lewiston,' she said, as they shook hands, 'I had not thought to see you at the opera. Do you have a box, too? Is it not delightful to be able to meet all one's friends with such ease? And Mrs Ramsey has ordered champagne, too. It is quite wonderful.' She beamed artlessly at Mr Lewiston. 'I have not seen Lord Amburley this evening,' she continued, ignoring the slight furrowing of

Mr Lewiston's brows at the name. 'I hope we have not offended his lordship, that he fails to come to our box.'

'Why, certainly not, ma'am,' protested Mr Lewiston, driven at last to speak of his friend. 'Amburley is not here tonight. Indeed, that was the cause of my own late arrival. He has left town on a matter of some urgency, I believe. He sent a message to tell me of it, but my good-for-nothing man failed to deliver it. So I waited for nigh on an hour before I discovered what was amiss. It is to that, Miss Winstanley, that I ascribe the blame for having missed Neroni sing.'

'But why has Lord Amburley gone—?' began Sophia.

'We must hope that nothing untoward has called Lord Amburley from town,' interposed Isabella politely. 'Do you stay in London for the rest of the Season, sir?'

'I shall certainly stay for some weeks yet, ma'am. As will Amburley, I believe, when he returns.' With a gentle smile for Sophia, who was looking quite crestfallen, he set about satisfying her curiosity. 'I expect him to return to town quite soon. Lady Amburley summoned him back to the estate, to deal with an unspecified crisis. Probably, she… Well, never mind. I doubt it will take long to resolve. He will be sorry to have missed paying his respects, particularly when you both look so splendid.'

Isabella accepted the compliment with a dignified

nod. It was not, she knew, directed at her. Mr Lewiston's eyes had been fixed on Sophia's face.

'Indeed they do,' echoed their host, as he joined them. 'Miss Winstanley looks particularly splendid in red, if I may make so bold as to say so.'

'You are too kind, sir,' smiled Isabella, recognising that her appearance was likely to be attractive only to gentlemen of an earlier generation. Mr Ramsey's extravagant attentions made her feel old enough to be Sophia's mother.

After a night's sleep, Isabella felt somewhat recovered from the desolation and disappointment of the previous day. Then, she had passed the events of recent weeks under review and had concluded, reluctantly, that Lord Amburley was pursuing Sophia. Now, in the clear light of morning, her conclusion seemed even more logical.

Isabella was sternly resolved to act in Sophia's best interests now. Her own desires were pushed into a dark corner of her mind where she turned the key firmly. No one would learn of her feelings for Amburley—not Lady Wycham, not Sophia…and certainly not the lord himself.

Having despatched Sophia and her abigail for a fitting at Madame Florette's, Isabella moved reflectively up the staircase to Lady Wycham's room, to broach the subject of Amburley and Sophia. It was, for Isabella, a matter of honour.

Lady Wycham accepted the news with equanimity.

'I was fairly sure she would attract the attentions of at least one eligible gentleman, in spite of her want of prospects. Amburley certainly seems to have been paying considerable attention to her of late. But, from what you tell me, his friend Lewiston has been rather particular in his attentions also.'

'That is true,' conceded Isabella, 'but Mr Lewiston shows no sign of wishing to come to the point, even though he has had opportunities—more indeed than Lord Amburley—to attach her affections.'

'Do you think either of them has done so?'

'Frankly, no, I do not. Though there is a degree of rivalry for Sophia's favours between his lordship and Mr Lewiston which has led to a marked coolness between them of late. It must be resolved soon, I think.'

'You say neither has attached her affection, but has she a preference, do you think?'

'I do not know, Aunt. She has not confided in me. In fact, I doubt she has anything to confide. She likes them both well enough, I dare say.' She paused as a vivid recollection came to her. 'I do recall, however, that she once said Lord Amburley frightened her.'

'Did she so?'

'Yes…but that was when she first knew him. I am certain he does not so affect her now.' Lady Wycham looked unconvinced. 'He is a man of honour and, I suspect, of deep feeling. She would grow to value him.'

'Hmmph. That's as may be. We shall see. For myself, I cannot see why he should have developed a *tendre* for Sophia. A singularly ill-assorted couple, in my estimation.'

Isabella swallowed and nodded dumbly. If only Mr Lewiston would make Sophia an offer quickly, be-fore— She stopped that thought in its tracks, admon-ishing herself sternly. It is not for Sophia's benefit that you would urge him on, she chided herself, but for your own. And what of Amburley? Does he not deserve happiness with the woman he loves, after so much early heartbreak? How can I wish for him to lose his heart's desire again? If that is the extent of my love, then it is no kind of love at all.

Lord Amburley, arriving back in London after an absence of over a fortnight, set about quizzing Lew-iston about his relationship with Sophia. 'I saw the report of the Hill Street ball. A resounding success, by all accounts,' he said, as they shared some fine burgundy over dinner. 'I scanned the *Gazette* regu-larly for your betrothal announcement. Do you tell me you do not intend to make Miss Sophia an offer?'

Lewiston turned the glass in his fingers, watching how the wine sparkled where it caught the candle-light. It was some moments before he spoke. 'To be honest, I cannot decide. She is surrounded by admir-ers, wherever she goes. I am merely one of the throng. I see no reason why she would look favourably on my suit. I have nothing to offer her.' He emptied his glass and reached for the decanter.

'You do yourself an injustice, George. You have

far more to offer her than most of that motley crew
of hangers-on. You, at least, are not after her fortune.
You have good family, a noble estate—'

'Nothing that she does not have already, Leigh. My
only advantage over the others is wealth—which she
does not need.'

His lordship sipped his wine meditatively. 'Does
she favour any gentleman in particular?'

'Not as far as I can see.'

'Then you have no clear rival. Come, George, look
at this in a positive light. If she has not yet formed
an attachment, it is up to you to ensure that her choice
falls on you. You *do* want her, I take it?'

'Yes,' admitted Lewiston, reddening slightly and
staring again at his wine. 'Yes, I do. But I shall not
make her an offer unless I am sure she will accept
me. I could not take a refusal, Leigh.'

His lordship concluded from this that his friend's
case was very bad indeed. 'There can be no absolute
certainty in such matters, you know, George. Women
are strange creatures, and unpredictable. If it would
be of any help, I could try to draw her out a little on
the subject of gentlemen in general, and you in particular.'

Lewiston accepted this unusual offer with alacrity.
'I am engaged to ride in the park with the Winstanley
ladies tomorrow morning, Leigh. Will you join us?'

'Not possible, I'm afraid. I must go into the City
to see the family lawyer in the morning.'

'Trouble?'

'Of a kind. My mother is in need of substantial funds, for which arrangements must be made.'

'I supposed that something of the kind was the cause of your sudden departure.'

'In that case,' replied his lordship, with a shrug, 'you supposed wrongly. When it is a question of money, my mother simply writes to require me to provide it. She went to the trouble of summoning me to tell me my father's uncle was reported to be dying. She wanted me to persuade him to change his will.'

Lewiston's question was written clearly in his eyes.

'No, of course not. I did not go near him. How can you think it? Silas Stansfield is a family tyrant, who uses his wealth as a weapon to enforce obedience from all his relations. He will live to plague us for years yet, but I refuse to dance to his tune.'

'Your mother could make the approach on her own behalf, I suppose, seeking his help for her good works.'

'Waste of time, George. The old man don't believe in charity, especially when it's organised by women.'

'So Lady Amburley has to turn to you again?'

'It is natural and right that she should do so, George, since I am the head of the family,' responded Lord Amburley, very much on his dignity.

'I did not for a moment mean—'

'No, of course not. I apologise for being so pompous.' Amburley sounded just a little sheepish. 'It's just that she's gone rather far this time—an orphanage is to be built by public subscription, with the costs underwritten by Lady Amburley, so that building can begin before all the money has been raised. The donations so far are pretty meagre. Unless building is to be halted, the Amburley donation will have to be both large and immediate.'

'Perhaps I might make a donation to Lady Amburley's fund?'

Lord Amburley looked hard at his friend. 'You have not the least interest in orphans, George.' He noted how Lewiston coloured, without attempting to argue. 'Thank you, but no. This is a problem I must resolve for myself.'

'Miss Winstanley's debt might help, if you could bring yourself to collect on it,' observed Lewiston shrewdly.

His lordship laughed. 'By God, I've missed your company, George. It's dull as ditchwater in the country at this time of year. Between the bailiff's interminable lectures about the state of the land, and my mother's urgings about Uncle Silas, it was a singularly dreary visit. Tell me how you have been going on while I was away.'

Lord Amburley then listened to a racy account of the progress of the Season, from which he deduced that his friend was paying court to Sophia Winstanley in much too timid a fashion. As soon as he had resolved his own business affairs, it would be necessary for him to take a hand in Lewiston's.

Lord Amburley's visit to the City firm of Dicks & Jenner next morning took much less time than he had expected. The arrangements proved to be remarkably straightforward—just the liquidation of part of his investments in the Funds which, Mr Dicks assured him, was simplicity itself. Even so, the visit might have lasted longer, if the lawyer had been allowed to deliver the homily that was clearly on the tip of his tongue. Like most of his kind, he strongly disapproved of his clients' dipping into their capital. Indeed, he was wont to say that expenses that could not be funded out of income should simply be forgone.

However, on this occasion, the client cut him short. 'Thank you, Dicks, but my mind is made up. Please go ahead immediately, and arrange for the proceeds to be transmitted at once to Lady Amburley. I take it you have all the authorities you need?' Lord Amburley rose from the hard chair on which he had been sitting.

Mr Dicks hurriedly followed suit. 'Indeed, yes, my lord. I shall set matters in hand immediately.'

Lord Amburley nodded curtly, turning to leave. Mr Dicks scuttled round the desk, only just reaching the door in time to open it and bow his noble client out of the inner sanctum.

'Good day to you, Dicks.'

Mr Dicks bowed again as the outer door closed.

Lord Amburley stood on the step, drawing on his driving gloves. Where was his curricle? After a moment's thought, he concluded that Brennan must be walking the horses in the nearby streets, since he would not have expected his master to appear again so soon. His lordship cursed silently. He could have accompanied Lewiston and the ladies on their ride after all, if he had but known how soon his business would be concluded. But it was too late now. Lewiston would already have made his excuses.

He leaned back against the door jamb, lazily surveying the bustle around him. No wonder Brennan had taken the curricle off. If he had remained here, the result would have been chaos, for there was barely room for a single carriage in the narrow confines of the City street. Most of the traffic was perversely slow, too—hand-carts and hugely overloaded vehicles drawn by single horses, fit only for the knacker's yard. If they met traffic like this during their race, the results would be appalling! It would be vital to avoid such narrow streets when they decided on the route. Not for the first time, he found he was grateful that no one knew what was planned. It was likely to do nothing for his reputation as a whip.

He was still musing abstractedly on Isabella Winstanley when his curricle appeared at the corner of the street. Brennan's consternation was evident. He was making excuses even before he was within earshot.

'Spare me the explanations,' said his lordship curtly, but without heat. 'You had no way of knowing I would need you again so soon.' Lord Amburley did not expect his retainers to number crystal-ball gazing among their accomplishments. He sighed resignedly.

'And now, I find I even have an hour or so in hand. I wonder… Ah, I know. Cigars.'

Brennan looked sideways at his master.

Lord Amburley was in a mood to be indulgent. 'I need some more cigars,' he said brightly, 'so we will pay a visit to Fribourg & Treyer in the Haymarket. It is not far out of our way. And someone has to pander to my filthy habit.' He laughed to himself. Cigar smoking was definitely frowned upon in polite society but he, like many of his fellow soldiers, found blowing a cloud much preferable to taking snuff, even if he did have to skulk outside on the terrace to do it. Perhaps, one day, it would become more acceptable.

It took some time to reach the Haymarket, because the traffic was heavy everywhere. It kept reminding him of the risks attached to his race against Miss Winstanley—if luck were against him, he might even lose his precious greys. He refused to consider such an eventuality.

'Shall I walk them up and down, m'lord?'

Lord Amburley shook his head. 'No. I am in no hurry now. Better you drive them round St James's and back again, so that they are not kept standing. I shall be here when you return.' With that, he passed the reins to the groom and jumped lightly down. He had already disappeared into Fribourg & Treyer's by the time his curricle was in motion once more.

Barely five minutes later, he was standing on the flagway with a box of cigars under his arm. It seemed he was fated to encounter only efficient tradesmen today. In normal circumstances, he would have been cursing if they had been otherwise, but today, everything seemed to be conspiring to give him time on his own—time to think—which he would have preferred to avoid. He began to stroll down the Haymarket, glancing idly into the shop windows as he passed. He hardly noticed what they offered, so preoccupied was he with his thoughts.

He had reached the corner of Panton Street before he paused to look around for his curricle. No sign yet. Ah, well. He turned back to look into the window of the shop on the corner.

Lord Amburley was not in the habit of frequenting jewellers' establishments, but Garrard's certainly offered an eye-catching display. The front of the window was filled with unusual items, obviously bespoke, which must have been made for wealthy clients. In addition, there was a tray of quite beautiful rings, some with oriental designs, and all containing the most exquisite stones. For several minutes, he gazed into the window, considering. Then, with a sudden shrug of his shoulders, he strode into the shop.

Chapter Fifteen

In the course of the next three weeks, Lord Amburley and his friend were often to be found in the company of the Misses Winstanley. Initially, the *ton* found it difficult to decide which of the ladies was being pursued, and by whom.

Mr Lewiston was mainly directing his attention to the younger lady, the heiress from Yorkshire, though he treated the elder Miss Winstanley with the greatest courtesy and danced with her often. Lord Amburley drove out pretty regularly with Miss Winstanley, though not more frequently than with other ladies. He did not drive Miss Sophia at all, but he danced with her at every event, sometimes twice. With the elder Miss Winstanley, he never danced at all.

The tabbies concluded, after much enjoyable speculation, that both men were pursuing the heiress, and that both felt they should seek the chaperon's support for their cause. The gossips would not stoop so low as to wager on the outcome—such activity was beneath them—but they did split into factions to argue the merits of their case.

Lady Sefton favoured Amburley's suit. 'Amburley offers a title. Lewiston has only wealth to recommend him, which she does not need. She will choose title and position.'

Mrs Drummond Burrell disagreed. 'She will choose wealth and the younger man, especially once she meets Georgiana Amburley. A young lady of Sophia Winstanley's background and style will never marry a man whose mother is totally immersed in good works. No parties, no entertaining, no London Season? A title is inadequate compensation for pious boredom.' Since she was the only untitled speaker in the group of patronesses, her words did not carry quite as much weight as she might have liked.

The speculation continued and came, inevitably, to the ears of Lady Wycham. 'Isabella, we must do something. Sophia has become the centre of attention since Amburley returned to London. They are all taking sides as to whether Amburley or Lewiston will win her. We cannot allow this to go on. She has the appearance of the most accomplished flirt, leading on two eligible gentlemen almost for the fun of it. I think I should speak to her. Do not you?'

'I do not know, Aunt. She does not flirt in any improper sense, I assure you, though she is clearly flattered by all the attention she receives. What can one say to her, when she is doing nothing wrong? She cannot be asked to choose between them, for neither has yet come to the point. And who is to say whether they will?'

Lady Wycham was silent for a while. 'I believe you may be right, my dear. If she were to discourage either of them, there is as yet no guarantee that the other would come up to scratch. And with her prospects, we cannot afford to offend *any* possible suitor. I shall not speak to her, then—not yet, at least. But when I next see Amburley, I shall ask him about his intentions.'

'Oh, no!'

Lady Wycham looked up sharply. Isabella flushed bright red under her aunt's penetrating gaze. 'Why ever not? He is not a man to run from such an enquiry. And if he once confides in me, he may bring himself to address Sophia.'

'I beg your pardon, Aunt. I… You will do as you think best, of course, only…I suspect that Sophia will feel duty-bound to accept the first eligible offer she receives, for fear there may not be another.'

'Do you tell me she favours Mr Lewiston?'

'I cannot be sure, but I fancy she may do so. Oh, dear, it is all so difficult.'

'Indeed so,' responded Lady Wycham with a shrewd glance at Isabella. 'Very well. I shall leave matters a little, but only a very little, longer. Meanwhile, you, Isabella, must find out what Sophia's feelings are. I shall speak to Amburley at the end of the week, unless you can assure me that she truly favours Lewiston. Are we agreed on that?'

'I shall do my best, Aunt,' promised Isabella.

After Isabella had left the room, Lady Wycham returned to her tapestry work. For several minutes, she set no stitches at all, staring blankly at the canvas. Then, with a little shrug and a long sigh, she began to ply her needle.

Isabella returned quickly to her own room. Her fiery blush had been replaced by a pronounced pallor, and her hands were shaking slightly as she closed the door of her sanctuary. For once, Mitchell was absent. Isabella had only her own disordered thoughts for company.

They were not pleasant thoughts. Three weeks of watching Amburley in pursuit of Sophia had depressed Isabella's spirits.

Isabella herself had had very little real contact with Lord Amburley since his return, except for their regular weekly drives in and around London. Although he had never once referred to her masquerade or to the encounter at the Fleet, it was becoming increasingly difficult for her to retain her composure in his company. She had often wished she were not committed to their private race. None the less, since it was unavoidable, she remained determined to show him she could be a worthy opponent. Partly for that reason, she had insisted that they avoid the simple, direct route along Fleet Street and the Strand. That would simply be a matter of speed—she would have no chance at all of mounting a respectable challenge.

Lord Amburley had eventually agreed, after much

discussion, that a more circuitous route, taking in Newgate and Lincoln's Inn Fields, would be a fairer test of their skill. They had driven it twice now, and the times had been wildly different. The outcome of their race might be purely a matter of chance.

Had it not been for the need to hide her feelings from him, she would have enjoyed their drives. His lordship was a well-read and much-travelled man, whose measured opinions marked his good sense and considerable intellect. Furthermore, he paid her the unusual compliment of discussing serious subjects with her. He knew how to provide amusing company, besides. His witty anecdotes of the lighter side of a soldier's life in the Peninsula often brought Isabella's laughter bubbling out, in spite of her inner melancholy.

He seldom spoke of Sophia. When he did, he seemed to Isabella to be trying to probe for information about her feelings. But, however obliquely he might approach the subject, Isabella was always on her guard. Privately, she sympathised greatly with his desire for reassurance before making another offer, but she owed it to Sophia not to give anything away. In any case, as she had now admitted to Lady Wycham, she really had none of Sophia's secrets to share.

It being Wednesday, she and Sophia were engaged for Almack's, with Isabella yet again in the role of chaperon. Isabella was tempted to play the *grande dame* once more, which she had not tried since the

night at the opera. But what would it serve? She
would look cool and dignified, to be sure, but it would
not make her the object of his affections. If anything,
it would widen the gulf that was already opening between them, and she had to admit she did not want
that. Being in his company might be purgatory; but
losing him forever would be like the loss of part of
herself.

She reviewed her situation as dispassionately as she
was able. Time was not on her side. She had no
choice, now, but to set about discovering what Sophia's feelings were. And if Sophia did favour Amburley, he would no doubt be brought up to scratch
by Lady Wycham within a very short time. Thereafter, private intercourse with him would be at an end.
He would be Sophia's betrothed. Isabella's only hope
was that Sophia might truly favour Mr Lewiston—
though it was not a wager on which she would have
hazarded much.

Twenty-four hours more, she concluded. That is all
I have—tonight at Almack's, and tomorrow, when we
drive out into London. Aunt Jemima expects her answer before Friday. Well, I shall endeavour to make
the most of every minute. The memories will be all I
shall have.

She reviewed her tactics in this new light. Not the
grande dame, she concluded, but the beauty. She
would be exactly as she had been at the Duchess of
Newcombe's ball, even as far as the aquamarines. He

had admired her then. Perhaps, just perhaps, he might do so again.

Lord Amburley and his friend dined in Jermyn Street before going on to Almack's. His lordship had very little progress to report.

'It is a little difficult on our drives because of the groom, of course, but I have tried on several occasions to draw Miss Winstanley out on the subject of Miss Sophia's feelings. Unfortunately, she persists in avoiding the issue. Have you been more successful?'

'Not really. Miss Sophia gives me vague encouragement, but nothing specific. And she seems to favour others quite as much as she does me. I tell you, Leigh, I cannot continue this posturing ritual for much longer.'

Amburley refilled their glasses. 'No,' he agreed slowly, 'it must be brought to a head soon. I wonder... Yes, I think that might serve. Provided I can create an opportunity for an uninterrupted private discussion with Miss Winstanley, I think the matter may be managed.' Lewiston looked inquiringly at his friend, but Amburley did not expand on the details of his plan.

Lewiston sounded a note of caution. 'That might be difficult, in the crush. It is so easy to be overheard. Still, you could always dance with her.'

That was treading on very delicate ground. The two men had reached an unspoken understanding, some weeks before, that they would not discuss Amburley's

reluctance to dance with Miss Winstanley. Amburley
had chosen to let his friend believe that it was a result
of a desire to avoid gossip, particularly during a period when he was driving out with her fairly regularly.
To himself, he was prepared to admit that the reasons
went deeper than that, but he would not probe them
too far. The truth might be painful.

'If it is the only way,' Amburley returned lightly,
'I shall certainly dance with Miss Winstanley this
evening. You, I take it, will be dancing with Miss
Sophia?'

'If I can. But that will be, at most, two dances and
precious little time to woo her.' He sounded almost
despondent.

'Come, let us talk of other things for now. There
is nothing more we can do about your courtship, until
we arrive at the Marriage Mart.' He sipped his wine.
'Lord, how I detest it. So many hopeful young things,
swathed in silk and hung with jewels, paraded to
tempt the eligible male of the species.'

'What an extraordinary man you are, Leigh. You
have certainly changed your tune of late. You make
it sound positively medieval—' Amburley's cocked
eyebrow indicated that that was precisely what he did
think '—but in any case, Miss Sophia does no such
thing. She dresses as becomes a young lady just out,
and she is never hung with extravagant jewellery. The
most I have seen her wear is a locket, or a single
strand of pearls.'

'Very expensive pearls,' remarked Amburley sardonically.

'But quite in keeping for a lady of her position. Miss Winstanley, by contrast—'

'What of her?' interrupted Amburley, rather too quickly. 'I have never seen her wear more than aquamarines.'

It was Lewiston's turn to win the war of words over jewellery. 'I'm afraid you missed the spectacle at the opera, Leigh. Miss Isabella Winstanley in a gown of unrelieved red silk and positively dripping with diamonds.' He paused, as shock registered on Amburley's face. 'I cannot imagine why she wore them or, indeed, where she had them. The effect was stunning, I may tell you. She looked like a queen—at least, to those who do not know what she really is.'

'Dear God,' muttered Amburley, half to himself. He reached for the decanter and concentrated hard on refilling their crystal glasses. 'The sooner we can have you safely riveted to Miss Sophia, George, the sooner Miss Winstanley will revert to her proper station and abandon this shameful imposture. I shall see what can be done tonight, I promise you.'

For several moments, there was silence between them. 'Come,' said Amburley at length, rising from the table, 'we had best leave now, so that we have ample time at Almack's. There is much to be done.'

Lord Amburley was set on seizing the initiative at Almack's—and keeping it. Barely had the Winstanley

A Poor Relation

party entered, than he greeted them. 'Good evening, Miss Winstanley, Miss Sophia.' He was delighted to see that his tactics were working. Miss Winstanley had clearly not been prepared to meet him the moment she entered the ballroom. He registered the shock in her eyes as he shook her hand. 'You see us both before you, reformed characters, ma'am.' His gaze warmed as he took stock of her stunning appearance. 'May I have the honour of this dance?'

Miss Winstanley gave a little gasp but made a quick recover, with a forced smile, as she accepted his arm to the floor.

There was not much opportunity for conversation during the country dance. Amburley fancied his partner was remembering the embarrassing silence of their only previous essay on the floor, for she forced herself into light-hearted banter each time they came together.

'You mentioned that you are reformed, my lord. Dare I ask from what wickedness you have turned?'

'Lack of self-interest, ma'am.'

He had surprised her into a laugh. 'I knew I should not ask. I am now even less enlightened than before,' she said as the dance parted them again. They passed down the set and came together again at the bottom, having completed the complex figures. 'Curiosity is my besetting sin, my lord,' she said, looking up at him through her lashes, 'particularly when my partner fails to satisfy it.'

'If you would allow me to borrow your favourite

epithet, ma'am, I should say "outrageous",' he said, ruthlessly stifling his natural desire to laugh. 'But then, it would be outrageous in me, so to describe a lady.'

'Oh!' She was trying to assume an expression of disapproval, but it was totally unconvincing. Her eyes were sparkling, and her lips twitched as she tried not to smile.

Amburley gazed down at her. She looked so radiant that he caught his breath. For a moment, he could think of nothing at all to say. 'One of the benefits of an early arrival at Almack's, ma'am, is the opportunity to ask for the hand of a beautiful lady for the waltz.' He had to clear his throat before he could continue. 'Will you do me the honour, after the supper interval?'

He felt her hand tremble a little in his. She failed to meet his eyes as she replied huskily, 'Thank you, my lord, I should be delighted.'

The dance ended then, and he led her from the floor, turning the conversation to everyday matters while he tried to fathom what on earth had come over him. He had fully intended to waltz with her later, but what had possessed him to say such a thing? Madness! An inner voice whispered that there had been hidden meaning in her reaction too, but he refused to listen to it. He must hold fast to his purpose.

Isabella left the supper room on the arm of a middle-aged admirer, unable to say what she had eaten

or what she had said or done. Since that dance with
Lord Amburley, his words kept running round and
round her head. She could not stop seeing his face
and the warm glow in his chocolate eyes. She could
not imagine why he now wished to dance with her.
She tried to tell herself sternly not to hope.

Lord Amburley came to claim her for the waltz.
She was perversely pleased, this time, to see that she
managed to control the quivering of her fingers when
she touched him. She had promised herself, besides,
that she would not stare in silence at the perfection
of his cravat—but she still found it immensely difficult to open the conversation.

'You waltz most elegantly, ma'am,' he began politely, expertly guiding her through the whirling
throng. 'It is a pleasure to have such a partner. And
it is a pleasure, too, to have an opportunity of private
conversation with you.'

She looked up at him, suspicion beginning to cloud
her sparkling eyes.

'I need to speak frankly on a delicate matter,
ma'am, and you are the only person who can advise
me.'

Isabella's heart was sinking rapidly in the direction
of her silken slippers. She forced herself to keep a
smile on her lips, politely assuring him that he might
continue.

'It concerns Miss Sophia, ma'am, as I think you
may have guessed. Forgive my plain speaking, Miss

Winstanley, but tell me, I beg you: will Miss Sophia favour Lewiston's suit?'

Isabella felt as if an iron hand had gripped her, so that she could not breathe. She had known he was pursuing Sophia but, somehow, particularly here in his arms, she had allowed her hopes to overcome her reason. Now, all was clear. He was waltzing with her, not for the pleasure of her company, but callously, to create an opportunity to quiz her about whether Sophia favoured Mr Lewiston over himself.

Her confusion must have been evident. And it was some moments before she found her voice. 'You are very blunt, my lord,' she said, in a strained tone. 'But your confidence is misplaced, I fear, for I cannot answer your question.' She had become rigid in his arms by the end of this little speech.

'I see,' he responded tightly. 'Forgive me for my impertinence, ma'am, I had thought you… I beg your pardon.'

Their dance continued in stiff silence. Isabella breathed a sigh of relief as he returned her to her party and took his leave. Thank God that was over. Being alone in his company had become unbearable. But how could she avoid it? They still had not completed their race. Oh, God! Tomorrow she was engaged to drive out with him again. Surely she would never be able to face him?

For a moment, she toyed with the thought of feigning illness on the morrow, but she soon dismissed that idea. She could not be such a coward. Drawing on all her inner resources, she smiled benignly on the gentleman who approached to invite her to dance. Whatever else Amburley may think of me, she vowed, he will never find me craven.

Chapter Sixteen

When Lord Amburley returned from his early morning ride next day, he found Sam shifting impatiently from one foot to the other outside his front door.

''Ere, guv'nor, I got what yer wanted at last. She—'

'Not here, Sam,' interrupted Lord Amburley sharply. 'Curb your impatience just a little longer, lad.' He gave the reins of his huge grey into the hands of the waiting lackey and led the way inside. 'Bring some madeira to the book-room, if you please, Wilson, and a pot of ale for young Sam.'

Sam made to blurt out his news as soon as the book-room door closed behind them, but Lord Amburley cut him short. 'Have you *all* the information this time, Sam?'

'Aye, yer honour, the 'ole fing. She's—'

'I suggest you wait until you've wet your whistle a bit and then give me it all from the beginning. Ah, splendid, here's Wilson with the madeira.'

By the time his lordship had poured himself a glass of madeira, Sam had emptied his pot of ale and was obviously itching to embark on his tale. But Lord Amburley would not be rushed. He wished to prepare himself for intelligence that he rather feared would be unwelcome. With deliberation, he took his accustomed place behind the mahogany desk and looked searchingly and sternly at Sam.

'Very well, young Sam. Now, tell me everything you have learned, from the beginning, if you please.'

Sam swallowed. 'Well, yer honour, like I told yer last week, the gentry-mort visits the Fleet at least once a se'enight, sometimes more'n once. Always ever so early it is, when she gets there. An' always with the same jarvey, 'im what I fixed when yer honour wanted 'im out o' the way. I got in under 'is 'orse an' cut 'is trace. 'E didn't even know I were there.'

'Go on,' encouraged his lordship, not wishing to interrupt Sam's flow, even though he was repeating facts from earlier reports—and boasting of his successes.

'She always wears them dark togs, wi' the shawl an' bonnet an' all. An' the jarvey comes back to meet 'er, by arrangement like, when she comes out again. I 'itched meself on the back o' the 'ackney outside the Fleet last week. Weren't worth the trouble. Went right back to the gentry-ken what she started from.'

Amburley's fingers were now starting to drum impatiently on the arm of his chair, and his stern look had developed into a frown. He was going to have trouble controlling his temper, if Sam did not soon come to the point.

Sam swallowed again. 'Yer honour wanted ter know 'oo the gentry-mort were visiting in the Fleet. I managed ter find a cove from inside last week, guv'nor, an' 'e agreed to watch 'er on 'er visits. Cost me 'alf-a-crown,' he added hopefully, looking at his lordship.

'Your expenses will be paid, Sam, *provided* you come up with the goods. Now...'

'This cove in the Fleet, 'e took a terrible long time ter find out about 'er doings, but 'e struck lucky t'day. The gentry-mort visits a cove name o' Graham.'

'What do you know of him? What sort of man is he?'

'Don't rightly know, yer honour, 'cept 'e's quite young an' well togged-up in a dreary sort o' way. Black, mostly.'

'You've seen him?'

'Aye, yer honour. 'E left just after the gentry-mort came out ter meet the jarvey.'

'He *left*?' repeated his lordship in surprise. 'I see. Do you know where he went?'

'Course I do. Followed 'im, di'nt I?' Sam gave a satisfied smirk. 'Went in ter that big church near the river.'

'Not an inmate, then,' deduced Lord Amburley, 'and, by his dress, a parson.'

'Dunno about that, yer honour. Di'nt fink yer

honour'd want ter know that. Thought it were the gentry-mort you was after.'

'I do want information about the lady, certainly. And for a lad who claimed to have "the whole thing", you have provided precious little so far.'

'I ain't finished yet, 'ave I?' countered Sam indignantly.

Amburley had to laugh at the defiant face of the urchin before him. 'I beg your pardon, Sam,' he said in mock contrition. 'Pray, do continue.'

Sam gave him a knowing look. 'I dunno whether this 'ere Graham cove's a parson or not, but I 'ave found out what they do in the Fleet.'

Lord Amburley leaned forward in his chair, tension apparent on his face.

'The cove's started a school for the nippers in the Fleet, them as is in there wiv their parents, like. The gentry-mort comes to teach the girls ter sew an' such like. I'd o' found out afore, only I never thought but that she were seeing someone in there more permanent, so ter speak.'

His lordship cut short Sam's recital of why he had taken so long to solve the riddle. He wanted, above all, to be alone, to think through this remarkable intelligence. 'Here.' He dropped two golden guineas into the grubby palm. 'Now, I'm going to send you down to the kitchen to get a square meal into that scrawny body of yours.'

Sam had hardly begun to voice his astonished gratitude by the time the butler appeared, summoned by Lord Amburley's bell.

Amburley let out a long breath as the door closed behind them and poured himself another glass of madeira. Sipping it meditatively, he began to piece together what he now knew.

She went to the Fleet to teach the wretched children there. Not surprising, really, in view of her passionate defence of Christian charity. She might be a penniless companion, but she would recognise that there were many who were even more disadvantaged than herself and, yes, she was the kind of woman who would wish to do something about it. Her wealthier sisters would simply give money to salve their conscience—if they had one. Isabella Winstanley was denied that easy option. She would give of herself. He should have guessed as much.

He smiled a little as he sipped the golden liquid. It was almost the colour of her hair. Unconsciously, his hand went to his waistcoat pocket to finger what he carried there. Her image rose in his mind as he had seen her last evening, a vision in the exquisite gown of gold and jade. She was beautiful, he admitted to himself, though not in the recognised sense. Hers was a more elusive quality that defied description. Beauty of soul, perhaps? He shook his head at such high-flown words and wondered, not for the first time, how it was that he had become so impractical of late.

After a moment more, he rose and began to pace the room. Doubts assailed him once more. If it were merely a piece of charity work, why had she not explained, when he picked her up outside the Fleet? The question nagged at him. He could not help wondering whether there was more than a shared interest in the education of hapless children between Miss Winstanley and the Reverend Mr Graham.

When he returned to Jermyn Street some hours later, having vented his frustration on various opponents at Gentleman Jackson's boxing parlour, there was barely time to change his dress before he was due to leave to collect Miss Winstanley. In a surprisingly short space of time, he was back in the hallway, impatiently slapping his gloves against his leg, while he waited for Brennan to return from the mews with the new team harnessed to the curricle.

No sooner had they appeared, than he was off.

'They're very fresh today, my lord,' said the groom, surreptitiously gripping the edge of the seat as Lord Amburley feather-edged the corner. 'Not best suited to town-driving, if I may say so.'

His lordship looked, for a second, as if he were about to deliver a very sharp retort, but then thought better of it. Brennan had served him too long to be the butt of his temper. 'I shall need you to walk the horses when I reach Hill Street. But I don't take you with me this afternoon. You can walk back to the stables.' Brennan did not attempt to argue. He always knew when his master was not in a mood to be crossed.

In spite of Amburley's hair-raising driving, they arrived in Hill Street a minute or so behind time, which certainly did not improve his lordship's temper. Brennan sat mute, a little pale around the mouth. 'What's got into you, man?' snapped Lord Amburley, losing patience at last. 'Go to their heads, dammit, I'm already late enough.' Brennan scrambled to obey.

As usual, Isabella was ready and waiting, dressed in the rich green she so often wore. If she looked a little pale, she hoped it would be attributed to her late night at Almack's. 'Good afternoon, Lord Amburley,' she said, rising to meet him and extending her hand. 'Punctual as ever.'

'That may be said of you, Miss Winstanley, but not, on this occasion, of me. I fear I was delayed by some business and am a little behind my time. Pray, excuse me.'

Isabella thought that his voice sounded a little strained. He could not, surely, be as tense as she was about this meeting? Unlike her, he had no cause.

Having settled Isabella comfortably in the curricle, Lord Amburley took the reins himself and, with a brief nod to his groom, let them have their heads. They were still very fresh, and it took considerable strength to hold them.

Isabella sat calmly with her hands clasped in her lap, admiring his skill and in no way incommoded when he took the first corner with barely an inch to spare. 'If you drive like that in our race, my lord, I shall certainly not best you, however generous the time allowance.'

Lord Amburley checked and slowed the greys a little. 'I beg your pardon, ma'am, I did not mean to alarm you.'

'But you have not done so,' protested Isabella, sitting totally composed.

That provoked a sidelong glance from Lord Amburley. 'I see I must beg your pardon yet again, Miss Winstanley. In my defence, I can only say that you seem to have nerves of steel, at least by comparison with my groom, who was not even trying to conceal his fright by the time we arrived in Hill Street.'

'An interesting comparison, my lord,' murmured Isabella, noting a slight tightening of his jaw at her veiled suggestion of impropriety. She chose to soften her strictures a little. 'I can well understand his feelings,' she continued. 'After all, he must do as he is bid, whatever your behaviour. I have always the option of asking you to modify it.'

'And do you so choose, ma'am?' he asked tartly, deftly steering his team through a gap that looked too narrow to accommodate them.

'Not at present, my lord.'

Perhaps it was her teasing smile, perhaps it was his own self-control, but, from that moment, he visibly began to relax. The horses seemed to sense their master's change of mood almost at once and became noticeably less skittish. They drove on in comfortable silence, until they reached St Paul's.

'As this is to be our last outing before the race, ma'am, I thought you might like to drive the route a second time. The corners between Newgate and the Fleet are a test of any whip, especially at speed.'

Isabella felt a little uncomfortable at the mention of the prisons, but she did not attempt to speak, merely nodding her assent. She took the ribbons and the whip from his hands and gave all her attention to her team, setting them in motion at a good but not cracking pace.

His lordship watched approvingly as she completed the circuit of the cathedral and started up Newgate Street. 'You are not planning to demonstrate all your skill today then, ma'am?'

'You shall not tempt me so easily, my lord,' she replied, expertly flicking her leader with her whip. 'I do not yet know what manner of time you will set me next week. It would certainly be foolish in me to give you an early indication of what I can do. Behold me, serious and sedate.'

'Indeed, ma'am,' he agreed, 'as you always are.'

Isabella could not immediately hit upon a suitable riposte, but her smile must have told him his barb had struck home. She was concentrating on threading her team through the traffic around the prison.

'The City seems very busy today,' he observed. 'It will not be much of a race if we face this again next week.'

'At this pace, I dare say we shall need wellnigh an

hour more to reach the Abbey. Does the traffic depend on the day, my lord? Markets or some such?'

'It certainly varies from day to day, ma'am, but I am at a loss to account for it. In London, there are markets almost every day.'

Although the traffic had eased somewhat, and Isabella's team had picked up a little speed, she was forced to go carefully in the narrow lane skirting the prison. When the Fleet itself came in sight, her hands tightened a little on the ribbons, making the greys resume their earlier restiveness as they made the turn into the main street.

'If you will forgive my saying so, Miss Winstanley,' began his lordship gently, 'your tension is conveying itself to the horses.'

'Oh!' gasped Isabella. 'Are you regretting your decision to permit me to drive them, my lord?' Her tone became even more haughty as she added, 'I shall of course return the reins to you at once, if you have the least concern for the welfare of your team.'

'No, ma'am, pray continue. I have not the slightest desire to take them from you. If I have a regret, it is only that you do not trust me enough to tell me what it is that so troubles you about this place.'

Isabella coloured and then grew very pale. Tension was now evident in every line of her body. 'You seek my confidence, my lord?' she asked at length, in a very low voice.

'Only if you are prepared to entrust it to me,

ma'am. I pray that you will. I should like to help you if I can.'

Isabella's brain was in turmoil. She did not know what his offer of help might mean, but she warmed to the note of genuine concern in his deep voice. Her heart longed to tell him everything, to confess every outrageous action and throw herself on his mercy. Her head warned her that there might be no mercy. Besides, why should a man in love with Sophia take such pains for her spinster cousin?

Her innate sense of justice reminded her that she *owed* him an explanation, whatever his motives for asking might now be. He knew she visited the Fleet in the guise of the poor relation. He could have pressed her for an explanation at the time; or he could have made her the subject of wicked gossip. Yet he had done neither, proving surely that she might trust him?

She slowed her team to a sedate walk while she made up her mind. She saw that he was smiling at her, beguilingly, so that her heart turned over and she was lost. 'I think I do owe you an explanation, if you wish for it, sir.'

He nodded encouragingly.

'It is a complicated tale, I fear,' she began hesitantly. 'I told you once before that my actions had been driven by foolish pride. Nothing can now be done about that, and I beg that you will forget about it.' She looked at him for some sign of understanding.

She could see that he was hesitating. She could not

wonder at it. It would be difficult for any gentleman to overlook conduct such as hers. She held her breath, waiting.

After a moment, he seemed to reach a decision. 'I can undertake to indulge in an appropriate lapse of memory, if you wish, ma'am.'

'Thank you, sir,' she whispered, closing her eyes for a second, before looking gratefully up at him. 'Pray, why do you smile so?'

His lordship considered a moment more. 'Well, ma'am, you have spent the last several weeks in studiously addressing me as "my lord". Until now, that is. I hope your reverting to the less formal mode of speech is a sign that I may be winning your trust.'

Isabella was now completely at a loss for words. She had not consciously chosen any particular mode of address, but it seemed that her formality had rankled. The unconscious change, she supposed, had dated from her discovery of her own feelings for him and her natural desire to salvage her pride in the face of his indifference. How difficult it was to deal with him. And how relieved she would be when these meetings were at an end.

She swallowed hard. 'You have asked me to confide in you, sir, and I shall do so. I feel that I owe you an explanation, I freely admit. Your forbearance has been more than I dared to expect.' Seeing that he was not about to make any reply, she screwed up her courage and plunged into the recital of her iniquities.

'You chanced to encounter me one morning outside

the Fleet prison, my lord, dressed as I had been when we met on the North Road. You have, no doubt, wondered about that incident. I must tell you, first, that I was waiting for a hackney that should have been there to meet me, but was delayed by some slight accident.'

Lord Amburley nodded.

'What you will not know, sir, is that I was outside the Fleet because I had just been inside it.' She glanced up at him then, but he said nothing. 'You do not ask why, my lord?'

'I see no need, ma'am. I feel reasonably confident that you intend to share your motives with me.'

'As you say, my lord. I should tell you, first, that I chanced to make the acquaintance of a curate, a Mr Graham, who is also a chaplain to the Fleet. His uncle is the rector on my brother's estate. Mr Graham is a man of great qualities, who burns to do good in the world. He has been much impressed by the beneficial changes which have been brought about in the felons' prisons, such as Newgate, by the Christian charity of a Mrs Fry, from the City. She is in fact a Quaker, I understand, and the wife of a banker. It would not normally be expected that our paths would cross and, indeed, I have never met her myself. But I know that she has wrought miracles among the Newgate women, in turning them aside from drunkenness— and worse.

'The position with the Fleet is not, of course, so dire. Some of the debtors there live in relative comfort by comparison with Newgate. But the women and children—some of them live in such squalor and want! Mrs Fry teaches a woman's skills to the females awaiting deportation. In the Fleet, nothing has been done. The little girls have no one to help them learn the skills they will need, if they are ever to earn an honest living.

'The prison needed someone who could teach them to sew and to mend, and the dozen other skills that most women learn at home at their mother's knee. Mr Graham besought me to find a lady who would undertake the role. I could not charge another with... Suffice it to say, I took on the task myself and, oh, I am glad of it, whatever other difficulties it may have created.' She ventured another glance at him then, but there was nothing to be read from his expression.

'I visit the Fleet in the early mornings, once or twice a week, dressed as you saw me. I go alone,' she added, with a note of challenge in her voice, 'though I do not want for chaperons, once inside. And, except on the single occasion when you took me up, my lord, I am carried to and fro in a hackney driven by my old groom, Tom.

'There, sir, you have it all,' she concluded, staring fixedly at a point between the horses' heads.

'It is surprising, perhaps, that the story of Miss Winstanley's good works has not got about,' he observed.

'I do not use my own name in the Fleet, sir. There I am Miss Winter.'

'Very wise.' He paused, obviously digesting this

new information. 'Miss Winstanley, I...I am grateful that you have felt able to confide in me. It is an edifying story. I wonder only why—forgive my presumption, ma'am—why you did not tell me at the time. Your reticence was bound to make me seek a much less laudable explanation for your presence at the Fleet. And I might have shared my ill-founded suspicions with others, to your detriment.'

They had reached Lincoln's Inn while he was speaking. Isabella tried to concentrate on her horses, pulling them to the side of the road and bringing the curricle to a gentle halt. She turned to face him then, for the first time since she had taken the reins at St Paul's. Her cheeks were a little flushed as she looked up at him, unable to read the veiled expression in his eyes.

'I had already made you one confession that day, my lord,' she conceded, almost in a whisper. 'I did not have the courage to make you another.'

Chapter Seventeen

When she arrived back at Hill Street some time later, Isabella had still not regained her composure. To be sure, she and Lord Amburley had reached a tolerable accommodation over her exploits in the Fleet prison. He had even gone so far as to look favourably on her charitable impulses, though she fancied he did not approve of her methods. She had no doubt that his Sophia would never be allowed to jaunter around town in a common hackney, or to venture into a den of iniquity such as the Fleet, however charitable the aim.

His Sophia! Oh, God! She had only a few hours left in which to find out whether Sophia returned his regard. Aunt Jemima might be beholden to Isabella for the upkeep of her establishment, but on matters of social propriety, her rule was absolute. Lady Wycham would speak to Lord Amburley precisely as she had warned.

Refusing to allow her feet to drag, Isabella climbed

the stairs to her room to change her dress. 'Is Miss Sophia at home, do you know, Mitchell?' she enquired presently. Even the most distasteful interviews had to be faced.

'No, miss. She is gone out driving with Miss Ramsey and has not yet returned.'

Isabella was not sure if such respite were welcome. Would she be able to keep her courage?

'I shall rest for a little while before dinner. But I do wish to speak to Miss Sophia, as soon as she returns. Be so good as to bring me word immediately, Mitchell.'

Sleep was impossible, of course. Her mind was in total disarray, with unrelated snatches of their conversation running round and round—images, too, like the quizzical lift of his eyebrow, or his strong hands controlling the greys with practised ease. And always—always—the clean scent of his skin whenever she was close enough to touch him…as she so often longed to do.

Now, faced with the prospect of losing him irrevocably, she at last admitted to herself that he would have been precisely the husband for her. He had a thousand good qualities. They could have shared so much together, laughed together over so many private jokes. He was, admittedly, a little taciturn in company, but that was surely to be preferred to the vacuous fribbles with which London abounded? So well suited. And she knew she could have made him happy, if only…if only he had loved her and not Sophia.

This melancholy reverie was interrupted by a message that Sophia had returned. Isabella hastily donned a dressing-gown and allowed Mitchell to restore some semblance of order to her hair.

'Shall I ask Miss Sophia to come, miss?'

'No, Mitchell, thank you. I shall go to her, I think.'

Sophia spent the first ten minutes regaling Isabella with the details of her day and her hopes for the ball they were to attend that evening. Isabella listened with only half an ear, absently watching the clever fingers of Sophia's abigail re-dressing her mistress's hair for the evening.

'That is most becoming, Sophia, dear. In your new blue gown, you will look lovely, I am sure. Have you some flowers for your hair?'

'Oh, yes. Madame Florette sent some silk ones, in shades of blue. And I have received such a pretty blue posy.' She rose to fetch it. 'Look. It will be exactly right, do you not think?'

'Why, yes,' agreed Isabella, eyeing the posy suspiciously for a sign of who might have sent it. 'But you will need some jewellery to wear also. Would you like to borrow my pearls again?'

At Sophia's eager nod, Isabella despatched the abigail to fetch them from Mitchell, who would know instinctively to hold the younger woman in conversation for a while.

'From whom did you have the posy, my dear?'

Isabella then enquired nonchalantly. 'Someone who knew what colour you planned to wear to the ball, I collect?'

'Oh, no! This one was from Mr Elworth, I think. There were several others too, but mostly pink or yellow, which would not do at all.'

'I see. And do you favour Mr Elworth?'

'Lord, no!' exclaimed Sophia. 'Why, he's as old as my father!'

Isabella frowned a little. Her charge's relative youth could not excuse such dangerous naïvety. She must learn to understand the importance of small gestures, where gentlemen were concerned. 'If you do not favour him, my dear, do you not think it a little unwise to choose his flowers over all the rest?'

Blushing, Sophia admitted she had not thought of that.

'Come, let us see what else you have. Perhaps one of the others may be made to suit.'

There were five posies altogether, two pink, two yellow and one white. 'Well,' said Isabella uncertainly, 'the yellow is clearly impossible, but the white would serve. And the pink also, if you were to change the flowers for your hair. May I ask who sent these posies?'

It transpired that one of the pink posies was from Mr Lewiston. The white one was from Lord Amburley.

Sophia hesitated self-consciously, touching first one posy, then another. 'Mr Lewiston's flowers are very pretty, to be sure. But these tiny white rosebuds in Lord Amburley's bouquet are exquisite, do you not agree? And I could add some of the blue ribbon from Mr Elworth's posy to the white one, which would make it quite perfect.' Sophia was beaming at her own ingenuity.

Isabella was determined that Sophia should not make her choice lightly. 'Lord Amburley will be gratified that your choice has fallen on him,' she said gravely. 'You are sure you should not favour Mr Lewiston, rather?'

'Oh, no! Decidedly not.' Sophia sounded very sure. 'Besides, he will need no explanation, when he sees that my gown is blue.'

Their discussion was interrupted by the return of Sophia's maid with the promised pearls. There would be no opportunity for any further conversation of a private nature before the ball. Isabella would have to rest on what little she had managed to glean.

She hurried away to Lady Wycham's room. 'She has not told me in terms, Aunt, but she has chosen to carry Lord Amburley's flowers tonight, in preference to Mr Lewiston's, even after I explained what could be read into her choice. Perhaps she does prefer Lord Amburley after all? Certainly, she cannot now dislike him. Even she must know better than to carry the flowers of a man she would wish to avoid.'

Lady Wycham nodded sagely.

'I should be better placed to judge this evening, I fancy,' Isabella continued, trying to keep all emotion out of her voice. 'I mean to observe them both closely, when he sees Sophia has accepted his posy.'

'And also Mr Lewiston, I suggest, when he sees that she has not,' observed the sharp old lady. 'Come to me after the ball, dear, and tell me what you have seen. I shall not be asleep, I promise. Now, you had best go and dress. It wants but half an hour until dinner.'

It did not take Isabella long to change into a splendid new gown of gold-spangled silk over an ivory underdress. The shimmering ensemble was completed by her gold filigree jewellery and a spangled scarf over her bare arms. She was critically assessing the overall effect, when a footman appeared at the door with a florist's box. Inside rested a tiny posy of exquisite rosebuds in ivory and gold.

'How on earth can this be?' exclaimed Isabella, searching for the card. 'Surely this cannot be coincidence?' She stopped in disbelief, holding the card in her fingers. It contained only a firm black signature—'Amburley'.

'Oh!' breathed Isabella, unable to tear her eyes from the card.

'What is it, Miss Isabella?'

'Just for a moment, Mitchell, I thought… But no matter. He sends me flowers in hopes that I may help him to win Sophia, I believe, that is all. She had a splendid white posy from him earlier. This, I think, was an afterthought.' With that painful conclusion, she went down to dinner.

* * *

Watching both Sophia and Amburley, when they met at the ball, was rather more difficult than Isabella had supposed. She could see all of Sophia's face; but part of Amburley's was in shadow.

Sophia was smiling brilliantly at Amburley and thanking him for the flowers. Isabella wondered whether the radiant delight arose from meeting his lordship, or from being at the ball. With Sophia, it was always difficult to tell.

Amburley was smiling down into Sophia's face with what seemed, to Isabella, to be real warmth and love. She was unable to see the expression in his eyes, but she was not at all surprised, a moment later, to learn that he had asked Sophia for the first waltz. A lover was bound to ask for the waltz, after all.

Mr Lewiston frowned a little, Isabella noted, on hearing that his friend's flowers had been preferred, particularly when Sophia naïvely admitted to having changed the ribbons on the white bouquet.

He thinks she could as well have added blue ribbons to his pink posy, Isabella concluded. As, indeed, she might have done.

Mr Lewiston's disappointment did not prevent him from securing Sophia's hand for the second waltz, however. Clearly, he was not yet prepared to give up hope.

Considering the situation, Isabella was beginning to feel more than a little sorry for Mr Lewiston, when Lord Amburley appeared by her side to interrupt her train of thought. 'A penny for them, ma'am,' he said.

'Oh! I beg your pardon, my lord. I fear I was wool-gathering. And I have not yet thanked you for the beautiful flowers. I admit I was quite astonished to receive a bouquet which exactly suited my gown.' She raised the posy to inhale the exotic scent. Something more to remember.

'I collect that you believe that ladies have a monopoly on intuition, Miss Winstanley,' responded his lordship smoothly—omitting to mention that he had bought the information from Florette's man.

Isabella had no answer for him. She merely smiled and breathed the heady perfume once more, while trying to think of something to say.

His lordship was before her. 'Will you honour me with the second waltz, ma'am, if you are not already engaged?'

She had not expected that. After all, he no longer needed to contrive moments of privacy with her, in order to further his cause with Sophia. For her own peace of mind, she should refuse him—but she could not bring herself to do it, even while she continued to wonder about his motives. He scribbled on her card and was gone.

Although the ball was a splendid affair, Isabella was not enjoying it much. She had to spend too much time spying on Sophia and her cavaliers. By the time supper was announced, Sophia had danced twice with Lord Amburley, including the first waltz, and once with Mr Lewiston. She seemed to stand on terms of intimacy with both gentlemen, which Isabella found puzzling, though she fancied she detected something special in the way Sophia looked up into Amburley's eyes. When Isabella herself danced with Mr Lewiston, she felt he was rather less at his ease than he had been previously. She supposed it must be jealousy. Poor Mr Lewiston.

Isabella was beginning to feel sick with apprehension as the second waltz approached and Lord Amburley came to claim her for, perhaps, the last time in her life.

'The privilege is mine, I believe, ma'am,' he said politely, offering his arm.

She hesitated before taking it. The sensations, she knew, would be just as before—strange feelings of heat throughout her body, and weakness in all her limbs. When they took the floor, she began to feel light-headed, even though she had taken no wine all evening.

He waltzed beautifully, guiding her securely but effortlessly round the floor. 'Are you looking forward to our race next week, Miss Winstanley?' he began abruptly. 'I must tell you, I am beginning to feel some qualms at the prospect of losing my favourite horses to you.'

'Fie, my lord! I do not believe for one moment that you expect to lose.' She had responded with more spirit than she had thought possible.

Lord Amburley looked a little guilty. 'Expect to lose? Well, no, ma'am. But, on the other hand, I am not wholly confident that I shall win. You are much too good an opponent for that.'

'Thank you, sir. From you, that is a compliment indeed.'

He then proceeded to explain all the details of the first leg of the race, which he would drive. Isabella mutely agreed to everything he proposed. Her own turn could take place at any time in the following three weeks, he said. Again, she simply nodded. She did not choose to tell him that she had privately resolved to be done with it as quickly as possible, certainly within the week.

As the waltz neared its end, Lord Amburley switched the conversation. 'How is Lady Wycham, ma'am? I note she does not often accompany you to engagements of late. I trust she is not indisposed?'

'Thank you for your kind enquiry, my lord. I fear Lady Wycham is not quite herself at present. She is recovering from a sharp attack she suffered a week ago and does not yet venture out.'

'Pray, give her my best regards. Indeed, if she is receiving visitors, I shall call myself to deliver them.'

Isabella glanced up sharply at that, but apart from the faintest gleam in his eye, his expression was unreadable. Devil take him! 'Lady Wycham received some callers today, I believe, my lord, while you and I were…otherwise engaged.' She smiled a little as her tiny arrow hit home and—if she were truthful—at the memory of their afternoon together. 'It is a great pity she is not yet herself again,' she added, after a moment's further deliberation, 'for she particularly wanted to accompany us to Richmond tomorrow. Unfortunately, it is not to be. Are you engaged for the party to Richmond, my lord?' she asked innocently, though perfectly well aware that he was not.

'No. I fear I shall not have that pleasure, ma'am. My friend Lewiston will be there, I believe,' he added. He seemed not at all concerned that Sophia might be stolen almost from under his nose. Then, leading Isabella from the floor, he looked into her eyes and added softly, 'Thank you for the waltz, Miss Winstanley. It has been my pleasure.'

On this last occasion, Isabella found that she wanted to believe him. But she could not—his motives were all too obvious.

By the time she arrived back in Hill Street, long after midnight, Isabella no longer doubted that Lord Amburley intended to offer for Sophia. She had watched the pair covertly for the rest of the evening. All his actions seemed, to the knowledgeable observer that Isabella had become, to betray the lover. Indeed, she wondered why there was, as yet, so little gossip about their burgeoning love affair. And, to cap it all, he had danced with Isabella, simply to find out whether and when he might approach Lady Wycham for permission to pay his addresses. Odious, odious man! She wished she might never set eyes on him again.

Isabella was soon sitting on the edge of Lady Wycham's bed, sipping (at her ladyship's insistence) a glass of warm milk. She had schooled her features to show nothing of what she felt. 'I spent the evening watching them, Aunt. I am as sure as I can be, that Sophia returns his regard, at least enough to accept an offer from him. *His* feelings are beyond doubt, I believe. There is such warmth and love in his face when he looks at her. He even created an opportunity to extract information from me about when you might be well enough to receive him.'

'Did he, indeed? And how did he contrive that, my dear?' Lady Wycham sounded rather sceptical.

A slightly bitter laugh preceded Isabella's reply. 'I own to having trapped him, ma'am. I baited my trap with the information that Sophia and I were going to Richmond tomorrow without you. I think you may expect him to call in the course of the day.' Her face was inscrutable as she pronounced the death sentence on her own love.

The old lady nodded. 'Well, at least it should be a more pleasant interview than my last, when Gradely came to seek *your* hand.'

Lord Amburley waited on Lady Wycham at noon next day. She fancied he seemed less than his normal assured self. Strange, for he had no grounds for concern, surely? An eligible gentleman, titled and fairly comfortably circumstanced, about to offer for a penniless chit barely out of the schoolroom? Sophia's father would welcome him with open arms.

Lady Wycham took pains to put her visitor at his ease, but she did not truly succeed. He declined her offer of refreshment. And he perched precariously on the edge of his chair. Lady Wycham smiled encouragingly.

'Lady Wycham,' he began, then paused to clear his throat. 'Lady Wycham, I seek your permission to pay my addresses to Miss Winstanley.' He sounded a little strained.

'It is a joy to me that your choice should have fallen on Sophia,' responded Lady Wycham, with a generous smile.

His lordship stared. 'Why, no, ma'am. I fear you are mistaken. I have no desire to wed an heiress. No, indeed. It is the regard of Miss Isabella Winstanley I seek to earn.'

'Isabella? Oh, dear…'

Lord Amburley launched into what seemed to be a prepared speech. 'Lady Wycham, I know her position is awkward, but my intentions are wholly honourable, I assure you. I am perfectly able to keep Miss Winstanley in a comfortable, though not an opulent style. She would be—'

Lady Wycham could not let him continue. 'Lord Amburley, forgive me, but you are labouring under a terrible misapprehension. I do not quite understand how it may have come about—and it is most distressing that I should have to disabuse you in such…delicate circumstances. I must tell you, sir, that Sophia is not an heiress. She has no expectations at all. Neither, to be precise, has Isabella.' She stopped, looking very concerned. 'Lord Amburley, I have to confess that Isabella and I have given currency to a falsehood, in order to protect Isabella herself from fortune-hunters. Since you ask for her, I must now tell you that she is *already* a very rich woman in her own right.'

Amburley looked stricken. After a moment, he excused himself and walked to the window where he stood immobile for some minutes, apparently lost in contemplation of the beauties of the house opposite. When he returned to his seat opposite Lady Wycham, his face was pale and set.

'I have made a grave error, Lady Wycham, for which I can only apologise. I pray you will allow me to take back what I have said to you today and to withdraw.'

Lady Wycham was astonished. 'Do you mean to tell me you do not wish to offer for Isabella after all? Such is not the conduct I should have expected of you, sir.'

His lordship flushed but stood his ground. 'I am no fortune-hunter, ma'am. When I marry, *I* shall be the one to provide for my wife. I ask you to try to understand my position, ma'am. To continue now would be impossible.'

Her ladyship was much touched by this honest appeal, in spite of an overwhelming desire to box Amburley's ears. How could a grown man be so stubborn?

'I ask you to grant me one favour, ma'am,' continued Lord Amburley, in a low voice. 'It is that you forget everything I have said to you today and, especially, that you say nothing of it to Miss Winstanley.'

'And you expect me to agree to this?'

'I ask it of you for Isabella's—Miss Winstanley's—sake, ma'am. Whatever her feelings may be, it can do nothing but harm for her to learn that I wished to make her an offer—but could not.'

Lady Wycham nodded.

'I should prefer to say, simply, that I called to ask after your health, as I promised I should. Will you do this—for her, Lady Wycham?'

'Yes, I will. But you will permit an old woman to tell you that you are a fool, my lord,' she added, shaking her head sadly. 'All kinds of a fool.'

Chapter Eighteen

None of the Hill Street ladies saw Lord Amburley for the better part of a week. According to Lady Wycham, he had called on her merely to enquire after her health. According to Mr Lewiston, he had departed for the country later that same day, presumably following another urgent summons from his estates.

Isabella could not understand it at all. Not for the first time, she taxed Lady Wycham on the subject. 'Do you tell me, Aunt, that he gave no hint at all of wishing to make an offer?'

'Isabella, it is quite unlike you to persist in asking questions that I have already answered. What are you about? Lord Amburley was not here above fifteen minutes. He asked after my health. He could quite easily have asked my permission to offer for Sophia. Indeed, I did what I could to encourage him to speak. He *chose* to make no offer for Sophia. Now, I hope that you will be satisfied at last, and that we need not return to this subject again. Speculation about what might have been achieves nothing.'

'Perhaps he is gone to Yorkshire?' ventured Isabella.

'I take leave to doubt that. Why should he go to her father, when he was already in my house and could ask leave of me? I imagine he has been recalled to his estate, or some such. No doubt he will return ere long.'

Isabella knew better than most that Lord Amburley must return, for he was due in London on the morrow, for the first leg of their race.

On the following morning, Isabella prepared with some care. She knew she must be practical in this, for the curricle would be moving at considerable speed through some of the least salubrious parts of London. It would be dirty and dusty; and if it should chance to rain, they would, no doubt, become thoroughly mud-spattered as well.

She ought to wear something eminently serviceable, of course, but she found herself laughing out loud when it occurred to her that the most appropriate costume would be 'Miss Winter's' hideous brown dress. Lord Amburley would certainly have some barbed comment to make about her appearance, if she wore that!

After lengthy hesitation, Isabella donned her newest walking dress, in Prussian blue with black frogging at the neck and cuffs. It was heavy enough to keep out the worst of what the weather might do and, if it did become covered in dust and dirt, it would no doubt brush clean. Isabella considered her reflection in the glass. She had to admit that her matching shako-style hat looked most becoming—but, at the last moment, she cast it aside in favour of a rather less daring blue bonnet. Unlike the shako, the bonnet could be securely tied under her chin.

By the time she was finally satisfied, it wanted but five minutes to the hour, and so she made her way downstairs, to await Lord Amburley's arrival. Somehow she knew he must come, that he would not cry off without sending her word. She was not surprised, therefore, when he was announced, promptly at the hour agreed.

'Good morning, my lord,' she said affably, shaking hands with him. 'I hope you have not interrupted your business out of town, simply to keep a frivolous engagement with me?' She observed with concern that his smile did not quite reach his eyes. He was troubled; but he was taking pains to conceal it.

'Nothing short of force would have persuaded me to fail you, Miss Winstanley, I assure you. Especially,' he added, with a rather more genuine smile, 'as my greys would then have been forfeit.'

Isabella laughed. Then, purposefully drawing on her York tan gloves, she led the way to the door.

The first part of the journey to St Paul's was completed in almost total silence. Lord Amburley seemed to be too preoccupied with his team to make any conversation. And Isabella, feeling suddenly both nervous and a little embarrassed, could think of nothing to say. She concentrated instead on the varied sights around her. Normally, they drove out together in the afternoon but, on this early morning excursion, the light made everything seem very different—Isabella found herself noticing things that she had previously overlooked.

It would be impossible to overlook St Paul's, of course, for its huge dome dominated all the City around it. Isabella promised herself that, if Lord Amburley still had not spoken by the time the dome came in sight, she herself would find something to say. She found herself looking out for it much too soon, as they threaded their way past the King's Mews towards the Strand. So far, the weather was being kind; the sky was blue and the sun was now shining directly into their eyes. Isabella was half-blinded, in spite of her poke bonnet.

Lord Amburley had his team well in hand now, since the fast trot along Piccadilly had taken the edge off them. He had been lucky with the traffic thus far, Isabella knew. Even the Haymarket had been less crowded than usual. She refused to think about what that did to her chances of winning, when her own turn came.

The Strand became more and more crowded, however, the closer they came to St Mary's church. The street was slightly wider there, but the buildings were much too tall for Isabella to catch even a glimpse yet of the great dome. And Lord Amburley still sat silent, his gloved hands delicately steering the greys between coal carts and carriages.

Isabella had to admire his skill as they inched past a laden cart—a very tricky manoeuvre, which she was not sure she could have undertaken herself. Just as they cleared the obstacle, a man ran out from behind a street-stall, bellowing something totally incomprehensible at the top of his voice. The nearside horse, startled, made to shy, but Lord Amburley controlled it instantly, and without apparent effort.

As he pressed on towards St Clement's, Isabella found herself saying, 'That was a very fine piece of driving, my lord.'

Lord Amburley half turned towards her, but he did not look her in the eye. 'Thank you, ma'am,' he said, before falling silent again.

Isabella was beginning to feel that she ought to be annoyed at his want of manners; a gentleman really should make some effort in a situation such as this. But she could not speak just then, for they were approaching Temple Bar—the entrance to the City. Lord Amburley had to rein in his horses to negotiate the narrow gateway, which left Isabella almost within touching distance of the fly-infested meat stalls at the roadside. She looked away quickly, trying to ignore the overpowering smell of blood.

Once through the gate, St Paul's was soon visible in the sunlight, its gold cross glinting and its dome forming a massive backdrop to the elegant black spire of St Martin's. Now, she must force him to speak.

'With so little traffic about today, you will certainly record a good time, my lord,' Isabella said calmly. 'You picked a favourable day, indeed. Another example of male intuition, perhaps?'

Her banter seemed to go wide of the mark. Amburley's jaw clenched visibly, and he seemed to be in the grip of a sudden passion. He turned on her with cold anger. 'Do you suggest, ma'am, that I play other than fair in this?'

Isabella was shaken by his harshness, but she responded immediately. 'Of course I do not, my lord, and you know perfectly well that I would not do so. I declare, you seem determined to pick a quarrel with me today.'

Her counter-attack deflated his anger. 'I beg your pardon, ma'am,' he said stiffly. 'I have offended you. Pray, excuse me.'

What on earth was the matter with him? Her teasing had never before provoked such a response. He must be under considerable strain to forget himself in such a way. Isabella resolved to tease no more that day and lapsed into silence again, while the curricle made its way up Ludgate Hill, finally drawing to a halt by the statue of Queen Anne in front of the cathedral steps. For a moment, Amburley sat taut, staring ahead; then he seemed to relax a little and turned towards Isabella.

She smiled generously at him, looking up into dark

eyes that seemed to warm, just a little, in return. 'I
had forgot to ask you when we last met, sir, about
how the timing is to be done. There are rules about
such things, I collect?'

'Indeed, there are, ma'am.' He took his watch from
his pocket and handed it to her. 'It is for the opponent
to give the word to start and to take charge of the
timing. It is perfectly in order, too,' he added, with a
hint of sarcasm in his voice, 'for you to wait until my
way is barred by traffic before you pronounce the
"off".'

'I should not dream of doing so,' protested Isabella.
'I shall win fairly or not at all.' She threw him a
challenging look.

He did not reply. He simply looked at her with
frank admiration for a long moment. Her flush of
wrath was in danger of becoming a blush of embarrassment. An awkward silence reigned yet again.

Isabella fixed her eyes on the watch, determined
not to look up at her companion. Out of the corner
of her eye, she saw him straightening the reins in his
fingers. 'I am ready whenever you say,' he said curtly.

Isabella waited. She had decided she would give
the word as soon as the minute hand reached the quarter, but the hand was moving so slowly it seemed to
be stuck. She looked up at the clock tower to check.
It showed the same time. She forced herself to concentrate again on the watch.

All around her, the noise and bustle of the church-
yard seemed to intensify. Every word spoken, every

tradesman's cry seemed to be magnified until she felt as if they were resonating in her mind like pealing bells. At her side, the warm, vibrant body of her companion was a magnet to her fingers; she had to clasp her hands more tightly around the watch to prevent them from straying towards his arm. His male scent filled her nostrils, overpowering even the memory of the earlier sickening stench. She closed her eyes. The effect of his presence became stronger still.

The quarter hour chimed. 'Now!' she cried, without pause for thought.

The horses leapt forward with such power that Isabella was thrown back in her seat, almost dropping the precious watch in the process. If his lordship heard her shocked gasp, he gave no sign of it. He was concentrating on his team.

In the relatively light traffic, the curricle moved fast, taking the corner of the cathedral with barely any slackening of speed and overtaking slower vehicles with ease. A movement opposite caught Isabella's eye: by the time they had rounded the second corner and were racing north towards Cheapside, several wide-eyed boys were staring down at them from the cathedral school window, pointing excitedly. Isabella cringed inwardly.

She had forced herself to resume her normal, upright position. She was both exhilarated and dismayed, for she knew she herself could never drive through town in such a fashion, however exciting it might seem. And they were already attracting far too much attention—not only from schoolboys, but from almost everyone else around. Two men on horseback had pulled up to stare. So much for Amburley's 'private race'. Unfortunately, there was nothing she could do or say now. He would slow down if she asked— she had no doubt of that—but that would not be fair. He would slow down, too, if he thought she was frightened—but she would not stoop to such a stratagem. She might as well live for the dangerous moment.

Isabella focused on the spire in front of her as they came up to the busy cross-roads. She could not remember the name of the church, which vexed her immeasurably, but she allowed herself a moment to admire the simplicity of its steeple. That reflection would help her to retain her calm during Amburley's headlong dash.

The junction was too busy to allow any vehicle to pass at more than walking pace, however skilful the driver. Horses and carts seemed to be crossing in all directions. Some of them were laden with freshly killed carcasses. Isabella swallowed hard. It was the first time she had seen traffic of this kind. By afternoon, she supposed, the market trade was usually long over.

It seemed that Amburley, too, had not reckoned on such heavy market traffic. He had slowed his team, perforce, but the set of his shoulders suggested that he was more than a little annoyed at the delay. Isabella found herself thinking that, if her own drive took place in the afternoon, she might have an easier run. Perhaps Amburley was thinking the same.

The curricle was forced to a standstill while yet another huge meat-cart made its way across the junction and into Cheapside. Amburley's hands tightened on the reins and he muttered something to himself. The horses had become rather skittish—probably unsettled by the smell of blood all around them.

Amburley's deep voice began to soothe them gently. It soothed Isabella too, she had to admit, for she had been getting as edgy as his team.

At last they were clear into Newgate Street, though progress was not much faster there. It seemed that every other entry led to a tippling house of some kind—one stumbling drunk almost fell under the horses' hooves. And then, there were the innumerable meat stalls to contend with, so close to Smithfield market. Thank God their route would avoid the bloody excesses of Skinner Street!

The curricle had barely edged above a walk by the time they reached Christchurch. Isabella dared to take a deep breath as they passed the neat vestry house. How could anyone live there among the noise and the appalling smells? Perhaps one became accustomed. After all, when she had first entered the Fleet, the stench had made her ill. Now, she barely noticed it.

Beyond Christchurch burial ground, the street narrowed once more, with high buildings and market stalls on both sides. At the corner, the looming walls of Newgate cast a deep shadow across the junction

towards St Sepulchre's great church. Isabella was perversely glad that she had remembered the name of
this one, at least.

They were approaching the turn when it suddenly
occurred to her that she had no idea what might confront her when they rounded the corner of the prison.
This, after all, was where public hangings took place.
She forced herself to think rationally. Hangings took
place at eight in the morning—it was now nearly ten.
Besides, there would have been a huge crowd around
the prison gate for a hanging, and St Sepulchre's bell
would have been tolling. She looked up expectantly
at the church, but the bell remained stubbornly silent.
Surely sometimes the corpses were left to hang on the
gibbet, as a warning? What if—?

Amburley feather-edged the corner into Old Bailey,
travelling rather faster now. Isabella immediately shut
her eyes, momentarily afraid of what she might see.
Then, feeling the increasing pace, she realised that
any obstructions outside Newgate must have been removed. Somewhat ashamed of her weakness, she
forced herself to look. All that was to be seen was
the gaunt expanse of Newgate's walls. Of course.

They were heading due south now, in the shadow
of the prison. Isabella shivered in the sudden chill but
refused to let it overset her. Instead, she raised her
eyes to the blue sky. She could just see the wedding-
cake tower of St Bride's over to her right, glistening
white in the sunshine. She smiled in recognition.

In a moment, the curricle must make the turn from

the breadth of Old Bailey into the narrow confines of
Fleet Lane. If Amburley were very lucky, he might
have a chance to race along its winding length; but
they had never yet managed to do so on any of their
practice runs. On every occasion, they had encountered at least one vehicle blocking their path. Isabella
fancied they might soon be brought up short.

In the event, Amburley made the turn rather faster
than prudence dictated. The turn itself was gentle
enough, but the entry into the lane was blind. Isabella
managed to overcome her instinct to grab for the side
of the curricle—but she did shut her eyes again for a
few seconds. Amburley would not be aware of her
weakness; he was fully occupied in controlling his
team.

The lane must be empty, Isabella thought, eyes still
stubbornly closed, as the curricle gathered speed once
more, racing down the slope to the first bend. It was
really cold now, for the lane was so narrow that
hardly any sunshine ever penetrated between its high
walls. She forced herself to master the urge to shiver,
even as she forced her eyes open once more. The lane
was indeed empty as far as the bend. Once they
rounded that, anything might happen.

Isabella steeled herself, feeling suddenly ashamed
of her earlier weaknesses. It did not matter that Amburley was unaware of it. Isabella Winstanley should
not show fear, even to herself! She resolved that she
would do so no more, however recklessly his lordship
might drive. She would *not* cling on to the curricle—

and she would *not* shut her eyes like a frightened child.

Amburley had not said a single word to her since they left St Paul's, apart from that unintelligible muttering at the Cheapside junction. As they neared the bend in the lane, Isabella heard him snatch a sudden breath and start to rein in his horses. A lumbering cart had just reached the end of the lane that joined from the right, barely thirty yards ahead of them. It was making to turn across their path, to precede them down Fleet Lane. Isabella fancied she heard a murmured oath; then the horses were whipped up again. Obviously, Lord Amburley had decided to squeeze through the diminishing gap between the turning cart and the stone wall. If he made it, they would probably have a clear run to the end of the lane. If he failed…

He must be mad, Isabella concluded. And I must be mad too, to be here with him. I have never known him to behave so rashly. What can have happened to make him behave so? It cannot be just the risk of losing his horses. Surely—

They were barely ten yards from the cart when the driver heard them. His head jerked round sharply. The vacant expression on his face changed to horror, as he registered the curricle bearing down on him. In a split second, he had thrown all his weight on to the reins, yelling to his horse to stop. Isabella had a momentary feeling of sympathy for the poor old animal, pulling such a huge load. No wonder it stopped at a word.

The gap between the corner of the cart and the wall did not look wide enough for the curricle to pass through, but Amburley gathered his pair and pushed them on, almost without a check. The carter's shouted abuse followed them down the lane. Isabella was glad she could not make out his words.

She felt Amburley throw a quick glance at her. She hoped—nay, she knew—that she was sitting proudly erect, showing no fear. She had determined long ago to salvage her pride, if nothing else. She thought he smiled, briefly.

Amburley's watch was still tightly clasped in her gloved hands. They were nearing the Fleet prison now. Its high walls were already visible on their left, behind the ramshackle houses in the lane. Isabella judged they had covered about a quarter of the total distance, but she had no idea of how much time had elapsed. She had rather lost track, because the watch cover had snapped shut when she almost dropped it. She must find the catch to open it again.

She could not quite see where it was. The watch was quite large, but delicately made. It was certainly not intended to be opened by heavily gloved hands. She began to fumble awkwardly, then paused, wondering whether she should remove one of her gloves. But how was she to do so without dropping the watch in the process?

Amburley's team continued to pound along the narrow lane to the turn into Fleet market. Isabella continued to fiddle with the watch, trying one last time to spring the catch with her gloved fingers.

The curricle reached the corner of the prison. The road ahead was clear. Amburley took the turn at a cracking pace. The horses started to gather even more speed.

Isabella had barely noticed where they were. She was still struggling with Amburley's benighted time-piece.

'Look out!' cried a man's voice.

A small girl had strayed into the roadway in the path of the oncoming curricle. For a moment, it seemed she must fall under the pounding hooves. But Amburley was quick to see the danger. He wrenched his horses sharply over, almost overturning the cur-ricle on the muddy surface. For several seconds, it seemed to hang in the air, precariously balanced on one wheel. Then it came to rest again on two. Lord Amburley, the child, and the greys were unscathed.

But Isabella—concentrating on the watch and un-aware of any danger—had been tossed out on to the roadway where she now lay, still as death.

With a groan of despair, Amburley leapt down from his place, flinging the reins to the nearest by-stander. He dropped to his knees beside her inert body and gathered her in his arms. His face was ashen. 'Isabella! Oh, God, what have I done? Isabella!! Speak to me, my love!'

Her body lay limp in his arms. She was intensely pale, with a tiny trickle of blood at her temple. It was impossible to tell whether she still breathed. Amburley himself was breathing very fast now, trying desperately to find a pulse, some hint of life, however faint. He laid his cheek against her lips, praying for a sign that he had not lost her. There seemed to be none.

'No, no!' he whispered, through clenched teeth. 'Please, God, do not let me lose her now!' Pushing aside her bonnet, he stroked her hair back from her pale brow, cradling her head in his arms as if she were the most precious thing in the world. 'Isabella! Come back to me! Do not leave me, my love!'

For a long moment, he simply gazed down at her mask-like face, his own contorted with anguish. Then, at last, as if in answer to his prayers, her eyelashes flickered a fraction, though her eyes did not open. She stirred a very little in his arms. 'Wh…what did you say?' she whispered, her voice barely audible.

Amburley was transformed as he looked down at her. In an instant, he seemed to have recovered his normal upright bearing, and the colour had returned to his face. 'Isabella. Oh, Isabella,' he responded gently, drawing her even closer into the protection of his encircling arms. 'Thank God you have come back to me. Try to open your eyes, my love. Please, try.'

She struggled to comply and finally succeeded. She felt dazed. Her eyes could not focus properly on his face, so near to hers. His seemed to be radiant with love, but that could not be, surely?

'What did you call me, sir?' she whispered again,

striving just a little to be released from her compromising position.

'Lie still, my love,' he replied, with a brilliant smile of relief. 'I can see that you are yourself again, but there is no call to struggle. I have you firmly now, and I mean to keep you.'

Isabella closed her eyes and sank back into his comforting embrace. Her mind was in a whirl. Had it not been for the warm pressure of those strong arms, she would have known she was dreaming. As it was, she simply stopped trying to think at all and gave herself up to feeling.

The curious crowd gathering around them was growing ever more pressing. There was clearly an urgent need to remove Isabella from the roadway. 'Do you think you are sufficiently recovered to be taken home, Isabella?' he asked anxiously.

She knew he was willing her to respond. When her eyes opened this time, her dazed look had been replaced by a glow of so much love that it almost took his breath away. 'Yes, my lord, if you will just help me to stand.' She made a move to rise.

'Be still, woman!' he commanded lovingly, smiling more broadly, now that her recovery seemed assured. He stood up with her in his arms and carried her to the curricle, where he placed her tenderly on the seat, supporting her back and head while he climbed in beside her. Tossing a shilling to the urchin who had taken charge of the greys, he collected them with practised ease and then set them in motion towards the Strand, very gently, with Isabella resting against his shoulder.

They had barely gone a couple of streets before she drew away from him to sit upright in her place. Her head was spinning, her bonnet was askew, and she knew she looked a fright. Amburley removed his supporting arm and gave his attention to his horses, watching her covertly from the corner of his eye.

Isabella, more or less recovered now, set about bringing some order to her dress. If she had been seen, all dishevelled, driving in a open carriage with Amburley's arm around her and her head on his chest... Suddenly, it burst upon her that she did not care. He loved her. He loved her! Above the noise of the London traffic, she would swear she could hear birds singing.

The journey was accomplished in silence until they reached Hill Street. Isabella was floating on a magic cloud, afraid to speak lest she break the spell. But when he halted his team and turned to look down into her eyes, she knew the spell was forever. 'My lord—' she began.

'Isabella,' he interrupted, in long-suffering accents, 'I will not be saddled with a wife who persists in addressing me by my title. Unless you can bring yourself to call me "Leigh", I shall have to withdraw my proposal.'

'But you haven't made one!' she protested. Then, at the sight of the wicked mirth on his face, she began to laugh. 'Ouch, that hurts,' she cried, putting her hand to her head.

'Forgive me, love. You are far from fully recovered. Let me bring you into the house. The other matter,' he added, giving her a meaningful look, 'can be resolved later.'

She made only a half-hearted protest, when he lifted her down from the curricle and carried her into the house and up the stairs to the drawing-room, where he laid her gently on the sofa. Having removed her bonnet and gloves, he knelt beside her, holding her hand until Lady Wycham appeared in response to his summons.

'My lord, what has happened?'

Amburley relinquished Isabella's hand and rose to meet Lady Wycham.

'Pray do not alarm yourself, ma'am,' he said swiftly, taking her outstretched hand. 'There was an unfortunate accident. A child ran under the horses' hooves. The child escaped unscathed, but Miss Winstanley was thrown out of the curricle. She landed rather awkwardly and sustained a nasty blow on the head, I fear.' Lady Wycham gasped and put her hand to her throat. 'I believe Miss Winstanley has taken no lasting harm, ma'am, but you will wish to see for yourself.'

'Do not worry, Aunt,' interposed Isabella from the sofa. 'I have the headache and some bruises, that is all. His lordship has been kindness itself. I am sure I shall be quite well by tomorrow.'

After a brief examination of her great-niece, Lady Wycham pronounced that it did not *seem* serious, though she doubted Isabella's hurts would mend in a day. 'I have some excellent salve upstairs. If you would be good enough to bear Isabella company for a few minutes, my lord, I shall fetch it.' Without waiting for a reply, she hurried away, closing the door behind her.

Amburley laughed softly, turning back to Isabella. 'I shall say it before you do, my love,' he commented, with a glint of mischief in his eyes. 'Outrageous to leave us together thus, without a chaperon. Do you think she is trying to compromise us, so that I may be forced to marry you?'

'I no longer know what to think,' replied Isabella, with as much of a smile as she could muster. 'Forgive me, Leigh, but my head aches so, I cannot—'

'Hush. Lie still,' he urged softly, dropping on one knee by the sofa. 'We have all the time in the world before us. What matters now is that you get well.' He raised her hand to his lips and kissed it. 'When you are a little recovered, I shall call to make my proposal in form. My token, then, shall be just what custom demands. For the present—' he turned her hand over and dropped a feather-light kiss on her palm '—I have a different token to leave with you.' He pressed a small metal object, warm from the heat of his body, into her hand and closed her fingers over it, just as Lady Wycham re-entered the room. 'Be sure I shall return,' he whispered. With the briefest of bows to Lady Wycham, he was gone.

Lady Wycham might not have known, at first, what to make of it, but now she was clearly in no doubt at all. She drew a chair up to the sofa and sat quietly by Isabella, helping her as she struggled to raise herself a little.

'Oh,' whispered Isabella in a long drawn-out breath, looking down at the object in her hand. Tears began to trickle down her cheeks, though she smiled as they flowed. 'Oh, Leigh!'

In her hand lay a tiny rectangle of gold and enamel, inset with rubies. A perfect miniature of the queen of hearts!

Chapter Nineteen

Lord Amburley called next day but, in spite of his protests, Isabella would not consent to see him. Lady Wycham received him in Isabella's stead, in order to reassure him about her niece's recovery. The interview soon progressed, of course, to Amburley's sudden change of heart—Lady Wycham professed herself delighted, but mystified. He had been so adamant that he would never marry where he might be branded a fortune-hunter. And Isabella was no less wealthy now than before.

Much embarrassed, Lord Amburley had no choice but to explain exactly how he had discovered the depths of his own feelings for Isabella—and of hers for him. 'I would gladly have taken her with nothing,' he said, 'but I was being totally selfish. I saw it as a grand gesture to raise my love from penury, without ever stopping to consider how she would feel.' He grimaced. 'Then I learned of her fortune, and I thought only of what the world would think of *me*—

when I should have been thinking of what I ought to do for *her*. Lady Wycham, I was blind until I thought I had lost her; and then I understood, at last, that nothing mattered except Isabella's happiness. Her money is of no importance. We shall find a way of dealing with it—together.'

Lady Wycham nodded, smiling her agreement. 'Very well, sir, you have convinced me. And I must tell you that I am delighted to learn that your regard for Isabella is as deep as hers for you. I really did believe, at one time, that it was Sophia's hand you sought.'

'Why, no, ma'am,' he began quickly, clearly much embarrassed, 'that was never in my mind.' At Lady Wycham's rather sceptical glance, he looked even more embarrassed. 'My friend Lewiston is... somewhat diffident, I fear, in spite of his wealth, and so I—'

'You did your best to help his suit.' Lady Wycham finished his sentence for him with a smile. 'And you have succeeded, I am glad to say. Sophia accepted him this morning. I suppose you knew?'

Amburley's expression was a mixture of pleasure and surprise. 'No, I did not. I am afraid that I have not seen Lewiston at all since I returned. But I am very glad to hear it. He is to be congratulated.' He, too, was smiling broadly now. 'I take it that Isabella is pleased by the news?'

'Yes, sir, she is. And when she is recovered, she will see them both to congratulate them. For the moment, however, she will see no one—not even you, my lord.'

With that, he had to be content.

For two more days, Isabella continued to receive no one. Lord Amburley called every day, impatient for sight of her, but she was always denied. On the fourth day, however, he marched straight past the butler, ignoring that worthy's protests, and mounted the stairs. He came face to face with Lady Wycham on the landing.

'Where is she, ma'am?' he demanded curtly, totally failing to observe the normal courtesies.

'In the drawing-room, my lord,' responded Lady Wycham, hastily adding, 'but you may not see her. She still has a black—'

It was too late. He had already thrown open the drawing-room door.

'A black eye,' finished Isabella, rising from her seat to confront him. 'How dare you force your way in, sir, when I expressly forbade all visitors? Is this the high-handed treatment I am to expect at your hands?' In spite of her stern words, she could not conceal her joy at seeing him.

'No, ma'am. You would be wise to expect much worse,' he grinned, striding forward and taking her in his arms.

Behind them, Lady Wycham quietly closed the drawing-room door and hovered, protectively, on the landing.

For a long moment, neither spoke; they simply clung to each other. Isabella felt deliciously warm and cherished in the circle of his arms. She was sure he must be conscious of the rapid beating of her heart through her fine cambric gown.

'Isabella, my love, queen of my heart, will you be my wife?'

She smiled at him, a little crookedly. 'Yes,' she whispered, looking up at him through her lashes. 'Yes, my dearest love. I will.'

The glow in his eyes at her words was almost more than she could bear. How could she ever have mistaken his feelings towards Sophia for love? She continued to devour him with her eyes, until forcibly distracted by his taking her left hand to slip a magnificent sapphire on her finger.

He lifted her hand to his lips to kiss it. He kissed her lips next, gently at first, being mindful of her bruises, but then more passionately, holding her wrapped tightly in his arms. By the time they broke apart, both were breathless and Isabella's knees would barely support her. Her dreams had never promised anything as overwhelming as this.

He guided her to the sofa, where she instinctively made to tidy her hair. 'Do not,' he said, removing her hands and raising them to his lips once more. 'You look—' he smiled, feathering a kiss into her palm '—enchantingly dishevelled. It reminds me of spring in Hyde Park.' Ignoring Isabella's rosy blush, he kissed her other palm and closed her fingers over it, just as he had done with the queen of hearts.

'You, sir, are a quite outrageous flirt.' She was trying to look—and sound—nonchalant, but she knew she was not succeeding. And she had not uncurled her fingers.

Amburley simply smiled at her. It was the kind of smile that made her insides quiver in response. The look in his eyes was so soft, so loving, so open, that she felt as if their souls reached out and touched. She should feel embarrassed, but she did not. She had given herself to this man completely and forever. She would conceal nothing of herself from him.

He put his arm around her, drawing her into the shelter of his arm and resting his cheek on her tumbled curls. 'Mmm,' he murmured contentedly, stroking her cheek with his free hand.

Isabella felt so safe, so surrounded by love, that she wanted to melt into him. She closed her eyes to drink in these feelings and the wonderful scent of him. For a moment, she was sure she could hear birds singing again. But surely there were no birds here, in a Hill Street drawing-room?

Without warning, there were tears flowing down her cheeks. Amburley's stroking hand pulled away as if it had been burned. He straightened to look anxiously at his love. 'Isabella, what is the matter?'

He looked so very concerned. She would have told him if she could, but the truth was, she had no idea what had caused her tears, unless it was pure happiness. Heavens, the practical Isabella Winstanley was become a watering-pot!

She scrabbled in her pocket for her handkerchief. There, her fingers encountered the little metal plaque which she had gazed at for so many hours in the last few days. She sniffed and blew her nose, trying not to look at him. Then she presented him with the little gold jewel, face up, on the palm of her hand.

'Have you an explanation for this, my lord?' she asked, trying to sound stern and forbidding.

He had the grace to look a little sheepish. 'Oh,' he said. There followed a long pause.

Isabella fancied he was trying to concoct a story to save her from embarrassment. 'It's easier to tell me the truth, you know,' she said, with a valiant attempt at an impudent grin. 'I shall, of course, accept whatever plumper you choose to tell me, but can you be sure you will remember to tell the same story on a future occasion?'

He seized her hand between his larger ones as if to capture the offending jewel and hold it fast. 'Madam,' he said, 'once we are married, I shall command that you believe every single word I say, even if I contradict myself in the same breath.'

Isabella laughed, without trying to free her hand. She said nothing, but her eyes looked her continued enquiry.

'Oh, very well,' he smiled, 'I yield. And the truth is not so very bad, after all.' He uncurled her fingers gently as he spoke. The little queen seemed to wink

up at them both. 'I chanced to see a display of en-
amels in a jeweller's and ordered this for myself, in
memory of a lady who plays a remarkably fine game
of piquet.'

Isabella knew she must be blushing. She was glad
that Amburley was looking at her hand, not at her
face.

'I had never intended to show it to anyone, least
of all you. It was just that when you were lying there,
all battered and bruised—and by my doing, too—it
came into my mind that I needed to show you that
you had always been in my thoughts. I had nothing
else to offer you,' he finished simply.

She bowed her head. 'That game of cards—you
knew what I had done.' It was a statement, not a
question. She felt, rather than saw, his gentle nod. 'I
fear that women are strange, unaccountable creatures,
my lord,' she whispered.

He drew her back into his arms. 'And women in
love are even stranger,' he said, pushing up her chin
with his finger so that he could start to kiss her again.
His lips fastened on hers and the queen of hearts fell
into the lap of her gown as Isabella raised her arms
to encircle his neck, drawing him closer. Since the
day she first set eyes on him, she had longed to push
her fingers into his thick, curling hair. But the joy of
caressing him was quickly overtaken. The impact of
his mouth on hers was so much more thrilling, as he
teased her lips apart with the tip of his tongue, darting
it into the honeyed recesses of her mouth. Isabella

clung to him, feeling as if her whole body was on fire. She was quivering in the strangest places, which seemed to be linked to her mouth by strings, like a marionette. She could not suppress a groan of pleasure.

Amburley raised his head. His eyes seemed to be out of focus. 'What is it, my love? Have I upset you? I go too fast…'

She was shaking her head before he had finished. 'I had not known…' she began uncertainly. 'When you kiss me, I feel so…' She did not know how to complete the sentence. She did not have the words.

His lordship looked suddenly very proud. He moved a little away from Isabella, leaving her space to compose herself, watching as she brought her emotions back under control. They sat in companionable silence for a moment.

Suddenly, Amburley frowned and took a deep breath. 'I have a real confession to make, Isabella,' he began very seriously, taking her hand in his once more. 'And you will have every reason to be furious with me when I have made it. I ask you only to hear me out before you vent your wrath on my head.'

Isabella nodded, bemused.

'I would have proposed to you before. Indeed, I was on the point of doing so, when I found out about your fortune.' He pressed her hand as she made to intervene. 'I had believed, you see, that you were precisely what you appeared on the North Road, a penniless companion. I came to love you, and I thought

I could offer you the kind of life that would otherwise be denied you. But when I approached Lady Wycham…' he would not meet her eyes '…when I spoke to Lady Wycham and she told me about your true position, I realised that I could offer you nothing but a title, and a minor one at that. I could not face the thought of being branded a fortune-hunter by the polite world, or by you…and so I withdrew.'

Isabella's face betrayed her shock, but she did not try to interrupt his recital.

'I had determined to leave London, to return to my estates, but of course I was honour-bound to complete our race, even if I lost my greys to you in the process. I behaved abominably in that race. No—do not try to defend my actions. There can be no defence. I was so stupidly determined to win, to best you there, at least, because I could not aspire to your hand. I behaved like a scoundrel!' Isabella was shaking her head vehemently, but he would not stop. 'It was only when you were lying in the roadway and I thought you might be dead, that I came to understand that nothing else mattered but my love for you. At that moment, I should not have cared if all the doors in London had been closed to me, provided I could hold you, alive, in my arms. Isabella, my dearest love, can you forgive me?'

Isabella's dazzling smile showed he had nothing to fear. 'Having made so many mistakes of my own, how could I refuse?' It was clear from his puzzled expression that he did not know what she meant. 'I promise to explain,' she said, squeezing his fingers, 'but later. We have to decide now what to do about my accursed fortune.'

'Nothing at all,' he replied blithely. 'Do with it as you have always done. Or give it to my mother. She would soon spend it. We shall have no need of it.'

This was going to be more difficult than she had thought. 'Might we not invest some of it in the estate, Leigh? It would be for our children, after all.' She coloured a little at mentioning such things. She still had not recovered from that devastating kiss.

He pulled her back into his arms, resting his chin lightly on her golden hair. 'Fortune has smiled on me, my love, in the most peculiar way. My great-uncle Silas, the family miser, died on the day after your accident. Oh, do not offer condolences, I beg of you. He was roundly hated in the family. I learned only this morning that his last act of defiance was to disinherit all those who had fawned on him over the years and to leave his entire estate to me, who refused to have any truck with him. I fear I may now be even wealthier than you are.'

In spite of herself, Isabella found she was laughing. 'Oh, dear,' she gasped, 'how can I behave so? I should be ashamed.' She giggled again.

'It does create one difficulty, I fear.'

Isabella's laughter ceased abruptly.

'As his heir, I am obliged to observe the mourning period. It will not be possible for us to be married until it is over, nor may I escort you to balls and assemblies and waltz you round the floor as I long to do. I had hoped for us to be married within the month,' he admitted wistfully, caressing her gleaming hair, 'but Uncle Silas has had the last laugh on me there.' A thought seemed to strike him. 'Unless, of course...' He let the words hang in the air.

'Unless what?'

'We could be married quietly now, by special licence, and travel immediately to the continent. There the mourning could be forgotten.' At her sharp intake of breath, he hesitated. 'But no. How could I suggest such a thing? It would be wrong to deprive you of the wonderful wedding you deserve. We shall spend the time in preparing a ceremony of suitable splendour.'

'Shall we, indeed? And if I do not want such a lavish affair? What then?'

'Isabella, do you mean that?' His voice had become a tense whisper.

Her shining eyes tried to tell him that she did.

'Rash woman. You shall be my wife within the week.' He kissed her again, long and lovingly, to seal their bargain.

'How can you possibly want to marry a woman who is covered in bruises?' she asked at last, drawing a little away from him.

'Are you? I can see only a black eye.' His gaze roamed caressingly over her slim figure. 'You mean there are more, that I cannot see?'

'You, sir, are outrageous. How dare you say any-thing so improper?'

'Madam, I wish only to be assured that my wife-to-be will be able to…fulfil her role.' He grinned wickedly at her.

Isabella's insides turned airy somersaults at his words. Nor could she control the fiery blush which spread to the roots of her hair. What a sight she must look, part red, part purple, part yellow—yet he seemed not to notice. 'Leigh—' she began.

'Ah, that's better.' He kissed her again, first on the lips, then on her good eye, then ever so gently on her bruises. 'I promise to be outrageous only when you forget my name.'

* * * * *

The Silver Squire
by
Mary Brendan

Mary Brendan was born in North London but now lives in rural Suffolk. She has always had a fascination with bygone days and enjoys the research involved in writing historical fiction. When not at her word processor she can be found trying to bring order to a large overgrown garden or browsing local fairs and junk shops for that elusive bargain.

Chapter One

'You little fool! You *will* speak to Mr Dashwood and what's more you'll show gratitude and a little grace in your address when you accept!'

Margaret Worthington's thin fingers locked with surprising strength onto an elbow that was ceaselessly jerking to free itself.

'You are wasting your time, Mama, and that of our... *guest*.'' The epithet was spat through gritted white teeth. 'I will not marry him, nor will I even deign to sit in the same room as that despicable roué.' Emma Worthington picked at her mother's clawed digits. The restraint was soon reapplied and Emma wearily sighed. 'Please let go of my arm.'

'I shall not! If you do not enter the drawing room of your own volition, you will enter from mine, or your papa's...or perhaps even Mr Dashwood's. He demands a biddable wife and one of unimpeachable virtue. Well, the latter condition you honestly meet, the former I own I've embellished upon. He might have to encourage that quality... And I'm sure he will now he's laid down two thousand pounds on your father's account.'

'Two thousand pounds?' The fury and disbelief in Emma's tone rendered her voice little more than an outraged squeak.

'You have allowed that…that vile man to purchase me for two thousand of his disgusting, blood-stained pounds?'

'Don't be so ridiculously melodramatic, Emma,' Margaret Worthington hissed. 'Besides, there should be another sixteen thousand of those disgusting notes to follow, when you are wed, and that should just about set your papa's finances to rights. How can you be so stubborn and selfish? Are you so determined to rip a modest comfort from your doting parents in their twilight years? I tell you, it's not to be borne!'

Taking abrupt advantage of her daughter's momentary daze, Margaret managed to swing open the drawing-room door with one determined hand whilst the other propelled Emma, with an ungentle shove, into the room. Margaret reclined daintily against the mahogany panels; a sturdy, unseen hand was planted at her daughter's back, preventing her retreat. It prodded her forward.

Emma tilted her chin, endeavoured to separate her grinding teeth and walked purposefully towards the gentleman who had gained his expensively shod feet at their ungainly arrival.

Tawny eyes of the most exquisite shade and oval shape met the dark gaze watching her. She politely extended pale, slender fingers to him and bobbed a curtsey. 'I'm so sorry to have kept you waiting, Mr Dashwood. Unfortunately, there appears to have been a misunderstanding between myself and my parents on the matter of your marriage proposal. I can only apologise to you for the confusion and beg you forgive us for detaining you.'

Emma just caught her mother's shocked gasp from behind but she kept her sooty-fringed amber eyes on the gentleman balancing the tapered tips of her ivory fingers on the swarthy blunt pads of his. His dark head angled out of his courteous bow a little and assessing olive eyes arrowed sideways at her.

Something in that low-lidded gaze slew her attention to where they held bodily contact. She curbed a shudder as she noted a few wiry hairs sprouting from sturdy knuckles. Jerkily, her hand recoiled to the folds of her skirt.

Jarrett Dashwood gave a low, unamused chuckle as he straightened into stiff-backed stillness. A piercing glance sliced over the top of Emma's honey-brown head to her mother's stricken countenance. 'I appear to be missing something here, Mrs Worthington,' he began, so smoothly amused, it almost belied the fierce glint in his eyes. 'On meeting with you and your husband earlier this week, I could have sworn you both gave me to believe your daughter was not only agreeable to my offer but "happy and honoured" was, I recall, the phrase you used…? Perhaps you have another daughter? One who more resembles your description of a shy spinster of advanced years with an amenable nature…ah, yes, and a fondness for reading frivolous romantic fancies penned by Jane Austen.' Barely pausing for breath, he drawled, 'Well, to bastardise that good lady's wise words: it is a truth universally acknowledged that a single man with a good fortune must be in want of a wife: most assuredly so once a little of said fortune has been transferred to his insolvent prospective in-laws.' With the same oiled ease, yet through lips that seemed motionless, came, 'Where is your husband? Fetch him, if you please.'

'My husband is unwell, sir.' The words were faint and breathy. 'I beg you will excuse him this afternoon. I beg, too, you will allow me a few moments alone with my daughter. She, too, I believe must be suffering the same malaise: confusion…muddled thoughts…'

'Your husband's usual complaint, then, Mrs Worthington? Your daughter, on the other hand, seems remarkably sober.' Jarrett Dashwood's silky sarcasm had Margaret squirming and blushing, then his disdainful olive gaze pointedly turned on Emma's dowdy appearance.

Despite her resolution that she would not, Emma also flinched beneath his distaste. She snapped her face up, unwilling to be intimidated, even by a man whose reputation as a black-hearted roué was unsurpassed. Their eyes clashed before his heavy lids drooped lower and an insolent look slid over her thin frame.

Emma bridled, clenching her hands at her sides. Let him check her over. He was sure to shortly be congratulating himself on a lucky escape!

She had never been praised as a beauty, even in her heyday nine years ago. When launched into society at eighteen she had found the superficial friendships and earnest rivalry between debutantes competing for male attention degrading and boring. She had never preened and primped at her appearance as other young ladies did, curling and rougeing and poring over the latest Paris fashions, even when her mother fair frothed at the mouth insisting that she did.

With her unusual fawn hair and eyes, creamy complexion and sculpted elfin features, she was never going to be a 'rage'. There was nothing extreme enough in her looks and colouring. She was only fair to middling in every way, as her mother had dispiritedly pointed out on numerous occasions. If only, her mother sighed, she were a petite, pink-cheeked blonde like Rosalie Travis who had had slavish gentlemen trailing in her wake for some twelve months before she'd settled on a Marquis; or she resembled Jane Sweetman, a tall, porcelain-complexioned redhead, who attracted beaus as bees to acacia. For her own part, Emma praised the raven-haired, grey-eyed perfection of her dearest friend, Victoria Hardinge.

Victoria was now Viscountess Courtenay, married to a man of her choosing, a man she loved, a man who adored her in return. And that was what Emma wanted. She was determined to settle for nothing less. And since the only man she had ever wanted to beguile had been totally impoverished, totally unsuitable and totally obsessed with someone else she had become reconciled to her quiet life in Cheapside, socialising on the fringes of polite society with a few sedate friends of similar tastes and circumstances. And she had believed that her parents had reconciled themselves to allowing her that simple, unassuming existence.

For affection and romance, Emma fantasised of fictional heroes: they were so much more reliable in providing her requisite perfectly happy ending.

Aware of Jarrett Dashwood jerking her a wooden bow, she returned a cursory bob, then he strode past and was speaking in a driven undertone to her mother by the door. Emma spun on her heel to watch. Her stomach tumbled as her mother's heightened colour seeped away, leaving her pasty-faced. The woman gestured in feeble apology, looking close to tears, and Emma's eyes closed in consternation.

She must not be browbeaten! she exhorted herself. She deserved better! Marriage to a man such as this would destroy her. The very idea was galling when she knew she could have attracted a worthier gentleman had she, in her prime, taken pains to court attention and flirt as other debutantes did. She had rebuffed several adequate suitors because she felt incapable of loving them. With arrogant idealism, she had determined to settle for nothing less than absolute bliss.

A few paying court had been pleasant enough and would have shown her kindness and respect. A sharp stab of guilt and regret…and ultimate understanding…pierced her. She now knew why her mother had ceaselessly nagged about security and status and marriage. It had been to protect her only child from a time such as this, when the only thing of value her irresponsible husband had left was his daughter.

Emma's tawny gaze raked over the side of the dark profile presented to her. Oh, Jarrett Dashwood was handsome enough in his way, if rather swarthy of countenance. His black hair was glossy and neatly styled. He was of medium height and a little stocky but his shoulder breadth was derived from muscular strength rather than portliness. His nose was a little sharp and hooked and his mouth too sensually fleshy, but overall he held the appearance of a dignified gentleman in his thirties. No stranger would have guessed that his wealth had come from plantation crops produced with barbaric slaving or that nearer to home he had a reputation as an insatiable lecher whom, gossip had it, beat inept mistresses. Even within the small, staid circle in which she socialised, Dashwood's meanness, his ruthlessness, his wealth were discussed with terrified curiosity and censure.

She had been reared with the consequences of her father's drunken antics, listening to her mother's sibilant stricture as yet another pile of merchants' bills went unpaid. Yet always they had survived. A business deal came good, a wager turned up trumps, a sympathetic friend loaned money at a good rate. Teetering on the brink of disaster, they had always managed to sidestep the abyss and find solid ground again.

To her shame, she realised she, too, had become complacent. When recent arguments between her parents had become exceptionally heated, she had simply retreated to the sanctuary of her room and a book. When meals had become meagre, she'd eaten less. When her maid had been dispensed with last month she had sadly bidden Rosie farewell with a small gift and tended to her own needs. Part of her had known disaster was again threatening but subconsciously she had trusted fate would again make it right.

Two nights ago when her parents had sent for her to join them in the parlour, she'd realised Lady Luck had finally deserted them. Her papa would not meet her eyes. Her mother had fidgeted ceaselessly on the chair-edge, and their unease had chilled her skin. Yet never had she imagined they would sacrifice her so callously in a bid to buy her father's extravagance another reprieve.

A marriage must be made, her mother had firmly decreed, while her papa had mumbled incoherent assent and blotted at his face with his handkerchief. Nothing Emma had suggested about further economies or a little time to think had made the slightest difference. And now she knew why: the marriage contract was already sealed and money had changed hands.

The sound of the door cracking closed as Jarrett Dashwood left started Emma from her miserable memories.

'Well, miss, you've done your work well!' was hissed

shrilly at her. 'Do you know what awaits us all now? Your spurned suitor has just promised your father an indefinite sojourn in the Fleet…and for us an indefinite sojourn in the nearest gutter. We are ruined…finished!'

'Mama, how could you consider turning me over to such an odious individual?' was Emma's broken, soft rejoinder. 'A marriage I would have agreed to. But you must allow me a man of my own choosing: someone I can at least respect, if not love. You know of Dashwood's reputation…assuredly better than I. He is reviled as a slave-master…and a whore-master. Yet you would force me to live my remaining years with him?'

'Some of the noblest, richest families in the land are built out of Jamaica, and have philanderers at their head. Are you to find fault with all of those too?' her mother impatiently snapped. 'You quibble unnecessarily, Emma!'

Margaret's tone honeyed persuasively. 'As his wife you would enjoy a life of pampered luxury. He would treat you well: after all, we all know how greatly he believes he has appearances to keep. Why do you think such a man would settle on purchasing himself a sedate spinster? He wants her virtue and gentility and the assurance she is never likely to humiliate him by shamelessly gadding about. Once you had provided his required heir or two, what more use would he make of *you*? A man so rich has his pick of beautiful courtesans to quench his lust.' A derisive, summarising stare preceded, 'You are fortunate to get any offers when you have so little to recommend you. You're too thin, you're too old—despite the fact you look like a gauche adolescent with your scrubbed complexion and buttoned-up gown. Even your hair has lost its rich hue as you've aged…your eyes too. I swear you're now all tea when once you were chocolate. Your musical accomplishments, I suppose, are adequate…' she allowed on a sniff.

'I hardly think Jarrett Dashwood is to be swayed to stay

home by cosy musical evenings about the pianoforte, Mama,' Emma mentioned on a sour laugh.

'How fortunate for you! In his absence, you could nestle into domesticity with a child on your lap and one of those soppy romantic novels in your hand.'

An impatient sigh escaped Emma at the ridiculously wholesome imagery. 'It might not be all so bleak for us, Mama,' she cajoled. 'You are right—Mr Dashwood does covet status and respectability. He will never sue Papa for fraud. Papa is known to be ailing. Dashwood would hate being seen as vindictive enough to dun a sick man without conceding him time to make amends. He will allow us a while to repay him… you'll see.' Warming to her theme, she enthused, 'I can work. I am educated well enough to be a governess…or a companion to a wealthy lady…or a housekeeper…'

'*Housekeeper?*' her mother choked, outraged. 'You have been gently reared! The success of your twenty-fourth-birthday ball was the talk of the *ton* for months afterwards. Had you deported yourself more…more becomingly to the gentlemen present that evening, you would have been wed these past three years or more and no longer draining us with the expense of your keep.'

As though unable to contain her fury or bitterness, Margaret's lips and eyes narrowed in exasperation. She approached her daughter on wobbly, stiff legs in the manner of a mechanised rickety toy. As she passed a side-table something caught a glaring eye and she grabbed up the leather-bound volume and looked at it with intense loathing. 'All this ridiculous daydreaming you do of love and heroes and happy endings…it is a shameful indulgence and not to be borne, Emma.' She snorted a sour laugh. 'It is a truth universally acknowledged,' she parodied in a shaking voice, 'that a wilful, selfish daughter of seven and twenty will prove to be a tiresome burden on her parents. Her presence should no longer be tolerated!' The volume of Jane Austen's work was skimmed abruptly towards her, and with chance accuracy smacked a hefty blow on a slender shoulder.

With a moan of recalled pain, Emma Worthington pushed herself upright in bed, her breathing fast and erratic and a pale hand instinctively seeking the tender bruise below her collarbone. Her head drooped forward, thick tan hair coating the sides of her face, as she waited for the pounding of her heart to steady and the vividness of the dream to recede a little.

A hand fumbled out to the unfamiliar table at the side of the alien bed and sought the candle, drawing it close to gain its weak, guttering light. She held it aloft in an unsteady hand. As she shook back tresses from her blanching face, wide, darting eyes surveyed the moon-striped tavern chamber, every gloomy nook scoured for spooks and intruders. But she knew it was nothing other than inner demons that had startled her awake.

The dream had so sharply, so accurately retraced events of two days ago that she might have been back in the drawing room of Rosemary House, facing her mother's spite and Jarrett Dashwood's menacing presence.

She drew her knees up close to her body, her slender arms hugged about them for warmth and comfort and she laid a cold shivering cheek atop them. A bar of silver light bathed her bent head as the moon again escaped scudding cloud. It shifted to incorporate her entwined fingers and she stretched them towards the pearlescence. Replacing the candle on the table, she quit the hard bed and padded softly over cold wood to the small leaded window.

A velvet night sky was visible through a net of shimmering nimbus. Her gaze swept the courtyard below. Immediately she shrank back. Her eyes had, by chance, located a courting couple by an outbuilding, their faces and bodies fused together. Compelled by an uncontrollable fascination, Emma slipped back, seeking again the shadowy outline of a tall man and a woman wedged between his sturdy body and the stable brickwork. She whirled away, her face stinging with hot self-disgust, and scrambled back into bed.

Shifting backwards against the crude wooden headboard, she distractedly picked up her book with one hand and the candle with the other. After a few minutes of mindless reading, she accepted that balancing the thin candle-flame this way and that to try and illuminate the pages was a pointless task. Her eyes were strained from deciphering print which seemed to merge into shapes like entwining lovers. Abruptly, she replaced the book and candle on the table and slowly sank down into the bed with a weary sigh.

Turning on her side, she stared wide-eyed and sightless at the perfect full moon as it emerged from cloud. She thought of Matthew and wistfully smiled as she wondered how he would react to her unexpected arrival; after all, they had seen nothing of each other for two years and she was still awaiting a reply to the last letter she had sent to him some six months ago now.

Perhaps it had been undelivered... 'Please God, don't let him have moved away,' she whispered at the silver orb. Doubt and guilt trembled through her as she thought of her parents in Cheapside. Were they anxious? Furious? Remorseful? She should have left a proper note...not just a few lines that begged them not to worry...or to try and find her.

She twisted restlessly on the soft mattress, frowning at shadows on the ceiling, while thinking of unrequited love and a man who had buried his heart with his first wife and of whether she would ever come to love step-children.

'Not been bit by the bed bugs, I 'opes,' the young man said. 'I seen folks wi' legs swole up an' as red as can be from the nasty blighters...'

'No, I'm quite well, thank you. Just a little tired still.' Emma responded to his query as to whether she had slept well. 'You seem very busy today.' A look through the window indicated the bustling courtyard.

The young potman inclined his dark head to conspiratorially impart, 'Quality wi' a queer name turned up late last night. His nibs be travelling on early wiv 'is family to Bath, so I 'eard. Get you anythin' else from the kitchens?' he offered cheerily, stacking Emma's plate and mug neatly together.

Emma returned him a smiling shake of the head. He swaggered off with a lewd wink for a girl sluicing tankards, and it was then that Emma, with pinking cheeks, recognised the young couple she had seen through her window.

Just as the sun was gilding the horizon, she had given up hope of sleep and made her way downstairs and into a small taproom. The cheerful landlady had served up tea and buttered crumpets, refusing to take payment, while patting at Emma's hand in such a knowing, sympathetic way, Emma had swallowed her protestations and pocketed her coins. She had savoured the delicious crumpets as she viewed unfamiliar sun-dappled countryside through dusty square panes, and pondered the woman's unexpected generosity. Was her unfortunate predicament so obvious? Was there something about her demeanour which branded her an impecunious spinster absconding from mercenary parents and a detested suitor? Or was the landlady simply a kind soul and, having been in the company of very few of those lately, she'd become cynical?

Collecting her carpet bag from beneath the rustic oak table, she made her way out into the fresh September morning to await the arrival of the coach and newly shod horses. She hoped the poor beast that had forced them to overnight at the Fallow Buck would be allowed to rest—one of its front legs had looked badly swollen as though more than just a black-smith's skills might be needed for it to continue pulling the cumbersome coach.

She was now keen to be travelling on. Even if her mother had at first dismissed her absence at mealtimes as a fit of sulks in her room, she surely would, by now, have found the brief note she had left on her dresser.

She doubted they would search for her. They had neither

the resources nor, she imagined, the inclination to send investigators after her. She was, after all, a spinster of twenty-seven, not a child in need of protection. Besides, her mother had declared her presence was no longer to be borne. Far from arousing anxieties, the reverse might be true, and her removal from Rosemary House deemed a relief. How they dealt with the odious Mr Dashwood and his recompense was their own concern. She would not dwell on it…nor feel guilty! The predicament was not of her making!

September morning mist was wreathed about the low brick and wood stables of the Fallow Buck posting house and with quiet appreciation she lingered to watch a spider, stealthy on the edge of its dew-beaded gossamer web.

As she strolled to the perimeter of the dusty gravel courtyard, her wide golden gaze roamed the recently harvested cornfields. Even denuded, they had a spare barren beauty to her unaccustomed town eye. She breathed deeply of the cool morning air, now mingling with a warm aroma of baking bread wafting from the kitchens, feeling unaccountably optimistic and uplifted. Sighing contentedly, she turned from the fresh, sun-dappled vista back towards the tavern.

Her confident step forward faltered, ground into gravel, halting her so abruptly she stumbled. Yet her eyes never relinquished the man. Something in his height, his breadth of shoulder and confident stature was unnervingly familiar, yet, try as she might, in those few, breathless seconds, she couldn't recall why. But whatever association it was produced an odd, terrified exhilaration that knotted her stomach and started her heart hammering.

Her eyes flicked over immaculate dark clothes to a silver-blond head, so unusual a shade that it ought, immediately, to have solved the mystery.

He was a wealthy, influential gentleman; that much was apparent from his attire and bearing. She was watching, analysing him with such rapt attention that she hadn't immediately noticed the child approaching. The boy clung to long, charcoal-grey legs and was immediately swung into his arms. She had sight of his profile now. His cheekbone and jaw were lean and angular and deeply tanned…an exotic contrast with his lengthy white-blond hair. He laughed at the boy in his arms, turning with him towards her…

Emma instinctively dipped her head and tilted her bonnet over her face before swivelling towards the fields she had recently admired.

Don't be so idiotic! she silently berated herself as she tried to steady the frantic pulse leaping in her throat. He was a stranger…probably a foreigner, judging by his sun-bronzed appearance. She immediately recalled the potman telling her of a nobleman with a queer name who had arrived late last night and was travelling with his family to Bath.

He was a French count, she dreamily decided. And the fact he seemed familiar was no doubt due to him resembling some romantic character in a novel she had read. Cocking her head to one side, she crossed her arms about her middle and sifted through plots and people, searching for a tall blond hero of devastating good looks. Possibly he was the villain, she mused, recalling how oddly apprehensive the sight of him had made her feel.

Long oval fingernails scored deep ridges vertically, horizontally, into bronzed skin and, with an impatient grunt, the man rolled them both sideways plunging hard and fast, at the same time unlocking gripping, silky legs from about his muscular brown thighs.

He ignored her frustrated squeal as she tried to drag his hips back to hers with her calves and make him shed his seed within her. With an easy shove he tipped her away onto her back and within seconds was seating himself on the edge of the tumbled bed. Tanned fingers swept across his shoulder and came away red and sticky. He looked dispassionately at the blood. 'Trim those talons, sweet…' he ordered with very little inflexion, yet the quiet, casual words brought her blonde head up off the pillow and she caught her full lower lip between small teeth.

Yvette Dubois narrowed blue eyes on angry weals tracking skin that looked like cold bronze and felt like warm satin. 'I can't 'elp it, *chéri*,' she purred breathlessly. 'You excite the wildcat in me, you know that. 'Ow can I be thinking and *sensible* at such a time?' She pouted at his broad shoulders, trailed a moist, apologetic kiss across the welts and then, still ignored, she huffed and flung herself back onto the sheets.

He picked up a tumbler, downing the few remaining inches of cognac in a swallow. 'A wildcat with sheathed claws is fine,' he commented drily, collecting his breeches from the floor in a fluid movement as he stood.

'Why won't you give me all of you?' she husked at him, casually lowering the sheet seductively away from her breasts as he finally turned to look at her. She peeked up through dusky lashes into cool silver eyes and knew he understood her perfectly.

'A swollen belly and sagging breasts?' he mused with ironic deliberation. 'I think I prefer you this way, Yvette.' His grey gaze swept down her curvaceous figure to where the sheet just exposed a tantalising rosy nipple.

Aware of his observation, she stretched sinuously, arms raised above her head. Small fingers clenched on the bedhead, making the thrusting perfection of her full, firm breasts impossible to ignore and openly available to him.

A tanned hand came out, fondling first one then the other until she was arching and moaning, her hands clenching rigidly on the brass bedstead. He choked a laugh, stepped into his breeches and was buttoning them by the time he reached the window and stood staring out.

'Richard!' Yvette furiously screeched from the bed. ''Ow can you go now? I want you…'

'Cut your nails…' he mentioned impartially as he drew a cheroot from his pocket, lit it, and stood staring absently into the dusk. He sensed he was irritated and that irritated him further for there was no reason to be.

It was nothing to do with Yvette Dubois or her savage passion or her transparently mercenary desire to make him impregnate her so she'd have a lasting role in his life. She was wasting her time on all counts: he had no desire for an enduring liaison or for children. He slanted a glance at her, a quirk of a smile softening his finely chiselled narrow mouth as he noticed how she immediately perked up with his attention.

A long blonde ringlet was slowly worked about a small finger and she rolled onto her back, impatiently kicking away the tangling sheet from her shapely long legs so the dark blonde curls between her thighs were displayed.

She was very good, very adept: the pulse in his loins was picking up tempo already, just as she was calculating it would. He drew deeply on the cheroot and reached for his shirt on the chair. If he hadn't promised to return to Silverdale in time for supper with his visiting relations, he probably would have stayed longer and let her earn her keep.

The irritation niggling at him intensified with that callous thought and he raked five brown fingers absently through his thick white-blond hair, unwilling to actually acknowledge that something so insignificant…so idiotic could disturb him so.

His mind returned to the Fallow Buck posting house and the image of a dowdily dressed woman standing with her back to him. There was nothing about her that could have possibly interested him. On first glance he would have guessed her to be perhaps a high-ranking servant—a governess or housekeeper travelling alone on business. What irked him was the unshakeable notion that, despite seeing nothing of her apart from an unattractive bonnet and dismal brown travelling cloak, he felt he knew her.

He was certain she had concealed her face just as he'd turned towards her, and that compounded the mystery. He'd been curious enough at the time to start walking towards her but had managed only a pace or two when his brother had distracted him to settle the landlord's bill. On returning to the courtyard, the Bath post was just pulling out into the road and he'd just known the woman was on it. He'd shrugged and walked away and forgotten it…for all of a few hours. Now, for some insane reason, not having crossed to the fields to look at her was a major aggravation and the sheer farce of it was killing him.

'I don't want you to go yet. You leave me too much…too soon. It's not fair…' was called softly from behind, breaking into his reverie.

Even white teeth clenched on the cheroot and he drew on it steadily, but he turned towards her with a smile. 'So what do you intend to do about that?'

Yvette swung long legs off the bed and posed with deliberate provocation on the edge. Her throat curved archly, her blonde head tilted as she viewed him between barely parted porcelain lids. Pushing herself slowly upright, she undulated towards him, each sinuous step swaying her pouting breasts. 'I think I shall make you change your mind about leaving…about a lot of things…' she purred as she came right up against him and grazed her naked belly against the hard proof of his full attention. A long fingernail trailed up his thigh, scoring into fine cloth as it neared his groin.

He caught at her hand inches from its target, brought her palm to his lips and dropped a brief kiss on it. Turning her away, he gave her a gentle push towards the bed. 'I have to go…'

'Business…business…all the time business,' she flung at him, whirling back in a cloud of shining blonde hair. 'I am sick with this business all of the while,' she complained, her accent thickening in her rage. 'I am alone too much. I need some company…I need you…'

'You can't have me, Yvette. Understand that,' he said with slow deliberation so that she digested all his meaning, then endorsed it with a smile that didn't warm his metallic eyes.

'If you're lonely, get yourself a companion,' he added carelessly as he moved past her and towards the door.

'*What…?*' she screeched. 'How shall I? A friend just drops from the sky?'

'Advertise in the *Herald…*' he suggested with an infuriating smile as he closed the door behind him.

Chapter Two

With a deep, inspiriting breath, Emma took another determined peek around the hazel hedge.

The dilapidated exterior of weatherbeaten boarding and slipping roof tiles had her optimism again ebbing. The cottage looked deserted. Perhaps he *had* moved away. Please no, don't let that be! she silently prayed. The London post was already lost to view as the road dipped below the shadow-racing field, and would be well on the way to Bath, some two miles further on.

She had been dropped in the village of Oakdene and had wandered the narrow, rut-scored lanes looking for Nonsuch Cottage with many a villager's curious stare following her. A bramble embedding in her skirt had quite literally brought her stumbling upon what she sought: it was an aptly named little place, she smilingly realised as her honey gaze weaved past the crude wooden name-plate on the gate, through foxgloves and scarlet roses entwined with bellbind and cow parsley, and on to the crooked door.

Gently reared behind the graceful brick façade of Rosemary House in Cheapside, she had hardly realised that such ramshackle-looking dwellings existed, let alone expected ever to enter one. As for gardening, nurturing delicate hothouse blooms had been her only experience of the demands of horticulture. The association of a conservatory and exotic plants and happier days with friends evoked a flash of memory, puzzling and niggling at the periphery of her consciousness. She gave it barely a further moment's concentration before again focussing on the grimy whitewash of the cottage.

On closer inspection it seemed structurally sound. In fact, she decided, it held a definite rustic charm. The interior of the building might be quite neat and tidy; one couldn't expect a widowed gentleman of straitened means to bother about weeds when he had to attend to the needs of his small children. Curtains were visible at dusty windows high under the eaves, she gladly noted, yet it was so quiet it could have been deserted.

As though to settle that anxiety a female voice shrieked out something unintelligible; there followed a child's thin wailing. So the property was inhabited, and by a Billingsgate fishwife by the sound of it! A sudden awful suspicion stopped her heart, and she wondered why it had never occurred to her earlier: had Matthew not replied to her letter of six months ago because he had remarried? Before she could torture herself further on the subject, the white-boarded cottage door was flung open. A small mongrel dog hurtled, whining, close to Emma's skirts then scampered out into the lane.

'Blasted cur!' the young woman barked, and was about to slam the door shut when she noticed Emma. Slack-mouthed surprise was soon replaced by a stony expression. 'Whatever you be sellin', we don't want none. Be off with you. We've got Bibles aplenty 'n sermons 'n pills 'n potions…'

Emma wasn't sure whether to laugh or display outrage that this young woman's first impression of her was as some sort of pedlar! Was her appearance really so drab that she was deemed to be touting from door to door? Her own impression now of this young woman was that she wasn't Matthew's wife but his housekeeper, a judgement backed by her rough local dialect and faded black uniform.

Aware of the woman still staring aggressively, Emma finally detached herself from the bramble with a tear to her skirt, a prick to her finger and a spattering of mauve berry juice to her palm. Drawing herself up to her full height, her slender shoulders back, and topaz eyes glass-cool, she haughtily informed the woman, 'I have just alighted from the London stage and would like to speak to Mr Cavendish. Is he at home?'

Emma's unexpectedly refined accent had the woman's jaw dropping again and a keen-eyed scrutiny slipping over her from serviceable tan bonnet to dusty, sturdy shoes.

'Close that blasted door, will you, Maisie? The draught is taking these papers all over the desk...' was bellowed from within.

'Matthew...' Emma whispered to herself at the sound of that well-modulated, if deeply irritated tone. But the relief she was sure would drench her at the first sight or sound of him was slow in coming. 'I should like to speak to Mr Cavendish,' she repeated firmly, with a nod at the door.

'Wait there,' the woman snapped discourteously, dark eyes skimming over Emma's modest attire, then the door was shut in her face. Within what seemed a mere second a tall man was stepping over the threshhold onto the grass-sprouting cobbled pathway. A hand was wiped about his bristly chin and across his eyes as though he was fatigued.

'Emma...?' Matthew Cavendish murmured disbelievingly as his fingers pushed a tangle of brown hair back from his brow for a better view of her. A white grin split his shady jaw and, with a cursory straightening of his shirt-cuffs and waistcoat, he was rushing towards her.

'Emma! How wonderful to see you!' He gripped her by the shoulders and warm hazel eyes smiled down into her upturned, uncertain face. 'Why didn't you send word you were coming? Oh, I'm so sorry...come inside...please. What an oaf you must think me, leaving you planted amongst the weeds! As you can see,' he added ruefully, gesturing at snaggled greenery, 'tending the roses isn't a fond pastime.' After drawing one of her arms through his they proceeded out of breezy late summer sunlight into the cool, dim interior of the cottage.

'Maisie will fetch some tea,' he directed at the woman while helping Emma to slip out of her cumbersome cloak.

Emma's eyes flicked to the small brunette and noted an odd, insubordinate stare arrow from servant to master. Then, with a twitch of her faded black serge, Maisie was gone.

After a brief pause during which only polite smiles passed between them, there was,

'I must apologise…'

'I should explain…'

They had spoken together and simultaneously laughed, embarrassed, too.

'You first,' Matthew invited, ushering Emma towards a comfortable-looking chintz-covered fireside chair and pressing her into it. As he leaned towards her and gripped her hands, displaying his pleasure at seeing her, a recognisable sweetish aroma assailed her nostrils. She had too often been about her intoxicated papa not to instantly recognise the smell of strong alcohol about someone's person. There was a hint of red rimming his eyes too, she noted, with a hesitant smile up into Matthew's undoubtedly hung-over face.

'I was about to say, Matthew, I must apologise for visiting you without proper warning. But I had no time to write, or wait for your reply.' She gave him a wry look. 'After all, it has been six months since last I wrote and still, daily, I expect your letter…'

Throughout the uncomfortably sultry atmosphere in the coach jolting its way to this village, all that had dominated her mind was Matthew: how she longed to unburden herself to him, beg him to reinstate his marriage proposal of five years ago. Now, oddly, the desperation had evaporated. What remained was simple relief that she had distanced herself from Jarrett Dashwood.

'You must rest awhile after your journey, then dine with

us,' Matthew said with an emphatic squeeze at her small hands within his.

Emma smiled her thanks; she was hungry; she was also grateful that Matthew was exercising tactful restraint. He had obviously sensed she needed a little time to compose herself before revealing the catastrophe that had forced her to break all codes of etiquette and arrive uninvited and unchaperoned at the home of an unwed man. Acknowledging that impropriety brought another to her attention: remaining with Matthew overnight as his guest, even if he had a female servant and children, was completely out of the question. She would need to find lodgings.

Emma glided small, unobtrusive glances at him as she looked about the untidy small parlour. Oh, he still appealed to her. He hadn't aged. But his unruly hair was tangled, his skin tone unhealthy and his attire dishevelled.

'I'll apologise for my appearance.' He shrewdly anticipated the reason for her eyes lingering on his unshaven jaw. A sheepish smile preceded, 'I attended a debate at the village hall last night. It was after midnight when I found my bed.' He made a determined effort to neaten his hair and clothes with slightly vibrating hands.

'Was it a literary debate?' Emma asked quite interestedly.

'Er…no,' Matthew laughed. 'Nothing quite so highbrow, I'm afraid, my blue-stocking Emma. It concerned the siting of a new water pump in the village and how division of the cost is to be made between tenants. Of course, once universal agreement was reached, we had to drink to it…'

'Of course,' Emma smiled, pleased and relieved that such an amusingly improbable incident was responsible for his hangover. 'And as the pump is not yet operative you were forced to settle for whisky rather than water.'

Matthew laughed. 'That's my Emma,' he said, with a gentle touch at her face. 'Actually, the toast was with ill-gotten geneva,' he revealed, sliding a finger to cover her lips.

Emma sensed her heartbeat quickening as their eyes held.

She smiled against the light caress, then asked quickly, 'And how are your children? I believe I've already had a quick brush with your little dog.'

'Ah, Trixie…' Matthew muttered with a laugh. 'I heard Maisie chiding Rachel for allowing the dog back onto her bed. She's a rapscallion…'

'Your dog, your daughter, or your servant?' Emma asked with a laugh.

'All three at times…but thankfully not usually together,' he answered, with a rueful shake of the head.

Their tea arrived and Maisie poured and distributed it all the while sending brooding glances at them both. Reproof, almost warning was apparent in Matthew's glassy hazel eyes as he and Maisie exchanged a look before she quit the parlour.

'My apologies for Maisie keeping you on the path,' Matthew smoothly said. 'She is a little wary of strangers. But she's a good girl…'

Emma's tawny head turned, alert to a muffled noise…a snort of humour or anger from the hallway. Matthew gave no sign he'd heard yet, passing idly by the door, he pressed it firmly shut.

'Well, Emma,' Matthew said with a distracting smile. 'Drink up your tea for there are things to be taken care of: the children above stairs, the dinner, but most importantly, you…'

'Well, do you think Rachel and Toby much grown?'

'Indeed. I should never have recognised either of them,' Emma truthfully admitted. Then, finding nothing positive to add, fell silent again. She gathered her cloak about her as the breeze stiffened and turned her head to gaze out over darkening hedgerows and fields.

The dogcart shuddered and swayed over potholes as they travelled on towards Bath, and her evening's lodgings. Matthew had not quibbled when, over dinner, she'd informed him that she must seek a place to stay. He had simply asked, quite gravely, whether she had the means to pay for her board. Learning that she did had seemed to relieve him.

Mrs Keene's rooms in Lower Place, on the outskirts of Bath, were the most fitting place for a gentlewoman to overnight, he had then decisively informed her. But now, as they journeyed on in amicable quiet, she knew Matthew was hoping for some complimentary comment about Rachel and Toby. Yet, on meeting the children again today, Emma had been surprised and disappointed.

Rachel was now nine years old and Toby seven and they no longer bore any resemblance to the bonny children she recalled meeting two years ago.

One mild autumn afternoon the Cavendish family had joined her in Hyde Park for a last stroll together before they quit London for Bath. She and Matthew had exchanged good wishes, reluctant farewells and promises to write, while two fair-haired children, neatly dressed in navy blue clothes, had refused to scrunch through the glorious red-gold carpet underfoot as others were, and stood quiet and solemn. On cue, they had politely shaken her hand before their father led them away.

Today, she had uneasily watched Matthew half-heartedly chiding two grubby-faced urchins for failing to wash or neaten their attire before they sat down to dine with their guest. Reluctantly, almost surlily, they had stamped away to be returned by Maisie some few minutes later in a slightly improved state.

Emma had freshened herself for dinner in a small upstairs chamber, thanking Maisie for the washing water and cloth and receiving little more than a terse grunt for her courtesy.

The meal, prepared by Matthew's cook—an elderly widow who lived but a few yards along the lane, he had conversationally told her as they ate—had been plentiful and delicious. Roast mutton and veal and a boiled chicken had joined dishes of steaming vegetables and sweet blackcurrant tarts on the dining table. Wine had been set out and although Matthew had poured a glass for both Emma and himself, his own goblet had remained virtually untouched—something Emma had found inordinately reassuring.

Despite Emma's attempts to talk to the children they'd seemed reluctant to cease chewing for the few moments a response would take. On asking about their lessons, Rachel had informed her with a grimace that Miss Peters at the Vicarage tutored them. As for a friendly enquiry on special aptitudes, neither had given the matter much thought before admitting to knowing of none.

Their fond father had then deemed them too modest and defended their ignorance with recalled good marks in English or arithmetic. But with lowered heads they'd simply set enthusiastically about their meals with an air of concentration that precluded further questions or table manners.

The elderly dun mare pulling Matthew's dogcart stumbled into a rut, throwing them together. Matthew steadied Emma with a sturdy hand, then raised her slender fingers, touching his lips briefly to them. 'It's so good to see you,' he said softly.

It was his tactful way of saying that an explanation for her presence was long overdue, she realised. 'I have quit London to avoid being married to a detestable man,' she informed him simply, gazing over a flat, dusky vista. Instinctively her fingers tightened about his, at the oblique reference to Jarrett Dashwood, as though drawing from his strength.

'I guessed it to be something like that,' Matthew said softly, reining back so that the mare slowed its steady trot.

Emma looked at her fragile hand resting in his large fingers. 'My parents have arranged for me to wed someone in the hope he will set to right my father's debts. The man is a notorious blackguard.' Her voice shook with strengthening outrage. 'I had never believed they would act so brutally. The matter was concluded before I had even a hint of it. I will have none of their plots. They have treated me shabbily…abominably…'

'They must be in grave trouble to do so, Emma, I'm sure.' His thumb smoothed gently at her wrist. 'I'm very happy and flattered that you felt you could turn to me for support.' His voice became husky. 'Does this mean that you would now reconsider *my* offer of marriage?'

The air between them seemed to solidify. It was what she wanted, wasn't it? She had fled Rosemary House late at night instinctively to seek him and these were the words she had prayed he would utter. She heard herself say, 'I need time to think, Matthew. I'm confused…plagued by ambivalence. I feel guilty for abandoning my parents, yet, at times, I'm sure I despise them almost as much as Jarrett Dashwood.' Even with the lowering dusk, Emma could discern Matthew's abrupt pallor. The cart jolted as he reflexively tightened his grip on the reins and the mare pranced.

'*Dashwood? Dashwood* wants to marry you?'

The disbelief was plain and made Emma smile a trifle wryly. 'He has expressed a desire for a sedate, mature spinster to wed. She must be biddable and, I've no doubt, so grateful to attain the marital state, she will not challenge him about any of his disgusting goings-on. I imagine he has no more use for her than as a brood mare.'

Matthew gave her an ironic, sideways smile. 'Biddable? *You*, Emma?'

'Exactly,' Emma agreed, matching his rueful tone. 'My mother has a persuasive way with my attributes when she scents a bachelor…whatever his character.' She sobered and gazed into the distance. 'Thank you for your proposal, Matthew. I will give it very serious thought in the next few days. And thank you for your kind hospitality and for bringing me to my lodgings tonight. I was so relieved on finding you still resided at Nonsuch Cottage and were not now…remarried.' An amber glance arrowed at his profile. 'I know you were keen for your children to have a mother's care and as I had not heard from you for so long…'

'I'm sorry not to have replied to your letter. I seem to find so little free time. A pathetic excuse, I know,' he admitted on a shake of the head. 'And there has never been anyone else that I've met who would suit the children so well as you.

You're so kind and dependable. You're a genteel lady and educated to such a degree you could tutor them yourself,' he enthused.

'And what of you? Do I suit you so very well?' Emma asked softly, sadly.

'But of course! That goes without saying, Emma.'

'This is a respectable house and we keep reg'lar hours. No gentlemen allowed in the parlour after nine o' the clock. No gentlemen allowed in the upper chambers at any time. Breakfast afore eight or none. Dinner in the parlour if you wants at a shillin' for a plate o' hot ordinary.'

'Yes, I understand,' Emma told Mrs Keene wearily as she glanced about the spartan room. But at least it looked clean and the bedlinen fresh.

'So wot's a nice young lady like yourself doin' alone in Bath?' the woman asked with friendly inquisitiveness, now she had laid down the rules of the house. 'Kin in the area, have you, wot won't board you?' The plump woman shelved her crossed arms on her ample bosom. A knowing nod preceded, 'I gets plenty o' such spinsters. Poor relations an' all they'll get off them wot's better sitchwated is mutton 'n porter once or twice a week an' a faded gown or two. Not that it's none of my concern, 'o course, or I'm complainin', like…for it suits me…' She wagged an emphasising finger.

'I'm seeking employment. I have no local family. Just a friend.' What had she said? Seeking employment? Why had she said that? Why not? echoed back. The logical answer to every pressing problem had helpfully presented itself. She had very little cash; she needed some time to think while she mulled over Matthew's proposal and meanwhile she needed somewhere to stay. There was little doubt in her mind that Mrs Keene would show her the cobbles as soon as she showed Mrs Keene an I O U.

Her landlady sucked at her few yellowing teeth. 'Seekin' employment, are you, miss? Well, not that it's none of my concern, o' course, but I'll keep me eyes and ears open for you. I'm known to run a respectable lodgin's for genteel ladies wot's on 'ard times, and it's not unknown for those as wants to take on to come to me first for their quality staff. No agency fees, you see. 'Course I accepts a small consideration—'

'Thank you…I should be grateful for help…' Emma cut the woman off. Undoing the ribbons of her bonnet, she dropped the dusty tan-coloured article onto the bed. She shook free her thick fawn hair, raking it back from her creamy brow, aware of the woman's gimlet eyes on her. Opening her carpet bag, she studiedly hinted, 'I'm a little tired…'

'O' course you are, miss. Will you be wantin' any supper?'

'No, thank you. I've already dined.'

'Tomorrow will you be wantin' any supper?'

'Yes, thank you.'

'Seven o' the clock in the downstairs parlour. Tomorrow's bacon 'n carrots. That'll be a shillin' an' you pay afore you eat.' With a gap-toothed smile at Emma, Mrs Keene was closing the door.

'You're late!'

'I'm here, aren't I?'

'Richard, you are becoming quite a trial to your mother,' Miriam Du Quesne stiffly informed her eldest son.

He seemed unmoved by her complaint and gave her an impenitent smile as he made for the stairs and took them two at a time.

'Come back! We have guests!' was hissed in a furious undertone at his broad, dark-jacketed back.

'And you're a wonderful hostess, my dear,' trailed back, bored, over his shoulder as he neared the top of the graceful sweep of mahogany bannisters.

'If you're not down these stairs and in the drawing room in ten…fifteen minutes,' she generously amended, in an enraged choke, 'well, I shall…I shall just…'

Sir Richard Du Quesne sauntered back to the top of the

curving stairwell and looked past the priceless Austrian crystal chandelier, suspended low, at the top of his mother's elegant coiffure. 'You shall what?' he jibed fondly. 'Beat me? Shut me in my room? Make me go without my supper?'

'Richard! This is no joke!' his mother screeched, small fists scrunching her elegant lavender skirts in her rage. Aware that she was creasing the satin, she flung it away and tried desperately to smooth it. She resorted to stamping a small foot instead, while almost jigging on the creamy marble in exasperation. Abruptly changing tack, she stilled, gave him a bright smile and wheedled, 'Please, dear, don't keep us all waiting longer. Dinner has been on the warm since eight o'clock. It is now nine-thirty and we are all quite ravenous.' A tinkly laugh preceded, 'I'm quite wore out with finding conversation to amuse us all. Besides,' gritted out through pearly teeth, 'nothing much is audible over the growling of empty stomachs.'

Her son gave her a conciliatory smile. 'I'll be but a few minutes. I'll just freshen up…'

'Oh, you look well enough,' she said irritably, gesturing him down the stairs. He did too, she realised as her blue eyes lingered on her tall, handsome son's appearance. His sun-streaked blond hair was too long, but suited him that way, she grudgingly allowed. His charcoal-grey clothes were expensive and well-styled; nothing she said or slipped to his valet seemed to make him dress in brighter colours. The bronzed skin tone he had acquired abroad had at first horrified her but, she had to admit, gave him a wickedly foreign air, and those cool grey eyes… A delicious shiver raced through her for they so reminded her of her darling John.

Miriam focussed her far-away gaze back on the top of the stairs to note that, while daydreaming of her late husband, their son had disappeared. She pouted, flounced about and stalked back towards the drawing room with the welcome tidings for their graces the Duke and Duchess of Winstanley and their daughter, Lady Penelope, that dinner was now, indeed, very nearly served.

* * *

'I know where you've been, you lucky, randy dog.'

Richard dried his face with the towel, lobbed it carelessly towards the grand four-poster on a raised dais and glanced at Stephen. 'Where have I been?' he asked as he fastened his diamond shirt studs and walked to the mirror to inspect his appearance.

'Come on, this is your dribbling sibling you're talking to. She must have a *jolie amie* for your best brother. Preferably blonde but I ain't fussy.'

'You're married.'

'I'm bored.'

Richard's icy grey eyes swerved to the reflection of his younger brother's shrewd, smiling face. 'You're married. You've got a lovely wife and two beautiful children. What more do you want, for God's sake?'

Stephen Du Quesne shrugged himself irritably to the window and gazed into the dusk. The fluttering silver-leaved whitebeams that lined the mile-long drive to Silverdale swayed like sinuous, ghostly dancers in the light evening breeze. 'A little excitement...that's what I want. A little of what you've got...that's what I want. You get risqué women and I get responsibility. It ain't fair, I tell you. You're seven years older than me.'

'No one forced you to propose to Amelia when you were twenty-one. As I recall you wanted her and nothing was going to stand in your way. Not even her constant rebuffs. You finally won her over and the proof that you were lucky to get it so right is just along the corridor, asleep in the nursery. Grow up.'

'That's rich coming from you,' Stephen moaned as he stalked his elder brother to the head of the stairs. 'You're thirty-three and still gadding around as though you've dropped a decade somewhere. Even that reprobate of a best friend of yours has been wed these past three years and is now as dangerous as a pussy-cat by all accounts.'

Richard turned a smile on him, knowing immediately to

whom he referred. 'That's love for you, Stephen,' he said. 'It can creep up on you when you're least expecting it…even when you're twenty-one and nowhere near ready. There's no shame in giving in to it.'

'Such an eloquent expert on finer feelings, aren't you?' Stephen ribbed him with a grin. 'Hard to believe most of your intercourse with the fairer sex is so basic and carried out while you're horizontal.'

'Shut up, Stephen, you are drooling,' Richard said, with a clap on the back for his sulking brother.

As they hit the marble-flagged hallway, Richard swung his brother about by the shoulder and studied him gravely. 'Look, if you're desperate for a little illicit entertainment, go ahead. But don't expect me to arrange it for you, or clear up the mess when it all goes horribly wrong. Amelia might just decide that what's sauce for the gander…' He trailed off with an explicit raising of dark brows.

'She wouldn't dare!' Stephen exploded, his face draining of colour. 'Besides,' he blustered as his older brother choked a laugh at the terror on his face, 'she'd never know…I'd be discreet.'

'Of course she'd know, you fool,' Richard scoffed. 'There'd be plenty of concerned ladies just itching to break the news. For her own good, of course. If you want a mistress, go and stand in the Upper Assembly rooms and look available. In five minutes you'll be knee-deep in frustrated wives, impoverished widows…' His long fingers tightened emphatically on his brother's shoulder. 'You're both envied, you know. You've a good marriage: you love your wife and she adores you and that's not easily found. It makes for a lot of green eyes and spiteful intentions. If you want to know the truth, *I* envy you.'

'Good,' Stephen said with slightly malicious relish. 'I think our dear mama is under the impression it's definitely time you were jealous no more.'

Sir Richard Du Quesne stopped dead and spun on his heel.

'God, she's not matchmaking again! Who's here? Not the Petershams?'

Stephen swayed his fair head, blue eyes alight with merriment. 'But of course not. We're aiming so much higher, dear one, now you're so much richer. Now you've added another million to the Du Quesne coffers, dear Mama scents a ducal connection…and as they were visiting in the neighbourhood…'

Stephen's drawling teasing came to an abrupt halt and the laughter in his eyes was replaced by horrified entreaty. For no more than a second he watched his brother striding towards the double oaken doorway, an exceedingly loud and awful curse flying in his wake.

Scooting after him, Stephen grabbed at his elbow and started dragging him backwards. 'If you disappear, so do I. I'll go and stand in the Upper Assembly rooms; you see if I don't. Mother will kill me if I let you escape!'

'*I* will kill you if you do not let go of my arm,' his brother sweetly informed him.

Stephen removed his hand and made a show of straightening the crumpled charcoal material of Richard's sleeve. 'Come on, Dickie,' he wheedled. 'Just smile and make them swoon a little.' Richard's grim countenance was unaltered. 'Well, just tell them about your money; that'll make them swoon a little.'

Richard tried to suppress a smile. He gazed at the rust watered-silk wall then back at his brother's anxious face. 'If I wasn't so damned hungry, I'd be out of here.' A tanned hand settled amicably on Stephen's shoulder as they turned towards the dining room. 'I suppose I should suck up a bit to his grace: I want the old bastard to grant me a lease on the land just east of the Tamar. There's a fortune in that clay-slate; I'll stake my life on it.'

'Better suck up to his daughter, then. You know the way to a fond father's heart is through his darling spinster offspring. And she is sweet on you, you know. You also know the old goat's concerned for his pheasants and won't let you disturb them with your noisy mining.'

'There's a fortune in copper there and I will have it some day. But don't tell Ross,' Richard laughed. 'He's convinced it's on the Cornish side in granite. Fool! Sometimes he lets his Celtic pride get in the way of his common sense.'

'Rival adventurers!' Stephen proclaimed. 'You'll bring him in on the deal, in any case. Me too, I hope! I've a growing family to support.'

'Make sure it's just the one legitimate family to support,' Richard told his brother, 'and perhaps I'll do that.'

Richard scowled at the ceiling. It was time he thought of marrying and producing an heir. A duke's daughter was soft on him. She was attractive enough to bed. The fact that she irritated the hell out of him with her vanity and her vacuous giggling was of little consequence: once she was breeding they need have little to do with one another other than on formal family occasions. Apart from exercising a little more subtlety, his licentious lifestyle need not alter. If Penelope found herself a beau it would not unduly worry him so long as she was reciprocally discreet. He could afford to be generous: her father was sitting, he was sure, on one of the richest copper lodes ever. And he was determined to mine the area.

The two brothers exchanged a rueful grimace before fixing smiles and entering the dining room. Richard's grin sugared for his mother as he saw her glower at him. Then he looked at the brunette, her face coyly concealed behind a fluttering fan. Brown eyes peeked at him over the top of ivory sticks. His teeth met but he bowed gallantly.

Damn you, David! he inwardly groaned as he thought of his best friend and his wedded bliss. He'd set a vexing precedent by marrying for love and being so nauseatingly happy and faithful. And he and David were too close…too alike… always had been since childhood.

Richard knew that aching void deep within David that only Victoria could fill sometimes yawned wide in him too. And the restlessness, the emptiness just wouldn't go away no matter how hard it was ignored or crammed full of commerce or self-indulgent lust.

Think of the copper…and beating Ross to it, he encouraged himself as he proceeded into the room, with a wry, private smile. He pulled a chair close and sat beside his grace the Duke of Winstanley. 'How are the pheasants?' he asked gravely.

Chapter Three

'What is for dinner today, Mrs Keene? Not bacon and carrots again, surely?' Emma frowned and sniffed delicately at the wafting salty aroma.

'Not at all, my dear.' Her landlady shuffled into her room, apparently unruffled by this aspersion on her unvarying menus.

Emma's tawny eyes brightened and she let her novel drop. She had been perched on the window seat for the past hour, hoping that perhaps Matthew might call again today to take her for a walk or a drive into the countryside. But it was nearly six o'clock and unlikely he would come now.

'What *is* for dinner, then, Mrs Keene?' Emma asked, her mouth watering in anticipation of some tempting mutton later.

'Er…it's hashed pork, my dearie. With a little herb and stock 'n so on.'

'Is it cured pork, Mrs Keene?' Emma asked on a sigh.

'I believe it is at that, Miss Worthington,' Mrs Keene admitted with a jovial smile. 'Now, I've got some good news. An' I expect, 'cos it is such a piece o' luck for you that a busy soul like meself's managed to put herself out on account of a nice young lady, that you'll be insistin' on showing me a small consideration for me pains. Now, not that it's none o' my concern, o' course, but I know for a fact you've been scourin' that *Gazette* for a position as would suit. Well, now—' chubby hands were planted on fat hips '—what did I hear today from a friend wot's been speakin' to a lady's maid?' She inclined forward from the waist and beady eyes rolled between fleshy folds.

After a silent moment when Emma realised either she guessed, enquired, or never learned, she obligingly said, 'I've no idea, Mrs Keene. What did you hear?'

With a flourish, a scrap of paper materialised from a greasy pocket. 'My dear young lady, the good news is that a gentle-woman in Bath is seekin' a genteel and modest companion. She is a pampered lady and bored…' Mrs Keene acted the part, shielding a yawn with a fat hand then simpering behind it. 'Soon as I heard I put meself out to speak to me friend and sing your very praises. She in turn spoke to the maid who had words with her *madame*. The lady has sent you this little note with her address. Now, what do you say to that good luck and good friends like meself?'

Emma's small white teeth caught at her full lower lip. What did she say to that, indeed? She had been at Mrs Keene's lodging house for a few days and had certainly been curiously flicking through the *Gazette* for local positions.

But it had been a half-hearted investigation: she had little idea where to start, or if indeed she wanted to start at all. She *had* been gently reared and nothing in that refinement had prepared her for at some time toiling for a living. She balked at the idea of being an assistant to a mantua-maker or a hab-erdasher and she had seen little else advertised.

Stung by her boarder's lack of effusive thanks and enthu-siasm, Mrs Keene huffed, 'Well, if it don't interest, I'll give this appointment to the new lady as arrived yesterday. She's fair desperate for a position and workin' for a foreign *madame* in quite the best part of Bath will probably seem like heaven dropped in her lap.'

'It's very good of you to remember me, Mrs Keene. I am very grateful.' Emma gave the woman a conciliatory smile as she held out a slender hand for the note. Interview details were written in an elaborate script. 'I *shall* attend and if it seems the position will not suit I can try elsewhere…'

'O' course…but I reckon it will suit, an' I reckon you'll always remember wot good friend managed to winkle it out for you.' Mrs Keene nodded good-naturedly at the subdued young woman smiling vaguely back at her. Sharp eyes dissected her waif-like appearance: a slender body that looked too delicate to tempt a man but such rich caramel hair and liquid honey eyes set in a complexion that was pure peaches and cream. Not that it was none of her concern, o' course, but it was puzzling for a body to decide if she was a raving beauty or plain as a pike-staff. Pike-staff, she plumped for; the pretty foreign *madame* wouldn't like a rival.

'Do you know what you're doing, Emma?' Matthew demanded shortly.

'No,' Emma admitted with a nervous smile as she straightened her bonnet and pulled on her gloves.

Matthew had called earlier that morning and on hearing she had an interview for employment looked startled and then disapproving. But he had offered to convey her in his little trap to South Parade on the opposite side of Bath to where Mrs Keene's lodging house was situated.

On now alighting at the top of a quiet, elegant crescent, Emma squeezed Matthew's fingers in thanks and affection. 'I need a little income while I decide what I must do.' She slid a glance at his tense profile and again lightly pressed his hand. 'And seeking employment doesn't mean that I am rejecting your proposal. Please understand that I need more time…'

With a slightly martyred air he offered, 'Shall I wait?'

Emma shook her head. 'I shall hail a ride. I've no idea how long I might be—perhaps only a few minutes, if Madame hates me on sight.' She sighed. 'Perhaps an hour or two if Madame tests my good nature with a protracted wait while she prepares to interrogate me.'

* * *

She had been jesting when she'd told Matthew she might be kept waiting. Emma raised her wide golden gaze to the sonorously chiming clock as it marked the half-hour she had been seated in a cool hallway on a hard-backed chair. It was now after three-thirty in the afternoon and she was becoming increasingly disillusioned and restless. She peered about for the dour-faced butler who had allowed her into the house. Madame Dubois was expecting her, he had intoned as he'd shown her to a seat, and had then disappeared with a stiff-legged gait.

Emma abruptly stood up and flexed her shoulders. She took a few tentative steps and peeked along the hall. When all remained still and silent, she meandered, admiring the tasteful decor, to the huge gilt scrolled mirror and studied her appearance. She straightened her bonnet this way and that, then glanced down at her fingertips trailing a glossy satinwood star inlaid into a rich rosewood console table. Swishing around with an impatient sigh, she returned to her chair. She would tarry just another few minutes then depart. A person inconsiderate enough to leave her totally ignored for so long would not make a good employer in any case, she impressed upon herself. She was on the point of reseating herself when a door along the corridor opened.

The figure that emerged was male and tall and very blond and had her gawping idiotically at his handsome profile. She had very recently seen those chiselled bronze features just visible beneath a fall of lengthy sun-bleached hair: it was the foreign count she recalled had been travelling on to Bath from the Fallow Buck posting house.

She quickly sat and folded her hands neatly on her lap, her thoughts racing. Of course! She had never made the connection that the *madame* in question might be this French nobleman's wife. The memory of the small blond boy he had lifted in his arms had her frowning at her hands. Would she be expected to nursemaid children? She had no experience of young people…but she could no doubt tutor, if need be…

Firm footsteps echoing against polished mahogany had her attention with the man approaching although her eyes stayed with her entwined fingers. His pace slowed and she knew he'd noticed her.

She glanced up demurely, politely, from beneath the shielding brim of her bonnet. Her face swayed back at once and she felt as though ice had frozen her solid to the chair. Her ivory lids drooped slowly in horrified, disbelieving recognition. French count! Her fingers spasmed as she sensed a hysterical laugh bubbling. No wonder he had seemed familiar! No wonder she had thought she knew him! She did!

But he had changed. It wasn't surprising she had not immediately been able to place him. His hair was no longer fair and stylishly short but long and white-blond, his complexion no longer city-pale but a deep golden-bronze.

An ostler at a rustic tavern had described him as Quality with a queer name...well, it had been perfectly correct. It was her whimsical romantic imagination that had concluded he must be a French nobleman instead of an English one.

On a misty September morning four days ago she had sensed meeting him somewhere before and fancied it to be in fiction rather than fact. Oh, how she wished that were so! For she had indeed seen him before. And on each occasion she had made it her business to insult him. Now she found herself sitting meekly in his house, hoping to be taken on. The sheer farce of it had the back of a hand pressing to her mouth to stifle a horrified choke.

She was aware of impeccably styled black hessian boots drawing into her line of vision. Please don't let him recognise me, she silently prayed, casually swivelling sideways on her seat, away from him.

He changed direction, veering off to the console table she had recently admired. From beneath the brim of her bonnet she watched long buff-coloured legs turn, the toes of his boots point towards her again and knew he was studying her.

It's been three years! she exhorted herself while an unsteady hand shielded her face by tidying stray tendrils of light tan hair into her dark tan bonnet. He'll never recognise you. Or if he does…he'll pretend he doesn't. They weren't married! This jolted into her consciousness at the same time. The woman's name was French-sounding, too, but not the same as his! God in heaven, she was auditioning as a companion to one of his…his women! Perhaps also as tutor to one of his bastards!

She sensed a writhing, seething indignation mounting. Three years ago when they had come together in London as social equals he had managed to instil in her just the same angry emotion. The fact that he had always been perfectly civil whilst with her, never meriting her hostility and sarcasm, had always flustered and shamed her. She could neither justify her aggression to him, when he'd casually enquired why she liked to insult him, nor to herself, nor to her best friend, Victoria.

She explained it away easily to herself now: it had been simple disgust at his hypocrisy and his condescension. Suavely charming he might have been to such homely spinsters as she, who he no doubt believed secretly swooned at the memory of his smile, but she knew him for a lecherous degenerate and had not been too coy to hint as much. She would have told him outright, in no uncertain terms, had the opportunity ever arisen.

Much to her mother's delight, he had seemed to show a friendly interest in her, but Emma knew it was all designing and insincere. For at that time his friend, Viscount Courtenay, had been laying siege to her own dear friend, Victoria Hart, and David had wanted Emma occupied so he could trap Victoria alone.

Despite the two men having infamously shocking reputations, they had been polite society's most popular bachelors, keeping the *ton* in a constant state of fascinated curiosity as to their philandering and drunken brawling. No scandal had seemed base enough to deter top society hostesses from fawning over them and sniping at each other to secure their coveted presence at balls and soirées. Once they were lured across the threshold, no freshly circulating gossip regarding that week's carousing had deterred ambitious mamas or their debutante daughters from beelining towards them with seriously immodest intent.

Emma felt her face stinging with heat on recalling how, at her twenty-fourth-birthday ball, her own mother had gladly foisted her upon this man as though she had been so much unsaleable baggage. Yet even now, despite that mortifying memory…or perhaps because of it…she could feel again the aggravating need to throw back her head and antagonise him. Perhaps acidly comment that it was obvious his morals hadn't improved along with his looks since last they'd met. What? What concern or consequence were his looks?

Her lids pressed closed again as the still silence throbbed with more intensity than the cased clock in the corner. *Why won't he go? Why won't he say something? I know he's staring*, she fretted.

'Are you waiting for Madame Dubois?'

His low, level tone was exactly the same; still it resulted in a jump and fluttering stomach. Her bonnet nodded at him. 'Yes, sir,' was stiltedly muttered in a voice even she didn't recognise. He remained quiet on learning that. Relief sang through her. Had he remembered her he would surely have mentioned the fact or swiftly removed himself.

Dainty footsteps tripped along the corridor and Emma managed to face the woman approaching without once revealing her face to the man standing opposite.

'So sorry to 'ave kept you waiting, *mademoiselle*… Are you still 'ere, *chéri*?' The woman interrupted her address to Emma on noticing the man, her voice taking on a completely different, husky inflection. The hem of a rose-pink gown was immediately sweeping away again as, ignoring Emma's presence, Yvette Dubois diverted her attention to him.

Involuntarily, Emma's head raised a little to watch them. She stared at the blonde woman's pretty profile, a delicate, pleased flush on a softly rounded cheek as she talked in a quiet, pouty way to her lover. An arch smile, then Yvette was onto tiptoe to whisper in his ear while a small finger trailed his dark sleeve.

Richard Du Quesne frowned at his mistress as though this untimely display of intimacy irritated him, then an icy grey glance shifted sideways. Emma was too late to avert her face and their eyes met and held.

He didn't know her! There was nothing at all in his expression that showed the least interest or recognition. The release was enervating, as was the desperation to be away from this house, these people. She glanced at her nervous hands on her lap, wondering how on earth she could extricate herself.

Yvette realised straight away that she had failed to lure Richard's eyes from the mouse-like creature seated on the hall chair. She was incessantly alert to a possible rival deposing her. Within a second a very female assessment had raked her prospective employee from head to toe. With intense satisfaction she concluded that the woman was as drab as she could possibly have wished, and no threat whatsoever.

A tilted blonde head draped ringlets over a pretty pink shoulder and a tight, malicious smile formed a rosebud of pink lips. Richard was unused to being in the company of such dowdy women and probably feeling some curiosity and sympathy for the thin little thing. *La pauvre* looked as though a nourishing meal would go down well, Yvette spitefully noted as her blue eyes narrowed on those fragile white wrists resting neatly on the girl's dun-coloured lap. It made her happily examine her own plump, bejewelled hands as she said sweetly, 'I must apologise for the delay, *ma'mselle*, and for 'aving forgotten your name. A moment ago I 'ad it and yet now…it is gone.' She gave a careless, continental shrug. 'Miss Woodman, is it, per'aps?' she guessed a trifle impatiently when Emma didn't immediately offer up her identity.

'Yes,' Emma confirmed after a further silent second. 'Miss

Eleanor Woodman,' she quietly, firmly lied, and raised her face to them both.

The doorbell clattered shrilly, making Emma start and the butler appear from nowhere. He opened the door and received the post.

An enticing glimpse of sun and sky and a rattling coach drew Emma to her feet and towards freedom. 'I'm sorry, I have another appointment and am already a little overdue. If you will excuse me…' The words tumbled out breathlessly, for she was obliquely aware of the butler starting to push shut the large white door, cutting off her escape route. She also glimpsed Madame Dubois's pout slackening as she realised she had been summarily rejected. But it was Richard Du Quesne's pitiless grey gaze following her that hastened her nimble dodge through the shrinking aperture.

Once in the air, she sped down the elegant steps and, skirts in trembling fists, was running without thought for direction. What halted her several streets away was the need to gasp in more breath to put further distance between herself and those narrowed silver eyes. She backed against a wall and wrapped herself concealingly into her cloak as though still afraid she might be exposed as an impostor. A trembling hand went to the coldness on her face and came away wet. She angrily scrubbed away the bitter tears and slowly, sedately walked towards an area of railed park she could see in the distance.

She had no idea where she was but had a depressing, sinking feeling that Mrs Keene's boarding house in Lower Place was some considerable way away and probably in the opposite direction. As she took a second slow turn around the small recreation area, she slipped unobtrusive glances at fashionable people promenading; nurses tending their young charges, while taking the late afternoon air. Most were now making for the exit, mentioning teatime or the need to be home now the air was cooling.

Emma scoured the skyline for a familiar spire or rooftop that would point her home. She sighed on finding nothing but lowering storm clouds in the west. She should really ask someone for directions but was loath to bring herself to anyone's attention.

She approached a small wooden bench as a young couple vacated it and strolled away arm in arm. Seating herself, she drew her cloak tight about her. The sun was setting behind that purply-grey nimbus, spearing golden rays into the chilling atmosphere. She'd obviously been lost for some while. She should have accepted Matthew's offer to wait and deliver her home, she inwardly chided herself. She would, by now, have been back at Mrs Keene's with the prospect of eating soon.

Thinking of food made her stomach grumble. The exertion of sprinting so fast and so far had sapped her energy and left her quite light-headed. She would be late and miss her dinner...and she had already paid her shilling for it. Well, it *would* be salt bacon again, she wryly consoled herself.

She searched in her pocket and drew out her small pouch. Tipping the coins into her palm, she carefully counted, wondering whether she could afford to purchase something to eat on the trek home. The idea of something tasty and different made her stomach roll hollowly again, yet even that consuming thought couldn't completely drag part of her mind out of that opulent, cool hallway and away from a man with piercing metallic eyes.

The shock and humiliation at meeting him again under such degrading circumstances were receding, allowing another worry to compete for notice. If Richard Du Quesne *had* recognised her but had been unwilling to embarrass himself in front of his mistress by saying so, he might not display such reticence in London on his return there.

He owned a smart residence in Mayfair; she knew that. Should he soon go to London and mention he'd seen her in Bath and Jarrett Dashwood came to hear of it... She recalled dark olive eyes sliding over her body with sly, nauseating inspection. That blackguard would make a vicious and vengeful enemy; of that she was absolutely sure. She swallowed a bitter lump in her throat, pocketed her coins and fairly bolted up from the seat as though the vile man might even now be on his way to fetch her. She would forgo food this evening and use her money for the safety of a carriage ride home, she decided.

'Miss Worthington?'

She stopped dead, her complexion paling in terror as she slowly turned.

Richard Du Quesne walked the path towards her and, as she instinctively stepped back, he gestured appealingly.

'Please, don't run away again…' he said, with a flash of a rueful white smile. 'It's taken me hours to find you as it is.'

Emma swallowed, still slowly retreating, even though her eyes had swept past him, taken in the plush phaeton visible beyond the railings that bordered the small park and digested the fact that it was, of course, his.

'I've no intention of running, Mr Du Quesne,' she lied quietly, while silently vowing that should the opportunity arise she would flee him with her last breath. 'How are you? Well, I trust? I'm sorry but I have no time to chat today, sir,' she fluently apologised, without waiting to discover how he did. 'I have to be going now. I have an appointment and am a little late.' She sketched a curtsey then spoiled all her confident ease by dithering over whether to walk back past him or turn and make for the opposite end of the empty park and thus enter yet more unknown territory. She settled for the unknown, whirled about and walked away.

A firm hand on her arm halted her and gently turned her about. 'Aren't you going to now allow me the courtesy of enquiring how you do?'

'Why? You know I don't associate you with civilised behaviour. I'm sure you're little interested in how I do…as, truthfully, I'm little interested in how you do.' She swallowed, bit her unsteady lower lip, ashamed of her unnecessary rudeness. All she had needed to say was that she did tolerably well, thank you.

She watched his light eyes darken behind lengthy, dusky lashes, then he laughed. 'For a while, I just couldn't conceive it to be you, Miss Worthington. Now I'm convinced it is. In three years you've not changed a bit.'

'Oh, but I have, Mr Du Quesne,' she said heartbreakingly huskily yet with a bright, courageous smile. 'I really have changed so much.' She felt a horrible, hot stinging behind her eyes. Please don't let him reminisce, she silently entreated; don't let him talk of their dear mutual friends, David and Victoria Hardinge; don't let him mention her darling goddaughter, Lucy, or any of those things that always brought a poignant mingling of gladness and envy to torture her.

Distraction came in the shape of a raucous cry that minutes before would have drawn her towards it. Her soulful amber eyes followed the progress of a woman hawking Sally Lunn's teacakes, a sweetish aroma strengthening tormentingly in the stirring evening air.

'Are you hungry?' Richard asked quietly, noting her exquisite eyes were fixed on the pedlar.

Emma shook her head and looked away immediately. 'The light's fading. I want to be home. I will be missed,' she lied again. She almost laughed. Who on earth was there here to miss her?

'I take it your mother is with you in Bath. Where are you staying? Why are you seeking employment?' His staccato questions were fired at her.

She avoided his eye. 'I…I'm not seeking work, sir,' she said slowly, while her mind raced ahead for plausible explanations. 'I must beg you to convey my apologies to your…friend. It was just a wager…a joke in very bad taste. Some acquaintances laid a bet that I should never have the audacity to seek a position or attend an interview. It was a stupid, inconsiderate thing to do. I bitterly regret getting involved at all.' She gained little solace from that small truth after such fluent lies and felt her face flame betrayingly.

When he remained silent, and all she was conscious of was

his muscular height and the moonlight sheen of his hair in the enclosing dusk, she began backing away again. 'Good evening to you, sir,' she tossed back at him as she twisted around and hurried on.

He didn't touch her this time, merely strolled unconcernedly behind her. It was as good as any physical restraint. Emma swirled about, continued backwards for a few paces then halted. 'Go away!' she snapped furiously yet with a hint of pleading.

'No,' he said easily. He passed her, circled her, examining her minutely then hovered close, like a patient predator awaiting the right moment to close in for the kill. 'Tell me where you're staying. What you're doing here in Bath.'

'It's none of your concern! Leave me be!' she raged in a hoarse whisper, yet with a lowered face as she sensed her exhaustion, her hunger, her fear of not getting back to her lodgings before it was really dark undermining her composure.

'Of course it's my concern,' he drily contradicted her. 'You know how upset Victoria will be if she hears I've neglected your welfare whilst you were with me. And when Victoria's upset David's unbearable…which upsets me.'

'I am not with you!' Emma flung at him desperately. 'Besides, they won't ever know. No one must ever know.' She looked up slowly, realising she had just, stupidly, given him all the information he needed.

'You're here alone…and in trouble.' The words emerged quietly, as though he couldn't quite believe it himself.

As the hawker retraced her noisy way along the street, still loudly advertising her wares, Emma's frantic tiger eyes flicked to Richard. If she could just get him to go away for a moment…all she needed was an unguarded moment. 'I am hungry,' she stated breathily. 'And feeling a little faint.'

He held an arm out to her. 'Come…' he urged gently. 'We'll find somewhere to dine, on the one condition,' he mock-threatened, 'that you tell me what problems bring you here, so they can be dealt with.'

'That's very good of you, sir,' she meekly thanked him. 'But I'm a little giddy and nauseated. Perhaps a quick bite of something now and a short rest on this bench…' Emma approached the seat and sank gratefully, gracefully onto it, her elfin features drooping into supporting hands.

Richard glanced at the vendor almost opposite them now on the other side of black iron railings. Then he arrowed a shrewd look at Emma. Either she was a consummate actress or she really was famished. The vision of a thin, pale young woman sitting in the hallway of his town house haunted him. He certainly didn't want her passing out on him.

A large hand rested solicitously on one of her shoulders, an instinctively cautious caress skimming over fragile shoulder bones beneath the enveloping cloak. Resisting the urge to simply swing her up in his arms and carry her to his phaeton, which he knew with a wry inner smile would no doubt earn him a slap for his pains, he said, 'I'll be but a moment. I'll fetch you a bun and a flask of brandy from my carriage.'

From beneath the brim of her bonnet, Emma slanted feline eyes at his powerful, retreating figure. He wasn't fooled at all, she realised. He turned, vigilantly, several times, walked backwards, giving himself the chance to return to her in a second. Her heart squeezed, lead settling in the empty pit of her stomach as she noted his crisp, athletic step. Should she not time it exactly right, she knew he'd catch her before she'd managed a few yards.

Apparently satisfied, finally, with her air of slumped-shouldered debility, Richard swung away towards the gate. As soon as the railing was between them and he was heading in the direction of his phaeton, she rose stealthily and, with never a backward glance, sped off into shadowy trees bordering the lawns.

'Ah, Frederick, so you are up and about today. How very nice to see you at last. How long has it been now?' Jarrett Dashwood mimed concerned thoughtfulness. 'A sennight, perhaps, since last we had dealings together?' The darkly suave man sauntered further into the drawing room of Rosemary House. Without waiting for an invitation, he flicked back his coat-tails and seated himself on a gilt-framed chair.

Margaret Worthington looked at her husband, looked at their tormentor and closed her eyes. 'Do have some tea, Mr Dashwood,' she urged in a thin, trembling voice, while thin, trembling fingers fumbled at the silver pot on the tray. 'It is freshly made in readiness for your arrival.'

'More tea, Mrs Worthington? I believe I am awash with your tea, dear lady.' His wide, sensual mouth smiled at her, his olive eyes did not. 'Now were you today to offer me, say, two thousand pounds, or a private interview with that intriguing daughter of yours, I would certainly be tempted to partake. As it is, I am heartily tired of trailing here each afternoon to meet with her only to be fobbed off with tea and excuses.' Leaning back into the chair, he stretched out his legs, crossing them at the ankles. 'Where is your daughter? The longer we are apart, the more desperate I am for some time alone with her. It is said, is it not, that absence makes the heart grow fonder?'

Margaret and Frederick Worthington exchanged nervous glances.

'She is visiting her aunt…'

'She is ailing in her room…'

The couple glared, horrified, at each other at these conflicting versions of Emma's lengthy absence, each sure that they had voiced the correct one for today. Both shifted uneasily back into their chairs and, apeing their sinister guest's lead, examined their manicures.

Jarrett Dashwood used a fleshy thumb to shine a perfectly trimmed set of fingernails. 'Well, what's it to be? Is she visiting? Lying abed with her smelling salts or Miss Austen's romances? Shall I go above stairs and discover for myself how my poor, ailing fiancée fares?'

'Please, sir, do not term her so,' Margaret forced out in a

high, wheedling tone. 'She refuses you; you know that. You have our sincerest apologies.' Margaret looked at Frederick, hoping for a modicum of assistance in dealing with this frightening man. Her perspiring husband simply gazed glassily into space. 'There is nothing to be done, Mr Dashwood.' Margaret emphasised her despair by crushing her handkerchief to her mouth. 'We cannot force her to wed against her inclination. Everything in our power…my power,' she gritted through the muffling linen, stabbing a glance at her florid husband, 'has been done to make the selfish ingrate see sense. But she is a woman grown and so stubborn she will take no heed of her fond parents' good advice.'

'Perhaps she will then take heed of me, madam,' Jarrett Dashwood smoothly said. 'Perhaps you both will do likewise. For this whole matter has now the stench of premeditated fraud about it. I have been fleeced, I believe, of my two thousand pounds, not only by you, good sir,' he mocked Frederick with a bow of his raven head, 'but also by you, madam, and your daughter. How many fiancés have you accepted for the chit in return for a little aid with pressing debts, only to find that she's turned coy afore the altar?'

Margaret's handkerchief dropped to her lap, her chalky complexion adopted a greyish-green tinge and her mouth worked like that of a beached fish. 'I beg of you, Mr Dashwood, never think it!' finally exploded from her. 'My daughter has received no other firm offers at all. She is accomplished at deflecting any gentleman's attention far sooner than that. It would be heaven indeed should she encourage just the one to come a-courting.'

'But I'm not convinced,' Jarrett Dashwood said easily, with a final lingering look at his flexing fingers. 'It is a truth universally acknowledged…' He laughed lightly. 'There…you see how the dear girl has affected me. I find I can continually bring to mind passages from her favourite books… Now, where was I? Ah, yes, with odd truths. Indeed, it is strange that the more one is denied something, the further it seems from one's grasp, the sweeter finally possessing it becomes. I believe I am developing a *tendresse* for your daughter which makes the money quite irrelevant. Even were you in a position to repay it, I would not accept. I want that spirited hussy as my wife. The documents pertaining to the marriage contract are signed and sealed. The marriage must go ahead.'

Finally bored with this polite charade, he said in a guttural voice, 'Find out to wherever it is she has absconded and furnish me with the news; I'm sure *I* can make her see sense. If you do not....' He smiled grimly at Margaret '...I understand that the Fleet is able to accommodate families...'

Chapter Four

'This is a respectable house, is it not, Mrs Keene?'

'Indeed it is, Miss Worthington. Oh, yes, indeed it is.'

'And no gentleman is allowed within it after nine of the clock, you said, did you not? So you will insist this gentleman immediately removes himself,' Emma prompted in a low, trembling rush.

Mrs Keene asserted nothing, simply gawked at the man to whom her lodger referred as though he were an apparition. Recovering her senses, she rolled her eyes at Emma, mouthing something completely unintelligible, before bobbing her mob cap and herself up and down as though in the throes of some palsy.

Emma watched her landlady's ridiculously obsequious display for no more than a second. Her furious glare turned on the blond man, lounging by the mantel in Mrs Keene's small parlour.

He looked right back. He couldn't take his eyes off her.

Sir Richard Du Quesne's jaw clenched…ached as he fought to keep his eyes from slowly stripping that virginal white nightgown from her slender body. Silver eyes returned sharply to her face and his angry attention had her valiantly, proudly tilting her chin. If it hadn't been for small, pearly teeth sinking steadyingly into her full lower lip he might have been fooled into thinking she was perfectly composed. He read her next move as it occurred to her and artlessly showed in those lucid golden eyes. Shifting away from the fire, he made for the parlour door.

A slow pulse throbbed low in his belly, spreading to tighten his groin, and he cursed at his feet in irritated frustration. He couldn't recall ever seeing a woman so simply attired—certainly none whose keep he was paying for and whose bed he shared. The women of his acquaintance, whether family or fancy, trailed about in lace with their hair in curls when ready to retire.

With a subtle air of disinterest he glanced at luxuriant, glossy fawn hair spilling over pristine, modestly embroidered cotton, tendrils curving into a gracefully narrow back. If her hair and eyes didn't resemble fine cognac she might not tempt him so much, he savagely mocked himself, shoving aside any ludicrous idea that she could join those whose bed he shared.

Emma turned warily on her heel as he passed, keeping him at the corner of a watchful tawny eye. His casual entrapment complete, he halted a few paces behind, forcing her to twist about to face him. Her eyes blazed copper beneath his silver stare until she abruptly looked away.

Mrs Keene's face was diplomatically lowered but her beady eyes were busy batting between the hostile couple. 'Ah, but that's no gentleman, you know, miss,' finally worked out of one corner of her mouth at Emma, while her eyes slid in the opposite direction.

A slender white hand flew to smother a hysterical laugh. Emma agreed through her quivering fingers, 'Yes, I *do* know that, Mrs Keene.' Very graciously she added, 'Nevertheless, on this occasion I think we shall allow him the sobriquet and insist on his immediate removal from the premises.'

'I can't do that, miss!' Mrs Keene whispered, horrified at the very idea. Her eyes slid to the tall blond man, who in turn had his sardonic mercurial gaze turned on her lodger.

'And why ever not?' Emma bit out, wrapping her slender

arms about her night-robed body to warm it and conceal its quaking.

'It's the silver squire,' Mrs Keene spluttered out, so low and fast it merely emerged as a sibilant hiss and Emma could decipher none of it.

'What?' she queried on a frown.

'She said I'm the silver squire,' Sir Richard Du Quesne told her evenly. 'Lightly translated, that means I own the freehold of this house and the rest of the street together with quite an amount of the city of Bath.'

After a stunned moment, digesting the awful news that she was actually attempting to eject him from one of his own properties, she fumed. 'And you think that gives you the right to come here and harass me, I suppose?'

'Your continual deceit earlier today gives me the right to come here and question you. So does a sense of duty to a close friend who cares about your welfare.' As though just noticing the goggling, hovering landlady, an explicit flick of a bronzed hand signalled her to remove herself.

'Don't you dare go!' Emma cried at the woman's back, noting she had immediately turned to do his bidding.

Richard shrugged easily. 'Please be seated, then, Mrs Keene, while Miss Worthington explains to me certain inconsistencies in her behaviour.'

'I am under no obligation to account to you for one thing, sir!'

Emma's thin hands tightened into fists behind her back. She could not believe herself to have been so stupid as to immediately race downstairs five minutes ago, on gleaning from Mrs Keene's garbled croak that a gentleman awaited her company in the parlour. Before she could interrogate the woman further her mob-capped head had disappeared from around her chamber door.

Pulling on her heavy cotton wrap, Emma had simply bolted after her, wondering how Matthew had managed to bribe her landlady to allow him entrance at this time of the night; wondering, too, why on earth he had not waited until the morning to enquire how she'd done with her interview. Then it had occurred to her, with a scattering of icy needles about her body, that it might be something more serious than the success of her job-seeking that had brought him here so late. Perhaps something pertaining to her flight from London…and Jarrett Dashwood… And she'd fair flown below.

Not once had she dreamed that Richard Du Quesne might be irked enough by her escape to bother discovering where she lodged and immediately track her. But then the novelty of being shunned by a woman, even a modest spinster such as she, had probably been enough to inflame a need for immediate retaliation.

'Did you walk back here?'

She glared at him, about to spit that he could mind his own business and go fly to the devil. A movement at one corner of a sensual, narrow mouth told her he was reading her mind.

'I hailed a cab,' she stiffly informed him.

'Why did you run away?'

'I was hungry,' she returned flippantly, gazing insolently past him, 'and couldn't wait longer for you to return with a measly bun. I decided to make my way home for one of Mrs Keene's delicious dinners before I faded dead away.'

He smiled at her churlishness, and at her long, slender fingers ceaselessly entwining then jerking apart.

'Are you going to tell me why you're here in Bath, unchaperoned?' he asked quietly so Mrs Keene was excluded from his dialogue.

'No,' Emma simply said, and disdainfully flicked away her tawny head.

'Very well. I'll send an express to your parents tomorrow and thus find out.' He was reaching for the door handle when she stopped him.

'Don't do that…please…' was forced out as her eyes squeezed shut.

He walked back, straight past her, seating himself in a chair by the small hearth. A movement of his long, dark fingers this time had Mrs Keene beetling for the door and Emma enviously watching her.

She didn't dare follow her landlady out, although he was taunting her with the opportunity. He had her exactly where he wanted her, she realised with impotent fury. Her face flung around, and she glowered her loathing.

He responded by smiling and settling back leisurely into the battered wing-chair, propping a booted foot on his knee. One dark hand was splayed idly against polished leather, the other against his face.

Emma sensed her teeth grinding, her fists curling. He was deliberately impressing on her just how easily he could keep her here, and that he was exercising patience in waiting for her to obediently disclose all to him. Her nails stabbed her palms as she suppressed a terrifying need to bound across the few feet that separated them and hit him.

'Do your parents know where you are?'

'My whereabouts are of no interest to them,' she snapped back. 'Why should they be? I am a spinster of twenty-seven and perfectly able to live alone.'

'I know how old you are, Emma,' he said softly. 'I attended your twenty-fourth-birthday celebration...remember?'

'Not by my invitation...' she sniped, then twisted away and closed her eyes. Do not antagonise him, she severely, calmingly chided herself. He is of no importance whatsoever. Just use half-truths and guile. It will satisfy his base curiosity, thus enabling you to rid yourself of his damnable presence...then all will again be well. He is simply a hedonistic fool ruled by lust and alcohol... She hesitated in her unspoken censure, recalling that there had been less of an inebriated haze about this man than about Matthew on their reunion in Oakdene this week...and several times since.

'Well?' His mild impatience shattered the tension after several silent minutes. When she steadfastly refused to look at him or speak because she still hadn't quite worked out which lies would serve her best, he added, 'Have you nothing at all to say?'

'Yes, I have something to say,' she announced, honey-voiced, as feral eyes pounced on him. 'And I do not think you will want to contact my parents to relay this. If you do not remove yourself this instant I shall scream and weep loud enough to wake the street and charge you with…'

'With…?' he prompted mildly through long, dark fingers curled against his sensual mouth, watching her from beneath heavy lids.

'With attempting to force your vile attentions on me…with molesting me. Now what do *you* say, Mr Du Quesne?' she flung at him, inclining slightly towards him in triumph.

He was out of the chair in a lithe second, making her jerk back and whirl away so fast, treacle hair flowed out thickly towards him.

'I'd say you're a little early with that complaint, Miss Worthington,' he purred as he walked right up to her. Smoky silver eyes eventually reached her white face, having leisurely mounted her body.

He watched real fear dilate her pupils. He also saw that she was still itching to slap him. His teeth met, shifting his jaw aslant, as he finally accepted that he wanted it too. He was just longing for her to touch him…in any way…in that way.

He forced himself away from her, cutting off her escape route, for she was now liable to flee and damn the consequences, then he still wouldn't know what the hell was going on. He stood with his back to her yet with her colouring, her sharp, sculpted little features imprinted on his mind. He laughed, low and private, in a way that had Emma swinging about, eyes raking the breadth of his shoulders to try and discover the reason for it.

Richard raised his sardonic dark face to the ceiling. So Yvette deemed herself a wildcat, did she? he mused ironically. Yvette was nothing more than a spiteful harlot…and spiteful

in a manner that had little to do with how she liked to brand
him as hers in a way easily recognisable to other women.

This was a wildcat, he realised ruefully…the genuine, un-
adorned article. She even looked the part with her spare, graceful body and tawny colouring: like a small woodland creature…too beautiful to touch…too beautiful not to. And he felt
a sudden drenching disgust at having resorted to subduing her
with the threat of violation.

He'd never in his life done that…never needed to. Women,
and plenty of them, came to him very willingly. Yet what
tormented him most was, now he'd acknowledged the desire,
self-discipline seemed to mock him. Angry frustration culmi-
nated in a dark fist cracking savagely against the door as he
moved abruptly past it.

Emma jumped and stifled a small scream; so did Mrs Keene
on the other side of the door, with one pudgy hand clamped
to her mouth and the other to her battered, ringing ear.

Giddy with fatigue and hunger, Emma leaned against the
wall to steady herself. She had eaten nothing since her meagre
breakfast and was now ravenous. Her stomach endorsed its
need for attention by growling loudly.

Richard arrowed a look at her as she instinctively pressed
both hands to her flat abdomen, bending over a little as though
to hide the offending noise.

'You've still not eaten, have you?'

'No.' There was no point in lying about something this trivial and obvious, she thought wryly. Deceit would be better
employed on major issues.

'Mrs Keene…?' Richard said quite normally.

After a momentary scuffling sound, the woman was in the
doorway, her apron polishing at the brass knob as though she
intended shining it away.

'Just afinishin' off me chores, sir,' she explained gruffly,
still managing to bob her head at him as she toiled.

'Quite…' he said very drily. 'I take it you have something
appetising to eat about the place?'

Emma choked a spontaneous laugh, making Mrs Keene look nervously at her and Richard arrow her a speculative look. Now why had that not occurred to her? she thought hysterically. Had she offered him one of Mrs Keene's delicious dinners, no doubt he would even now be halfway home.

'Why, o' course, your lordship. I'd be happy to fetch it direct,' Mrs Keene hastily offered, elevating Richard's rank in her enthusiasm. 'La, miss, you missed out on your supper, didn't you now? You should've said for it slipped me busy mind. Now, there be beef silverside and vegetables roastin'. Or mutton hotpot on the hob…an' a dumplin'…'

Richard looked at Emma questioningly for a choice but she simply held onto her newly gurgling stomach and stared at Mrs Keene in amazement. Beef? Mutton? Dumplings? Where was salt bacon and carrots?

'Now, not that it be none o' my concern, o' course, as to what you choose, but the beef do look a treat an' fit for a conasewer o' fine fare…'

'Fetch two plates of the beef and hurry, if you please,' Richard clipped across Mrs Keene's recommendations, making the choice for them both.

Mrs Keene was like a whirlwind. Within a few minutes of her leaving them alone, she was back, accompanied by the young girl who helped in the kitchens. Cutlery, bread, butter, pickles, wine and beer all decked the small parlour table while Emma watched. Then, just as she was about to get a grip on her pride and her senses, and tell him he could dine here alone for she wanted none of it, the steaming plates appeared and she was lost. The beef certainly looked and smelled as good as her landlady had lauded.

Mrs Keene hovered in the doorway with her knees bent and a piece of her skirt held daintily out at an angle in thumb and forefinger.

'Thank you, Mrs Keene,' Richard said graciously. 'And your chores for the day are finished now, are they not?'

'Yes, sir, indeed they are, sir,' she emphatically declared, and at his peremptory nod she was gone.

Emma remained by the wall, her eyes on the table, still striving for the courage to reject it…and him. Just a chunk of that aromatic bread would suffice, she realised, if she could snatch it on the way to the door.

'Sit down.' His order sliced evenly through her half-hearted abstemiousness and for some reason she immediately obeyed. Approaching the table, she sank into the chair he had pulled out. Seating himself opposite, he pushed one laden plate of beef and vegetables towards her, lavishly buttered a chunk of springy warm bread and, unperturbed, started eating.

After a silent moment when Emma simply stared hatefully at the tempting savoury repast as though wishing it all to be stringy, salty bacon and carrots boiled to a mash, she picked up her knife and fork.

They ate in silence yet Emma refused to meekly avoid his eyes. From time to time, she forced proud topaz eyes to meet steady silver, desperate to match his mild, expressionless demeanour. But she knew it was impossible. Every time he pushed bread her way or refilled her glass with sweet wine she tensed, wanting to throw it back at him. And he knew it, too, she realised as her eyes again rose valiantly and swept past dark, sardonic features on the way to glare at the fire.

When she was full and simply shook her head at him as he offered her more, he finally said, with absolute calm and reason, 'I think that it would be wise for your family to know of your whereabouts.'

'Leave us all be,' Emma responded with quiet civility, sensing an unspoken truce between them that she was willing to momentarily honour. 'You will cause us more grief by interfering. No one will thank you for broadcasting this matter, least of all my parents.'

There was a new, narrow-eyed intensity to his gaze. 'Have you been sent away? Banished from London?'

Emma averted her face, feeling it heat in indignation on

comprehending his obtuse meaning. So he classed her morals as no better than those of the women he consorted with, did he? But his base imaginings might just serve her purpose, she realised, her refreshed mind back to investigating devious tactics.

Yes; why not comply? It would be sure to disgust and alienate such a hypocritical degenerate. If there was an infallible way to rid oneself of a gentleman's presence, it must be the hint of an approaching, illegitimate birth. Speculation as to the child's paternity was sure to be bandied about.

'It is a very delicate matter, sir, for a lady in my position…' Emma whispered. *And at least I am a lady!* she would have loved to raucously screech at him, but resisted and demurely lowered her face. 'And I do not wish to say more. I'm sure you understand…' she timidly concluded, pressing her lips tight to conceal a small, satisfied smile.

'But I wish you to say more for I do not understand,' he rejected with silky steel. 'Have your parents sent you away to avoid a scandal?'

She remained diffidently quiet yet was aware of his absolute stillness, his absolute attention. When the silence between them dragged interminably some of her smug confidence evaporated and her stomach's mellow satiety began to curdle.

'Are you with child?'

'I beg you will not press me on the matter, sir,' she pleaded shrilly, agitatedly, swivelling sideways on her chair. He hadn't leapt up and excused himself as she'd expected; moreover, he seemed content to simply sit and singe the top of her head with a quicksilver stare.

'What of your lover? Where is he?' he asked quite levelly, yet on shoving himself back from the table the chair almost tipped over.

She was aware of her body receiving a disturbingly thorough assessment. No doubt he did know of such things, she realised acidly. She'd seen him at the Fallow Buck with a child. Whether it was born of his wife or his mistress was anyone's guess. As Victoria had never mentioned Dickie—as she affectionately termed him—marrying, the child, she presumed, must be the offspring from some base union.

She and Victoria exchanged letters quite often. Via one of those, Emma had learned that this man had moved abroad a year or more ago to oversee his foreign estates. Such a shame he ever brought himself back! she viciously thought, squirming beneath his unrelenting observation.

'Is he married already or refusing to support you?'

'Please, do not ask for I…I really cannot say…'

Well, how lucky can you get? Richard sourly mused. You wanted her and now it looks as though not only can you have her but another man's bastard, too. For God's sake, leave now! he urged himself. You've done your best. You've fed her…offered to help. She doesn't want your aid. She's never liked you. Even at your mannerly best, she never liked you, he mocked himself, recalling how attentively civil he'd been to her three years previously in London when he and David Hardinge had been the bane of polite society. And there, of course, lay a prime reason why he was loath to abandon her: he owed it to the best friend he had ever had to protect her, for David's wife, Victoria, cherished this woman as a very dear friend.

In fact, he was quite surprised that she hadn't fled into Hertfordshire to seek support from Victoria rather than head this way where she seemed friendless and alone…unless… He twisted on his heel. Of course, you fool, he silently berated himself. If she's headed this way, that's because her lover lives locally. 'How long have you been in Bath?' he asked abruptly.

'Five days,' Emma answered honestly, yet looked warily at him.

So she'd been here five days and was starving and seeking employment, which meant that the bastard had no intention of taking on his responsibility. If he was already married the least he could do was settle her in her own establishment somewhere as his mistress.

Oh, no! Don't you dare give it a minute's pause! he inwardly raged. *A pregnant mistress?* In three months' time when her belly's swollen you'll be visiting Yvette and counting the cost of it all. *A mistress with a child?* You don't even like children! You like your nephew well enough, an inner voice argued back. He likes you too. Stephen says you're good with children. But they're family…they share your blood. This flyblow could be sired by a criminal…drunk…gambler. Should suit pretty well, then, echoed back drily as he recalled his duelling, his long nights spent heavy-eyed at card tables and numerous drunken brawls in his misspent youth.

Besides—he swivelled on a heel to look at her—at some time she's going to be this beautiful again…perhaps filled out a little too, he thought wryly as he discreetly surveyed delicately curving breasts and hips. 'You need someone to care for you,' he heard himself say. 'Even if you manage to get employment, you'll be put off as soon as your condition becomes apparent.'

Emma merely nodded, not knowing what else to do, for her stomach was in sickening cramps as she anticipated what would come next. But then, it had been niggling at the back of her mind since she'd stupidly threatened to cry rape to frighten him off. He'd looked at her from beneath his long, dusky lashes in a way he had three years ago…in a way he no doubt looked at all women who aroused his lust. And she knew she did that for some odd reason.

No other man had looked at her in that steady, intent way, as though the backs of his eyes were afire. Certainly not Matthew. Yet, even with so little experience of men, an innate sense warned her that throbbing, silent stare was a prelude to lechery. She slowly stood, quickly said, 'Thank you for your concern but I have made my own plans… If you will excuse me…'

They seemed to be pacing towards the door at the same time, at the same speed yet he reached it first from further away. A solid dark fist was planted casually against it and slitted silver eyes gleamed down at her. 'What plans?' he asked idly.

'Private plans,' she returned sweetly.

'Plans that include absconding from here as soon as I'm out of sight?'

'I have nothing further to say, sir,' she said with great dignity…yet alarmed, for he had a disturbing ability to read her mind. 'I can only ask you not to cause my family further distress by…by mentioning this to anyone at all. My parents are quite ill with worry.' And that was the truth, too, even if their anxiety stemmed from a different source entirely.

'You can't stay here; it's hardly fitting. Besides, as you and Mrs Keene insist, it is a respectable house,' he mentioned satirically. 'I'm sure you'll soon be asked to leave.'

'Mrs Keene need never know!' She realised immediately how naive that sounded. A pregnant woman was quite easily identifiable as she neared her time. 'I shall not be here for very long,' she quickly amended.

Richard looked meaningfully at the door. 'Oh, I'm sure a hint of it might already have reached Mrs Keene's ears.'

Emma glanced, horrified, at the door then actually caught a muffled shuffle of receding slippered feet.

'You need someone to care for you, Emma.'

She felt the soft words stir the hair at her brow, sensed the distance between them close and solidify with tension. She swallowed, trying to dredge up some clever snub, but nothing came. Nothing at all. Her volatile mind was unusually lethargic.

The fist planted by the side of her head slid down the panels on the door, dark knuckles brushing against fawn hair close to them. His long fingers uncurled slowly, moved a trailing tress back from her brow, then another with a mesmeric gentleness that would have rendered objection superfluous.

Her copper eyes were slowly raised, magnetised by eyes like tarnished silver stars. 'Let me care for you, Emma,' he said huskily before his moon-pale head dipped and his lips touched a feather-light caress to her brow.

Entranced, her body felt immoveable, her limbs heavy. Even her ivory lids felt weighted and drooped as warm, skimming kisses trailed her cool skin from temple to cheek.

Hit him! Push him away! resounded in her mind, but hollowly, as though from far, far away. And the tantalisingly soft caress was so soothing. Suddenly, it felt as though she'd been starved of human contact and this man's touch was as essential as the food she'd eaten.

A dark thumb traced her lower lip, a hand wound into thick tawny hair, tilting her head those necessary few inches. His mouth touched hers with infinite gentle persuasion, and Emma felt herself melting into it.

He knew it, too: unbelievably, her acquiescence seemed a mere kiss away. 'I'll care for you and the child,' he murmured confidently against her mouth. 'You'll want for nothing, I swear. I'll make lasting provision for you. Even if I marry at some time, you'll want for nothing.'

A glacier of icy feeling, bright and invigorating, seemed to meander from her pulsing lips to her rigid toes. As his mouth slid forcefully on hers and his hand spanned her jaw, manoeuvring it apart, she finally wrenched her head aside, simultaneously swinging small, clawed fingers up towards his face.

Swift reflexes had him ducking so the worst her nails did was glance off a bronzed cheek before her wrist was encircled by five tanned fingers and slammed back against the door beside her head. Her breathing was so fast and shallow, the cotton of her nightrobe chafed her soft breasts, tautening her nipples, but fiery feline eyes boldly held his as she cautiously primed her other hand for a like assault. This time he was prepared and those slender, curled fingers partnered the others on the opposite side of her head.

After a few moments straining her wrists against his easy imprisonment she cursed beneath her breath and flung herself back against the door. 'I do realise I deport myself unbecomingly with gentlemen,' she sweetly said through closed teeth. 'My mother tells me so all the time. I've omitted to thank you, haven't I, sir, for the offer of your kind protection? I do thank you, of course, but must, unfortunately, decline your generosity. My private plans are not negotiable—something I'm sure Madame Dubois will appreciate… Oh, and your future wife, whoever the poor fool may eventually be.'

She watched his eyes narrow, his jaw tighten but he laughed deep in his throat with a lack of amusement. 'It seems you've deported yourself extremely becomingly with one gentleman, sweet. Would that it had been me,' he said as his face lowered tormentingly towards hers. She fought against his captivity in earnest, but refused to look away from those savage silver eyes.

Her valour was her undoing. As she finally ceded and swung her head aside it was too late and his mouth slanted exactly over hers. The more she tried to shake her head free and avoid him, the more his mouth pursued and clung. With insulting ease and leisure, both her wrists were trapped in one large dark hand while his other spanned her jaw and stilled it.

No man had ever kissed her like this. Not one of the stolen kisses she had received following her debut nine years ago had made any lasting impression. On the few occasions Matthew had kissed her it was with an odd brevity, as though he was sorry for troubling her. She had never guessed kissing could be so disturbingly appealing that she knew the memory would brand itself on her mind to be remembered for ever. His mouth was warm and wooing, his tongue-tip lightly caressing the clamped line of her lips, tempting them to part. They did, curiosity subduing pride. His tongue tasted hers then traced the silk of her lower lip. Then, just as her breathing slowed and she felt that anodyne enchantment dooming her to whatever he wanted, it was over and he was wheeling away from her and into the room.

Strolling to the fender, he planted a booted foot against it. 'Good evening, Miss Worthington,' he said quite normally.

Emma put the back of a hand to her mouth. It clenched into a fist and angry knuckles scrubbed as though to remove his taint. He was actually now dismissing *her* from *his* presence! And the fact that part of her no longer wanted to go...wanted him back close to her...was unbearably humiliating. She fumed inwardly and then outwardly. 'When you leave this lodging house tonight you will pay for one meal...yours. I have already paid for my dinner this morning and you will pay nothing more for it.'

Richard watched her, amused, through a mesh of dark lashes. 'As you say,' he agreed solemnly, 'it is paid for.'

'And...and I am counting on the affection and friendship we both have for Viscount and Viscountess Courtenay to keep you from...from repeating any of this. You know Victoria would be deeply upset and anxious on my behalf if she came to hear of such gossip. I will tell her all in my own time. I hope I haven't overestimated your character in even that small respect. Whatever else I may believe you to be, I trust you are a loyal, true friend to them.'

'As you say,' he bit out, 'a loyal, true friend.' A brief pause preceded, 'In exchange for my promise I expect you to vow to stay here until some proper arrangements can be made for your future.'

'Goodnight, Mr Du Quesne,' Emma said shortly as she pulled open the parlour door and exited the room, with absolute aplomb.

She climbed the stairs sedately, chin high, yet on legs that felt weak and wobbly. On entering her room she lit the small candle by the bed, turned down the covers neatly with shaking hands and sat on the edge of the mattress. Her eyes squeezed shut, her mind jumbling with so many tumultous emotions that coherent thought was impossible. As she drooped sideways onto the bed, her hands covered her face and she felt hot tears wetting her palms. 'I hate him,' she whispered. 'I hate him...hate him...' she cried, muffling the sound with knuckles rammed against her sensitive, pulsing lips. How dared he treat her with such disrespect, such abominable familiarity, as though she were some…some shameless trollop like that Frenchwoman? She had been gently reared; a social equal to men such as he. Yet he had the gall to proposition her as though she'd emerged from some dockside tavern!

But you've made him believe you're a shameless trollop, a small inner voice justified. You've implied you've lost your virtue and your wits by getting with child, then impudently refusing his aid. He's been a rogue for years; you would have been a schoolgirl when he started philandering. It was sheer folly to imply you're a fallen woman. A man of his arrogance and experience probably believed you were inviting…begging his protection. No doubt he's now feeling pious for attempting to rescue a stupid strumpet from squalor.

He had offered lasting provision, and she believed he'd meant it. Out of the duty and affection she knew he felt for Viscount Courtenay, he would have honoured that promise. When his lust for her was expended and all she aroused was pity and disgust he would still have supported her financially.

That mortification was too much to bear. Emma rolled over onto her front and her small fists banged into the pillow in frustration and fury as she dried her face by scrubbing it against the linen. You could have been truthful. You could have explained you were here in Bath to marry an honourable man. Instead you've let three year old prejudices addle your wits. You've acted without due caution and brought all of this shambles down on your own head, you reckless idiot!

'Mrs Keene?'

The woman leapt up from her rocking-chair, sending it oscillating crazily. Her gin tot banged down onto the scrubbed surface of the scullery table which she careered into in her haste. 'Oh, your lordship, I didn't hear you come in. Is there somethin' else I can get you?' She bobbed, balancing on one foot, with an unobtrusive rub at her smarting knee.

'It was a good dinner,' Sir Richard Du Quesne said with an

appreciative nod and a lazy indication that nothing further was required. 'I have it from Miss Worthington that she has already paid for her meal. What do I owe you for mine?'

Mrs Keene raised her mobcap to peer at him. The little hussy thought she'd paid a shilling for a crown special, did she? 'Why, nothin' o'course, sir,' she said humbly. 'It be a very great honour to have your noble self partake of me victuals and do return at any time to—'

'Thank you.' Richard cut off her fulsome invitation and gave her a smile. 'While Miss Worthington remains here, I should like her welfare scrupulously attended to. I imagine she forgets to eat at times…or to pay her way. I will settle any balance due on her account but would not want her to know that.'

'Ah, yes, sir; proud, studious little thing that she is.' Well, Mrs Keene mulled over shrewdly in her mind, he wants her looked after, an' no mistake. Jauntily she added, 'She fair forgets to come below for her meals when she's got her head in one of them books. Reads novels all the time, don't you know. 'Cept when her friend comes acallin' an' takes her for a drive.'

Richard pivoted slowly back towards the woman. 'Ah, yes…that must be…Mr Sullivan, her cousin and a good friend of mine. Dark hair…quite short and squat.'

'Oh, no, sir,' Mrs Keene said innocently, 'this be a different gentleman. Tall, he is…not so tall as you, though, with light brown hair. Sometimes he brings his children with him and they all ride in his little gig together. I believe I heard Miss Worthington call her friend Matthew,' she helpfully supplied with a sideways look. 'Not that it be none of my concern, o' course…or I tattle…'

'That's right, Mrs Keene, it is none of your concern, and I'd hate to learn you tattle…' Richard subtly warned.

Chapter Five

'So would you be likin' some mutton hotpot for your dinner this evenin', Miss Worthington?' Mrs Keene asked with a gap-toothed grin from the doorway.

This unexpected disturbance had Emma relinquishing Elizabeth Bennet's misfortunes, and focussing again on her own. Where was Matthew? Why had he not come calling? Clapping her novel shut with a sigh, she inclined forward to again peer along the street, hoping for a sign of his gig. Was he still vexed with her for attending that farcical interview yesterday? It was ironic—now she no longer wanted time to consider his proposal his absence was preventing her telling him so!

'Dumplin's are fresh made with a little herb 'n onion...' Mrs Keene's persuasive tone cut across her thoughts.

An awful inkling of the reason for her landlady's solicitude was followed by a flash of angry humiliation that seared Emma from head to toe. That disgusting lecher had, after all, last night paid for her dinner! If possible, she now hated him even more. *No, she didn't!* she scolded herself. He held no such power to disturb her. What he aroused was simple contempt. It was a decision, made in bed, that had soothed her inner turmoil enough to let her drift into an exhausted slumber as dawn approached. So had the comfort that her hateful reunion with Richard Du Quesne served a purpose: it made her appreciate more than ever the solid, upstanding qualities of a man such as Matthew Cavendish.

'Did Mr Du Quesne pay for my dinner yesterday?' Emma asked frostily.

'La…no, m'dear. You'd already paid me for yourn!'

A tad mollified, Emma, nevertheless, arrowed a suspicious amber glance at her landlady. 'Did he ask you to lie?'

Mrs Keene's crossed arms shivered, propped up her bosom, and a look of absolute affront preceded, 'O' course not! I, bein' the honest kind o' body I am, felt obliged t'inform *Sir Richard*—' she emphasised his aristocratic status by inclining forward '—that you'd squared with me earlier for your board.'

'A shilling was enough?' Emma asked, amazed. Obliquely she realised she had forgotten Victoria's postscript on a letter two years ago informing her that Sir John Du Quesne had died as a result of the grave illness that kept his heir from attending her baby daughter's christening. A proxy had taken on Richard's role of godfather while he remained at his father's bedside.

'Er…yes…yes, a shillin's right,' whistled through yellowing stumps.

'The mutton and dumplings tonight…that is also a shilling?'

'O' course…' was again ejected in a persuasive purr. If a poor widow could sell a crown special with all its juicy profit, a shilling-a-plate hot 'ordinary' could go hang. Why, the silver squire probably wouldn't quibble at a half-guinea a plate for this lucky young lady. She'd heard gossip that he was right generous to his women.

Emma rose from her chair by the window and approached the door. 'Excuse me, Mrs Keene.'

The landlady gathered her greedy thoughts, then her greasy skirts, and wobbled after Emma along the musty corridor. Emma halted at another door, knocked and, when summoned to enter, did so. She smiled at her fellow lodger, a young lady she guessed to be some years younger than herself. But, without consulting a mirror, she knew that this fair-haired, modestly dressed young woman had the same air of dejection and a haunted, hungry look.

Now, of course, *she* had recently been sated with delicious, nourishing food, and had drunk sweet, expensive wine—and at no extra cost, it seemed!

'Miss Jenner,' she greeted cheerfully, 'Mrs Keene is here to relay her shilling menus for tonight. Shall we listen and choose together?'

Emma was aware of Mrs Keene's head quivering in denial but ignored it. If the *silver squire*—she mockingly recalled his nickname—wanted to supplement her meagre meals with his…well…silver, she would let him. The thought of later sitting at the same table as this young lady, eating heartily while her fellow boarder picked over the unpalatable scraps that served as dinners night after night…the injustice of it set her small teeth ascrape. Either they both enjoyed mutton hot-pot or neither of them did.

Mrs Keene was sure to charge him exorbitantly and that was so hugely gratifying she chuckled. It made her want to run into the street and invite every ragamuffin she laid eyes on into the house to dine courtesy of their generous local lord at a shilling a plate.

Felicity Jenner smiled back with shy friendliness and definite interest in what was being served up.

At Mrs Keene's slow backwards shuffle along the corridor, Emma called out, 'Oh, please don't disappear yet, Mrs Keene. Tonight is to be mutton hotpot with savoury dumplings or…what was the rest, Mrs Keene? Is it beef and roast vegetables, as yesterday? Saddle of lamb? Steak and oyster pie, perhaps? Such exceptional value is sure to tempt many customers into your eating room. Miss Jenner and I are both at a loose end. We can go into the street and drum you up some noon trade. Now what do you say to that?'

A burbled croak was all a horrified Mrs Keene was capable of emitting. Then, with a poisonous glare over a slumped shoulder, she was scurrying below.

* * *

Sir Richard Du Quesne looked at the list in front of him. A quill trailed the column of names, settled again by Matthew Drury and the nib tapped idly.

He looked up, at nothing in particular, then grunted a laugh. It couldn't be: the man was hardly tall and his hair was more red than brown…besides, to his knowledge he had no children. He glanced back at the listing of all the men he could bring to mind named Matthew, who seemed of about the right social status, lived locally and who in some shape or form fitted Mrs Keene's description. None seemed right.

If Emma Worthington's *friend* wasn't a figment of her landlady's wily imagination, it seemed reasonable to assume he must be living somewhere hereabouts. Perhaps they'd travelled from London together. Perhaps, on learning of her condition, he'd bolted first and she'd followed him.

He pushed himself back from his desk with an irritated sigh, a tanned hand at the nape of his neck easing the tension beneath pale gilt hair. He was beginning to wish to God he'd never been at Yvette's when Emma had shown up. He'd not had a minute's peace since. Even that first glimpse of her at the Fallow Buck posting house—and he knew now with absolute certainty that it had been her—had left him unaccountably restless.

He wouldn't have been in South Parade at that time in the afternoon had he not succumbed to Yvette's erotic thanks for the bauble he'd bought for her during their shopping trip an hour earlier. The fact that he had been very actively employed with Yvette while Emma sat patiently awaiting an audience barely twenty yards away both humbled and harassed him.

The idea that the two women might ever have dealt 'companionably' together caused him to smile. Had he not been there, and Emma had been taken on, sparks would now be flying fit to burn his Palladian town house down. Miss Spitfire Worthington made Yvette…made most women…seem insipid. In fact, he acknowledged with a scowl, Miss Worthington was once again fascinating him too damned much, and continuing to justify his involvement in her welfare as simply duty to his friend, David, was self-deluding. His body was constantly reminding him just how interested he was on his own account.

He had become interested on his own account three years ago when David had been pursuing Victoria. Initially he had turned his attention to Emma to assist David and separate her from her friend. After one memorable meeting with Miss Worthington, when she'd stunned him as much with her beautiful golden eyes as with her memorable insults, he had been, for no sensible reason, smitten and planning his own courtship strategies. But she was having none of it. Every tentative friendly overture had resulted in a withering snub.

For an eligible bachelor hounded by tenacious debutantes and demi-reps alike, the novelty of unequivocal rejection had had him reinflating his crushed ego in a time-honoured way, thus fully meriting Emma's allusions to his turpitude.

She had made it clear she didn't like or trust him then; neither did she like or trust him now. And yet he just couldn't put her from his mind…or body. He'd kissed her now and that told him all he needed to know: she wasn't nearly as cold and indifferent as she wanted him to think. He'd experienced far more erotic kisses but nothing matched the satisfaction of her spontaneous surrender. It had both excited and gentled him, stirring something completely new: he *wanted* her to like him. He wanted her approval and respect because she had his…she had always had his. So he'd let her go.

When they'd first met, he had been struck by her beauty and wit. But her courage and honesty had captivated him too: she'd dared what no other woman ever had, even his mother. She'd flouted at his licentious lifestyle.

Three years on, she'd lost none of her spirit, which probably meant her pregnancy was the result of an ill-starred love-affair rather than ravishment. While that gave him a sense of quiet relief, it also agitated a burning resentment of this faceless man who had won her affection and esteem.

With an impatient curse at such singular sentimentality, he reached for the brandy decanter and the cigar box. One innocently alluring kiss…one clawed cheek for his noble self-restraint and eccentric generosity, and he was behaving like a languishing hero in a romantic novel. She was expecting another man's child, for God's sake! The sensible course of action was to keep her respectably lodged until this Matthew, if indeed he was her lover, could be found and persuaded to take her on.

He irritably jammed himself back in his chair just as Stephen entered his study with a companion. They were of approximately the same lofty height, yet the dark-haired man with his blond brother was of impressive muscular stature.

'Ross! I had no idea you were here. Where have you been hiding? Have you been in Bath long?' Richard greeted his friend and business associate recently arrived from Cornwall. In an instant he had risen from his desk and was striding towards him. The men shook hands and embraced warmly.

'Well, long enough for Stephen to introduce me to a rather fine claret and his very fine new addition to the family,' Ross Trelawney said with a grin. 'The child's going to be a beauty like her mother.'

Noting his younger brother's wide grin and proud, puffed-up demeanour, Richard said drily, 'Have a cigar.'

Stephen took one; so did Ross on being offered the box.

Sauntering idly to the desk, Stephen frowned at the column of names on the paper. He picked it up, perusing it. 'What's this?'

'Just someone I was trying to bring to mind: a man named Matthew who lives locally—quite tall, I'm told, with light brown hair. He's probably reasonably well-connected and might have two children.'

'What's it all about? A woman? A lynching?' Stephen chortled.

Richard smiled at the fingers holding his smouldering cheroot. *'Touché…'* he murmured wryly to himself. 'Just some gossip I heard,' he said aloud. 'It's needling me that I can't recall the man. I'm sure I must know him.'

Stephen let the paper drift back to the leather-topped desk. 'We thought we'd go into town to Bellamy's, then perhaps on to the theatre…are you coming?' At his older brother's hesitation, Stephen slyly hinted, 'Or have you and the comely Yvette more exclusive plans for tonight?' A suggestive elbow nudged Ross's side. Stephen winked, slow and lewd, at the same time pouring himself a generous measure of brandy.

'You're not going,' Richard mentioned idly to his younger brother.

Stephen looked crestfallen, his jaw dropped and his untasted drink plonked onto the desk. 'Whaaat…?'

'You're not going. It's your wife's birthday this week. She's been left alone most evenings while you've been carousing in town. It's time you took her out. I'm sick of going into one room or another and seeing Amelia on the verge of tears and Mother clucking over her having a nervous attack.'

'Oh, Amelia's well enough,' Stephen dismissed cheerily. 'I'll take her to the opera on Saturday. I recall her being moody for a few months after Jake was born. It must be a female thing…a malaise that follows confinement. It makes her vexed and weepy.'

'Perhaps it's you that makes her vexed and weepy,' Richard coolly suggested.

'Am I missing something here?' Ross interjected, waving his cigar between them as he aimed perfect smoke rings at a scintillating chandelier.

'Stephen thinks he's in line for a little extra-marital entertainment. I expect he's hoping you'll show him the best places to find it later. He's bored, bless him.'

'Is that so…?' Ross said, with a thoughtful look at Stephen. 'And Amelia? Is she bored?' he asked.

'Of course not. Women don't get restless urges like men… like that…' Stephen blustered.

Richard and Ross exchanged looks of surprised enlightenment.

'Well, if she does get restless urges…like that,' Ross said with gentle gravity, 'be sure and let me know, won't you…?'

Stephen stalked off a way and stared out of the window. 'What is this? A conspiracy? Here I have under one roof, in the same goddamn room, no less, two of the most notorious Lotharios of my, or anyone else's, acquaintance. Do I get a little manly advice? Do I get a few tips on where the best muslin congregates? Oh, no! I get moralising and I get jokes…' His arm flung out, emphasising disappointment and disgust.

'Oh, I wasn't joking, Stephen,' Ross said.

Stephen stared at him as though he didn't fully understand, then he launched himself across the room, screaming, 'You filthy bastard…'

Ross adroitly sidestepped his flailing fists and put out his hands placatingly. When Stephen still swung savagely at him, a muscular arm gripped him restrictingly about the shoulders and held him close. 'Listen, Steve…' Ross soothed. 'Your wife's a very beautiful woman. I'm not blind or alone in noticing that. Once it's gossiped about that you're seeking diversion and neglecting her, she'll be approached. And there'll be plenty of eager young bucks ready to console her. Who would you rather it was…?'

Stephen wrenched himself free of Ross's comforting embrace and stalked, stiff-backed, towards the door. He glowered over his shoulder at the two tall men of strikingly dissimilar colouring. 'Enjoy yourselves…' he snarled before the door crashed shut.

Richard's grey eyes met Ross's green-flecked gaze over the rim of a brandy balloon. 'Yes, I know. We're a pair of rank hypocrites,' he muttered, before abruptly throwing the cognac down his throat. He smacked the glass back onto the desk. 'Thanks anyway. She's the best thing that ever happened to him. Unfortunately, she happened about ten years too soon. If he didn't love her I wouldn't bother. But, God knows, a love match is too rare and precious to be discarded lightly. If he takes a mistress things will never be the same between them. If she retaliates and takes a lover and he finds out…well, you just saw his reaction to the possibility. The reality might have him committing murder and I don't want my nephew and heir growing up in the shadow of some sordid scandal.'

Richard sighed and stared out of the window into a mellow autumn afternoon, his head angling so long fingers could massage the tension in his neck. 'I know it's been difficult for him…Amelia's been out of bounds for a while. The least I can do is throw a few obstacles in his way until she's recovered from the birth and he's retrieved his brain from his breeches.' Another hollow laugh choked out of him. 'The proof…I am a rank hypocrite,' he sourly observed then stuck the cigar in his mouth and drew deeply. His bronzed hands were braced at either side of the window and he watched an endless avenue of silver-leaved whitebeam shimmering in the light breeze.

'Sounds like that came out of experience and straight from the heart, Dickie,' Ross drawled with a small smile and a shrewd look. 'And I never imagined I'd be saying that to you. Is it anything to do with this Yvette?'

Richard snorted a laugh. 'Hardly,' he said to the blue sky.

'Who is she?'

'A talented whore, my friend. That's who she is. And yes…you're very welcome…'

The door slammed back against the wall, cutting off further conversation.

Richard pivoted on his heel to see Stephen posed regally in the opening. 'I am taking my wife and my mother to the Upper Assembly Rooms,' he announced in a crisp, martyred way. 'I shall endeavour not to stand around looking available, lest I receive unsolicited female attention. And it's Cavendish,' he gritted, before putting wood back in the aperture with a resounding crack.

'Cavendish?' Ross echoed, then shook his head and shrugged his total bemusement at all of it.

'Cavendish!' The name resounded like gunshot as Richard's eyes flicked to the list on the desk. He swore beneath his breath then said with slow, measured vehemence, 'Good God! Why the hell didn't I think of him…?'

Emma frowned at the note then reread it, a simultaneous warm joy and chill suspicion assailing her as her fingers unconsciously comforted a burning cheek.

'Is everythin' all right, m'dear?' Mrs Keene asked, quite disturbed by her lodger's alternately receding and heightening colour.

'Oh, yes. Thank you. Thank you, Mrs Keene, for bringing this. Was it delivered a while ago?'

'No, miss. Just a few short minutes since. Sir Richard's man be waitin' below for a reply. What shall I tell him?'

'Tell him…tell him…' Oh, God, what was she to tell him? raced through her mind. She needed time to think what to tell him. 'Tell him to wait, please, Mrs Keene. I shall endeavour to pen a reply as quickly as I can.'

'I could give to him your spoken reply,' the woman slyly offered as she squinted sideways at the letter, wishing she could decipher a few words.

'That won't be necessary, thank you, Mrs Keene,' Emma said, with a flash of sooty-fringed topaz eyes.

The woman sniffed and flounced out. She flounced back again. 'If you be soon movin' out, I'll start reckonin' up your account, shall I?' she said, letting Emma know she could make a good enough guess as to a certain gentleman's intentions, written or otherwise.

'Yes, and please also reckon up what Sir Richard owes you.'

Mrs Keene slanted her a look. 'Just you remember, I never said nothin' to you about the silver squire bein' generous on your account.'

Realising that her landlady was quite seriously anxious, Emma reassured her. 'I shall have no qualms in letting Sir Richard know I guessed he offered to supplement my board. Include every extra cost on your bill and I shall willingly present it to him…' She added gleefully beneath her breath, 'And test his generosity.'

'Well, not that it be none o' my concern, o' course, miss, but you're too sharp. Mark my words, you'll end up cuttin' yourself bad.' A plump finger wagged warningly. She hesitated on the way to the door. 'Every cost?' she asked uncertainly.

Emma nodded, her eyes on the succinct note she had received from Richard Du Quesne conveying such startling yet welcome news:

I wish to inform you that I attend the arrival of our very dear mutual friends, Viscount and Viscountess Courtenay, at Silverdale. I imagine you would not wish Victoria to quit Bath before you have had the opportunity to meet with her and perhaps discuss certain pressing matters; thus I should be pleased to have you join us as house guest this weekend.

My mother, the dowager Miriam Du Quesne, and my sister-in-law, Amelia, are currently in residence. We are also graced with the presence of my mother's sister who shows as little inclination to return home as do my closer kin. In short, Silverdale is at present overflowing with suitable chaperons for a virtuous single woman: you need not fret for your reputation.

Send word with my man, Gibbs, if you are to honour us with your presence and a carriage will collect you at six of the clock this evening.

Yours etc.

P.S. Should you decide not to attend, please indicate how you would wish me to respond if drawn into debate on how you go on. You seem adept at evading those ques-

tions; thus it might be in your best interest to deal per-
sonally with such enquiries for I can't promise to match
your skill.

Emma folded the paper and closed her eyes. Even the sar-
castic references to her reputation and her virtue and her dis-
sembling could not dampen her happiness. Victoria was soon
here in Bath! Perhaps already here. It had to be true! Why
would he lie?

A few evenings ago he had quite tersely dismissed her from
his company. He was hardly likely to bother plotting to lure
her back into it. The tone of his invitation was hardly persuasive. It was as wearily dutiful as had been his offer of aid.
She could imagine him, in private, heartily bemoaning her
arrival in Bath, her embarrassing presence at his mistress's
house. No doubt they laughed at her together.

Now he had done his best: offered her his protection and
supplemented her keep with his money. What more could he
have done? he would no doubt shrug and sigh sanctimoniously
if pressed on the matter. As a shrewd opportunist he had attempted to discharge his duty and still exploit her predicament
to some advantage. After all, it was costing him dear…even
if he didn't yet know quite how much. Emma smiled to herself
with a certain malicious satisfaction, thinking of Mrs Keene
even now totting up his account.

The chance to see Victoria was too tempting an offer to turn
down. If there was one person she knew she could confide in,
it was Victoria. Victoria had three years ago been through
hardships and heartbreak herself before finding such bliss with
David Hardinge, Viscount Courtenay. She would understand,
she would sympathise, she would not judge her.

And Emma felt now in desperate need of some advice. For
she had still not seen or heard from Matthew. It had been
several days since he had dropped her off at her interview. He
had not called at Lower Place even to enquire whether she
was now employed.

In the immediate aftermath of her skirmish with Richard Du Quesne, she had been determined to accept Matthew's proposal. As the days dragged on with no opportunity to tell him so, niggling doubts again set in. She knew he did not love her in the way she wanted; indeed, she was no longer sure she still loved *him* in the way she wanted. But...it was security of sorts and if it were to come to choosing between marriage to him or vile Mr Dashwood...or being housed and intermittently used by Richard Du Quesne when the fancy took him...she knew very definitely which shelter she preferred.

But now she was close to being able to share all her problems with someone she truly loved. And she did love Victoria as the sister she had yearned for but never had. Enduring Richard Du Quesne's company for a few days was a small price to pay for spending precious time with Victoria, perhaps even seeing darling Lucy, too.

She grabbed at her quill, drew a sheet of paper close and while dipping for ink mulled over her reply. Her first instinct was to match his mordant tone, but...she would rise above it and be civil, she decided; after all, she was accepting his hospitality, however reluctantly it was bestowed.

Topaz eyes squinted up lazily through dusky lashes at a million leaves fluttering like sinuous pearly wings in a cobwebby canopy. The avenue of trees undulated into the distance like a discarded silver necklace. Emma's tawny head swayed sideways on the squabs and she stared out over verdant swards to wooded horizons, the first vibrant autumn tints tipping gold into the dense foliage. Then, as the carriage rattled over planked boards, fording a crystal-clear, rushing stream, it swung to the left and she saw the house.

Shifting forward on the seat, she tilted her head for a better view. Cream bathstone gleamed mellow honey in the setting sun, a bank of high windows afire with low, slanting rays. A wistful amber gaze meandered from majestic chimneys to raked gravel. It was magnificent in every aspect: its grand size, the perfect symmetry of its spare Palladian architecture, its central positioning with neatly manicured parkland sweeping gracefully away on three sides. Somehow she had known Silverdale would be this wonderful; ultimate confirmation elicited a small wry smile: the injustice…the irony of it all! That such a degenerate should be allowed to reside within such splendidly decorous walls.

The coach rumbled on, finally scrunching to a halt before an imposing porticoed entrance. A footman opened the door for Emma and politely assisted her to alight.

A smartly uniformed butler was sedately descending a flight of flared stone steps. Halting by the carriage, he executed a stiff bow. 'Simmons, at your service, Miss Worthington,' he formally introduced himself. 'Sir Richard is expecting you. Please come this way.'

Emma reached down for her carpet bag but Simmons shot her an alarmed look. 'Gibbs will get that,' he reproved, with a haughty glance at the hovering footman that sent his eyebrows shifting in opposite directions.

Emma started to demur but, on noting Simmons's shocked look, eyebrows jiggling, quickly dropped her bag to the driveway gravel and smiled her thanks. 'When in Rome…' she muttered beneath her breath.

'Are Viscount and Viscountess Courtenay arrived?' she asked pleasantly on gathering her skirts in her fists and following Simmons's starchy black figure. As she climbed wide stone steps, a niggling anxiety returned to disturb her. She had fled London with very few clothes: she had quickly pounced on a few gowns with no thought other than they must be serviceable and versatile. She was sure to feel quite dowdy amid such grandeur. But then, she sighed, she wasn't here to parade in finery, simply to see her dear friend, and perhaps, with Victoria's fresh eye, discover a solution to her problems.

But then, logically, there were only two options and she was sure practical Victoria would soon point them out: she could return to London praying that Jarrett Dashwood had meanwhile taken himself off elsewhere in pursuit of a drudge to wed; alternatively she could finally contact her parents and inform them she was to marry Matthew Cavendish in Bath…assuming Matthew still desired her as a wife. There *was* a third possibility, or rather a probability: Victoria would insist on offering financial aid.

Viscount Courtenay would loan her father money—primarily because Victoria asked him to, but also because he was a very wealthy and very generous man. Emma's eyes squeezed in mortification. She wouldn't be able to bear the prospect of her wastrel father shamelessly accepting charity. She knew he would have no qualms in using another man's cash to pay his way at the card tables or the gin houses he frequented while he left a mountain of bills untouched on his desk.

Yet, as much as she despaired of her shallow parents, in her own way she loved and missed them too. It was some while since she'd decamped and now every passing hour increased her guilt and worry as to how they did.

With a sigh she allowed dresses to again monopolise her thoughts. No doubt, even in that inconsequential respect, dear Vicky would help out. They had before, on happier occasions, swapped gowns. Abruptly recalling that her query as to the Courtenays' arrival was still unanswered, she angled her face to Simmons. As they proceeded over the threshold into a spacious hallway she repeated, 'Are Viscount and Viscountess Courtenay yet arrived?'

'No.'

Emma stopped dead. Just one quietly spoken word yet she immediately recognised the voice. Momentarily blinded by the shadowy interior after such strong evening sunlight, she squinted in the direction of slow, approaching footfalls. She was obliquely aware of the great doors being closed behind her and that light now entered through a many-faceted window well set high in a domed ceiling. Sunbeams shafted into a central pool, gilding creamy marble flags between soaring marble pillars.

Sir Richard Du Quesne stepped through the dusty radiance, the top of his blond head momentarily incandescent, and then he was into the shadows again and closing with her.

Emma immediately raised her eyes to his, seeking to read something positive in his face despite his negative response.

She dipped a curtsey but refused to demurely lower her face. Instead it tilted a little to one side. Her chin came up, her full, soft mouth pursed aslant, proud and challenging. If he thought for one minute he had intimidated her with that proposition…with that kiss…he would find he was much mistaken. She had barely let it worry her. She had scarcely given it a second thought.

'How have you been?'

'Very well, thank you, sir. And you?' Emma politely returned.

'Do you care today how I do, Emma?' His expression was unreadable, his tone laden with irony.

Emma felt her colour rising as he alluded to her past discourtesies. 'No,' she retorted, impenitently, and her eyes slid away over stately furniture she could see looming against distant walls.

She could sense his sardonic amusement, his unwavering attention searing the side of her face as she studied her opulent surroundings. And suddenly she knew she couldn't possibly stay here, with him, longer than was absolutely necessary. 'I thank you very much for your invitation to spend the weekend here,' she stiltedly began, 'but I must decline your hospitality. I have simply come to speak to Victoria before I return to my lodgings. Is she soon due?'

'No.'

Emma's face jerked up to his dark, handsome features. 'No?' she breathed.

'No,' he repeated, his argentine eyes as cool as his tone.

'In your letter you wrote that…' She trailed into silence as her face pricked with an awful icy suspicion. 'You lied?' she whispered, unconsciously taking an unsteady step back.

'Yes.'

'Why?' she demanded, unable to keep a hint of panic from her tone.

'It's my turn,' he said.

Chapter Six

Emma took two faltering backward steps then swished about and made for the double doors. Her small hands lunged at heavy brass handles and frenziedly yanked, rattled. 'Open these doors! At once!' she hissed, lashing out at dense oak panels with a small clenched fist.

Approaching footsteps had her twisting about. Her head shook back, violently dislodging her bonnet to hang on unequal ribbons. One hand instinctively prevented it falling from tumbling, tawny hair; the other snaked behind to a cold metal knob and recommenced frantically jerking at it.

'Running away again, Emma? Where to this time?' Richard softly taunted.

'It's none of your concern!' Emma shrilled. Where was she going? Even if she had a destination, how on earth did she intend reaching it? She judged the city of Bath to be five miles distant from the estate of Silverdale. The nearest cottages she recalled passing must have been at least two miles away through that winding avenue of whispering silver-leaved trees.

She would walk back to Mrs Keene's lodging house, she intrepidly decided. But her fragile valour crumbled with the memory of her confrontation with this man in that parlour: she had brandished charges of molestation; he had disquietingly responded that she was a little early with such a complaint.

Her reckless stupidity that evening dominated her thoughts. Why on earth had she used empty threats and insults? Or scratched his face? Or brazenly led him to believe she was with child?

'Is your mother here? Or your other female relatives? Or was that lies, too?' was quaveringly flung at him. Then, twisting about to face the massive doors, her small palms slid on brass fittings too huge for her grip. As betraying heat pricked the backs of her eyes her head bowed. As the first wet squeezed through her lashes, a small foot frustratedly kicked out at impenetrable oak.

'Come here, Emma…' Richard's voice was as thick and soothing as honey, all trace of humour gone.

She faced him at the soft command, her sculpted little chin immediately coming up and small teeth clamping into her wobbly bottom lip. Silver eyes narrowed on her proud white face, seeking contact with her fugitive eyes, but they were now riveted to one side of him.

Richard pivoted on a heel to see Ross Trelawney on the stairs, tossing and catching a coin single-handedly in slick rhythm as he descended. On seeing Richard he pocketed the sovereign and walked over, smiling.

A dilating amber gaze slid between two powerfully virile men of similar height but contrasting looks. Emma swallowed and stiffened against the door, her mouth too arid to again demand if ladies were present. But then she already knew the answer: Silverdale seemed shrouded in a solitude that scorned her panic. Only servants and these two men were within its stately walls.

Three years ago Richard Du Quesne had had a reputation as a profligate. The fact that he had taken himself off abroad for a while in no way indicated reform. When in London together, he and Dashwood might be colleagues who frequented the same sordid haunts. Drunken orgies…young, friendless women abused then discarded…she knew of the whispers, if not the perpetrators, and had dismissed it as salacious scandalmongering… Her desperation to see Victoria had made her negligent. Momentarily she had lost sight of the calibre of heartless rake she was dealing with.

You *encouraged* him to think you a fallen woman! reverberated through her, making her quake on the spot. Why *should* he now bother maintaining a sham of consideration or respect? This stranger with the dark hair and wickedly laughing eyes is probably a rogue in the same mould, too… The hysterical suppositions streamed together, converging into a maelstrom of plausible horror threatening to engulf her. She was aware of a hand reaching for her and instinctively shrank back against the door, slapping frantically at long bronzed fingers.

Dark hands fastened on her arms, restricting them to her sides as Richard jerked her against him. 'Listen to me,' he soothed, yet with such a razored edge of steel to his voice that she actually did so. 'This is a good friend of mine, who is presently a house guest…as you are.' A glance flicked at Ross. 'Ross Trelawney, meet Miss Emma Worthington. Emma is a close friend of the Courtenays. She's recently arrived from London and is to honour us with her presence at Silverdale for a while.'

Ross prised free one of Emma's small hands from Richard's restraint and raised it gallantly to his lips. 'I'm very pleased to meet you, Miss Worthington. No doubt we shall see a deal of each other in the next few days…if I'm allowed.' He slanted a canny glance at his friend and despairingly shook his head. 'Not you, too, Dickie… I'm off to Bath for an hour or so…' drifted back as he strolled away to collect his hat and gloves.

Emma strained ineffectively against Richard's imprisonment. 'I wish to return to Bath. May I beg a ride with you, please, sir?'

'No, you may not,' Richard bit out quietly.

Ross hesitated and said amiably, 'Dickie, you can't keep the lady here against her will.'

'I don't intend to,' Richard whiplashed back, his eyes like shards of ice.

Emma sensed the atmosphere leadening with tension and knew she was the cause of it. She could depart with this stranger she didn't know at all, or stay with this man she knew a little…and distrusted a lot. He had lied to her…tricked her.

But she had lied to him…tricked him.

Richard's eyes locked onto hers, warning, threatening… He was allowing her to choose yet she knew if she rejected him at some time she would pay.

A terrified exhilaration caught a ragged breath in her throat as she stressed for Ross, 'I should be most *grateful* for a ride to Bath, sir.' Long fingers reflexively bit into her arms and then they were gone.

Ross grimaced, gesturing himself innocent of influencing her decision with spread hands. Noting his friend's murderous expression, his dark head lolled back and he mouthed an expletive at the ceiling.

'She stays here with me,' Richard said very reasonably, very coolly as he slowly paced to confront Ross in the centre of the marble hallway.

Emma watched in awe, absently rubbing at lingering phantom pressure on her arms. Minutes ago she had believed herself in peril of degradation; now, for some inexplicable reason, she knew she was not…and never had been.

Ross Trelawney didn't want her to share his carriage into town; he wanted harmony with his friend. But his decency obliged him to offer whilst hoping she would decline. And she had been so quick to brand her champion a rogue! Guilt and chagrin made her complexion flush rosily, yet the few, required words of reparation refused to relinquish her throat.

Shunning Richard Du Quesne's company in favour of a stranger she had never met before was an insult to his character, his integrity and his hospitality. He was utterly enraged: she could see wrath in every harsh, rigid angle of his bronze face, in his light, purposeful step as he approached Ross. He wanted to punish her; instead he would fight his friend to soothe his ego.

'Richard…be sensible…' A disarming smile and conciliatory tone from Ross elicited no response other than a vague elevation of dark brows.

'The blue silk was preferable, Diane. You look like a complete fright in that…that… What is it, in any case? Is it a pink…a purple? A poor choice, indeed, with those fractured veins on your nose.' A cultured female voice penetrated solid wood, mingling with the scraping of footsteps on stone.

Abruptly the double doors swung inwards, forcing Emma to hasten away from them. Two liveried footmen took up position in the wide aperture and a party of chattering people trooped through the wedge of sunlight.

Emma gawped at the sight of two stylish middle-aged women picking and flicking at a red bonnet as they proceeded into the hallway. The shorter of the two rotated it in her hands to aid inspection. Behind came a young couple: the woman blonde and pretty and the man also fair and tall. A small boy slouched at the woman's side, attempting to wriggle his hand free of hers.

The more regal-countenanced of the matrons abruptly batted away the hat as if bored with it. Her short companion smoothed the skewed crimson feathers then settled it atop her head.

'Ah, there you are Richard,' Miriam Du Quesne observed, spying her eldest son stationed in the centre of the sun-glossed marble flags. Her encompassing gaze took in his friend close by. 'Never say that you and Ross are about to bolt! I won't have it, you hear! Guests are due. The Petershams are to arrive at eight. Everyone is to sit down at nine. Now what is the time?'

Miriam gazed about and spied Emma hovering uncertainly in the shadows behind the door. She frowned, then comprehension widened her blue eyes. 'Oh, my dear… It's Miss Worthington, is it not?' A thin, pale hand flew in consternation to

her delicately rouged mouth. 'I completely forgot you were to
come earlier at six. Richard reminded me of it this morning,
too. How awful of me not to be here to greet you!' She rushed
to Emma and took her hands. 'I'm so sorry, my dear! We
would have been back from shopping sooner but my sister,
Diane, insisted on returning to the first ever shop we went into
to purchase a Parisian hat…monstrosity,' she breathed at
Emma with an expressive roll of her blue eyes.

'And then dear Jake—' a languid hand-flap indicated the
young boy '—took a tumble and skinned his knee.' Miriam
continued with her explanations. 'We were into the apothe-
cary's sorting through the potions. Then on to the confec-
tioner's to find a treat to cheer him up…and stop him howl-
ing.' Her lids fluttered, a tortured expression wrinkling her
smooth, powdered features.

The young invalid trotted to his uncle and solemnly displayed his wound. With a final glare at Ross, Richard swung
the boy into his arms, inspected the damage and gravely
praised his bravery. Jake settled his small bright head against
a powerful shoulder and sucked his thumb.

Emma looked at them together; the beautiful child she had
believed to be his bastard son was obviously his nephew.
Jumping so readily to a base conclusion was reprehensible and
added to the remorse already choking her. She had misjudged
so much! Even to thinking that he had lied about his female
relatives being in residence.

'Now come along with me, Miss Wor…may I call you
Emma?' Miriam asked. 'I feel as though I do know you. Every
time dear Victoria is here she talks of you. We'll do proper
introductions later, but for now…' Turning Emma by the arm,
she wagged an elegant, indolent finger at people, listing, 'My
younger son, Stephen, his dear wife Amelia and my sister,
Diane, and sweet little Jake, my grandson.' She indicated the
boy drowsing in his uncle's arms. 'Oh, stupid!' she chided
herself. 'I, of course, am Richard's mama. You may call me
Miriam.'

Emma moistened her lips, about to speak…say something, anything for her shock had receded enough for her to begin feeling uneasily dumb. But then she hadn't rallied quite enough intelligence to decide what to say…or do. And even if she had, slipping a word into her hostess's chatty monologue was not going to be easy. She drew a deep breath, managed a wavering smile and…

'The Courtenays are such a lovely couple. They visited me even when Dickie was abroad…oh, that's what they call him but then I expect you do, too, although I prefer Richard. And they brought that darling child especially to see me. Of course you are godmother to little Lucy and Richard is godfather, even though he missed the ceremony because of his beloved papa's ill health at that time. David, of course, is very fond of me. And I of him, rogue that he is…was, I should say. Such a change in a man I've never before witnessed! But then he *is* so in love…'

'I want to speak to you.' The clipped words sliced icily through Miriam's rambling discourse, making her cease, open-mouthed.

For a moment the hallway's occupants were united in silence. All eyes were riveted either on Richard's saturnine features or Emma's steadily heightening colour, for it became obvious from his relentless stare that he was addressing her rather than his gregarious mother.

'Now…' Richard purred into the crackling quiet as he set the child back onto the flags.

Ross exchanged an explicit, amused look with Stephen. With a hasty farewell, he was then through the door and on his way down the stone steps before Emma could launch even an appealing glance his way. With a perfunctory peck for his wife, Stephen was soon after him in the hope of catching up with some gossip.

Diane and Amelia drifted away to the mirror, apparently accustomed to the brusque dictates of the master of the house, and assisted each other in positioning the *chapeau* to its best advantage.

Miriam shrugged stiffly. 'He has his moods…just humour him, my dear, or he'll storm off out and not be back in time for the Petershams. I expect he wants to talk privately to you of your mutual friends.' A weary sigh preceded, 'He can be so churlishly impatient at times…'

Emma felt like laughing hysterically and stating that unforgivably rude was her opinion, but there was no time. Her elbow was gripped in firm fingers and she was being propelled across the hallway at some speed. She tried to carelessly shake herself free. On glancing back, Miriam beamed a smile and flicked a hand in a dismissive, eloquent way. *Just go along with him,* Emma read in the languid signal, and some mouthed encouragement, before Miriam, too, was at the mirror and it was her turn with the scarlet headgear.

As soon as they had rounded the corner into a seemingly endless stretch of sumptuously carpeted corridor, Emma wrenched free and backed against the watered-silk wall.

Richard made no attempt to touch her again but a glimmering silver gaze scorched down at her. After an aggressive moment molten copper eyes finally flinched from his, and he pointed along the hallway. 'Second door along on the left-hand side. You can walk or I can carry you…'

She looked scornfully up at him, about to dare him to try and do so with his mother barely yards away, but something in the sardonic enquiring lift of one eyebrow told her he would do as he pleased in his own home. She'd already gleaned as much: his mother might demand his punctuality at dinner, but she guessed it was entirely at his own whim whether he even graced them with his presence.

She flung herself away from the wall, marched proudly to the appointed doorway and halted with her chin tilted. He opened the door, mocked her with a bow and indicated she should precede him in.

The spacious library soared upwards and outwards and for

a moment held her quietly spellbound. She took a few paces within, her amber eyes clambering up library steps, sliding along polished shelves housing neatly ranged books within a mellow wood gallery then down the stairs on the opposite side of the room. She had never seen such a magnificent collection of books. It took her breath away and the fact didn't go unnoticed.

'Well, well,' Richard remarked drily, having allowed her a few moments of fascinated quiet. 'Had I known how a stocked library affects you, I would have had you brought into the house this way.' A bronzed finger flicked idly at large double doors that opened out onto a terrace.

Emma sensed her cheeks burn and her clinging gaze tore reluctantly from the tomes to study her feet. Then a cool, aloof gaze lifted to his dark face. 'I want to go home,' she stated.

'Home? You're ready to return to London?'

'No. I want to return to my lodgings.'

'You class that as home?' he asked quietly.

She turned away to hide her flushed confusion, for the fact that she subconsciously referred to such a lonely, soulless place as home was, indeed, disturbing. 'Temporarily…yes,' she murmured at some leather-bound spines.

He seemed about to speak then shoved his hands into his pockets and frowned at the ceiling. 'I'm sorry,' he said tightly. 'I shouldn't have misled you about David and Victoria being soon due. It wasn't actually a lie; I am expecting them in a fortnight. And I'm sorry I hadn't realised just how sincerely you despise me. I don't want to frighten you…quite the reverse.'

'I'm not frightened,' Emma choked fiercely but in a voice that was unevenly pitched.

'You were terrified,' Richard contradicted with a hollow laugh. 'If I'd known you seriously considered me capable of luring you here for some depraved purpose, I'd have arranged for my mother to collect and accompany you. But then I truly believed she would be about to greet you when you arrived. I apologise for that too.'

Emma sensed her own guilty regrets sharpen with his unexpected grace and honesty. She moistened her lips and raised topaz eyes to his face. He was watching her steadily, keeping his expression quite neutral.

'Why did you imply Victoria would be here?' she asked huskily, her disappointment keening in every word.

'Was there anything else I could have tempted you with? It was the only sure way of getting you here.'

'Why do you want me here?' she demanded in the same hoarse tone.

'I've told you…you need someone to care for you,' he returned impassively. 'You can't stay in that seedy hole, especially not in your delicate condition.'

Emma felt her face burn at the allusion to yet more of her deceit. It made her lash out defensively. 'And why should you worry about my accommodation? Why should you care at all? There's nothing in it for you…'

His eyes arrested hers as they attempted veering past. Her oblique reminder of spurning his proposition tautened the space between them.

Long, dusky lashes fringed low over silver eyes. 'Well, perhaps I'll let you entertain me in other ways. That acid tongue of yours for a start—maybe it sweetens when you sing.' A hand reached out so quickly she had no time for evasion. He raised slender, quivering fingers in his and looked at them. 'Perhaps these can set about an instrument more kindly than they do me.'

He abruptly released her and strolled to stare out into the garden. 'If you're going to fret over the cost of your keep here at Silverdale,' drifted back to her, 'just divert my mother's attention, and be a friend to Amelia; that'll repay me tenfold. They seem to have taken to you.'

'I think I shall like them, too,' Emma replied quietly, but her nervous thoughts were elsewhere. The mention of the cost of her keep reminded her she had in a pocket of her cloak two leaves of paper covered in Mrs Keene's sums. She was now loath to present him with that fraudulent account…and yet she had promised Mrs Keene she would.

She couldn't be sure how many of Lower Place's hungry residents had enjoyed fine dinners over four days courtesy of this man. She did know that in that time Mrs Keene had twice run out of meat and sitting space in her eating house. She also knew there was a grand total of ninety-five guineas at the bottom of a page followed by a flourishing signature.

'I…I have something for you.' She firmly withdrew the account with tremulous fingers and valiantly proffered it, watching with bated breath as his eyes leisurely descended first one, then the other page, without a flicker of expression.

'You have a good appetite, Emma, I see,' he eventually said. 'Over two hundred meals in four days. I'm not now sure I can afford to keep you here,' he solemnly added.

It was impossible to prevent the sudden rush of blood from staining her cheeks. 'I'm eating for two and get very hungry,' she returned flippantly, then floundered for she hated compounding her deceit. She hated feeling so wretchedly mean, too, after his chivalrous apology and offer of care and hospitality. 'I told you not to pay anything to Mrs Keene on my account. You insisted on interfering so you should take the consequences or…or Mrs Keene will sue you.'

'Will she?' he asked, with a flash of a white smile. 'How do you know?'

'I told her to. I told her how to go about it and that I would stand witness. I know how it's done.' Oh, she knew well enough! If there was one thing Emma had learned during twenty-seven years in her papa's wastrel company it was the process of being dunned.

He looked at the papers again and his smile transformed into a silent laugh. He had a team of the finest lawyers on retainer who would bury any such claim and counter-sue punitively if he let them…once they'd ceased guffawing.

'You will pay it, won't you?'

'What's it worth?'

He arrowed a sideways look at her and then frowned in regret. How many times had he heard that phrase? He'd responded spontaneously…as he always did on being presented with an outrageously extravagant bill by a woman he desired. And usually she was more than happy to suggest ways of repayment. Only this time, as he'd already been told, there was nothing in it for him. A brown hand flicked dismissively. 'My apologies. Just for a moment I forgot myself.' The papers were neatly folded and slipped into a pocket. 'Of course I'll settle it,' he graciously agreed, as though he'd never confused her with a mercenary harlot.

Emma burned in earnest, feeling more wretched than ever. Had she behaved in a way that a greedy, scheming mistress would? She believed he had, indeed, forgotten himself…and who she was. The money hadn't been spent on her own account! she wanted to shout. It had benefited people much worse off. She shouldn't have done it! Now she felt…

'I'm sorry,' she whispered. 'I shouldn't have done it. It was…it started as a joke. I just wanted Mrs Keene's other lodger to be treated as I was and then…there are many people who live in that area much hungrier than I have ever been and I was annoyed at you…'

She was unaware he had moved away from the window and approached her until a dark hand lifted into her line of vision. It drifted to her face, touching with just enough pressure to tilt it to his. 'Well, I'm not annoyed at you. I admire your philanthropy. I will pay it. But I don't want to hear any more of it. Now what's that worth?' he said huskily as grey eyes merged with amber. 'I'd say it must be worth at least…' He deliberately hesitated, looking thoughtful, then, as she flushed, concluded innocently, 'A truce?'

Her tongue-tip moistened her lower lip and she was aware of him unwaveringly watching its movement. Her soft lips immediately pressed together as though she could conceal them.

'I said a truce, Emma,' he said wryly, releasing her face with a trailing stroke of a finger. He extended a hand. 'Shake on it.'

After a momentary hesitation pale, slender fingers lightly curled about long bronzed ones. She gave him a wavering smile and, on doing so, realised it was the first time since their reunion in Bath that she had smiled at him with friendliness rather than sarcasm. Even three years ago in London she couldn't remember directing an amiable smile his way. Her fingers fluttered within his, endeavouring to tactfully withdraw, and finally he allowed it.

She backed away a few steps, hunting in her mind for some bland conversation as a prelude to escaping. 'The nickname Mrs Keene used…silver squire…is it because of how you look?' Emma blurted out chattily.

'How I look?' he echoed with a smile.

'Your blond hair and grey eyes…' She rattled off her observation so fast and quietly, she hoped he would dismiss it and change the subject, but his amusement increased.

As though savouring her revealingly intimate remark, he allowed a silent, lingering moment before teasing very gently, 'You've looked at me long enough to notice I have grey eyes? I'm amazed!'

Emma flushed in earnest, frowning through the window. All she'd intended was a little civil dialogue. Why could she never get anything right? As she was about to hurtle from the room and devil take pleasantries, he came to her rescue.

'It's been used by locals for generations. I've always assumed it grew out of the Du Quesne's involvement in silver mining in Devon. And the house was named after the avenue of silver trees. But, now you mention it, there has been a preponderance of blond-haired, grey-eyed baronets in the family…several of us with sterling qualities…'

She nodded quickly, hoping he would mock her no more

on the subject, wondering how she could escape to his mother and thence, she hoped, to a chamber and rest. She felt drained and in need of solitude and the opportunity to sleep for a while.

Recalling Miriam's preoccupation with dinnertime, she exploded quietly, 'I won't keep you. I expect you were going out with your friend. Your mother will be upset should you return late to dine with your guests.'

'I'm not going out,' he demurred, an air of latent amusement still about him.

The thought of Ross Trelawney's gallantry made her dart a look at Richard. Would they now avoid each other because of the antagonism she had fired between them? She had almost caused them to fight! The memory was simultaneously shameful and oddly thrilling. Even in her youthful heyday, no man had ever seemed desperate to retain the pleasure of her company. Of course, Richard was simply minding his masculine pride by insisting she stay with him. She might distract him with her gaucheness but she was sure the primary reason he kept her close was onerous duty to David Hardinge.

A few days ago he had punished her with a kiss then dismissed her as though she bored him. Today, she had nearly caused havoc in his stately vestibule, fearing a dowdy spinster of twenty-seven could incite him to act the lecher in his own home. Considering the circumstances calmly now, and the fact of his pretty young mistress housed in the neighbourhood, she knew her ridiculous arrogance should have provoked hilarity; instead she cringed. Aware that he was observing her pink-faced pensiveness, she garbled out, 'I...I hope that you and Mr Trelawney will not be... I didn't mean to cause you... That is, I should hate there to be friction between you,' she finally settled on.

'Ross and I are used to a little...er...friction between us.'

Uncertain she had correctly understood the subliminal message, she ventured, 'You have fought Ross before?'

'Oh, yes,' he said with a grin.

'Over…over a woman?' she audaciously asked, but her inquisitiveness was too great for indelicacy to matter.

'Oh, no,' he said with a gentle smile.

Emma's wide glossy gaze was on him, thoughtfully assessing the lean angles of his handsome dark face. She recalled Victoria saying that David would have been killed abroad, in the war, but for this man fighting alongside him. David owed Dickie his life, Victoria had gravely told her.

Richard stared back, feeling the heat in his groin rage beneath her liquid golden gaze. His long lashes dropped low over his eyes. God, she was captivating, with those beautiful doe-eyes and fawn hair wisping untidily about her face. Her bonnet was still askew about her shoulders and he wanted to remove it and the drab cloak that obscured the slender lines of her body. But he knew if he touched her now he'd break the spell. She'd bolt, or lash out at him like some skittish little creature.

He inwardly groaned his frustration. The only way he could get her to relax, to look straight at him without wariness or disgust but with frank interest, was to discuss the various brawls he and Ross had participated in over the many years of their acquaintance.

'What did you fight over?' Emma asked almost brightly.

'What over?' Richard echoed huskily. 'Well…there was the time he cheated at cards. The time I did. The time he wagered on copper prices rising then reduced his mines' output to ensure they did. Then there was the time I did something similar with my mines and he was furious not to recognise the plot. There was the time he took my Highflyer out without asking and turned it over then brought it back…over several trips…' He hesitated, smiling at her engrossed attention. 'Do you want more instances?'

'Are there more?'

'Undoubtedly…if I care to set my mind to it.'

'Who wins these fights?'

'I think…at last count…it was about eight to five in my favour. One of those he claims against me I disallow, though,

Emma,' he said with studied gravity. 'He waited until I was… er…a little inebriated before throwing the first punch. Very ungentlemanly. Besides, since I turned thirty and became a baronet a little more decorum is called for. We try to settle our differences with dignified discussion…initially,' he added on a slow smile.

She choked a little laugh, her eyes as warm and honeyed as cognac pools in her creamy complexion.

'Today, the fear of losing a truly unique woman to him, made me entirely disallow dignified discussion,' he admitted huskily.

Her smile fled. 'There's really no need to humour me.' She fiercely rebuffed his quiet compliment. 'I'm now quite composed. I'm also twenty-seven and no longer impressed by flattery. I apologise for causing a rift between you and your friend. And thank you for your hospitality which I should like to accept for a few days until I can implement my plans…my private plans,' she amended coolly. 'May I go now, please? I should very much like to freshen myself.' She walked quickly to the door yet hesitated by it, unsure if he would prevent her leaving.

Slow footfalls had her nervously removing her straggling bonnet and unsteady fingers winding the ribbons neatly into coils.

'Why do you keep reminding me how old you are, Emma? Do you think I forget? Do you think I'm likely to bother with flattery? Me?' he taunted. 'A callous lecher with money and sin enough to purchase sordid pleasure? Why, there's no need for me to notice you at all, is there?'

Emma flung herself about and glared up at him with sparking topaz eyes. 'Good. The less you notice me, the better I shall like it!' she choked.

He smiled but no humour warmed his icy eyes. 'Three years ago I brooded over what it was I did to make you dislike me so. I always treated you with respect and courtesy. Now I'm more inclined to think that was the problem. It wasn't anything

I did, it was what I didn't do.' A hand moved towards her and she defensively recoiled. He watched her, his mouth slanting mockingly as his touch skimmed past to open the door.

'I'm older…wiser now, Emma—not nearly so easily affronted…or deterred. As for your private plans, you'll have the opportunity of sharing those with me later,' he softly stated. 'Wait here for a moment while I find my mother. She'll show you to your room,' he concluded, closing the door quietly behind him.

Emma stared at the wide mahogany panels, feeling absurd tears burning, stinging at her eyes, her throat at his infuriatingly calm authority. She marched to the nearest bookshelves, scrubbing a furious hand across her dewy eyes. Jerking a book from the shelf, she stamped to a chair, sat down and sightlessly turned pages while she did his bidding.

Chapter Seven

'*Merde! Merde! Merde!*'

Neither the butler nor the maid understood French but from Madame Dubois's raucous tone they knew the recently received note contained no welcome news for her but some most excellent tidings for them.

The elderly butler jigged, stiff-legged, on the hallway flags. The young maid looked less jovial and he was sympathetic: he could now disappear below stairs, and spread the word; she, poor thing, would no doubt take the brunt of *madame's* rancour for a few days more.

He shook his old head to himself. They rose from nothing to the heights and couldn't accept that eventually they would finish between the two. A very agreeable middle ground it was, too, by his reckoning.

The silver squire was renowned for his generosity: all departed, testing the coach's axles with trunks full of fine new clothes, decked with jewels. Their final, flouncing descent down the elegant steps of number three South Parade was often in a blinding flash.

None went willingly. The pattern was always the same. A brief note, a brief visit, a copious amount of weeping and pleading and within a day or so they were gone. Thankfully this foreign one had been here but a few months. The shortest stay of all that he could recall. That really made him smile as he made for the kitchens on his bowed legs.

Yvette Dubois screwed the note in her fist then raised it to her mouth and screamed at it. She immediately uncrumpled it and reread it but there was nothing ambiguous in the few lines. Pacing between window and table, she mulled over recent events while absently toying with a gold and ruby bracelet on her wrist, and malice and retribution slowly dried her tear-sparkling blue eyes.

Richard had bought the bracelet for her a few days ago and had seemed happy enough that afternoon to receive her amorous thanks for it…until he spied that drab woman cloaked in tan. The little mouse had run off without being interviewed and Richard had followed almost immediately. She must mean something to him. There was no other explanation for him staring at her, or later returning in the foulest mood imaginable, to demand to know where she lodged. Yvette's rosebud lips tightened indignantly as she recalled him impatiently repulsing all her erotic little tricks. Nothing would make him stay and he had not visited since.

A blonde ringlet was twirled about a plump finger, then yanked at in sheer peevishness. To be discarded for a woman prettier was insufferable…to be discarded for one so plain was *abominable*! An insult! In return she would insult him! Hurt him! Perhaps even win him back…she slyly calculated.

Yes…Richard might be very vexed if she played with that lascivious-eyed little brother of his. She could lure the panting cub tomorrow! On the occasions she had seen Stephen his limpet blue eyes had been so full of lewd imaginings, even when his pretty little wife was close by his side. Coyly, she had acknowledged his interest with just enough encouragement to sustain and whet his appetite. He might not be as handsome or as wealthy and influential as his big brother, but she was realist enough to accept that such a man as Sir Richard

Du Quesne happened along but rarely. It made losing him so soon the more infuriating.

Since her sixteenth birthday, when her father had sold her to an elderly, wealthy merchant, Yvette had been pleasuring gentlemen. Far from being disgusted, she had relished her first lover's slow, sensual attention. He had taught her much: groomed her for the bedchamber and the drawing room, fashioning a quality courtesan his peers would envy. He'd tutored her in English, music, dancing, even imparted a little knowledge of cultural disciplines so she could act with refinement at supper before performing bawdily at bedtime. Reluctantly he had passed her to his son with his business when his health had failed and he had no further use for sex or commerce other than as a spectator. His lusty son had been happy to show off the savage energy he introduced to Yvette's repertoire, until his marriage and his heiress wife's prohibition on all shenanigans had resulted in Yvette being banished.

She had been keen for adventure, and a kindly ancient mariner had agreed to bring her sailing to England with him. At Bristol Yvette had seen Richard Du Quesne, just disembarked from foreign parts, and had been immediately smitten. For days she had inveigled to hook him, finally coaxing her sea captain to engineer an introduction. Still he'd been impervious to her overtures until her sailor friend had endorsed her story that she had been one family's hetaera for nine years and was not some sly jade. After two nights of momentous passion that had rendered her French lovers fumbling novices, she had managed to coax Richard to take her with him to Bath.

She'd been certain he was as enamoured as she was, for no indifferent man would make love in such a way. But within a week she'd realised that he was unlike any man she had known: Richard could be an attentive, expert lover one minute and a cool, ruthless stranger the next. He might give her *incroyable* pleasure for hours at night but he would never otherwise give her much of his time at all and he would never at any time give her his heart. So she had decided to settle for his child. Such an upstanding aristocrat would always make provision for his bastards and thereby their mothers. Yet even that he'd denied her. The sheets or her belly had received his seed; in the throes of passion, when she was spent, he'd retained absolute control. The fact that she'd believed he might not had seemed to amuse him.

And now…now she was to be returned to Bristol or France—the decision was hers, he had written. Well, she had chosen. She wanted a Du Quesne for a lot longer. He would be protective of his brother…of his sister-in-law. She could read the signs that he was paternalistic. She picked up his note from the table then flicked it away with careless fingers. He would come to his senses. The little brown mouse would soon loose her hold on him when he discovered his brother was receiving the brand of exotic passion at which she excelled. She flounced happily into a chair to write a letter of her own.

'May I come in?'

'Please do.'

'We didn't have a chance to talk earlier. I've just come to welcome you properly and see if there's anything you need.' Amelia grimaced guiltily. 'That scarlet bonnet really is the most hideous thing, and purchasing it made us so late back to Silverdale to welcome you.'

Emma smiled in acceptance of the oblique apology. She had been shown to this luxurious guest chamber by a servant toting her bag and a relentlessly gregarious Miriam. Having snoozed for a while in a comfortable armchair, lulled by a view of verdant landscape that stretched away as far as the eye could see, she now felt a little refreshed. She glanced at the tea-tray. She had left all virtually untouched: even those delicious little cakes had not tempted her to stay awake.

'Would you like me to find you a maid to assist you in your toilette?'

'No, but thank you, anyway. Miriam kindly offered earlier to send me her maid.' Emma indicated her few gowns draped over a chair. 'I'm travelling light and have nothing suitable for dining in distinguished company.'

'You are coming down to dinner, though?' Amelia queried with a frown.

'No. I shall eat here, if I may, and retire early. A headache too, I'm afraid…' It was the truth! It wasn't cowardice born out of a very great desire to avoid another confrontation with the master of Silverdale. Her head did feel heavy and she had no stylish gown with her.

Her tawny gaze lingered on Amelia, a stab of something akin to envy tightening her stomach, and that worried her for she had never coveted other ladies' looks or attire. Every drape and shimmer of cornflower satin highlighted Amelia's fair colouring and blue eyes and clung with an alluring elegance to her curvaceous figure.

Hastening towards the gowns on the chair, Amelia sorted through the dull, serviceable garments, tactfully silent until exclaiming, 'This is lovely!' She drew forth sheeny amber fabric. 'The colour is so unusual. It must suit you very well,' she said, swishing about and holding up the gown while glancing between it and Emma's autumn-gold hair and eyes. 'You have the most unique colouring, Emma…'

Emma felt her face heating. It was the second time today she had been termed unique. From this young lady she readily accepted the description was complimentary. Her eyes and hair were a strange colour; her mother had often told her so, with other disparaging remarks on the dismal lack of pink in her sallow complexion. It had always concluded with how stupidly obstinate she was in continuing to shun the rouge pot.

Richard Du Quesne said she was unique and she knew that meant he found her quaint. She was an engaging little oddity to divert him for a while. She might only have seen the one, but she knew she was nothing like the women he chose to consort with: far too thin, and plain, and dowdily dressed. Well, she'd no ambition to conform to his ideals, of that she was quite sure!

The memory of their skirmish in the library was shoved to the back of her mind then immediately retrieved with a malicious little smile. Their truce hadn't lasted long and she was glad. And if he thought for one moment he could bully her into disclosing her plans for the future…or details of her lover… *What lover?* Fingers were pressed to her mouth to contain a silent burst of laughter. She no longer felt guilty about deceiving him over that either. How dared he talk to her of his…*his sordid pleasure*, as though she were some lowlife trollop? He had no right to feel superior! No right to patronise her as though she were some insecure *ingénue* either. And how dared he insinuate she was craving his hateful attention?

But then, his conceit didn't surprise her: she knew men with such power and wealth who were continually fawned over considered themselves quite irresistible. Well, she found him utterly resistible and was perfectly capable of organising her own life, as he'd discover when she married Matthew. She was confident Matthew wanted her as his wife and as mother and tutor for Rachel and Toby. More for the latter than the former, she knew, but it no longer piqued her as sharply as once it had…

Forcing herself out of her wistfulness, she gave Amelia a smile. 'Unfortunately, that gown is badly creased, but it is a favourite…' It did suit her, too. She could clearly recall wearing it on the first ever occasion she and Richard had met—not that he was likely to remember any of it .

As she stroked the iridescent silk, her mind wandered to a soirée in London that she and Victoria had attended with her parents. She recalled their overbearing hostess, Petra Blair, and her blonde daughters preening and presiding in their hot, stuffy salon. The very welcome, very unexpected arrival of the *ton*'s most charismatic and eligible bachelors had caused a definite stir of excitement amongst the ladies present. Only she and Victoria had been dismayed by Richard and David's abrupt appearance. Discreetly they had whisked themselves off to the cool sanctuary of the Blairs' small conservatory to devise a plan to slip away home.

Emma smiled nostalgically: David had had no intention of letting Victoria escape him quite so easily that evening. In order to aid and abet his friend in his amatory pursuit, Richard had ambushed her…and she had insulted him…and thus the pattern of their very brief, very prickly relationship three years ago had been set.

'We can find Mrs Braithwaite; she'll arrange for your dress to be pressed,' drifted through to Emma's consciousness. 'Silverdale's housekeeper will make light work of these creases. She's also a marvel with her pills and potions. She'll find something for your headache.'

Amelia slipped an arm through Emma's and led her towards the door, crumpled amber silk draped over her other arm. 'You seem preoccupied, Emma. Have you troubles?' Amelia asked sympathetically.

'Well…a few, I suppose,' Emma admitted, with a nervous golden glance at the pretty woman. 'As everyone does, of course,' she dismissed lightly.

'Yes…' Amelia said on a sigh.

Emma looked keenly at Amelia; her attractive features seemed momentarily wan and drawn. A pang of guilt at her selfish introspection made her hastily say, 'I suppose you are anxious about your little son. Is his cut knee healing well?'

'Oh, yes,' Amelia reassured her, but with a melancholy smile. 'When married, one's children are sometimes the least of one's problems…' More cheerfully she added, 'Come…I daren't return downstairs with the news that you shall not be dining with us all. Richard already has a face like thunder.'

Emma felt the more determined to eat in her room with that news and was about to say so, but Amelia was already into the corridor and busily urging her along. 'We can call in at the nursery and see Alice.' With a throb of maternal pride, she explained, 'Alice is my beautiful little daughter. She is now four months old and really is the most darling thing.

Stephen dotes on her, as he does his beloved Jake. Would you like to see the baby?'

'Oh, I'd love to,' Emma said simply. 'Thank you.'

His mother was matchmaking! Emma realised.

A surreptitious glance slid from beneath dusky lashes and slanted across glossed candlelit mahogany to where Miriam sat at the head of the table. She appeared at her elegant best in a lavender silk gown with her pale gold hair elegantly coiffured. Seated next to her was Squire Petersham. Opposite the squire was his wife, Susan, and seated between, at either side of the long grand dining table, was the rest of the Du Quesne family, Ross Trelawney and then the Petershams' daughter Veronica, positioned close to their host and opposite Emma who had been allocated a seat close to him too, much to her chagrin.

Aware of Veronica's dark scrutiny, Emma managed a small smile. It went unreturned. Veronica's attention was already sliding away to hover on the man seated at the head of the table, opposite his mother.

Emma had but briefly spoken to Veronica in the drawing room as polite introductions were made. Then Stephen Du Quesne had gallantly offered both his wife and Emma an arm and sedately led them into dinner. With barely two sentences having passed between Veronica Petersham and herself she knew she didn't care for this young lady. She judged her to be nineteen or twenty and she was certainly pretty. In fact she had similar colouring to her dear friend Victoria: her skin was pale, her hair and eyes dark, and her scarlet gown was a very effective foil for her colouring. But she had nothing like Victoria's ethereal beauty or sweetness of countenance or nature. Her features had a hard, sharp edge and her eyes, unless trained on the gentlemen, were cold and watchful.

Good! Emma thought maliciously. I hope his mother succeeds in pairing the two of them! They make an excellent couple! Very deserving of each other!

She avoided looking at the male of the prospective match although she knew she often came under his study, even if he had barely spoken to her. Perhaps he finds me ill turned out for such a grand banquet, Emma sourly mused. All the other ladies were richly bejewelled and had made elaborate toilettes. Her thick, glossy hair was simply twisted into a neat chignon and her amber silk gown was a plain empire-line style. Her only jewellery was a pair of modest silver and topaz eardrops.

Well, she didn't want to be at Silverdale! And a sandwich in her room would have suited her very well, she proudly thought. She glanced down at the delicious mixed viands on her plate. She had lost count of the number of courses served so far. Her hunger now sated, she simply tasted morsels from each dish from curiosity and politeness, leaving the majority of it untouched. Her thoughts turned uneasily to the residents of Lower Place she had so recently lived amongst, and what they would think of such sumptuous, endless fare. Or what her parents would think, for that matter. Their family meals at Rosemary House had dwindled to little more than reheated leftovers. The thought of her parents and how they did brought with it that stabbing cramp to twist at her insides. With each day now that passed the necessity to contact them, if only to let them know she was safe, tore at her conscience.

'Would you allow me to show you some of Silverdale's grounds tomorrow, Miss Worthington?' A low, well-modulated voice addressed her from the opposite side of the table, cutting into her guilty thoughts.

Through a gap in the bank of shimmering candelabra, Emma returned Ross Trelawney's smile. 'Thank you, sir. I should like that,' she quietly replied.

Laughing dark eyes strayed sideways to their host. Ross sipped from his crystal goblet then gestured his pleasure at her consent with it. 'Good. The Italian garden and gazebo are quite a pretty sight. Then the lake and summer house are well worth a visit. As are the knot garden and the maze, of course. We could take a picnic…' he suggested softly, intimately. Their conversation was exclusive, all the other diners seemingly engaged in their own cosy chats. Ross turned his dark head towards the blond man seated at the head of the table, smiling at a bubbling Veronica. 'Perhaps Richard might like to join us?' Ross whispered across the flickering candle-flame with an air of studied enquiry. 'Shall we ask him?' Without awaiting a reply he dismissed, 'No; we ought not to trouble him. Such a courteous chap would feel obliged to agree when he'd rather attend to business without distraction. I recall now he has much to do…'

Their host dropped his knife back to his plate with such a resounding clatter that it masked the curse ejected through his even white teeth. All conversation abruptly ceased and all eyes swivelled, startled, towards him. 'Why don't you and I take a stroll outside now, while I do have the time and don't feel courteous?' Richard bit out with an unwavering glimmering glare at Ross.

'Oh, not now, thanks, Dickie. I've not finished eating.' A smile of immense charm accompanied the remark, directed at the table as a whole.

'Later, then…I insist…' whipped back in a purr.

'Oh, well, if you're desperate for some air, of course I'll accompany you, old friend,' Ross agreed, all innocent affability. 'I must say, you look a little overheated,' he mentioned, with a concerned peer along the table at Richard's icy features.

'I should like a little air later,' Veronica trilled into the conversation, glancing at Richard through her lashes.

Ross shrugged easily. 'There you are…a far fairer companion. But I think, Miss Petersham, I shall challenge him for the pleasure of your company.' Ross treated the young lady on his left to a suave smile. 'You can tell me all about your visit to Lyme Regis last week. Was there seabathing?' He inclined close and Veronica dimpled and fluttered her lashes.

Emma sensed the side of her face prickling, burning. She slanted a glance sideways and her eyes clashed immediately with a threatening steely gaze. She stiffened indignantly. It wasn't her fault if his friend chose to tease him in company. Her chin tilted, prompting a twitch of amusement to soften his mouth, then he turned away as Stephen addressed him.

Emma also looked away…for all of a second or two, and then her eyes slid back. She might hate him but she couldn't deny he looked wonderfully handsome with his lengthy blond hair glinting silver in the candlelight.

Her appraisal dropped to a hand resting idly on the table. Lash-screened eyes travelled over long, well-shaped dark fingers to a cambric shirt-cuff. It ruffled starkly white against his tanned skin. Her covert observation took in a sleeve of charcoal superfine wool then a silver silk cravat set with a fiery diamond before reaching a shirt collar as razor-sharp as the bronze cheekbone above it. Tawny eyes again flitted to his hair, trailing lengthily over linen…then swerved to silver eyes to find them watching her. She spontaneously burned with heat and dropped her cutlery, much in the way he had done moments before. Cringing at the clatter, then again at the ensuing quiet, she managed a small apologetic smile for everyone.

Ross dropped her a discreet wink before resuming conversation with Veronica. A general chatter recommenced about the table. It was only her host's attention that stayed, making her squirm uncomfortably in her seat.

'And I think you look very nice, too,' she heard him eventually say, gently amused.

Emma felt her blush increase and was never more grateful for flickering candlelight mellowing her complexion. 'I thought we had established that I find flattery boring,' she rebuffed acidly, turning away.

'I thought we had established that I never bother using it.' His eyes skimmed the light swell of her petite breasts beneath her gown's square neckline. 'That dress always did suit you. The colour matches your eyes.'

Sheer astonishment that he should remember it made her face him again and her clamped lips involuntarily soften.

Reading her thoughts, he choked a laugh. 'Oh, I remember

it all, Emma. Every meeting, every insult. You called me a novice that first evening. I'd still be interested to know exactly what experience you think I lack. I'm keen to prove myself proficient...' Richard watched her feline eyes sidle from his to ensure no one was listening then creep back to pounce.

'Perhaps a little discipline in restraint and moderation might benefit initially,' she hissed angrily, yet feeling guilty too at those three-year-old slanders and wishing that he had forgotten them all.

'I'm sure you'd make an excellent tutor in restraint and moderation, Emma. Finding out might be pleasurable enough.'

'Indeed,' Emma jibed softly. 'And you might become a model of propriety overnight!'

'Well, it might take several nights...unless *you're* very proficient at discipline,' he taunted huskily. He smiled at her blank-eyed concentration as she scrambled in her innocence for his meaning. As she guessed his intention to be ribald insult, her face tipped down and she glared at her plate.

'I also seem to recall you leading me to believe that you were practically betrothed.' He spared her blushing confusion and changed the subject. 'Your mother was soon expecting an offer for you, you said.'

'My mother was always soon expecting an offer for me,' she snapped in a low breath. 'She was ceaselessly optimistic of becoming some man's mother-in-law. It never mattered who he was.'

'I wish I'd known. Perhaps I might have obliged her.'

Emma stared at him with huge shining eyes. 'At times I very much hate you,' she whispered.

'Why? Because I tell you that with a little encouragement I might have offered for you three years ago?'

'That's a lie!' she choked while stabbing viciously at morsels of food on her plate. 'You had no real interest in me then!'

'And that lack of real interest forced me along to your birthday celebration, I suppose.'

'David forced you along. It was obvious he was only attending to pursue Victoria and obvious you came along to keep me well out of his way as usual.'

'David wasn't due to attend. He'd decided to change tactics with Victoria. He was going to play hard to get and stay away. I knew he'd never manage it, but then again I didn't expect him to turn up at close to midnight, either.'

'Why would you come on your own...for no reason?' Emma scoffed.

'I've no idea, Emma,' Richard said very drily. 'I'll own it certainly wasn't a habit of mine to attend young ladies' birthday tea parties.'

Emma stared, scanning his dark face for falsehood, for cunning. Was this how he set about trapping his prey? She had no experience of men but she suspected it was: flattery...a sham of liking and interest...offers of protection and financial help. She'd experienced all that now. He believed her so grateful and gullible, she'd yield like all the rest.

'You've lost your hearty appetite tonight, I see.' Richard cut smoothly into her frantic suppositions. His fingers toyed with silver cutlery and his eyes rested on her virtually untouched plate of food. 'And I've made a point of arranging for fifty courses...just to ensure you were adequately filled.'

Brilliant eyes shot to his face. 'You've not!' she whispered, horrified.

'Fifty dinners a night, wasn't it, by Mrs Keene's reckoning?'

Emma sent a flick of a glance about the table but everyone seemed happily engaged. 'Tell me that's a joke!' she squealed furiously, her glossy golden eyes shielded by thick inky lashes.

'It's a joke,' he said softly.

Emma looked up slowly, thankfully.

'Of course it's a joke. We're under truce at the moment... aren't we?'

She blinked and looked away.

'Aren't we, Emma?' he softly demanded. 'We shook on it, didn't we?'

Emma remained silent.

'Say yes, Emma, or I'll call in the remaining courses,' he said to the ceiling, with a husky laugh.

'Now you've monopolised Emma quite enough, Richard,' Miriam called, sliding a look at the matron seated on her left.

Susan Petersham had her gimlet eye resting on this unexpected rival to her daughter. Their eligible host seemed to be paying her unusual attention, even if she was nowhere near as modishly turned out as her own dear Veronica. Nowhere near as young either, she guessed, with a satisfied sniff. And that hair? Heavens, what sort of shade was it? Nowhere near as richly brunette as Veronica's elaborately teased tresses, that was obvious.

As though guessing her neighbour's shrewd imaginings, Miriam explained, 'Oh, Miss Worthington and Richard have very dear mutual friends: Viscount and Viscountess Courtenay, you know,' she informed, with an emphatic wag of her fair head. 'They are both godparents to the Courtenays' darling little girl and of course they have so much news to catch up with when they get together. It's a while since you saw Emma, is it not, Richard?'

'Indeed it is…too long,' he returned levelly.

Miriam widened her blue eyes and nodded meaningfully at Susan Petersham. 'Emma lives with her parents in Cheapside as a spin…single lady of educated pursuits. We had a wonderful chat together earlier. She has told me she loves to read. And so do I. Oh, yes, I love a romantic novel, as Emma does. We share a favourite author in Miss Austen, you know, and a favourite work in *Pride and Prejudice*. Anyway, Emma is visiting Bath and, of course, had to make a point of seeing Richard whilst here. They are such old friends…'

'Are your parents here with you, Miss Worthington?' Susan Petersham sliced through Miriam's speech.

'No, ma'am,' Emma ventured quietly. Heavens! What was she to say when asked whom she was with? It was highly irregular for a gentlewoman to be travelling alone…even one of advanced years. She had wondered why the Du Quesne family had so far made so little of it: the subject of her lone status had hardly been broached at all. After some silent debate she guessed it was because Richard had decreed no questions were to be asked. And she rather guessed that what Richard said was law at Silverdale.

'Not even your mother is accompanying you?' Susan Petersham interrogated.

'My mother is not well enough to travel at present, ma'am,' Emma returned quietly. And that was the truth! When she had quit Cheapside, her mother had been barely able to stir herself from bed in the mornings.

'Miss Worthington is in Bath specifically at my invitation. When the Courtenays visit, there shall be a happy reunion.' Richard cut into the conversation with such an air of icy finality that Susan Petersham nervously fiddled with her ringlets.

'Well…quite…' she was heard to murmur.

Into the ensuing silence came plaintively, 'I'd love to walk to the lake with the flares alight, Richard.' Amelia looked appealingly at her brother-in-law. 'Might we do that? It's always so romantic.'

'That's a good idea, Dickie,' Ross chipped in laughingly, and the atmosphere immediately lightened.

Stephen pulled a face. 'It's a bit chilly now, my dear,' he moaned to his shining-eyed wife. 'Besides, gentlemen like a cigar and a tipple and a chat after dinner…'

'Go and ask Simmons to have them lit, so you can take your wife for a romantic stroll,' Richard directed firmly at his brother, with a nod at the door. As Stephen scowled, he returned him a smile, and continued looking at him until his brother moodily shrugged himself up from the table.

'I'd love to go, too,' Veronica announced, glancing coyly at Richard.

'Well, you shall, you shall,' Miriam said, exchanging a sly

look with Susan Petersham. 'You wanted the air earlier, Richard. You must accompany Veronica,' Miriam decreed.

Ross shoved back his chair. 'I insist,' he said in a husky growl, 'that Miss Petersham allows me that privilege.'

Veronica visibly shivered beneath his intent dark gaze and rose, trance-like to stand close to him. They slowly strolled arm in arm from the table, Veronica's dark eyes widening on the piratical face smiling down at her.

Emma glanced at Richard to see a large, spanning hand in the process of soothing his brow. Beneath shielding fingers, he was laughing silently. He tipped back his head to smile at the wavering light on the ceiling.

'I expect you're going to say you'd rather jump in the lake than walk to it with me,' he remarked exclusively for her and with laughter still apparent in his tone.

'At last…something to admire about you, Sir Richard!' Emma gushed with mock wonderment. 'How marvellously perceptive you really are.' She dropped her napkin back to the table, ready to rise to her feet. She could finally escape to her room. Yet she felt ashamed of her insolence: he had so recently rescued her from the probing and prying of Susan Petersham.

The other diners were already away from the table, talking of fetching shawls and cloaks.

'Do come along, Richard, and you, my dear,' Miriam directed over her shoulder at them. 'I shall have Simmons fetch you one of my cloaks, Emma, and save you a trip to your chamber.' She was gone from the room before Emma had managed to draw in breath to offer up the excuses of fatigue and headaches.

'Well, is it romantic?'

Emma looked about at the shadowy swaying foliage. She gazed out over a sheet of rippling black silk patched with yellow, listening to the gentle lapping of water beneath the boarding she stood upon, the soporific rustling of a million leaves. Turning her head, she gazed back the way they had come. A pathway illuminated by parallel breeze-lengthened flares pointed up to the house, its honey aura enhanced by sconces aglow on its majestic walls. The hood of her cloak fell to her shoulders as she tipped back her head to marvel at a sky of velvet blue studded with glittering stars. Tepid wind stirred her hair, smoothed her face. She just couldn't lie. 'Yes,' she said simply. 'It is…'

Richard smiled and nodded, still staring out over the lake.

The other night-time strollers were some way off, keeping to the formal paths, whereas Richard had led her onto the landing stage where several small boats were moored for trips out to a large, densely wooded island. Emma squinted at what appeared no more than an immensely ragged floating boulder. Beneath her feet she glimpsed the hypnotic rocking of deep water.

'I imagine you had fine times here as a child,' she said pensively. 'Fishing and boating and swimming.'

'Very fine,' he agreed. 'David and I spent many summers without moving far from here. Sometimes it was days before we ventured back indoors, and then only for more supplies. We'd camp, shoot, sleep on that island.'

Emma gazed up at his shadowy profile fringed by strands of pale hair. It was so easy to imagine two small boys, one very dark, one very fair, grubby and dishevelled, with fishing lines, smelling of woodsmoke and sporting scraped knees. 'It must have been wonderful. I should have liked to be a boy…'

He choked a laugh and shot a look at her.

'Why is that funny?' she demanded haughtily.

'It's not…' he said wryly. 'Especially for a man who likes you as a girl.'

Emma disdainfully turned her head away but admitted soulfully, 'I should especially have liked a brother or sister. You were very fortunate. Even when David was not visiting you here, you had Stephen…a companion to play with.'

'David and I were inseparable…closer than kin. We were

at school together or we were here at Silverdale or at his home, Hawkesmere, together.' He paused. 'I feel quite guilty that I spent so little time with Stephen. But then he is seven years younger than me. When I was thirteen he was barely out of skirts. I'd never allow him into my camp. He used to throw a tantrum to get Mother to persuade me.'

'I should have liked to go away to school. I had a governess at home. A young ladies' academy or boarding-school might have been nice. Then I might have had a friend to spend the summer with…'

With great solemnity, he announced to her sweetly wistful profile, 'I'd have let you into my camp…you're only six years younger. If you'd known Victoria then, I expect David might have been happy to accommodate her too. Perfect… Fishing, shooting, swimming, boating…girls…'

'I was but seven or eight when you were thirteen!' she snapped icily. 'And Victoria was nine.'

'Old enough,' he said, with a white smile over the lake, then arrowed a look at her. 'I was able to cook over an open fire when I was eight. You'd have managed. Why else would we let two girls into our camp?'

Emma tutted disgust but to hide her smile flounced her face away and spied Miriam's pale head and a waving hand, some way off on the bank. 'I believe your mother wants you.'

She just caught his muttered curse. Aloud he said, 'Just ignore her…'

'You can be very rude to your mother, I've noticed,' she let him know.

'Don't nag, Emma,' he said with a smile in his voice. 'It's far too soon for that.'

'I think she's hoping you will take a turn about the walk-ways with Miss Petersham.' Emma vainly tried to suppress the malicious amusement honeying her tone. 'Or are you con-tent to allow Ross to do that?'

Richard glanced down at her. 'I'm very content to let Ross do that…and he knows it. That's what good friends are for,

Emma. He would have had access to my camp too, had I known him then.'

Emma allowed a small smile. 'Ross really is the most terrible flirt, isn't he? I imagine he is another accomplished rogue...although a charming, likeable one,' she qualified, unaware how satisfyingly insulting it sounded.

'He comes from a very long line of accomplished Cornish rogues. And, yes, he's a practised flirt. In comparison, I'll admit to being a novice in pointless dalliance,' he said with biting irony.

'Well, you wanted to know earlier which qualities you lack,' Emma taunted. 'Pay your addresses to Miss Petersham and polish your flirting and charm.'

'That's what you think I should do, is it?'

'Indeed. You make an excellent couple.'

Richard looked over her head at nothing. 'If you're keen to foist her onto me, I now know for certain how much you dislike her.'

'Again, I can only marvel at your shrewd perception, sir. Oh, please don't let me keep you from her,' she sweetly said, and stepped back quickly along the planked boarding.

Richard grabbed at her and jerked her forward to teeter on her toes. 'When I said you might prefer a dip in the lake to my company, it was a joke, you know.'

Emma cautiously peeked over a shoulder to see inky water undulating directly below. She could feel just the tips of her shoes on solid wood. Her hands gripped frantically at muscular forearms and she squeezed shut her eyes, wondering why he didn't move backwards and take her with him. Her lids flicked up to see moon-silver eyes on her face. 'Your mother is waiting,' she desperately reminded him.

'I am waiting,' he returned softly.

'For what?' she squeaked.

'Lots of things: an apology...an explanation...another kiss...'

Her fingernails reflexively stabbed through the fine wool of his sleeves into his arms, trying to gain purchase and pull herself forward and away from danger. But he refused to help, holding her rock-steady at arm's length.

'Let's start with your private plans,' he said. 'Why don't you tell me about Cavendish?'

Emma's astonishment was so great, she almost relaxed her grip and tottered backwards into the water.

She felt his support increase but watched an awful, sneering smile twist his features. 'Good God, it really is him, isn't it?' he ground out, at the same time swinging her easily about to gain sure footing. He pushed her away from him as though disgusted. 'Matthew Cavendish?' he grated. He turned away and swore, then looked at her again as though he just didn't believe it.

'How did you find out?' Emma fumed. 'Who told you?'

'It's him, isn't it?' he repeated in amazement as though still hoping she'd deny it. 'Is the child his? Is it?' he hissed, completely ignoring her interrogation. When she remained silent he drawled in a stone-cold voice, 'He doesn't even know, does he? You've not told him, have you?'

'I've…I've said I won't talk of any of that,' she flared. 'It's nothing to do with you… It's none of your concern!'

A steely grip on her shoulders yanked her off the ground and slammed her against him, then shook her into silence. Her head swayed back, exposing an arc of slender throat, and she was staring up into vicious metallic eyes. 'Don't ever say that to me again, or I swear I'll live up to every sordid expectation you have of me. You'll discover just how unconcerned I can be.'

Emma opened her mouth to speak but something in his brutal gaze, in the pitiless line of his mouth, his rigid jaw, made her clamp it shut again.

Her heart fluttered like a caged bird against her ribs yet she couldn't think what it was she usually said or did to gentle him. He was utterly enraged; more angry than she'd ever known him. Yet she didn't understand why. He had somehow learned what had brought her to Bath: her relationship with Matthew. But surely that news would relieve him? At Mrs Keene's he had wanted to know whether her lover was prepared to support her.

'Take your filthy hands off me now, or my future husband will kill you,' she lashed with icy contempt. 'He'll kill you anyway when he hears of you insulting me with an offer to join your whores.'

'Will he, my dear?' was silkily queried. 'When will that be? Next time he's sober enough to stay on his feet? Had I known you'd already joined his whores, I'd have looked higher... Haymarket, perhaps.'

A small fist whipped out with an outraged gasp. 'Well, I'm sure you'd know where the cheapest harlots tarry,' she spat. 'The amount you've had you'd have lost this fine place to the brothels years ago.'

Long, harsh fingers anchored her flailing fist back to her side. Without another word he made for the path, dragging her behind him. Once on solid ground, she was shoved away in the direction of the flickering flares. 'Get back to the house,' he directed coldly, imperiously, and with flint-eyed amusement watched her resentfully comply, before striding in the opposite direction.

Chapter Eight

'Richard looks so angry; have you quarrelled with him?' a shrill voice called from behind, making Emma stop and spin about. 'I've quarrelled with Stephen,' Amelia continued, then burst into tears.

Emma placed a comforting hand on Amelia's arm but her mind was in turmoil: she felt furious, so blazingly irate that for two pins she would have raced back down the firelit path to find Richard Du Quesne in the vain hope that this time her fist might surprise him and find its mark.

Had it been simply spite that had made him imply Matthew was a drunken womaniser? But why should a man such as Sir Richard, with power and wealth, stoop to vilify a man so far beneath his notice? She couldn't deny his shock and contempt had seemed genuine on learning that she was, indeed, involved with Matthew Cavendish. Neither could she deny that she'd already spotted signs of drunkenness about Matthew's haggard features, or that his housekeeper, Maisie, behaved in a decidedly familiar way with him. She had previously found plausible excuses: Matthew liked to relax with alcohol as most men did. His housekeeper was simply a little sluttish in her ways.

Amelia's soft weeping finally penetrated her chaotic thoughts. Slipping an arm through hers, she set a quicker pace along the path. 'Don't fret so, Amelia,' Emma kindly soothed. 'I'm sure you and Stephen will make up.'

Amelia shook her head, wiping her face with her fingertips and sniffing loudly. 'We argued because he…he has another woman, I know it. And he didn't bother to deny it. He…he just said I was too possessive and should never question what company he keeps. He said I should be dutiful and modest as other wives are. He said he is entitled to have his freedom as other men do. Other men have mistresses…that's what he means.'

'Seven years between them, maybe…such similar brothers nonetheless,' Emma muttered. Aloud she reasoned, 'But he didn't actually say so?'

'Do…do you think perhaps I'm mistaken?' Amelia asked hopefully.

Emma bestowed an optimistic look on her while her heart sank. If Stephen even slightly resembled his older brother, his infidelities were probably more prolific than his poor wife could ever imagine.

'May I talk to you in your room for a while?' Amelia pleaded as they entered the house.

'Yes, of course,' Emma replied gently, yet feeling that she had no more advice to give. She sorely needed a confidante of her own and her thoughts immediately turned to Victoria. Oh, Vicky, she inwardly whispered, I so wish you were here for me.

The following morning at ten o'clock a note arrived summoning her to his study. It found the fire. So did the second bearing the same command and a veiled threat of retribution should she again ignore him. The third—stating that should she attempt to leave the house in his absence dire consequences would ensue—she kept and perused thoughtfully.

An hour later Emma was peeking down at the two riders on the circular gravel drive.

Richard, garbed in a long vented riding coat that reached

down to his boots, swung athletically into the saddle of a golden stallion. Even to Emma's inexpert town eye, the animal looked to be such a sleek, graceful creature she unconsciously let go of the veiling curtain she was stationed behind to better her view of it. Ross was astride a chestnut horse that seemed quite wild. It restlessly pawed at the ground and flung up its head as though keen to be off. As she watched, the animal skittered sideways before being brought under control. Chill September air froze the animals' steamy breath and that of the riders as they shared some conversation which caused them both to laugh.

A fair head turned, angled. She screened herself with rust damask curtains just moments before he looked up at her window. As soon as the two riders were lost to sight along the shivering silver avenue, she grabbed a shawl and raced below.

She knew the directions of the stables and hurried along the shingle path to the coach house. A groom was chatting idly to one of the young serving girls and they sprang apart as Emma approached. The young maid dipped a curtsey at Emma then skipped over the dewy grass towards the kitchens.

'It's a fine day,' Emma greeted, looking about at the mist-wreathed landscape. 'I'm sorry, I don't know your name.'

'It's Martin, m'm,' he supplied while yanking at a lock of auburn hair flopping over a freckle-dusted brow.

'Well, Martin, I should like to take a little drive in the countryside. It's such a pleasant, fresh morning. Would you oblige me with a driver and conveyance, please?'

'Can't, m'm,' the young groom burst out, crimsoning with embarrassment.

'I shall take responsibility and speak to Sir Richard…' she coaxed, guessing what ailed him.

'Can't, m'm,' Martin repeated, his face screwing in remorse. 'Sir Richard said as you might ask and that I should tell 'im if you did and that I was to tell you that's what I must do.'

Emma strained a smile over gritted teeth. She spied another young stablehand watching, fascinated, from the coach-house doorway. 'If I ask that young man instead you need not be in trouble…'

'Master's told 'im 'n all. Master's told all of us in stables.'

Emma dredged up another stiff smile, before marching back to the house.

She found Amelia alone in the morning room stabbing list-lessly at some embroidery. 'Might I speak to you?' Emma asked quietly.

Amelia let her sewing drop to her lap and she nodded. Her face was blotchy from crying and Emma directed her fury and hatred at both Du Quesne men.

'Amelia, I know you would like me to accompany you to the Assembly Rooms later and I know I have said I am re-luctant to go, but I have been thinking…perhaps we ought to try and do each other a good turn. It seems we are both in need of a little kindness. If I promise to accompany you for an hour or two this evening…might I ask a favour in return?'

'Of course…anything, Emma,' Amelia said huskily.

'Would you please go to the coach house and ask for a conveyance to be brought round to the front door so you can go to Bath? And please don't mention that I am to accompany you.'

Amelia perked up. 'Is it some intrigue?' she breathed. 'Where are we really to go?'

'I'll tell you on the way,' Emma said with a satisfied smile.

'Are you in love with this man?' Amelia whispered as she leaned towards Emma, agog with curiosity.

Emma shrugged and smiled wistfully at her hand brushing lazily through leaves trailing against the landau's glossy coachwork. Now the early morning haze had lifted the sun was warm, early autumn tints singeing the overgrown hedge-rows. She plucked at some blackberries as they passed a laden bramble, handed one to Amelia then popped the other into her mouth.

She unfastened her cloak and removed her bonnet. A fall

of tawny hair tumbled free, honey and copper lights glinting in its sheeny thickness.

Martin was driving them and only occasionally turning to bestow on Emma a melancholy look as they bowled along the back lanes of rural Bath towards the village of Oakdene. Emma felt a little guilty: she hoped she had not caused this young man to fear reprimand, or, worse still, losing his position. But then, despite hating Richard Du Quesne, she imagined him to be a fair employer. Martin would surely not be punished for her deceit.

'It's why you're here in Bath, isn't it?' Amelia interrupted her reflection. 'You're here specifically to see your friend; not to see Richard, as he said at dinner yesterday. How romantic! You've travelled alone from London, risking all, to find your heart's desire,' she murmured theatrically. 'Richard knows, of course, and would try to help as you are such good friends.'

Emma's choke of sour laughter went unremarked upon. 'I wondered why Richard was so adamant that no one should quiz you about your being in Bath unaccompanied. What of your parents?' Amelia asked. 'Do they like this man? Do they object to him?'

'They probably hold no opinion, and only vaguely recall him from when he resided in London years ago. He has never been a wealthy man. My parents had every hope of me marrying well and thus easing their financial burdens, so he would be a disappointment in that respect.' Emma turned to gaze at the countryside, hoping Amelia would probe no more. She didn't want to fib.

She sighed and closed her eyes as a jumble of thoughts spilled into her mind. Let Matthew be an honourable man. Let him still want me. Let me be satisfied with my lot. Don't let Richard spoil it by maliciously interfering.

He was sure to be furious that she had disobeyed him and that she had involved Amelia in deceitfully obtaining a carriage. But he had forced her to it with his tyranny, she immediately justified.

* * *

'So it's you again.'

'Indeed it is,' Emma snapped, feeling indignant at Maisie's surlily amused expression. 'Is Mr Cavendish at home? I should like to converse with him.'

'Oh, he's home right enough. Whether you'll be able to converse with him…now that be a different matter,' she jibed darkly.

Emma glanced back at the landau to see Amelia and Martin diplomatically turn away their heads.

'Very top-notch now, ain't you? 'N all thanks to the silver squire, I'll be bound,' Maisie sneered, sheer envy coarsening her country brogue. 'Makes me wonder why you're here at all bothering with the likes of him.' Her brunette head jerked towards the cottage's interior.

'What do you know of the silver squire?' Emma demanded sharply, her tawny eyes scanning Maisie's sullen features.

'What's the likes of me likely to know of him?' Maisie snorted. ''Cept he's got money 'n influence aplenty. When he was here with Matthew, he scared him straight back into a bottle.'

'When was he here?' Emma gasped, completely overlooking Maisie's audacity in using her employer's given name and disclosing his chosen comfort.

'Earlier in the week. Then again this morning. Frightening, he were, both times, if quiet. Don't much raise his voice at all yet he were angry, right enough. Angry 'cos of you, I reckon. Wonder why that might be?'

Emma blanched and her heart started to hammer erratically. 'Tell Mr Cavendish I wish to speak to him,' she ordered in a shaking tone.

'Tell him yourself,' Maisie retorted carelessly, swishing away.

Emma hesitantly followed her towards the back of the cottage and entered a small kitchen. Maisie ignored her and continued supping tea, seated at a battered pine table.

'I don't want us to be enemies, Maisie,' Emma sighed. 'I'm sure you care well for Mr Cavendish…'

'You've got no idea just how well I cares for him, Miss Uppity. An' he don't want such as you to know,' she burst out bitterly. 'Just go away and leave us be. He's worse than ever since you came troublin' him…' After a gulp of tea, she blurted, 'He's upstairs a'bed.' A jerk of her head indicated the rickety stairs set at the back of the kitchen.

Gaining a creaking landing, Emma tried the first door she came to. It opened onto the children's chamber. Clothes and toys were strewn on the floor and bedding draped untidily from two rough-hewn pine beds. She tried the other door and found him.

Matthew was sprawled, fully dressed, on the bed with his forearms flung up, framing his head. His eyes were closed and his breathing was stertorous.

The cloying smell of alcohol hit her with nauseating force as she proceeded into the room. As she tiptoed closer she noticed the flush on his features and sweat beading on his brow and top lip. Her heart hit her stomach, but mixed with grinding disappointment was pity and sorrow, for she knew even her treasured London memories of this man were doomed.

'Matthew…' she called softly. When there was no response she lightly shook his arm. A muttered blasphemy was ejected but he remained dozing. Emma shook him quite vigorously and then leaped back as he abruptly shot into a sitting position.

'What in damnation are you about, Maisie? You little bitch!' he rumbled. 'My head feels riven in two!' A massaging hand lowered from his brow and his lids were raised to reveal bloodshot eyes. He stared, unblinking, as though she were an apparition and twice his lips formed her name before it actually emerged. 'Emma?' he croaked. 'What in all that's holy are you doing here?'

'I've come to see you, Matthew,' she choked through the tears in her throat.

Matthew worked his way gingerly to the edge of the bed as

though every movement pained him. Emma watched his hand hover over a glass with dregs of alcohol in it on the side table. His fingers clenched then withdrew, leaving it untouched.

He grunted a noise that could have been laughter. 'I never wanted you to see me like this, Emma,' he said hoarsely. 'I can control it,' he stated quite seriously, while red-rimmed eyes stared out of the small paint-peeling window to one side of him. 'It's just…since Sara died, it's been a solace of sorts. It helps me sleep…then when I'm asleep she comes back to me.'

Emma felt tears prick at her lids and quickly closed her stinging eyes.

Matthew turned his head to face her. His gaunt grey complexion split in a grin. 'So you're keeping quite exalted company with Sir Richard Du Quesne at Silverdale. He's been here twice, if I rightly recall it,' he mocked himself. 'For I was a little under the influence on both occasions. How do you know such as he, Emma?'

'We share very dear mutual friends,' Emma told him huskily. 'I was acquainted with him some years ago; but we have little liking for one another. He found out I was in lodgings and insisted I stay at Silverdale with his mother and sister-in-law.' She managed a weak smile. 'He deems Mrs Keene's lodgings an unseemly place for me to stay. Mostly he frets that our dear friends might find out and accuse him of neglecting me.'

Matthew swiped a tremulous hand about his stubbly jaw. 'I'm glad you dislike him as much as I. He can be… intimidating…'

'Oh, yes…' Emma endorsed bitterly. 'Very…'

'Despite his probing I told him nought, Emma. You must not trust him. That devil Dashwood and he are of the same breed…such as they stick together. Once he feels he has done his duty by you he may be glad for Dashwood to take you off his hands.'

Emma felt her heart and stomach squeeze at that for it so exactly confirmed her own fears.

'I thought maybe you'd guessed of my secrets when you withheld your consent to our marriage. And I had no right to be annoyed at that.' Matthew looked up at her sheepishly. 'I intended coming to Lower Place to talk to you but I've been too bad in drink to get below stairs some days—' He broke off, a palsied hand dragging through his matted hair. 'I would never have told Sir Richard of our mutual affection, Emma. Such a sophisticate would misconstrue: take the fact of your fleeing London and couple it with your visit to me and draw conclusions of a base liaison. He was trying to prise as much from me, I'll swear. I have done everything in my power to shield your reputation.'

'Thank you, Matthew,' Emma choked past the ache in her throat, as the first tears trailed her cheek. 'Thank you very much for that.'

She had falsely insinuated to Richard that she was no longer chaste and because of that deceit this man's integrity had been called into question. In return Matthew had done his utmost to protect her, even whilst raddled by drink.

'Where are the children?' Emma asked in a bright, brittle voice.

'At the vicarage. Maisie takes them there for their lessons. They'll be home soon and glad to see you,' he said, but with little conviction.

'I can't tarry, Matthew.' The relief in his face made the lump in her throat thicken. 'I have a friend waiting in the carriage outside. We are just out for a drive in the countryside and I thought to call in…' she concluded in a ragged whisper.

Matthew nodded. 'I'm so sorry about…'

Emma rested a hand on his tangled hair. 'I'm so sorry too, Matthew…'

'I'll show you out, shall I?' Maisie walked boldly to the closet and drew forth a nightdress and deliberately placed it on the bed. She then moved to the small dresser and picked up a comb and began tidying her hair. Her eyes met Emma's in the mirror with meaningful challenge.

But Emma already understood. With a last squeeze at Matthew's hand she murmured, 'Goodbye, Matthew,' and was quickly out of the door and down the stairs.

'I shan't come here again,' Emma promised with apology underlying the words.

Maisie smiled at her with something akin to wry humour. 'I can't say as I blame you. If I had such as the handsome silver squire looking out for me, I wouldn't be here either.'

Without another word, Emma turned and walked into the September sunshine.

Amelia had decided to journey on and join Miriam and Diane at the Petershams' for afternoon tea. She had attempted to persuade Emma to accompany her but the thought of spending time with those awful women while she felt so low was unimaginable. On alighting from the landau on the circular driveway it pulled away and disappeared along the avenue of whitebeam.

As Simmons opened the door to her, Emma tentatively enquired, fingers crossed in her pockets, 'Is Sir Richard home, to your knowledge?'

'To my knowledge, he is not, Miss Worthington,' he answered while his eyebrows tilted in opposite directions at the odd notion that something might yet occur at Silverdale that escaped his notice. 'Ah, now…' the butler began as he leaned sideways to peer past a mightily relieved Emma.

As she heard gravel spit and scrunch she spun about. She froze, determined not to flee, even as she glimpsed the sleek, champagne flanks of a large horse. She still held her ground when she saw the recently dismounted rider striding with long, purposeful paces towards the house.

She wasn't frightened, she impressed on herself as she watched him mount the stone steps two at a time with his riding coat flapping about long, muscular legs. Nevertheless she decided speeding across the hallway to the stairs might be a prudent move.

Sir Richard Du Quesne strode into the house, his blond hair glinting in the afternoon sunlight, his dark face thunderous. 'Have a groom brought round,' he flung at a stoical Simmons as he passed him without slowing his pace. His scouring gaze found Emma hovering by the bannisters. He continued walking with daunting deliberation and a satisfied smile curving the ruthless line of his mouth.

It was then Emma conceded that she was too shaken by the day's events for any further heroics. She *was* frightened and she no longer cared if he *did* know it. Turning on the bottom step, she launched herself upwards with a deep breath and her skirts gripped in shaking fists.

Before she'd managed three stairs she was jerked backwards into mid-air and against a hard, broad torso. She squirmed, attempting to twist about, but her arms were lashed to her sides with insolent ease by one arm encircling her body. He carried her as though she were a china doll…very carefully and very easily.

His study door was treated to no such attention: it was kicked inwards with such brute force that it crashed back against the wall, allowing them entry, then bounced back to seal itself.

Richard deposited Emma on the Persian rug and a hand nudged her forward away from him.

She swung about and immediately flew back at him.

He caught at first one then the other of her hands as they swung for his face and held her at arm's length. When she still kicked and fought, he took them behind her back, forcing her heart-stoppingly close.

So close, she could distinguish the clean sandalwood scent of him mingled with leather and a disturbing searing heat that seemed unnatural. Her wriggling immediately ceased. Her breathing was coming in short, sharp bursts and she gasped out, 'Let me go, this instant, or I shall scream.'

'Go ahead,' he said quietly while quicksilver eyes flowed over her and her soft body seemed to be melding to the hardness of his.

She strained at her imprisoned wrists, trying to force them out of his grip. 'I hate you…*I hate you*,' she raged against his chest.

The sadness that had been steadily strengthening since she'd first faced Jarret Dashwood in the drawing room of Rosemary House was no longer containable. Her melancholy meeting barely an hour before with Matthew had left tears betrayingly close to the surface and after the first jerking sob she was lost. She wrenched at her hands again and again, her head working this way and that in despair as she tried to free herself and conceal her wet face with thick, tawny hair. Finally submitting, she stilled, burying her face down against her shoulder.

He stepped back a few paces to the desk. Kicking his chair back from it, he spun her about abruptly then sat and pulled her down onto his lap. 'I think, Miss Worthington, it's quite likely you'll render me insane before too much longer,' was murmured huskily against her bent head. That wry observation seemed to increase her anguish, so he soothed, 'Hush, it's just a joke. I know you worry for my health.'

For what seemed an age they sat like that; the only noise disturbing the silence was Emma's weeping, the only movement a large dark hand smoothing against her face, her hair. As she quietened he searched his various pockets and eventually brought forth a handkerchief. Tilting her face up to his, he leisurely picked away damp fawn tresses stuck to her cheeks.

'Look at me,' he ordered, and she did. Luminous golden eyes fringed by clumps of wet black lashes glanced up at him. Richard closed his eyes, dropped his head forward and swore softly. 'Looking that appealing after crying gives you an unfair advantage, Emma.'

White linen moved gently across her face, removing salty wet, and she sat rigidly, a little sense and composure creeping back. He seemed momentarily mellowed by her angry tears and acting quickly would be wise. A tentative attempt to rise was thwarted. Immediately his eyes flicked to hers, narrowed and amused. 'Not yet,' he denied her, dropping the handkerchief to the floor. 'I really would be mad if I let you go without an explanation…or an apology. You've jeopardised Martin's livelihood and involved Amelia in your deceit.'

Emma made to twist her face away but a dark hand spanning her jaw arrested it. 'So tell me…was it worth it? Was he sober when you got there?'

Her lids drooped so that mercurial gaze couldn't mock her. But she felt drained of aggression and lies and so awfully guilty at the thought that he might, after all, put off the young groomsman simply to punish her. She merely answered his question with a shake of her head. 'I apologise for disobeying you and borrowing a carriage. But if…if you put Martin off because of it I shall never forgive you, I swear I won't. Nor if you make trouble for Amelia. If you want to wreak your paltry revenge,' she flung at him, 'then do so with me.'

'Not a wise invitation, Emma,' Richard observed sarcastically. 'Never forget I'm that callous lecher you love to malign.'

As his hand moved away she turned her head to stare out of the window.

'You knew Cavendish in London, I take it?'

She nodded.

'Was he coherent enough when you got there? Have you told him now of the child?'

Emma stiffened in his arms, her heart thudding. Matthew's sweet defence of her virtue played over in her mind. She would show him the same respect and kindness and never allow this man an opportunity to vilify him once she had left the area. 'We were not lovers in that way,' she informed him coolly. 'But we like each other very much and Matthew had asked me to marry him. I came to Bath hoping he would again propose, and he did. I had no idea he drinks too much. But then the grief of losing his first wife has never left him. Alcohol helps him cope as, I suspect, does the company of his housekeeper. He is not a lax hedonist as some…' she darkly hinted. 'But he is a very sad man. I expect you know all of that,' she added bitterly. 'Matthew said you had visited and tried to make him admit to some base liaison between us.'

'Did he?' came back quietly. 'Well, which lax hedonist is responsible for a base liaison with you?'

'That's none of your con…'

A dark hand covered her mouth. 'I thought we had agreed you would never again say that to me.'

'I never agreed,' she snapped pettishly, jerking away from his touch.

Silver eyes clashed with sparking topaz. 'Don't bait me needlessly, Emma,' he gently warned. 'I could break that aggressive spirit of yours so easily.'

Emma felt icy fingers trail her spine. It was no idle threat. She had known as much for a long while. As long ago as her skirmishes with him in London. She slid on his lap, trying to get her feet flat to the floor to flee.

'Sit still,' he grated, hauling her backwards against his chest, and the rough command in the words petrified her.

A narrow mouth moved close to a delicately shaped ear. 'I shall ask you this just one final time; thereafter, I contact your parents and ask them for an answer…as I should have done days ago. Who is your lover?'

Emma stared out of the window, her mind racing. Again, Matthew's recent words came back to haunt her. 'You must not trust him… Once he feels he has done his duty by you he may be glad for Dashwood to take you off his hands…'

Richard's patience with her had expired and, in fairness, she couldn't wonder at it. She *had* been a nuisance and he would gladly rid himself of her. But if he relayed to her parents that she was pregnant… She dared not even contemplate what damage that would wreak on them. It would be best to bluff out this nightmare charade she had idiotically begun. Strive to be amenable for a day or so longer and then return to London and pray Dashwood had shown leniency in her absence. But which man was she to condemn? A character her lies could never harm was the only answer…

'You would not know him so it is pointless naming him. He lives in the north…in Derbyshire…and visits London at times.'

'Is he married?'

'No, but he is spoken for.'

'Have you told him of your condition?'

'There's no way I can do that.'

'You love him that much?'

'I've always held him in great affection.'

'What's his name?'

Emma took a deep breath and said quietly, 'William…'

At a raise of dark brows requiring the rest, she murmured, 'Fitz.'

'William Fitz?'

'I said you would not know him,' she uttered agitatedly. 'He lives in Derbyshire and would never move in the circles you do. He is an honourable man…quite shy in a way.'

'Very shy…' Richard said drily. 'Very honourable…' he muttered with increased cynicism.

'I have told you now,' she quavered. 'You have got what you wanted, for what good it will do you.'

After a pulsing silence, Richard said solemnly, 'What has happened to our truce, Emma? It's not yet a day since we made it yet still we snipe. I think we should reinforce it.' A dark hand flipped over, palm up, waiting.

Be amenable, she reminded herself. Humour him until you can devise a way out of this maze of deceit you've stupidly concocted. Long fingers immediately curled over the small hand she placed atop his.

'Perhaps some affection to seal it and help it last this time,' he suggested softly.

Emma's golden gaze flicked warily to his dark face. Oh,

no! The humiliating memory of how easily he had subdued her with that last kiss…how she had hungered for more…the detached abruptness with which he'd released her…still needled mercilessly. She attempted to snatch back her hand and turn her burning face away.

But determined fingers laced into hers. 'Yesterday, by the lake, I wanted from you an explanation, an apology and a kiss. There's but one left for you to bestow. Come…I did save you from a watery fate,' he reminded her with humour in his voice. 'That alone must be worth a token of thanks…'

'I'd sooner be up to my neck in pond weed and kiss a frog!' she snapped, but her heart was pounding so much, the words were breathy.

'I think that's another lie, Emma,' he softly laughed, with a touch of cool lips to her hot cheek. 'I think, too, you'd not deem a casual kiss more important than Martin's acquittal of insubordination.'

She swung her face towards his, forgetting how close he was. Their lips were mere inches apart. 'That's blackmail!' she gasped, and tried to tilt away from him but a hand speared into her thick hair, holding her close.

'I know,' he said impenitently, a finger smoothing over her trembling lips. 'But then you expect no less of me, I'm sure.'

Fawn eyes were riveted on his narrow mouth as it approached and her head strained against the sturdy palm cupping her scalp.

His lips caressed over a cheekbone. 'You taste salty,' he whispered, and she watched his tongue slide over his lower lip, savouring her tears. That prompted an involuntary sweet smile, and as her lips softened and parted he immediately covered them with his.

Resisting his narcotic charm was impossible. She felt pliant as he tilted her face, made no objection as he manoeuvred her jaw until their mouths perfectly fused. His lips gentled at first then increased pressure, moulding her soft mouth beneath his as he sensed her entrancement.

'Kiss me back!' The hoarse command was breathed against her skin and then he roughly showed her how and waited.

She copied what she could recall unstintingly, skimming her lips along his, touching her tongue to his lower lip, inserting it to touch the tip of his. With a low growl he crushed her closer, yet still her mouth hovered, parted, beneath his, tempting with light, inexpert touches, until he took back control, plundering the soft sweetness of her again with seductive skill.

Emma didn't hear the study door open. It was the abrupt removal of her source of drugging pleasure, the vehement curse of the man responsible for that ecstasy, that brought her jerking to her senses and then to her feet. Scarlet-faced, she glanced at Ross who had turned sideways and was grimacing his absolute remorse at the ceiling, hands linked behind his head.

'Emma…' Richard pleaded, but she was already backing towards the door. 'Emma!' Richard ground out imperiously, with a stabbing glare at Ross.

'Please don't go,' Emma addressed Ross in a shaking voice. But with a double-handed gesture of sheer apology he was closing the door quietly.

'Come here,' Richard demanded. 'We have things to discuss.'

'Leave me be…'

'To do what? Even if you decide to settle for your drunken swain, there's the matter of his concubine. A *ménage à trois* in a tumbledown cottage? I don't think it would suit you, Emma.'

'Neither does a Palladian town house and an allowance,' she forced through her bruised, pulsing lips, frightened that fresh tears were imminent and she would never control them.

'I'll think of something that does suit you.'

With her hand on the door knob she turned to glance at him. 'There is *nothing* you could think of that would suit me,' she managed disdainfully before closing the door.

Chapter Nine

'You seem a little happier this evening, Amelia.'

'Stephen has been so agreeable,' Amelia brightly disclosed. 'We chatted this afternoon for an age and although nothing was mentioned of those *suspicions* I told you of he seemed very attentive. He took Jake out on his pony…and spent time in the nursery with Alice and us all.'

Emma breathed a sigh of relief. 'Good…you were perhaps mistaken in your reasons for arguing by the lake, then.'

'I do hope so,' Amelia sighed. 'And I'm glad you managed to slip out and see your friend Matthew. It was very mean of Richard to deny you a carriage just because you had quarrelled. Unlike him, too. He is never usually petty when cross with someone.'

Amelia linked arms with Emma and they strolled away from the sets forming on the dance floor and towards some chairs ranged against the wall.

'Richard never accompanies you all to these dances?' Emma asked casually, yet praying that the answer would be in the negative. Her wanton behaviour in his study that afternoon was so fresh in her mind that her lips pulsed and her face flamed anew with the memory of it. It must have been the stress of the day that had caused her to act so, she consoled herself. There was no other explanation for acting like a mindless fool, obeying his every command.

'Heavens, no!' Amelia broke into Emma's pensiveness. 'You would have more chance of spying him at one of Mrs Petersham's afternoon tea parties!'

'I'm sure Mrs Petersham and Veronica would be very happy to see him,' Emma returned a little sourly.

Amelia tinkled a laugh and flapped a hand. 'Oh, that is nothing. Miriam has no real wish for an alliance there. She simply hopes that by placing Veronica constantly in Richard's way he might surrender and finally pay his addresses to the woman he will eventually marry: a duke's daughter. As you are friends he will no doubt tell you himself of his intentions towards Lady Penelope—and her dowry, of course. Stephen says the settlement will bring Richard copper-mining rights in Devon that he is desperate to have.' She lowered her voice. 'Apparently there is a fortune to be unearthed on the Duke of Winstanley's land.' She smoothed her gloves, then continued. 'Naturally, it is no love match...although Penelope seems quite smitten. But Richard will not worry...he has his...*lady friends*.' She glanced at Emma from beneath her lashes. 'As you know him of old...in his London heyday...you know that he and David Hardinge were most terrible scoundrels. Richard is improved, but not cured of bachelor excesses. He and Ross are no doubt carousing about town as usual.' Amelia sighed. 'I think, at times, Stephen hankers after their permissive lifestyle...'

'I'm sure it's no more than an idle envy,' Emma reassured her friend, but her voice was thin and an odd chill seemed to seep through her veins. Richard, married? For some reason it had not occurred to her that a serious alliance might be brewing. Yet it should have: had he not mentioned it himself when propositioning her at Mrs Keene's? Words paraded mockingly through her mind...*I'll make lasting provision for you. Even if I marry at some time...* Three years ago he might have considered a modest spinster with little to recommend her, but now he had his birthright and family commitments. He would want a wife of status and dowry and an heir.

She deliberately shook off the melancholy, rubbing at her arms briskly. Brightly she resumed their conversation. 'I think that Ross perhaps envies your husband. He seems rather taken with you, Amelia. Stephen watches carefully when he pays you attention.'

'Ross is rather taken with every woman over fifteen and under fifty. He is the most prolific flirt I have ever met. But he is rather captivating…in a buccaneering sort of way.' She added mischievously, 'I'll admit I do encourage his interest…especially when Stephen is in the vicinity.' Amelia dipped her head quickly towards Emma's and shielded their faces with her fluttering fan. 'He is coming again!'

Emma peeked curiously about the fan. A soft groan escaped her lips. Since arriving at the Upper Assembly Room in Bath some half an hour ago, Emma had, for some reason, attracted the attention of a rather dashing young man she guessed to be about her own age. His dark eyes had fixed so unwaveringly on her that at first she had believed she must have a smudge on her face and had asked Amelia to check. Amelia had laughed and said he was staring because she looked most alluring in her amber silk gown with her sleek tawny hair and lovely eyes.

'I do believe he is soon to ask you to waltz,' Amelia squealed. 'He is rather good-looking, Emma. I wish he would ask me. Stephen might be utterly miffed!'

Spying Stephen's tall figure weaving through the crowd, a glass in each of his hands, Emma laughed. 'Well, let's hope our beau approaches you now, then, for never would there be a more opportune moment.'

'Your servant, ladies,' Stephen greeted them, proffering glasses of lemonade.

Amelia inclined towards her husband. 'Emma has an admirer, Stephen. He is sure to soon wangle an introduction.'

Stephen grinned. 'Well, he'd better make his move before

Richard does. I have a feeling my brother is a little protective where Emma is concerned.'

'Richard?' Emma and Amelia chorused.

'An amazing sight, I have to own,' Stephen conceded, still grinning. 'But yes; he and Ross are just arrived and causing quite a stir among the ladies in the ante-room. Not least amongst our own kin. I believe dear Mama practically hit the floor when she spied her eldest son surrounded by muslin. It's the venue that's astonishing, of course, not the yards of petticoat…' Belatedly recalling to whom he spoke, he reddened a little and cleared his throat. 'Emma knows him well enough.' He pacified his pink-faced wife. 'Good Lord, she's not deaf to gossip, and she was in London three years ago, you know.' Distractingly, Stephen added, 'He should soon have fought his way through the throng, if only to assist Diane with the smelling salts. It is the least he can do after causing Mother to have an attack.'

Emma glanced nervously about and did indeed spot an unmistakable silver-blond head. He looked strikingly imposing dressed in elegant back tailcoat with such contrastingly fair hair. A press of colourful ladies and just a few gentlemen, she acidly noted, presently entrapped him. Although he was smiling and chatting his eyes were scanning the room. Emma deliberately looked away.

Aware of Amelia and Stephen's engrossed conversation, she diplomatically swivelled about on her chair, allowing them privacy, and unintentionally faced her admirer. Yes, please do come over and talk to me, she silently encouraged, with a coy smile. I should like to annoy him a little more before the day is out. Mostly I should hate him to think that kiss in his study affected me in the slightest. It means as little to me as it does to him.

The young man's features adopted a smouldering intentness which abruptly fixed, mask-like, making Emma choke a soft giggle. After a stiff bow, which seemed not for her, he was dashing in a different direction.

Emma turned slightly, eyes slowly climbing long legs en-
cased in dove-grey material; a black sleeve was passed over
on the way to glimpse a hard, dark profile. Steely eyes were
fixed on the man's retreating figure. A tanned hand was braced
casually on her chair-back and then he looked down at her.

Emma darted glances about the room, noting that many people were either staring at them quite openly or discreetly peeking at intervals. 'Don't look so…so…' she hissed in an underbreath. 'Just don't look like that; you're making people
stare,' she resorted to muttering.

'How do I look? Annoyed to find you flirting quite outrageously with a man you're not even introduced to?'

'I was not flirting! Merely being friendly. And how dare
you preach so sanctimoniously? I doubt you're formally introduced to any woman you consort with,' was spat out in a
whisper.

He sat in the vacant chair next to her, looked at her and
smiled. 'Very well. I concede. The women I used to consort
with don't expect niceties, just nice things. Is that what you
want to hear?'

Emma choked and shielded her heating face with a cool
hand. 'Do you have to be so…so extremely vulgar?' she
fumed.

'If you don't want to know, Emma, don't probe until I tell
you.'

'I was not!'

'Yes, you were.'

She speared a glance at him to see he was still seriously
amused. He slanted back an intimate look, dusky lashes
screening his eyes as they targeted her still swollen ruby lips.
Heat coursed through Emma and she shifted backwards on her
seat.

'I want you to dance with me.'

'When? Why?' Emma asked nervously.

'Now. Because I want to,' he replied.

The orchestra played the opening bars to a waltz and, standing abruptly, he offered her his hand. Emma slipped white fingers onto lean, bronzed ones and allowed him to lead her away. Suddenly he diverted from the whirling couples on the dance floor so abruptly, it gave cause for blatant whisperings.

'I shall be but a minute...' he murmured apologetically, inclining close, on returning Emma to her chair. A thumb traced a lingering caress on her soft palm as he reluctantly relinquished it, and then he had turned away and was weaving swiftly through the throng.

Amelia looked at Emma and shrugged her bemusement. 'I see we've both been abandoned. Stephen has disappeared, too. They obviously have some men's gossip to catch up with.'

'Men's gossip?' interjected a familiar, laughing, voice. 'Do tell me more.' Ross seated himself next to them both with a raffish white smile.

Emma managed to greet him adequately although she blushed, recalling how mere hours ago she had been discovered by this man on his friend's lap looking for all the world like a wanton hussy. Ross seemed oblivious to any impropriety that might make her uneasy. In fact, despite his charming demeanour, he seemed unusually preoccupied himself as he chatted, yet kept watchful eyes on the entrance.

Richard's fingers closed vice-like about the woman's arm. Without slowing his pace he spun her about in the Assembly Room doorway where she had boldly stationed herself, and pushed her in front of him as he made for the stairs that led below.

Once out in the cool evening air, and concealed at the side of the building from prying eyes, she was released with a small shove.

'I wasn't sure you would be 'ere, *chéri*,' Yvette Dubois purred at him. 'I didn't think such tame entertainment was what you liked.'

'Just listen,' Richard bit out. 'Go home. I'll come in an hour or so. You can then explain the reason for your impertinence.

By the time I arrive, make sure you to have begun packing up to leave tomorrow afternoon. Make sure you to have chosen which side of the Channel you prefer…or I shall choose for you. Now get into that carriage.' His blond head jerked at a conveyance close by, a young maid's face visible at the window.

Yvette shivered beneath the stone-cold fury she could sense emanating from him. He terrified her when he was like this. But she forced a shrill laugh and jittery confidence, for she was determined to provoke his jealousy and win him back. 'Per'aps it is you who should listen, Sir Silver Squire,' she mocked. 'I am come 'ere to tell you that I 'ave done my choosing. This Bath suits me so ver' well. The *monsieur* I 'ave chosen to replace you suits me so ver' well, too.' Innocently, she asked, 'You did not think I am 'ere just to see you? My new lover is 'ere tonight…with his so *charmante* wife. She knows nothing of me, *naturellement*. As always I am so discreet…'

Blonde curls were twirled round a finger as she peeked slyly sideways at him. 'And I think you must forget your little visit to me later…unless…three people together excites you. Does it? Per'aps a new pleasure…something you never try before…' she throatily coaxed, pink tongue trailing her lower lip, a long fingernail trailing his black sleeve.

'How sweet,' he drawled, harsh boredom curling his lip. 'You think there's something I've never tried before. Unfortunately, my dear, there's nothing you can tempt me with…you've nothing I want.'

Yvette felt her temper firing, her vanity crushing. But she managed a Gallic shrug. 'I'm not so certain, Richard…I think per'aps I 'ave in my power something you do want so ver' much… Ah…' she purred contentedly. 'See, 'ere 'e comes now…'

Richard pivoted on a heel. Stephen was approaching, peering about as though seeking someone.

Yvette chuckled huskily, with intense satisfaction. The

astonishment on Richard's face was mingling with conflicting emotions of anguish and hopeless rage. They might fight over her, Yvette happily mused. How *merveilleux* that would be! Two handsome brothers fighting on the cobbles because of her, while inside the polite people who shunned her presence at their gatherings wondered where the two dignified brothers could be.

As Stephen noticed his older brother, he approached uncertainly. 'What's going on?' he demanded nervously of Richard. 'She told me you'd finished with her.' A suspicious look was arrowed at Yvette. 'And she was free to find someone else to…to care for her.'

'And you think that should be you?' Richard asked, deadly quiet. 'She contacted you, I take it? Suggested as much, then let you know what delightful attention you'd get in return? Sampled any of it yet?'

Stephen reddened and his eyes narrowed. 'You sound so damned righteous it makes me sick. Don't lecture me! Never once in your adult life have you been in a position to moralise!'

Richard put up dark hands in acceptance. *'Touché.'* he said gravely. 'And I know you have. You put me to shame…I admit it. You've been a good husband and father.' Richard paced away then swung back to look at his brother. 'And now you think you're due a little recreation. Who am I to deny you? But the thing is, Stephen, I'm not sure how I feel about letting her go…especially to you.' An uneasy laugh and rub at the bridge of his nose preceded, 'Unfavourable comparisons might be made. Besides, I've always been bad at sharing things with you…you know that.'

'I shall see how Diane is faring with the smelling salts,' Emma announced, feeling unaccountably uneasy. She left Ross and Amelia innocently flirting as she wandered to the ante-room where refreshments were set out. She spied Diane; seated next to her was Miriam, feverishly fanning herself. And standing nearby, conversing heatedly with them, were the Petershams. With a sigh and a steady smile, Emma approached.

Apart from a distracted welcome from the Du Quesne women she was virtually ignored. Soon she discovered why. Juicy gossip-mongering was in progress.

'Never say so!' she heard Miriam whisper at Susan Petersham. 'It cannot be true!'

Susan Petersham inclined forward. 'I have it straight from Mrs Jones who is just arrived from London. Dashwood is so enraged at the turn of events that it is likely the mother will still end in the Fleet. The daughter too if these investigators winkle her out. He is out for blood!'

'I feel so sorry for the girl's mother… What a terrible thing! To first lose a daughter then a husband!'

At the first mention of the name Dashwood, Emma had become petrified, straining to hear every snippet. Now she could hardly make out anything other than the pounding of blood in her ears. They were talking of her family, she was sure. And had mentioned that her mother had lost her husband! She grabbed behind her double-handed at the wall as she felt her legs weaken.

'Someone must know the family,' Miriam probed.

'Dashwood is so infuriated by being made to wear the jester's cap that he is keeping all close to his chest. The father is absconded too and one never knows what he might do to avoid the Fleet or pistols at dawn. It would be one or other and no mistake! The family's name will never survive the scandal. I imagine they are people of some station, but not of the first stare.' Mrs Petersham drew breath then hissed, 'I say it's disgraceful of the chit to leave her parents in such disarray! Thousands of pounds had changed hands, too, you know, with more to follow after the nuptials.'

'I have a little sympathy for the poor thing,' Miriam whispered with a shake of the head. 'I have heard such diabolical tales of that man as make a saint of the devil…'

Susan Petersham endorsingly wagged her head. 'I should

not like to be in that chit's shoes when eventually she and Dashwood come face to face…'

Emma retraced a few steps from the gossiping women in the manner of a sleepwalker. She tottered woodenly about, obliquely aware that they had not noticed her withdrawal. She walked, not knowing where she headed, and twice bumped into people. Automatic apology was whispered through a throat that felt too tight for her even to breathe.

She found some stairs and quickly descended them, instinctively heading towards fresh air and comforting, obscuring darkness.

Richard's steady, sensual gaze had Yvette visibly drooping against the wall for support. 'So we disagree a little…' he murmured, eyes stripping her. 'I threaten to put her off. But the idea of my brother touching what's rightfully mine…'

Yvette swayed towards him. She clutched at his arm, grazing herself wantonly against him. ''E will never touch what's rightfully yours, Richard,' she fervently vowed. ''E is a boy compared to you! Three notes I send before 'e contacts me once. It is you I love. You won't regret keeping me, *chéri*. I will show you later just 'ow much you will not regret it, in every way you like,' she whispered, in so thick an accent the words were almost indistinct. 'I never wanted anyone else… only ever you. I like you to be jealous…I say it. I knew you would 'ate 'im to 'ave me.'

Richard backed her against the wall, arms stationed at either side of her, and bent his head. She immediately wound herself about him, jerking his face to hers and kissing him with a desperate ferocity, a little moan of pleasure and triumph breaking in her throat as his tongue filled her mouth.

Richard pulled open her cloak, exposing a thrusting cleavage, the skimpy muslin bodice cut so low, crescents of dark aureolas were visible. He lowered his face again. Before he'd touched her she was arching to meet him, eyes half-closed, sighing in anticipation.

'Still want her?' Richard asked idly as he pushed himself away from the wall and turned to face his brother.

Stephen's face was taut with mortification, white with rage. 'You bastard! You've tricked her into saying all that. She would have settled for me.'

'And that's what you want, is it?' Richard ground out in slow, measured tones of utter contempt. 'A whore who'll settle for you. You're my brother, goddammit! Look at her! I could take her back tomorrow…next week…next month.' He spun away from Stephen in sheer disgust, ignoring Yvette's darkly furious face. 'That arrangement suits you, does it? Sharing her when the fancy takes me?'

Stephen stared stonily for a moment, then, with an enraged cry, he sprang forward, fists raised. Richard deflected the blow easily and pushed him away. 'You want her…you have her. I've never yet fought over a whore and I'm damned if I'll start now. She leaves for France tomorrow. You want her so damned much, bring her back at your own expense,' he sneered, before striding away.

Emma backed away in the shadows as she saw him approach. Although she felt rigid with shock and disgust, she knew to avoid him. What was best? Turn and run? Hide and hope he would pass? She shuffled backwards on weak legs, close to the brickwork, praying that the deep colour of her gown and the shadow cast by the wall gave her adequate protection.

As she retreated, all she'd witnessed…every revolting part…undulated before her eyes, whispered in her mind more woundingly than the matrons' gossip about her parents.

A silver-blond head dipping to kiss a woman was what she'd seen from afar and despite her cold dread she'd paced forward, mesmerised, out of sight. Then she'd recognised the woman's identity and seen Stephen, in the shadows, watching them.

'That arrangement suits you, does it? Sharing her when the fancy takes me?' she'd heard Richard suggest in a cold, careless tone. It had been enough to make her twist about, nausea churning her stomach, and immediately distance herself from the foul exchange. When she'd glanced back, she'd seen that Richard was moving away too, and it had sent her rushing to hug the wall for cover as she'd stepped back, for she was appalled she might appear a voyeur.

Emma froze. His pace was outstripping hers and she realised he would soon draw level. He was far more likely to notice her moving than stationary. Flattening herself motionless against the brickwork, she waited, barely breathing, for him to pass so she could flee. And she knew she would; at dawn she would quit Bath for London.

Snapping his head back, Richard spouted savage curses at the stars. His head whipped around to glance at the face of the little maid at the carriage window. She immediately dipped her bonnet and he looked away…and hesitated. He looked again. Then stopped. Pivoting on a heel towards the wall, he stood perfectly still and stared.

Emma moved first. She just couldn't endure the suspense any longer. She walked, head high, towards the entrance to the Assembly Rooms.

Richard proceeded too, at an angle, so he'd cut off her path within seconds. He braced his arm against the wall and she immediately tried to pass him, but he blocked her way with his body, forcing her back against the brick. 'Were you looking for me?'

Emma swallowed twice, desperate to act coolly, rationally. Still her throat wouldn't work so she shook her head and again made a move to pass him.

'Will you listen if I explain?' An odd hint of plea roughened the words.

'I needed some air,' exploded in a gulp. 'I came below for some air because I felt…I felt…' A tear trickling from the corner of an eye was smeared away without conscious thought.

A dark hand skimmed towards her face but she slapped it so swiftly and savagely, it spun up and away from her. It was

controlled and on its way back so fast, she flinched, sure he
would hit her, but his fist smashed into the brickwork above
her head with such force that she felt the tremor at her back.

His moonlit head inclined a little. 'What did you hear…
see?'

He asked it quite normally, she thought. In the way one
would enquire after a diverting tableau. 'Enough,' she reported, striving for the same bland attitude. 'Enough revolting,
loathsome…' She trembled into silence and stared past his
shoulder at the starry night, her lower lip so tightly held by
her teeth, she tasted coppery blood.

'Are you going to let me explain?'

'Why? I would not believe you if you told me the time of
day. I would never listen to pathetic lies about why you share
your mistress with your brother.'

A grunt of mirthless laughter met that and the sound shattered her fragile control. She lashed out at his face…and he
let her. She hit him twice and each time he simply turned with
the blow, making no attempt to stop her or protect himself.
When she finally restrained her shaking fury and flung herself
back against the wall, he looked at her.

'You *will* listen to me, Emma.'

'*You* will listen to *me*,' she quaveringly countered, a vestige
of composure scraped together. 'Never think I came out here
seeking you. I did not. I was not spying. When above stairs,
I heard some…some gossip of people I know that upset me
and I had to get away for a moment. I wish I had never seen
you…her…or Stephen. Not because your disgusting debauchery has wounded me or surprised me, but Stephen's has. And
Amelia already suspects that Stephen is unfaithful. She has
spoken of it; asked my advice, and if she does so again, I shall
not know what to say…' Her hoarse voice trailed into silence
and she smeared away another tear before it left her lashes.

Richard inclined his head, sightlessly inspecting his torn and
bleeding knuckles. Absently he turned the fist vertical, rested
his forehead against it and swore with vehement abandon.

Aware of Stephen approaching, he abruptly pushed himself away from the wall and grabbed Emma's wrist. She twisted in his grip but his fingers brutalised just enough to make her cease straining. 'Let the others know we're on our way back to Silverdale,' Richard bit out without once looking at his brother as their paths traversed.

'Don't you dare manhandle me, you…you perverted bastard!' she spat.

'Don't make a scene, Emma. And don't, for God's sake, provoke me further.'

With a snap and an imperious flick of long fingers a carriage was soon drawing up close to them.

The journey to Silverdale passed in total silence. Emma watched the passing of pearly scenery as though branding it on her memory. She would see it a final time in dawnlight when she left for London and then no more. Once or twice she snatched a glance at Richard's profile to find him staring through the coach window in the same vacant-eyed, preoccupied fashion she imagined she had been.

When the avenue of ghostly whitebeam widened on to driveway shingle and the footman opened the coach door with an exceedingly wary glance at his master, Emma dismounted with the servant's help and an insulting tap at the dark hand that was extended towards her.

Richard followed her into the hallway. 'Go straight to bed, Emma. We'll talk of this in the morning,' he said with weary dignity.

She ignored him, but did, indeed, head immediately for the stairs without once deigning to look in his direction. Halfway up the sweeping staircase, the explosion of a door below slamming made her jump and grab at the bannister. She actually stopped dead for a few seconds to allow her heart rate to settle before continuing to her room.

Emma looked at the letters she had written: one for Amelia, one for Miriam and one for Diane. Each held virtually the same wording: that she was pleased to have known them and sorry to leave so abruptly, but pressing matters in London required her immediate return. She felt inordinately pleased that there was no hint of untruth in any of it. She raised her eyes from her writing table by the window and looked out over a pink-streaked dawn sky. She had not slept at all and felt quite light-headed with an odd mingling of fatigue and nervous energy.

If Martin refused to take her to the general coach office in Bath to catch the early London mail coach, she would walk. She judged she would still make it in time for seven-fifteen. She and Victoria had rambled for miles through Hertfordshire countryside at times, and her carpet bag would not be that much of a burden. She collected it now, and, with a deep breath and a closing of her tired eyes, knew she was ready to depart.

A light rap at the door had her welded to the spot, heart hammering. Who on earth would be up and about at this hour? It was far too early for one of the maids to rouse her.

The tapping came again, then a plaintive voice called, 'Emma? Are you awake? Please open the door if you can hear me.'

Emma turned the key at once and Amelia rushed in, her face white and her eyes red-rimmed. She, too, was fully clothed.

'Stephen didn't come home with me last night. He is still abroad. He has a woman; I know he has.'

Emma felt chill seep through her. 'You can't be sure, Amelia,' she whispered…hoping.

'Oh, I can. Look!' She thrust a vibrating piece of paper at Emma. 'I went through to his chamber to see if he had returned and found this under a book. He hadn't even bothered to properly conceal it!' she hysterically squealed.

Emma took the cloyingly scented note, her heart sinking as she immediately recognised the elegant script to be the same as that on the interview details she had received from Yvette

Dubois. She scanned the invitation to meet then dine privately later that evening at South Parade. It was all couched in coy, suggestive terms and its purpose was indisputable.

As though just realising that Emma was not in nightclothes but actually cloaked and bonneted, Amelia cried softly, 'Are you leaving? Why?'

Emma nodded. 'I had written you a farewell note.' She turned her head indicatively towards the writing table but her eyes instinctively sought the brightening skies. 'There are urgent matters in London I must deal with. I'm so sorry, Amelia, but I must be going. If Martin refuses me a carriage, I shall need to walk to Bath.'

'I'm leaving too!' Amelia choked, too concerned with her own problems to ask further about Emma's. 'And I'm never coming back! He can keep as many cyprians as he pleases!'

Emma stared at her, aghast. 'Amelia, be sensible. You're a married woman. What of your beautiful children?'

Amelia's drawn face hardened intractably. 'He is a married man. Yet he conveniently forgets it! And my children will be well cared for. Miriam loves them. There are nursemaids, wet nurses, every conceivable help here at Silverdale.' She whispered brokenly, 'And their papa dotes on them…more than he does on me. They will be well cared for.' A bitter blue gaze was turned on Emma. 'I am leaving and if you will not let me travel with you, then I shall travel alone. I have a spinster aunt in London; we always deal well together. She won't tell of my whereabouts. Not even to her sister, my mama. For she is sure to rant and rail about duty and modesty—' She broke off and whirled about for the door. 'Well, I am done with duty and modesty!' she hissed. 'He pleaded with me to marry him, you know. A dozen times at least he must have proposed before I said he could approach my papa. I know how men are…even married men with their mistresses. But I believed we were different.' She added soulfully, 'It was a love match…is a love match…or so I thought…'

'Please consider what you are doing, Amelia,' Emma implored. 'You are being a little irrational. You might feel it impossible to abandon Jake and Alice in a few hours' time when you are calmer. It is a very great step to take: there may be no way back to your children.'

Amelia tossed her head and merely replied, 'Please wait, Emma; I should rather travel with you than alone. I'm sure you'd like a companion, too.'

Emma did wait, in the shadows in the spectral marble hallway, with thumping heart and dry mouth. All was eerily quiet until the sound of Amelia whisking down the stairs made her start.

Amelia, now cloaked and carrying a bag, grabbed at her hand and led her to a side door. 'At least you will not now have to walk to Bath, Emma,' she joked with muted hysteria. 'Martin will never refuse me a ride in the landau. We can take it directly to London. It will save time. If Stephen wants the vehicle back…he can blasted well search for it himself.'

Chapter Ten

The sound of the study door knocking back against the wall brought Richard's blond head up off his arms. As he pushed himself upright, a dark hand caught against the empty glass. He calmly righted it and slumped back in his chair to blink at the man by the door. 'What do you want?' he snapped irascibly.

'Amelia's left me,' Stephen croaked disbelievingly.

Richard drew a hand across his bleary eyes. 'Left you? What do you mean? How do you know?'

Stephen paced forward and let the note drift to the desk from his shaking fingers. 'The bed's not been slept in. She must have found this. It was lying on her pillow.' He choked an awful laugh. 'It's not the place I would have put it. She's run away. She's abandoned me and the children.'

Richard glanced over Yvette's note then flicked the perfumed paper away, grimacing in distaste. 'You've been out all night, I take it?'

'Yes, but…'

'He's been with me,' Ross chipped in from the doorway. 'We stayed at Bellamy's playing hazard and faro.'

'Why has she done it?' Stephen demanded, fingers dragging through his flaxen hair, tears glossing his blue eyes. 'Why?'

'Why?' Richard mimicked scornfully. 'She's done it so

you'll follow her, you bloody fool. And you'd better make sure when you do catch up with her that your excuses and apologies are word-perfect.'

'I never did anything, I swear. You can ask that French trollop. All I did was write her a note and meet her outside the Assembly Rooms. I never touched her. I swear it!'

'They left at dawn, in the landau,' Ross interjected quietly.

'They?' Richard repeated, a slow realisation focussing his intoxicated grey vision. He was halfway towards the door in seconds. The stairs were taken two at a time, but he slowed as he noted Emma's chamber door was ajar. On entering, he approached the writing desk and glanced down at the three letters arranged neatly. So she'd intended fleeing alone, he realised with a taut smile. It would have been pointless leaving Amelia a note if she had planned for them to journey together, or had known Amelia also intended bolting.

He aimlessly wandered from window to bed, then back again, feeling bereft already, and on quitting the quiet, tidy chamber smashed his fist into the door in sheer frustration, breaking open the crusty wounds on his knuckles.

'Well, I'm getting myself some breakfast,' Ross said cheerfully as he glanced from a coldly exasperated man to one who looked on the point of blubbing.

'You have to come with me,' Stephen pleaded. 'I need an alibi. Amelia will never believe I was gambling after reading this!' He flapped Yvette's note.

A wry look softened Ross's piratical features as he indicated Richard with a hand and a meaningful elevation of ebony brows.

'Oh, no one believes me,' Richard snarled sarcastically. 'I'm a perverted bastard…'

Ross blew out his cheeks and looked quizzically at them both. 'Are you sure there really is some point to this being in love?'

Richard stared, scowled and stalked off. Stephen dropped

his head into unsteady hands and ambled behind his brother towards the stables.

'*Derbyshire?*' Stephen cried in astonishment a few minutes later. 'For God's sake! Why there?'

'That's what I heard, Sir Richard,' Martin offered nervously. 'I'm sure I heard the lady with Mrs Du Quesne say about setting directly on the road to Derbyshire.'

Richard smiled grimly at the brightening horizon. 'No doubt she was aware you'd recount it to me,' he muttered. 'And I'd have reason enough to believe it plausible.' He mounted the palomino with swift agility. 'Let's try the London road,' he said, and was off in that direction.

'Horses could do wi' a drink 'n a rest,' the groom said. 'Fallow Buck be just up ahead, m'm. We can stop 'n you can take a drink too, if'n you fancy.'

'I should like a drink, Emma. It's getting quite warm now,' Amelia said.

'Are you sure you want to continue to London, Amelia?' Emma asked for the hundredth time. 'It is still early enough for you to change your mind. You could set about now and be back at Silverdale before you are properly missed.'

Amelia shook her head vigorously, setting blonde ringlets asway. 'I hate him,' she informed Emma calmly, chin tilted. 'I utterly hate him…'

'But what of your children?' Emma gently reminded her. 'I don't mean to nag you, Amelia, and it's not that I don't want your company, but…'

Amelia leaned towards her and squeezed her hand. 'I know. You want what is best for me. But I truly would have run away whether or not you'd departed for London. Don't feel guilty that you set the idea in my head.'

'I sat here in exactly this spot by this window when I journeyed to Bath all those days ago,' Emma told Amelia soon after as they sipped tea and ate cake and gazed out through tiny-paned, leaded windows into the inner courtyard. 'It seems like eons since I left London.' She smiled at her companion. 'And, strange as it may seem, I saw your dear little Jake here, although of course at the time I didn't know him. He and his uncle were on the forecourt. I was waiting for the mail coach to leave and saw them moments before I boarded it.' At Amelia's quizzical look, she added, 'I only glimpsed Richard's profile and didn't recognise him. He looked…looks very different now. His tanned skin and sun-lightened hair make him appear quite a stranger.' She added quickly, 'Were you here too that morning, Amelia?'

Amelia shook her head. 'Richard and Stephen took Jake to the seaside for a few days. Miriam has friends at Lyme Regis whom she wanted to visit. I couldn't travel for I was still indisposed with my confinement.' She paused. 'Little Jake adores Richard; he would make a good papa. I shall miss my Jakie,' she murmured with a throb to her voice. 'He is a good boy…'

With an anxious frown at Amelia's tear-bright eyes, Emma tried again. 'You see, you are pining for the children already. I think you should turn about and return home…'

'And I think that sounds like sensible advice, sweetheart,' came huskily from behind them.

The two women exchanged startled glances before twisting about on their chairs.

Stephen was standing directly behind, Richard was in the process of handing the landlord a sum of money for the small taproom's private use, and Ross was seating himself on a rickety stool by the bar. Helping himself to a bottle and a glass, Ross nonchalantly commenced making good use of both.

'I believe it is time we resumed our journey, Emma,' Amelia said with icy deliberation. She stood and had managed two regal steps towards the door before Stephen stepped in front of her.

'You're my wife and you're going nowhere at all but back home with me,' her husband growled.

Ross winced and shook his head at his drink. Richard leaned

against the bar, helped himself to the bottle and poured while slanting a flint-eyed gaze at Emma.

Emma stared through the taproom window. Her weary lids dropped in sheer hopelessness. Why had it yet again all gone so horribly wrong? If only she'd been selfish! If only she'd refused Amelia's company and departed alone this morning from York House coach office: she would have been well on her way home.

As it was, her only means of continuing to London would be via a mail coach, if one stopped, sporting a vacant seat, to refresh its passengers and horses. Failing that, she might be stranded at a countryside inn or taken back to Bath by the detestable lecher she was keen to escape. Perhaps Richard believed she had cajoled Amelia into accompanying her by recounting what she'd witnessed outside the Assembly Rooms last night!

'Do you expect me to believe *that*?' sliced through Emma's feverish thoughts in a savage hiss.

Stephen's coaxing response to his wife's outrage was also audible. 'Ross will tell you it's the truth! I *swear* I was with him…I *love* you, Amelia…'

Feeling unbearably intrusive, Emma abruptly got to her feet and made for the door. She kept her head high as she passed the two men at the bar, even managing eye contact and a quavering, 'Good morning.'

Ross gave her a lopsided smile. Richard looked so sardonically triumphant that it almost caused her to halt and wipe the smile from his face.

As she emerged into warm Indian summer sunshine, honey and copper glints flared in her fawn hair. She sped away towards the road and stared along it, willing a coach to appear right now…*this minute*.

There was nothing; all was pastoral and peaceful. It was a hauntingly glorious morning, she glumly realised. Dispiritedly she turned back to see a groom lead away the handsome stallion. Then its owner appeared in the tavern doorway and strolled towards her.

He stopped a little distance from her and stared along the dusty, rutted track in much the same way she had moments before. 'What are you looking for?'

'The mail coach,' she stiffly informed him, staring across haystacked fields.

'Ah,' he grunted in wry comprehension. 'Still intent on taking the scenic route to Derbyshire, then. Proceeding via London, are you?'

Emma flushed. She had forgotten about that little deceit.

Reading her thoughts exactly, he said softly, 'You see, I'm coming to know you well, Emma. If you want to outwit me, try telling the truth. I swear the surprise will kill me.'

'Indeed I shall, then, sir. The inducement is too great to ignore.'

He laughed at that and turned fully towards her, and as she looked properly at him she recognised the dissipation in his dark face. 'You're drunk,' she snapped.

'Not any more. I'm hung over,' he explained easily. 'And feeling much better now I've had a hair of the dog that bit me.' As though sensing her suspicions, he said softly, 'I was at home all night, drinking alone.'

'I really couldn't care less where you were or who you were with,' she dismissed with a shrill laugh.

'Well, persevering with my new wisdom that the truth is usually the opposite of what you say, I conclude you care very much.'

'That's not wisdom,' Emma shot back, startled, 'but conceit. And there's nothing new about it. I dare say it's been with you your life through.' She swished about to glare along the road.

'Well, enough of these pleasantries.' Richard laughed with an amount of contentment. 'It's time to be getting home. Between them, Stephen and Ross should have managed to persuade Amelia that her husband's not an adulterer but an idiot. There's been time enough for tears and making up.'

'Unfaithful in heart, unfaithful indeed,' Emma muttered.

'That makes you sound sweetly innocent, Emma,' Richard softly mocked. 'And I'd really like to think you were…rather than simply naive.' A searing silver look was levelled at her slender body from beneath low black lashes. 'It's got nothing to do with his heart. His heart has always been with Amelia. Stephen's only vice last night was gambling.'

'And his vice tonight? Or is it not yet his turn to visit South Parade?' she bitterly lashed out. 'Will Ross speak for him when it is? Will you? Will you both help him lie and cheat and deceive his wife?'

A dark hand spanned his brow, easing tension beneath a fall of sun-bleached hair. 'Are you now willing to let me explain about that?' he sighed.

'There is no point,' she whipped out haughtily. 'I still wouldn't believe you if you told me the time of day.' That jolted her thoughts to the morning passing. She peered again along the track for sight of the mail coach. 'I wonder how late it is? It surely cannot yet be noon,' she muttered to herself, with a squint at the sun.

'It's almost a quarter to eleven,' Richard informed her with studied gravity. 'Would you care to check my watch?'

As she glowered and blushed simultaneously, he said on a choke of a laugh, 'Come, I'll get the landau brought round.'

'I'm going to London,' Emma breathed at his back as he walked away.

'You're going to Silverdale,' he smoothly contradicted her without bothering to turn around.

'Don't give me your orders! I have to journey to London.'

'Why?'

'I want…need to see my parents.'

Richard turned towards her. 'Will they want to see you?'

'Yes, I'm sure they will now.'

He slowly retraced his steps. 'Well, come back to Bath today and I'll take you to London tomorrow. We have to return to Silverdale for a coach, in any case, and I have some business to conclude.'

'Thank you for your concern,' she said tightly, 'but I can board the mail coach. I wouldn't dream of imposing on you…'

'That means go to hell…'

'Indeed,' Emma said.

'I'll get the landau brought round; we'll discuss it all at Silverdale.'

'I'm not returning there.'

'This is foolishness, Emma,' Richard gritted with straining patience. 'I can't spirit you to London without transport. You can't be sure a mail coach with space will pull in here this week.' He stuffed his hands into the pockets of his long leather riding coat. 'Anyway, it makes no difference if the damned coach arrives empty and within the next five minutes—you're still not boarding it. You're not travelling to London alone.'

'I travelled from London alone!'

'Well, you're not travelling back in the same manner!' he suddenly roared. The grim exasperation in his face had Emma taking two hasty backward paces.

'Sorry.' He held out a hand, palm towards her, in placation and reassurance. As it moved to span his brow, massaging at his temples, she noticed the wounds crimsoning his knuckles.

'Is your hand sore?'

'Yes. I'll try and remember to use the other one next time you provoke me into sparring with a brick wall or a bedroom door.'

Their eyes met and held, silver engulfing amber as he walked back slowly towards her. 'I was peeved that you'd run without due thanks for my hospitality.' He ironically explained away the bedroom door incident. His fingers rose towards her face, then nimbly dodged the slap she aimed at them. 'That's very cruel, Emma,' he reproached her, with a pained look. 'You'll make me bleed again.'

Despite herself, she *felt* cruel, and ashamed. Seizing his

damaged hand, she inspected rusty, crusty lacerations to make sure none had been caught. 'I'm sorry you hurt yourself,' she said quietly. 'You should ask Mrs Braithwaite for some salve. She has potions…' Becoming aware of his stillness and silence, she quickly released the injured digits.

Both dark hands curved about her upper arms, stubbornly drawing her close. 'You know, you can be incredibly sweet to me at times…when you forget you ought to hate me.'

'I was simply concerned that I had worsened your hurt,' she burst out, turning her face to study the ground as she sensed him getting ever closer.

'I love your concern. It's worth being hurt. That's the first time you've touched me with kindness.'

The sound of approaching footsteps and conversation had Richard blaspheming through closed teeth and Emma hastily breaking free.

She showed him a little sympathy and his damnable conceit made him think there was more to it! Just as it made him think she cared with whom he spent a drunken night…when of course she did not! It made no difference to her whether it was Ross and Stephen or a dozen French courtesans! She swallowed and made a conscious effort to unfurl her fingers and prevent her nails digging any deeper into her tender palms.

'Emma!' Amelia, face aglow with contentment, tripped daintily away from her husband. Drawing Emma aside for privacy, she whispered, 'Stephen has explained everything and Ross has said it is all true. And I do believe them.'

'Good…good,' Emma breathed. 'I am happy you are to return home.'

Amelia linked arms with Emma and urged her along the track. 'Come, let's take a little walk by the hedgerows and we can be as deliciously immodest as we like while I tell you all.' Amelia peered back over her shoulder at the men watching them. She sighed happily at her husband's smouldering-eyed semi-smile, flounced her blonde ringlets around and began, 'The note I showed you that I found in Stephen's chamber was sent by Richard's mistress! The shameless trollop was soliciting Stephen's protection because his brother had put her off. She actually attempted to peddle her vile services to my husband!' Amelia squeaked in outrage. 'For two pins I'd go to South Parade and scratch her evil eyes out. But I'd be too late: Richard is sending her back to France, thank heavens!'

Amelia narrowed her blue eyes. 'I saw her once or twice when she was at the theatre with Richard and she did slyly eye Stephen. The impudent hussy has got her comeuppance and will soon be gone. It was just so droll, Emma,' she confided breathily. 'Stephen was so desperate to convince me that this baggage is now out of favour, he revealed that his brother must already be coaching her understudy! The house of sin is apparently rarely vacant!' Hugging at Emma's arm, she squealed, 'Scandalous of us to talk so, isn't it? Miriam and my own dear mama would be utterly outraged by such indelicacy and have a wondrous fit of the vapours!'

Emma forced a brittle smile. 'Yes; but perhaps no more might be prudent. You should forget it for she is not worth further time or thoughts.'

So, Yvette Dubois was to be banished because Richard had someone in mind to replace her. Emma swallowed. She had an ominous feeling she knew who that might be! No wonder he was adamant she return to Bath with him. Though she doubted he had any intention of taking her to Silverdale. Her destination was likely to be a vacant Palladian town house in South Parade!

As they strolled on in September sunshine Emma's mind was in turmoil. She could return to Bath and choose between a temporary position as a gentleman's mistress or a lengthy labour as a drunkard's wife; or she could journey on to London and face Jarrett Dashwood and her mother's wrath. She thought of her pathetic, weak-willed papa and wondered in which direction he had absconded and whether Dashwood had yet tracked him there. Perhaps he had fled west, too, and was unknowingly close to her.

A tremor shivered through her as she recalled Susan Petersham's unwitting warning: 'I shouldn't like to be in that chit's shoes when eventually she and Dashwood come face to face…' And yet it seemed every passing moment proved, that for her parents' sake, and, yes, even her own, it would have been prudent to settle for the future he offered. The past several days had been a catalogue of her deceitfulness and trickery and the outcome was further jeopardy and harrowing self-disgust. Nought had been gained! Now she was scheming to return and right the mess her flight had caused. Her behaviour was reprehensible: utterly selfish and stupidly immature.

Dashwood had appearances to keep, she recalled her mother saying. Susan Petersham had implied something similar in that he was loath to name her family in this scandal or to reveal much of any of it. Even if it was for his own wounded pride's sake, she could only feel gratitude for the reprieve.

Her mother had been right all along: she was a fool to hanker after love when security was attainable. One couple of her acquaintance was blissfully happy and she coveted that for herself, ridiculously supposing *she* could live a romantic ideal. With hindsight, she saw she had allowed gossip to prejudice her views of Dashwood before she had passed five minutes in his company. Had she been pleasant to him he might, in turn, have been perfectly fair and civil.

Half an hour later, displaying maternal and wifely duty in abundance, Amelia was desperate to again be at Silverdale with her husband and children. Emma returned Amelia and Stephen a double-handed waving salute as the landau crunched over the Fallow Buck's forecourt and disappeared up the lane. Her amber gaze then slid sideways to the tall blond man standing close by. 'I shall do very well here,' she brightly told him. 'I was alone here once before and quite safe.'

'Yes, I recall seeing you here alone. I'm not likely to forget that morning. I've not had a moment's peace since,' Richard added ruefully.

Stunned that he had even noticed her hunching into her

cloak and bonnet that misty morning, let alone remembered the drab sight she must have presented, she garbled, 'Thank you for your kind hospitality at Silverdale. I shall impress on Victoria just how attentive you were to my needs.'

'I'd like to return the compliment and impress on David just how attentive you were to my needs,' Richard rejoined smoothly. 'I shall have a carriage brought here from Silverdale and accompany you to London. *En route* you'll have a little more opportunity to redress the balance and be kind to me. It is time I checked on my London residence, in any case.'

Emma lowered fiery, tawny eyes. She was right! Be *kind* to him indeed! Once alone in a carriage with him, she would be seduced…tricked back to Bath and installed in that house as his mistress. Well, she wanted no more of his attentiveness! And he was certainly receiving none of hers!

Even should she be wrong, and he returned her to London, his presence would be hazardous: he might allow some of her stupid lies to leak out. Just the slightest rumour circulating that she was with child and Jarrett Dashwood was sure to believe himself duped into giving a bastard a name. The ensuing furore and ostracism would devastate her parents! What on earth had possessed her to contribute to the fallacy that she was ruined? Now the only way back was to admit she had intentionally misled him.

'I realise you have business concerns,' she burst out, trying a different tack. 'You will want to conclude those before quitting Bath. There is no point in us both returning to Silverdale whilst you do so. I shall wait here for you to return with a carriage.'

'There is only a minor concern,' Richard informed her, hard-pressed to keep laughter from his voice as he recognised her strategies. As soon as he was out of sight, she would be off in the opposite direction. 'Ross is to conclude that matter. It will be no hardship for him…' he added drily, recalling Ross's speculative look on being charged with ensuring Yvette Dubois was packed up and shipped out with her belongings and a banker's draft. Ross was certain to appease any tantrums with a little consideration of his own.

'Don't fret on my account, Emma,' Richard gently mocked. 'There is nothing else pressing. I shall not be terribly incommoded by accompanying you. However, a little show of gratitude for my pains would not go amiss…' He slanted her a smile then laughed at her narrow-eyed irritation.

'Come…pax,' he said softly. 'Our truce is still in force, you know. I'm determined to honour it a while yet.'

'Well, I am *not*,' she choked at his leather-coated back as he headed towards the tavern, with talk of feeling hungry. 'Our truce is over. *I* am ready to resume hostilities,' she impressed upon him, half running behind to keep up with his long stride.

'That's not an option following our truce, Emma.'

'Oh? What is, then?'

'Surrender.' He turned to face her so suddenly that she shoved her hands against his broad chest to prevent herself crashing into him. Topaz eyes flared beneath silver gleaming down at her. A nervous flick of a tongue moistened her dry lips and then she dodged past him and entered the tavern.

'Not like that!' Richard chided as the cards flew in all directions. A large hand swept the small baize-topped table, collecting them. He stacked them quickly, neatly cut the pack, shuffled them expertly then cupped a hand to square them.

Emma concentrated carefully, her sharp little chin resting on curled fingers. She held out a small hand, received the pack with a supercilious look and set about matching his mastery. Her thumbs seemed to stick to the card edges: instead of freeing them to neatly interleave they clumped down thickly without rhythm.

Dark fingers covered hers. 'Hold then lightly…let them flow.'

She watched their fingers flexing together and the cards did, indeed, mesh. With a confident smile, she cupped the pack in her hands and tried to adroitly flick them back as he had. They

spattered across green baize. The few she still held were
dropped onto the table with a wry grimace.

They had been playing piquet. The first occasion she had
been dealt four sevens and he'd received four eights she had
accepted it *might* be odd chance. She had resolved to shrewdly
observe next time the cards were distributed. She'd noticed
nothing up his sleeve or slipped from under the table…yet
he'd then received four tens and she four nines. Sulkily, she
had flounced back in her seat, snapping that he ought to have
dealt himself the four knaves, he was such a Captain Sharp.

'That's fighting talk, Emma,' he had warned with a soft
laugh, and next dealt her a hand devoid of royalty: a carte
blanche.

Naively, she had been pleased, believing it might win, and
was about to triumphantly display it…until he asked what he'd
given her with an air of innocence and latent amusement that
made the French term freeze on her lips. 'Nothing worth having,' she'd petulantly retorted, discarding the hand.

That had made him laugh outright and say softly, 'Very
wise…I'm sure we'll manage better than that.' He'd proceeded to deal her four aces next time around. It was the first
game she'd won and, gratified, she'd omitted to chide him for
his chicanery.

He had taught her two card tricks; leaned across, empty-
handed, and drawn forth the queen of hearts from behind one
of her small ears, then idly erected a winding trail of barely
touching dominoes. The last he'd flicked over and a sinuous
line had gracefully bowed down. It was only when collapsed
on the table she'd noticed it formed the shape of a heart. She
had been entertained, impressed, too, until the heat of liquid-
mercury eyes on her had cooled her humour. It was obviously
his heart, she had acidly commented, as it was black.

Richard collected the scattered cards now and idly shuffled
them, observing her sculpted, pensive countenance while she
watched his nimble fingers.

'It's rude to stare,' she muttered at his hands.

'You're beautiful; why shouldn't I look at you?' he reasoned mildly.

Emma stabbed a fierce golden glance at him, sure he was jesting, but there was no hint of mockery in his face. But there was something else: it made her heartbeat check then start pumping erratically. 'My mother says I've faded as I've aged...I'm now quite near thirty,' she emphasised. 'I must admit when younger...much younger...my hair was darker... my eyes too, I'm sure.'

'Is that supposed to make me see you differently?' he asked gently. 'You looked exactly the same three years ago. You've not altered a bit. Your hair...your eyes are just as exquisite now as then. Don't you like it that I find you beautiful, Emma? Does it frighten you?'

She stood abruptly and wandered to the window and gazed out into the mellow afternoon. He was definitely attempting to seduce her, she realised, and she could feel some traitorous response to his flattery deep within her, ready and willing to succumb to his blandishments.

Matthew's compliments praised her kindness, her wit, her ability to tutor his children. No man had ever told her she was beautiful. This silver-tongued squire said it and made her believe it, too. But then, of all the men who had shown a modicum of interest in her since her debut, he was by far the most dangerously sophisticated. He was well versed in all aspects of seduction, she was sure, including pretty, contrived speeches. And it was simply stupid vanity that made her want to believe him sincere.

With a wistful sigh Emma gazed onto the courtyard, watching a young ostler grooming a child's pony. She guessed the time must now be about four in the afternoon and there was still no sign of a mail coach pulling in.

Since the others had left for Silverdale, she and Richard had enjoyed a fine meal and animated discussion about the Courtenays and their cherished goddaughter, Lucy, and Richard's intention to soon bring about an overdue reunion with them now he was finally back home.

She had learned that Richard had spent most of the past two years, following his father's death, in the West Indies. He had no wish to keep the sugar plantations that his great-grandfather had bought more than a hundred years previously. Slave labour and all its barbarism was abhorrent to him, he had said, and besides, the abolitionists would eventually get their way and outlaw the practice. He had been content to live there for a time while he ousted the corrupt overseers and managers who had been left in charge. Then there was the lengthy process of selling on the vast acreage to a neighbour planter and issuing his workforce with manumissions which made them free men and women.

Emma had listened with awe, feeling quietly astounded by his humanity; disturbed, too, that he must, indeed, be acquainted with Dashwood. Dashwood had plantations in the Indies and a reputation as a very harsh master. She had practically had to bite her tongue to prevent her demanding whether all the foul gossip she had heard of her spurned fiancé was true. But she knew that any mention of Dashwood would arouse Richard's curiosity and suspicion and prompt an interrogation…and then all her tapestry of deceit would surely unravel. So she'd simply listened, engrossed, learning that Richard had no inclination or need to return abroad and was home at Silverdale to stay.

To an outsider they would have appeared what they were supposed to be: close cousins breaking their journey with refreshment, rest and absorbed conversation.

It had been Richard's idea to introduce them as kin. They were, after all, sharing a private dining room on the first floor and, as she was supposed to be a virtuous single lady, her reputation would suffer if it got out she had been closeted alone with a bachelor for some hours. It was a trifling deceit amongst so many, he had meaningfully said with a penetrating look, and would serve a purpose.

Emma picked up her novel from the window sill where earlier she had dropped it and idly flicked the pages over. She felt a prowling restlessness. She wanted to be gone from here. Wanted to be far from this man for he set such conflicting thoughts spinning in her mind. She wanted to hate him, yet she recognised feelings of immense respect that he had placed philanthropy above commercial gain. He had not brought it to her notice, but she knew he could have sold his slaves along with his acreage to his fellow planter.

Yet weighted against all that was his debauchery. She knew his history: he'd certainly been a scandalous rakehell for years. But he was no worse a rogue than David Hardinge had been, and Emma gladly admitted to being very fond of him. David was now a devoted husband and father. Perhaps Richard would be, too, when he married his duke's daughter. Despite Amelia dismissing his nuptials as no love match, he would surely reform enough to give his bride dignity and status and keep his paramours well out of sight.

Thoughts jumbled in her head…thoughts of when he'd kissed her and how it had made her feel—as though she would willingly join their numbers, remain in that entrancing, pleasurable limbo he sent her to and let him do what he would to her. That fearful, unwanted perception made her face flame and an involuntary 'No!' broke from between compressed lips.

Richard arrowed a look at her and then unwound himself from the chair he sat in and strolled towards her. Two dark hands braced either side of her, trapping her against the skewed black oak window frame. She felt hair stir at her nape as he bent towards her and said, 'Come, don't sulk. If I'd said you were ugly as sin you'd have a reason to be broody.'

That made her smile wanly at the autumn afternoon. A dark hand slid to cup her cheek, his thumb smoothing across a ridge of delicate high cheekbone. Her smile faded and she tried to twitch away from his touch.

Gently he turned her about and held her still. 'Look at me, Emma.'

Fawn eyes flicked to his, wary…suspicious.

'I want to explain about yesterday evening. Why I was with Stephen and Yvette Dubois outside the Assembly Rooms.'

Emma stared past his shoulder. 'There's no need. Amelia has done so. You had decided to discard your mistress and she approached Stephen to replace you.' She made to sweep past but he wouldn't allow it.

'That doesn't explain why I appeared to be kissing her. In fact it makes the explanation seem false.'

'Appeared?' she snapped. 'Are you inclined to striking poses, then?'

'No. Just walls and doors, since you came back into my life.' Barely pausing, he continued, 'She was kissing me because she hoped I would be persuaded to take her back. It was a little unsuccessful seduction, nothing more. For my part, I went along with it because I wanted to convince Stephen he'd be a fool to jeopardise the love he and Amelia share for such a fickle, paltry liaison.'

'So noble of you to endure it all, sir, I'm sure,' Emma ground out caustically, and again vainly tried to pass him.

'Do you know why I didn't want to endure it?' At her careless show of ennui, he listed softly, 'Because I wanted to return above stairs to you. I wanted to dance with you…go home to Silverdale with you…kiss you… I want you.'

Emma sensed his lips closing with hers and jerked back.

'Don't do that, Emma. You know you love it when I kiss you,' was breathed huskily, warmly against her cheek.

'Don't you do it!' she whispered back hoarsely. 'Don't you dare! There's nothing you can say…no eloquent lies that will make me go to that house with you…' The rest was lost. This time she did put up a token resistance. As his mouth slanted warmly across hers she raised her hands, pushed at his shoulders, raised them further till her knuckles raked his face. Her nails *did* press against his lean cheeks, and she sensed his skin dipping beneath the pressure, but she couldn't do more.

And he realised it, too. His kiss was rewarding, gently courting. Her arms rose and for the first time she embraced him properly, slid quivering fingers into his beautiful pale hair, felt its silky glide against her skin.

Firm fingers skimmed her sides, drawing her close to his hardening body, massaging tantalisingly close to tautening breasts, and the moan tore from her, exploding softly into his mouth.

Richard pulled his hot mouth away across her cheek, nipped at an ear, fanned steaming breath against her neck, making her twist her head, writhe her body to merge with his.

'Does he make you feel like this?' was rasped against her ear. 'Does he?'

'Who?' Emma whimpered as her throat arched temptingly towards him.

Tormenting kisses were trailed against the creamy column of her neck. 'Your Derbyshire lover. William Fitz,' he gritted out, his hands tightening on her hips, thrusting her close to his rigid groin. 'Tell me. Can he arouse you as I do…with just one kiss?'

Emma jerked back, looked up into grey eyes blackened by lust. 'Yes. Every time he kisses me,' she choked. 'Every single time. It's so much better than this…'

She attempted to squirm free, but a lean, dark hand wound into her thick, glossy hair, brought her face back to his. He fused their bodies, holding her unmoving. 'Thank you, Emma' he breathed with clean, raw satisfaction against her lips. 'That means he doesn't even compare.'

Chapter Eleven

If there was a perfect time to escape it was now: he would never suspect she might disappear while her only mode of transport was in full view in front of the tavern.

Wandering away from the pump where she had stationed herself, Emma broodily watched the passengers alight from the mail coach. To add insult to injury, there was one vacant seat that she could discern. She took another slow promenade about the white-washed building, rays of late afternoon sun weaving gold into her reflectively bowed tawny head.

She tried to focus on the urgent need to travel but her mind recoiled time and again to fix on her humiliation above stairs minutes ago. Her complexion was still flushed with the memory of it, her lips puffed scarlet, her pupils so dilated her eyes resembled amber-ringed obsidian. Pearly lids shielded a mortified brilliance on recalling how he had unwound her tenacious arms from about his neck and gently put her from him. Not that he wanted to stop, he had softly sighed, but if he didn't they might finish being more than simply kissing cousins at this roadside tavern. And then, with a shattered little laugh, he had left her, saying that he needed some air to cool off.

By the time he returned, ten minutes or so later, Emma had salvaged a modicum of dignity and pride and with great aplomb informed him that she, too, needed to refresh herself, and immediately quit the room.

Out in the balmy autumn afternoon, she was soon grinding her teeth in vexation as the mail coach swayed to a halt. Of course, he would have noticed it too but was probably smugly confident she was now so in his thrall she would gladly surrender and go to South Parade. Well, he was vastly mistaken in imagining she would submit so feebly!

Be first to move; take the enemy by surprise! her papa had used to chortle when absconding from Rosemary House minutes before his creditors hammered at the door. That rhetoric had come good for some twenty years. When victory seemed unattainable, avoid the battle, was Frederick Worthington's hypothesis.

True to his word, her papa had again removed himself from the fray and disappeared and she would do likewise—perhaps in the process secure for her papa another twenty years' dun-shunning, she heroically fancied.

But how? Walking to London was hardly an option. Even if she possessed the courage and energy, she'd not manage more than a mile or two before Richard caught up with her. And bolting into woodland on foot would be idiotically reckless. She might be accosted by gypsies while getting hopelessly lost. She needed to keep close to the main road. She needed a ride, too.

Sensing eyes on her, she swung about and peered over a rough wood door into semi-darkness. A stable lad with a mop of curly flaxen hair peered back. A curry comb was in his hand and he had obviously been grooming the flanks of Richard's horse, silhouetted in the murk.

He looked to be little more than fourteen yet had a confident, cocky air. But he tugged a forelock politely at her. 'Yer cousin's 'orse be a fine animal, m'm,' he judged knowledgeably.

'Indeed,' Emma snarled in irritation. The lad looked abashed at her brusqueness, prompting a surge of remorse. 'He has quite wonderful colouring, don't you think?' she conversationally made amends. 'Just a few shades lighter than a new sovereign, I would judge.'

He nodded. 'And 'is tail and mane so near white. 'E's an Arab in part, I'll be bound. I should like t'ave rid such as 'e,' the boy wistfully said, patting a supple side with a reverent hand. ''Ave you rid 'im?'

Emma stared at the boy and then at the horse, her mind feverish in its machinations. 'Why, yes,' she fibbed. 'And a good rid…ride he is too. It is the reason I am here…for a little exercise. I am feeling a trifle restless while waiting for my cousin's transport to arrive.' Swallowing, she glanced uneasily back at the tavern. Encouragingly, the upper window of their small private chamber was not at all visible.

The stable boy was quizzically regarding the way she was garbed. Hardly riding attire, she gleaned from his face.

'Oh, these will serve.' She carelessly twitched her plain brown travelling skirts. 'Would you saddle him, please?' she charmingly commanded.

'What's 'is name?' the boy asked, obediently unhooking the saddle.

'Name?' Emma neared the animal and as it bobbed its head around she noticed the ivory shape on its golden nose.

'Star,' she blurted with a smile. 'Leastways, that's what I call him.'

Rather belatedly the boy asked cautiously, 'You sure yer cousin knows, m'm, an' won't be objectin'?'

Emma bestowed on him her haughtiest look. 'Knows? Objecting?' she spouted, with a scornful little laugh.

''Ave to ask, m'm,' he apologised, his smooth cheeks reddening. 'Master might be right mad if'n 'e don't know and do object.'

'Oh, but of course he will know of it…' Emma reassured him. *Eventually*…whispered through her mind with frightening reverberation.

The lad nodded his head and heaved the saddle across the animal's back. 'Can you ride wi'out side-saddle, miss?'

She hadn't thought of that. 'Oh, yes. It's no problem at all…' In for a penny, in for a pound…scuttled deliriously through her mind.

There seemed to be an inordinate amount of buckling and tightening to be done and Emma felt some of her nervous exhilaration sapping. She bit at her tongue to stop herself scolding him for sloth while congratulating her foresight in having donned her cloak against an early evening chill before coming below. She checked its pockets for her money pouch then glanced anxiously back at the courtyard. All seemed tranquil…almost too quiet.

Aware the groom was finished with his task and eyeing her expectantly, Emma surveyed the statuesque stallion with a wary eye, hoping she could recall all that David had taught her about riding.

She had owned a pony as a child when she and her parents had lived in Surrey. But as soon as her papa's gambling had become excessive their rural home had been lost and they'd lived permanently in Rosemary House, in Cheapside. Rumour had it that her papa had actually wagered the deeds to their modest country retreat on one throw of the dice. That had been when Emma was nine years old and she had not again mounted a horse until she'd visited Hertfordshire and stayed with the Courtenays at their opulent mansion.

Victoria wasn't an accomplished rider either so they had both been under David's expert tutelage and had had fine times trotting happily about together on gentle-natured beasts while improving their rusty skills. She imagined her friend would be an able horsewoman by now.

Emma looked fearfully at the palomino…anything less like those mild-mannered mares she could not conceive. With an inspiriting smile and her skirts bunched into her fists, Emma threw modesty and a shapely leg to one side. Once settled on the saddle, she decorously smoothed her clothing and gave gracious thanks, and a coin from the few left in her pouch, to the grinning young groom. He tugged his forelock, face aglow with admiration as he watched Emma proceed sedately, then at an easy canter into the distance.

He'd give her a while to sulk and feel ill-used and then go to find her, Richard decided with a wry smile. And when he did he might as well tell her. As he'd accepted it now himself, it was pointless not reassuring her that his intentions were entirely honourable. Yet he would rue the passing of these sparring sessions she manoeuvred them into…there was a definite sensual satisfaction in converting all that aggression to sweeter passion.

He sat in the armchair by the small fire, pulled the wine table close and rested his booted feet upon it while drawing deeply on his cheroot. Flickering logs held his attention as he acknowledged he was feeling undeniably content. Which was odd considering he'd obliquely acceded to another man's bastard, if male, being heir to Silverdale and all his vast estates and wealth. But then such madness was, he supposed, the price one paid for indulging in this bewitching torture that was love.

He could recall pitying David for succumbing to the ravages of that thankless emotion. Now here he was, three years on, gladly wallowing in it himself. He choked a laugh and blew a lazy blue haze at the ceiling as he wondered how she would react to his declaration. Astonishment…definitely, for he was still a heartless philanderer in her estimation. Suspicion… definitely; she would no doubt think he was lying to trick her back to his town house.

Reciprocation was what he wanted. He wanted her to look at him with those beautiful feral eyes, sheath her claws and melt sweetly against him, as he knew she could. But he wanted her to do it of her own volition, without him touching her. He wanted her, unreservedly, to love him back. Cynicism twisted his sensual lips. Which brought him neatly to a faceless man from Derbyshire and the uncertainties that plagued him.

Did she love this William Fitz? She didn't appear to be pining and seemed to have readily accepted that he was pledged elsewhere. Yet he knew she would never have indulged in a casual affair. It just wasn't her way. But it had been his way, for far longer than he cared to recall. That was why, in his heart, he knew her censure and distrust were justified.

His riotous past was wedged between them. He and David *had* been disreputable scoundrels for very many years. But watching David's father die from the pox had been a salutary lesson for them both. Time-served courtesans had never been of interest. Of greater attraction had been fresh young women, fallen on hard times, who were delighted to escape the penury of widowhood or the rigours of long hours toiling as seamstresses in favour of a position as pampered paramour until they were pensioned comfortably off. And they applied in droves. It had rarely been necessary to seek them out; both he and David were regularly propositioned by ambitious young women.

Yet since David's marriage and move to the countryside he had curbed his excesses and rarely kept more than one mistress at a time, rarely gambled, or drank to excess. In fact, yesterday evening was the first time in a long while that he'd imbibed too much to get to bed. Most of his fighting was now restricted to organised bouts at Gentleman Jackson's or the fencing academy.

He envied David: seeing him so serenely happy, so relaxed and content, with a wife he adored, had been one of the reasons he had opted to deal with his Jamaican interest himself rather than send an agent. Their friendship had been so intense he'd known he had to get away and allow the bond to loosen for both their sakes. And while overseeing the sale of his Jamaican estates he had often brooded on whether he wanted to return to such orgiastic excesses or whether David's marriage had neatly closed a youthful era for them both.

Relaxing some evenings beneath a heavy tropical moon,

he'd reminisced about Emma too, yet dismissed sentiment and longing as being some contagious reaction to what David felt for Victoria. The idea that he and his best friend would neatly fall in love with the perfect harmony they did most other things was just too ludicrous. So he hadn't allowed himself to contact her again, discover whether she was now married, and his bruised pride had reminded him time and again that, in any case, she had never liked him.

Now he knew how stupid he'd been. Just one glimpse of a cloaked woman at a rural tavern and he'd been overwhelmed. His mind hadn't known it was her, but his heart had... instinctively. When he'd seen her waiting patiently in his hallway at South Parade, he'd known: fate had brought her to him. She had raised those extraordinarily beautiful eyes and her wild panic as she'd recognised him had aroused the strangest sensation: a welcome tranquillity.

After three restless months on English soil he felt truly home.

Wryly acknowledging that what couldn't be undone must be endured, he stood abruptly, wandered to the window and scoured the courtyard for sight of her. He smiled at the stationary coach. Perhaps she was ensconced within it, waiting for it to depart. A laugh throbbed in his throat. Hardly! With her temperament she would have attempted driving it off herself! It was as well one of the horses had pulled up lame.

He made to turn and his hand knocked against her novel, discarded on the window ledge. Collecting it idly, he carried it back to his seat. Sticking the cigar between his teeth, he flicked over pages and read: 'It is a truth universally acknowledged, that a single man in possession of a good fortune, must be in want of a wife...' He smiled past the cheroot...feeling mellow as he did, it seemed a reasonable enough assumption.

The knock at the door some time later had Richard dropping the book on the table. 'Well, I'll be damned!' he muttered, low and vehement, and shook his head in disbelief.

Stephen sauntered into the room, a grin livening his boyish

features. 'What excellent service is this? What effusive thanks do I deserve?' he ribbed his older brother.

'What effusive thanks do *I* deserve?' Richard drily countered, reminding Stephen he was due a little gratitude for his part in recovering his wife and his senses for him.

Stephen had the grace to blush a little. 'Mmm…thanks for helping out with that. I've been a blasted fool of late, I admit it. But it's all finished now…' He shuffled uneasily, studying his nails.

'I'm glad to hear it. I'm sure Amelia is, too…'

'Not only does your carriage await, m'lud—' Stephen swiftly changed subject '—but I bear tidings.'

Richard raised dark brows as he lit a fresh cigar, waved the match about to extinguish it then flicked it towards the fire.

'Ross has attended to your business with his usual flair and speed. Yvette has set sail…apparently looking mightily content once your banker's draft was in her hot little hand…or perhaps it was something Ross put there that pleased her,' he drolly suggested. 'I can't now quite recall… Anyway, Ross sends word that he is to visit his brother, Luke, in Brighton and will see you in London in a few days.'

Stephen paused to help himself to a brandy from the decanter. 'Now the bad news…' He grimaced. 'Mother is fair prone with nervous fatigue. I've managed to persuade her that Amelia was missing due to an early morning drive to see Emma partway home and that Emma… Where is she, by the by?' he interjected, glancing about. 'And that Emma has important matters to deal with in London. Does that sound right?' he ventured.

Richard had risen while his brother was speaking and walked, frowning, to the window and looked down. The mail coach was still there, and his elegant carriage was close by. Of Emma there was still no sign.

'Not only has that vexed dear Mama,' drifted over to Richard, 'but I am bid to order you back by nine for dinner with the Duke and Duchess and Lady Penelope.' A taunting grin preceded, 'I'm sure you'll make that.'

A lewd suggestion as to how his Grace could amuse himself in his absence escaped Richard. But a stirring uneasiness was tightening his chest as he scoured the empty courtyard.

'Oh, and Mother's fretting she might have offended Emma, prompting her to quit Silverdale. Apparently in the Assembly Rooms last evening she and Diane and the Petershams were having a gossip about Dashwood. One moment Emma was with them then the next she had disappeared without a word.'

'Dashwood? What is it that foul bastard's about now?' Richard felt a knot of cold suspicion churn his stomach. He recalled Emma saying she had been upset by some talk of people she knew. He had wanted to believe her tears yesterday evening had sprung from jealousy at how she had come upon him with Yvette. Perhaps his arrogance had got the better of him...

'Dashwood has been made to look a monkey, by all accounts. He bought himself a genteel spinster to breed with. Money changed hands with a prospective impecunious father-in-law before the dowd of a bride had been informed of any of it. It was assumed she'd be so pleased to get off the shelf, she'd simply go along with it all. No more ado, she's shown more mettle and a clean pair of heels. Dashwood has investigators out on the hunt. The contract was signed and sealed and he's bent on revenge. The girl's father has now absconded, too, avoiding Dashwood's blood-letting, I imagine. What scandals we miss in this neck of the woods... Are you ailing? You look ghastly...' he tacked onto the end, splashing more fine cognac into his glass.

'I thought you might be out riding, actually,' Stephen added conversationally. 'I swear I saw Shah away in the distance as I turned in. What a coincidence! Two palominos in the neighbourhood!'

Richard stared, his lean cheeks ashen beneath bronze. He stood perfectly still for a moment then calmly walked to the fire, discarded the cigar butt and said, 'Have you brought along a ride back?'

At Stephen's nod of confirmation, he picked up his leather riding coat, threw it over a powerful shoulder and walked to the door. 'Thanks for getting back here so quickly. I'll be back in a week or so—or send word from London.'

Emma glanced behind at the fiery horizon, trusting that as long as she headed east and kept the road in sight she would be fine. Not that she was intending to ride *all* the way to London, she impressed upon herself, while jogging along. That was a futile expectation. What she would do was journey to the next posting house, leave Star in the landlord's care and charge him to get her note to Sir Richard Du Quesne. In it she would make her apologies for borrowing his horse and let him know where it was available for collection. Then she would buy a ride to London on the first conveyance heading that way able to accommodate her. By her increasingly optimistic calculations, she should be in London early in the morning. By this time tomorrow all her family's problems should be solved.

As the setting sun streaked the skyline a rich russet, she slanted a squinting gaze at a cluster of cottages and small farm buildings. She hoped soon a hostelry would come into view. It was rash for a lone rider to risk travelling at night. And this handsome steed would be enough temptation for a felon to accost a man. A woman would be easy pickings.

She patted at Star's head again and leaned forward to run a slender hand across the milky mark on his nose, while murmuring his name. He bobbed his head in acknowledgement. Perhaps she had correctly guessed his name for he indeed responded to it.

But he didn't seem to want to respond to her urgings to increase his pace. He ambled along and she refused to dig her heels into his flawless sides. Perhaps she had tired him...but then they had not galloped. She hadn't felt confident enough for that, and the covering trees and shrubbery they weaved through, in any case, made speed difficult. Perhaps he was hungry or thirsty, she mused as the horse slowed to a walk.

Emma tapped a creamy flank and made clicking noises with her tongue. After a few vain encouragements she huffed and sat still, deciding to allow him to crop for a while. Slackening her hold on the reins, she waited for him to dip towards sparse, coarse grass. He did no such thing, simply raised his head and curled his upper lip, scenting the air. He snorted and pawed at the ground then walked about in an aimless circle.

Perhaps he was above eating grass, Emma thought. Perhaps he was so used to feeding on sweet hay and oats in a stable he didn't know how to chew this thin, reedy stuff. He was altogether too indulged, she sniffily decided. Altogether his master's beast!

Warily eyeing the forest floor, she wondered if, once dismounted, she would be able to get back up. Trusting she would, she gathered her skirts in a hand, arced a bare leg nimbly over Star's head and slithered to hard earth. A controlling hand gripped the reins while she tore at grass stalks then offered them up on a flat palm.

Emma heard the sound properly this time, acknowledged it as significant, rather than again dismissing it as breeze-wafted pastoral melody. She peered nervously about. There were wild creatures in woods...foxes and deer and small, scurrying things. The eerie, high-pitched ululation was unidentifiable, but then all animal calls were uncommon to her urban ear.

Star acknowledged it: his ears pricked and he whinnied, bobbing his head excitedly. Perhaps he would take fright and bolt. She wound the reins round a hand and looked about for a boulder or tree stump she could stand on to aid clambering back astride him. Ready to discard her offering of grass and get moving, the stallion dipped its head and nuzzled her palm. She smiled at his gentle nibble, while smoothing his velvety nose. 'You were hungry...'

The hair at her nape prickled and icy needles assaulted her

cheeks at the unmistakable slow clop of hooves. The approaching horse stilled and stamped and the rider remained silent…and she knew.

She had difficulty detaching her tongue from the roof of her mouth. It finally came free, allowing her to croak at Star's muzzle, 'I…I was just borrowing him…'

The ensuing quiet was shattered by a horse's soft snorting. That seemed to rouse Star. He nudged Emma firmly aside and trotted past, spinning her about and forcing her to run a few steps until she shook herself free.

Richard was sitting atop a grey mare, one leg bent and resting on the animal's neck as though he had happened upon an interesting spectacle and settled to watch it. In fact, he seemed so comfortable, so impassive, she was almost lulled into believing he wasn't angry.

'I *was* just borrowing him…' she emphasised in a quavering voice, her tilted chin wobbly. Her ragged murmur this time prompted some reaction. He swivelled, leaped down and abandoned the mare to Star's increasingly amorous attention.

Still he said nothing. He didn't need to; Emma could read wrath and retribution in every taut plane of his sardonic face, in every light, skimming pace that brought him purposefully closer. Swallowing jerkily, she stepped back clumsily, then spontaneously turned and fled.

She bolted into woodland, her skirts held high, away from the snatching briars. Thorns tore instead at her petticoats, her nude legs. She winced as sharp barbs nipped at her flesh. Still she swerved on, running and dodging the dense shrubbery that tweaked at her glossy fawn hair and loosened it to tumble in a tangle about her shoulders.

The blood was pounding so heavily in her ears, her sobbing breath hacking so sharply at her throat that she was conscious of nothing else. She expected any moment a grip on her shoulder…her neck, to jerk her about or push her to the root-heaving ground. She desperately wanted to know if he had given chase but turning to find out would lose her precious time.

The stitch in her side twisted relentlessly into torturing needle stabs until eventually she could endure no more. She plunged towards a large oak, almost fell against its rough, scabby bark and concealed herself.

She waited, her lungs pumping fit to burst, her rib-cage jerking so wildly she pressed trembling arms across it to forcibly restrain it. Unfastening her hampering cloak with clumsy fingers, she let it fall to the ground then scraped her back against wood to peer about the tree.

He was nowhere in sight and it was silent apart from muted forest sounds: rustling undergrowth and a crow cawing somewhere overhead. She closed her wide, fawn eyes. Perhaps he was glad enough to recover his horse and be finally rid of her. She couldn't blame him; he must be heartily rueing the day she'd ever appeared in Bath and caused havoc in his ordered life.

A sudden stinging sensation moistened her eyes and nose. She didn't want him to hate her. She didn't want him to think badly of her at all; but he would…and she deserved that. She had lied, abused his generosity, hit him on numerous occasions, stolen his horse…shown him no gratitude or respect… when in fact even her own papa had never provided for her so unstintingly…so uncomplainingly. She owed him so much. Yet some innate sense bade her escape him again rather than remain and explain.

She twisted her head sharply against bark, needing the spiteful abrasion against her scalp to drive out the weakness. He was a selfish lecher and she would do well to remember it! He had shown her such largess to protect his friendship with the Courtenays; she would do well to remember that, too, and forget any ideas that his kisses and flattery had been more than idle amusement as he'd sought to groom a quaint new paramour.

Slow minutes passed and finally, as her breathing and heart

rate steadied, she swooped, gathering up her cloak, forcing her mind back to practicalities. She must travel urgently to London and her parents. In which direction were the farm buildings she had recently noticed? She might get assistance there. At the very least the locals would point her towards the nearest coaching inn.

She squinted up at the canopy of leaves overhead. The sun was gone and the evening was now drawing in. With a sigh and a shove away from the oak she ventured out from behind it.

'Why steal a horse when you can gallop like that…?' was drawled sarcastically from her left side.

Emma swirled towards him, stepped back in readiness…but a bronzed hand stretched out. 'Don't do it, Emma,' he gently warned. 'I swear, if you run or provoke me further… Come here,' he tacked onto the end without concluding the threat, long, autocratic fingers beckoning.

Emma moistened her lips, blinked her doe eyes before they veered around him, seeking escape routes. 'I didn't steal Star…just borrowed him. I intended to get word to you where I left him stabled, I promise.'

'Shah…'

'What?' Emma breathed.

'His name is Shah…'

'Well, I prefer Star.' Emma defiantly bristled.

Richard smiled and took an easy pace forward. When she remained unflustered by that he took another, all the while glancing idly about at his surroundings. 'For a woman in the early stages of a pregnancy you take remarkable risks with your health, haring about like that.'

'I am healthy…very healthy. I'm robust, my mother tells me…'

'Your mother says a lot I don't agree with.'

'Well, none of it is your con—!' Emma broke off as silver eyes streaked to hers and melded with them. 'I've never been frail,' she resorted to muttering.

'I imagine your lover might not approve of your hoydenish antics either. Tell me about him again. I believe I might know of him, after all.'

Emma flung him a scornful glance. 'And I tell you you do not!'

'He is betrothed, you say?'

A curt nod and pout laden with ennui answered him.

'To whom?'

'A respectable lady. Assuredly no one you would know!' was delivered in the same bored, impatient vein.

'Not a daughter, is she, of a certain Mr Bennet with four other girls to offload and a shrew of a matchmaking wife to contend with?'

Emma's tawny head flew about, glowing tiger eyes raking darkly ironic features.

'Very novel, Emma…' he said drily. 'But then I'll own Dashwood's no ideal personification of a raven-haired romantic hero. I can see why a fiction would prove preferable.'

Blood seeped from her complexion, ice shivered her spine, yet she met his gaze unflinchingly, trusting brashness might confuse him.

But his eyes and mouth narrowed at her reflexive reaction to mention of her spurned fiancé. 'If you lie to me again over this, Emma…' The vehement threat trailed into silence but she recognized ultimate retribution in his flinty eyes and a profound sadness in the thick timbre of his voice.

'Are you with child? Has Dashwood violated you? Or have you simply fled to avoid marrying him?'

Emma chewed at her trembling lower lip, wondering whether now to be honest; tell him everything: confess to deceit, cowardice, selfishness at having jeopardised her parents by reneging on a hateful marriage contract. But she didn't want him to know. She didn't want him to despise her for her disgusting failings.

'Tell me, dammit!' he thundered. 'Tell me if that bastard's touched you…whether you're carrying his spawn!'

'Mr Dashwood has not *violated* me. I might have been a little…startled by him initially…but not any more. I am travelling home to wed him. And that is all I shall explain. The rest is…*none of your concern*,' she whispered, quavering challenge mingling with the peace of ultimate defeat. 'Go away and leave me. Go and find your horse before he runs away.'

'Oh, he won't run for a while yet. He's being entertained…' he told her in a calm, quiet voice.

The air between them seemed to solidify, the evening birdsong and woodland hum to fade, leaving sheer silence. It was shattered with his ruthless need. 'I think it's high time I was…' he dulcetly stated, and started to approach so lightly it seemed he skimmed the peaty ground.

Her eyes were wrenched from his to dart glances left and right: an obstructing hazel thicket to one side and a tangle of bracken and bramble to the other. Beyond him a clearing. But that way lay easy capture… *Turn and run…turn and run* her reason whispered. *Escape him while you still can…*

Small, shaking hands spasmed on tree bark directly behind them, then, with an anguished cry, she hurtled instinctively forward, trusting destiny.

He sprang as she did, intercepting and catching her to him then driving her back against the ancient, sturdy oak. Wood and the granite pressure of his body kept her off the ground, breast against breast, thigh against hip, mouth welded to mouth with grinding, punishing force. Her head fell back into supporting, protective fingers pitilessly abraded against wood as she squirmed to liberate her face. She fought energetically, kicking and twisting, her pinioned hands bunching into futile fists, tirelessly seeking freedom to claw at him.

Long brown fingers speared into her thick tawny hair, winding just enough to make her cease straining and keep her face tilted to his.

He plundered her mouth with savage abandon, teeth and lips erotically barbaric in every nip, slide, stroke, his tongue thrusting with uncurbed lechery to explore sleek, moist velvet.

A marauding hand hoisted her higher, parted her thighs so he could wedge between them, then coiled her calves about him. He pinned her like that—the full weight of his strong, muscular body inescapable, the iron of his erection pulsing raging heat at the heart of her vulnerable femininity.

Emma ground her head violently against his palm, trying to free her mouth, and each frantic evasion shredded his injured knuckles, and was countered with increased lust. Long fingers ripped free the buttons on her bodice, then leisurely peeled back first one then the other side to expose fragile ivory shoulders, the plump swell of small, firm breasts. His fingers worked at the laces on her chemisette and she gasped her outrage into his mouth, her head swinging in denial. Still he was relentless. A tormentingly slow disrobement followed, until she was naked to the waist, cooled by evening air, scorched by expertly teasing touches. The insolent, selfish assault on her mouth ceased and his face lowered.

Her head rolled to one side, air was gulped into her starved lungs, while her tongue gentled lips that felt excoriated. Then the first languid tasting at her breasts had her tensing, arching, whimpering like an animal in pain. Tantalising wetness traced puckering rosy skin with aching slowness, dried in the balmy breeze to be reapplied within moments. A flick of hot damp at a rigid nipple had her sobbing deep in her throat and fighting to work free a hand trapped between them, not now to hit but to hold. The torturous sensations were undeniable. She was defenceless against a barrage of carnal skill consummated over two decades. His tongue, teeth, lips at first one breast then the other taunted her with exquisite delirium and her slender back arched bow-tight, begging for what she couldn't, wouldn't say.

He deliberately tempted back, lingering with butterfly brevity, drawing her leisurely to a peak of moaning pleasure. When finally he allowed her hands free they slid immediately into his soft hair, holding his cruel face against her exposed, swollen flesh. He rewarded her by giving her what she wanted, suckling deeper until some inner part of her seemed to detach and float in liquid ecstasy. His fingers plucked at the strings of her flimsy drawers, freed them so his fingers could smooth in long, hard strokes over her buttocks, her lissom thighs, slide torturously close to the dewy, petalled core of her before drifting away. She groaned and bucked against him, not knowing what she wanted but demanding it, sure it was his to give.

A gentle knuckle grazed artfully against the damp curls between her thighs, collecting the honey there, moistening the sensitive small bud blooming, before rotating, nudging a little way into her, repeating the action with slow, breathtaking rhythm.

Richard dipped his head, tipped her lolling face around with his so he could bring their mouths together, and his tongue leisurely mimicked the pleasure his fingers were giving her. A thumb circled slickly, making her writhe and whimper.

Calculatingly, he studied her flushed complexion, her mouth scarlet, sleek and parted, begging more attention, her eyes no more than fiery golden lustre beneath a net of jet lashes, and he realised he still wasn't absolutely sure. She responded like a woman already awakened to sensuality…yet she was overwhelmed, simply a recipient of whatever he next chose to give her. 'Shall I stop, Emma?' he roughly taunted her.

In response her lids squeezed in anguish and her head lolled further back but speech was impossible. The notion that he might finish enslaving her with this untasted delight simply left her breathless.

'Are you pregnant with Dashwood's child? Tell me!' he begged huskily.

Her lids flew wide and a wild fawn gaze was focussing on him…staring…and then she struggled.

Richard saw her concentration, her valiant attempt to fight free of the voluptuous web he'd spun, to gain some sort of control. He waited no more. His mouth meshed with hers, luring her back into the dark heart of desire. 'Hush. It makes no difference. I swear it makes no difference,' he breathed time and again against her febrile, fragrant skin until he sensed the tension he could feel in her was all for him. Her desire…her need was just for him.

'Tell me something else, Emma,' he whispered hoarsely. 'Tell me you want me as much as I want you…' As though to prompt her his mouth secured an erect nipple and laved it with such leisurely, loving attention, a sob rasped her throat and she instinctively thrust her pelvis into contact with his. He pressed her back against chafing bark, holding her still, lazy, teasing fingers trailing the sensitive, satiny skin of her inner thighs.

He raised his head, traced her pulsing, battered lips with a slow, soothing tongue, inserted it gently between her lips to taste hers before kissing her with pure, pitiless seduction.

'Tell me! Say you want me, Emma…please,' tore rawly from him.

'I do…' Emma wailed.

A shattered gasp of a laugh warmed her face. 'Save that for later, sweetheart. Say you want me like this…lie again. Just say it.'

'I want you like this,' burst out in a despairing whisper.

His eyes closed in peace…in gratitude…and he allowed the rampaging need to dominate and shake him. Coiling his arms about her fragile form, he turned them slowly about then sank, supporting her, to his knees before lowering her back onto her cloak, discarded on musky earth.

Chapter Twelve

It was the scent of woodsmoke that woke her.

Emma squinted through screening lashes at wavering yellow warmth. Forcing a leaden hand up, she touched soft material bunched beneath her cheek but couldn't rouse the energy to lift her tangled tawny head. She wondered how long she had slept; the dusk had deepened although, on flicking up drowsy eyes, patches of slate sky were still visible through branches overhead. A mournful soughing swaying the topmost foliage rippled shivers through her. She imagined it must be about seven of the clock and she had probably slept for an hour.

Agitated eyes flitted over murky undergrowth, seeking a tall, dark figure, a blond head, but beyond the fire's flickering orbit was mere shadow. Her naked limbs shifted position beneath his leather coat, causing the burn between her thighs to rage and ignite a flare in her wan face.

Despite sleeping she still felt enervated by the slow, insatiable intimacy to which she'd been subjected. Her whole being had been quaking, raw with sensitivity when, finally compassionate, he'd tipped her over the edge, allowing sapping spasms of ecstasy to spiral her towards a shattered peace.

And she knew that what most drove his need to torment her and seek such thorough satisfaction was nothing to do with any festering slights or swindles that had gone before. She recalled a stabbing pain that had made her shriek, instinctively squirm beneath him to free herself. Through waves of palliative excitement had throbbed painful vulnerability; she had realised why he'd stopped and sworn savagely at odoriferous earth: one deceit had certainly fooled him. Until that moment he had believed her no virgin.

Even though conscious of reprisal in his ensuing sensuality, she couldn't fight him again. She had been his to mould. Where he'd positioned her she had stayed, instructions he'd whispered she'd obeyed, mindlessly, absolutely, even though each was calculated…proven to notch her arousal to a new excruciating height. Nothing had mattered other than that the source of her punishing pleasure be sustained and she taste its ultimate explosive finish.

Exhausted, she had slept almost immediately, with their loins still in congress, with hard-muscled ribs still pressed to her breasts, long, ruthless fingers cradling her drooping head.

A slender shaking hand covered her eyes as though to blot out further mortifying memories. She rolled onto her stomach and jackknifed onto hands and knees, clutching his coat to her nudity, wondering apathetically when he had covered her with it, used his fine black jacket to cushion her head. She cast about on the ground for her clothes and tugged them close to her.

Dusty dark boots appeared at the edge of her vision and she scrabbled faster, hugging garments up against her as though he might snatch them away.

Richard crouched close by and Emma immediately sank back onto her heels.

A dark hand moved towards her grubby white face but she recoiled and it dropped away. It was back within moments, with the other. Grasping her by the shoulders, he pulled her closer. 'Look at me, Emma,' he requested hoarsely. When she refused to cease staring over a shoulder, he barked harshly, 'Look at me, dammit.'

Glass-bright topaz eyes sliced to him.

'I'm sorry,' broke gruffly from him. 'I didn't want it to be that way…'

'Yes, you did,' she countered, the bite in her voice blunted by an odd passivity. 'I know now. That's always what you intended. Even three years ago you wanted to shame me for insulting you.'

One dark hand released her, and his fingers pinched at the strain between his eyes. 'You're wrong, Emma…so wrong…'

'Go away so I can dress,' she begged in a brittle snap.

A travesty of a laugh preceded, 'Have you found something I've not seen?' Abruptly he stood, turning his back.

'I said go away!' she pleadingly screeched, wanting him out of sight so she could clean herself. She touched an inner thigh and her shaking hand came away stained. 'What have you done to me?' she whispered at her fingers as she stared aghast at the blood.

'You know what I've done to you, Emma,' he returned patiently. 'I've taken your maidenhead. And had you honestly told me it was still there to take…I wouldn't have…' His blond head fell back and a hand covered his eyes. 'Perhaps that's a lie…I don't know. But I swear it would have been different. I would have been different.'

He swung about to see her mesmerised by her hand. With careless savagery he ripped a strip of cambric from the bottom of his shirt, then again went down beside her. He slowly wiped her quivering fingers before pressing her back against her spread cloak. Unfolding leather from the curve of creamy hips, he carefully wiped her, holding her firm as she flinched from the intimacy of his methodical, impassive handling; he might attend to one of his injured animals so, she dully thought.

He walked to the fire and discarded the soiled rag and Emma used his absence to hastily commence pulling on her clothes. Her gaping bodice she managed to close with its one remaining button. She donned her cloak and was straightening it over her torn, crumpled dress with fussy precision when she started at the high-pitched whistle.

She watched him draw back his lips and signal again and realised blankly that he must have been following her and Star for some while earlier before locating them. Star…Shah had, of course, obeyed his master and refused to travel further when he'd heard his call. The noble creature, in his unwitting way, had betrayed her and that seemed to make her desolation complete.

As thudding hooves became audible and shrubbery was knocked aside, she blinked blurrily at stars intermittently visible through fluttering leaves. The two animals trotted obediently close and halted away from the fire.

She gasped hurriedly, huskily, 'I…I should be grateful if you would deliver me to the nearest posting house as it is now dark…'

Silver eyes glittered at her, his lean, angular face visibly tensing. 'Did you believe I might leave you here? Make you walk?' he suggested in a soft, liquid voice that dried her mouth. 'What villainy are you next expecting? That I'll act the heartless rake to the hilt and abandon you to all and sundry now I've had my wicked way? Is that what you think, Emma? Is it?' exploded in a strangled voice.

At her solemn silence, Richard strode to the fire and the toe of a boot savagely shovelled earth, smothering the flames. Eerie darkness shrouded them, prompting a hollow sob to swell, suffocate her. She stuffed a muffling fist to her mouth as it quaked her chest. All her aggression, her independence, her resourcefulness seemed to have been whipped from her at one and the same time and she felt utterly bereft…utterly alone… utterly useless.

He had threatened this, she forlornly recalled… 'Don't bait me needlessly' he had said. 'I can break that aggressive spirit of yours so easily…' And so he had and she had nothing left, not even the ability to hide from him his victory.

Shah's spectral shape approached through the gloom, the mare tied behind the stallion. Richard leaned down. 'Give me your arm.'

Praying for the courage to be defiant just once more, to manage flippantly telling him to go to hell, kept her unmoving…waiting. But it was hopeless. Suppressing her crying took all her energy, and left her dithering.

Dismounting, he closed the space between them. An unsteady dark hand lifted to a wet face, smoothed tentatively over cold, quivering cheeks. Abruptly she was pulled close, rocked comfortingly. 'Don't cry, Emma…' he groaned into her hair. 'It'll be sweeter next time, I promise. I'll love you tenderly… Please don't cry…'

And that was all she needed. Had he said again he was sorry or he had lost control, she might have accepted it. But not that…anything but mentioning that, for it was, she realised, all she craved hearing. He had coupled with her without once uttering a word other than to tutor her shame. No affection, no trifling endearment had passed his lips.

'You bastard…' she choked, wrenching free. 'Don't you dare ever touch me again or patronise me with your stupid lies…' The rest was lost in a gasp as firm fingers girdled a slender waist. She was abruptly lifted and plonked atop Shah's back. Richard swung up behind her, wordlessly kicked Shah into action, then they were plunging through undergrowth towards the London road.

She was approaching home. Emma's eyes sought out the gates to Hyde Park as they passed in the splendid carriage. It was the first proper landmark she had recognised. From here she knew it would be but a few miles…a few minutes more until she alighted at Rosemary House and was confronted by her mother.

She swallowed her anxieties at the coming reunion and concentrated instead on her papa. Please let him be safe and well, whispered in her head as soulful amber eyes scanned a blue sky.

It was another beautiful autumn day, close to three in the

afternoon, she guessed. They had made good time from the Fallow Buck posting house where they had overnighted.

On returning there yesterday evening, Emma had been allocated the same chamber as on her journey to Bath some eleven days earlier. Despite fretting she would never manage a wink of sleep, she had succumbed to sweet oblivion as soon as her aching head touched crisp, clean linen. A young maid, bearing a tray laden with food, had woken her about an hour later, then returned to fill a tub with warm, lavender-scented water for her to wash in.

Emma had not queried whence such consideration came for she already knew. Where Richard slept or ate she did not know…neither did she care, she told herself.

Feeling composed and refreshed after her meticulous bathing and drying on a spotless warm towel, she had attempted reading her book, but found that Elizabeth Bennet and Fitzwilliam Darcy no longer captivated as once they had and she'd wistfully pondered that loss, too.

She had once more snuggled into the white sheets and faced the window, staring at the moon, as she had on her outward journey. When last she'd wished upon it, she had thought of another man and felt optimistic about a future with Matthew. Now she'd stared at the silver sliver hating it, wishing it to be any other colour, as she'd flung herself onto her back and tears had dripped slowly from the corners of her eyes to soak her fawn hair. And time and again she'd told herself that she didn't love him; that the idea of it at all had only been prompted by his perfidious words, and that tomorrow, when back with her mother and all the mayhem that must ensue, things would seem so much better…

Emma sighed deeply and settled back from the window into sumptuous leather upholstery as the carriage slowed behind a press of vehicles ahead. A discreet glance was slanted sideways at the man she knew had watched her for practically the duration of the journey. For her part, she had endeavoured to avoid looking in his direction at all.

She could no longer meet those silver eyes without spontaneous colour staining her cheeks. No longer speak to him without stuttering or uttering stupid things. Once, stinging rebuffals and witty slights had slipped easily off her tongue; now she found basic dialogue difficult. Refusing or accepting food or drink when he asked if she was hungry or thirsty caused her to become tongue-tied. Replying that, yes, she was sleepy or, no, she needed no rest caused her to stammer. So she'd withdrawn from conversation. Withdrawn from him.

Huddled into her private world, only thoughts of her family's predicament had been allowed as she'd whiled away the journey with bouts of snoozing and sightless staring through the carriage window while he, sitting opposite, had made himself comfortable, propped in the corner, with his long legs raised and his booted feet stationed close to her hip.

Several times before they'd left the Fallow Buck posting house she had politely refused his coach, his escort to London. A public conveyance and her own company was adequate, she had insisted. When he'd continued calmly preparing for the journey and only brooding dark looks had met her quiet rejection of his aid, she'd eventually retreated to sip tea while he made arrangements for Shah to be returned to Silverdale in his absence.

First one then another highly polished top-boot withdrawing from the upholstery at her side dragged her thoughts back to the present.

Richard slid along the seat so that he sat directly across from her. Leaning forward, he rested forearms on knees, dark fingers loosely linked. 'You're nearly home.'

Emma nodded her knowledge of it facing the window, a frown puckering her brow.

'Are you going to talk to me before we finish our journey?'

'Yes, of course, if you want,' she politely replied to a passing curricle.

'I do want…' he said quietly. 'So look at me.'

Emma glanced at his dark face then at the seat then at the squabs, noting how very supple the hide was.

A heavy sigh preceded a dark hand spanning her face, holding it still so she couldn't avoid his eyes. 'Don't you think I'm due an explanation, Emma? Don't you think I deserve at least that courtesy?'

She sank back into the squabs, and his hand dropped to his knee.

'Yes, of course,' she repeated civilly while her fingers ceaselessly entwined. 'I hadn't bothered…expounded it all… for I believed you must have heard the gossip from your mother…or perhaps someone else has told you. But I was with her when she learned of the scandal in the Assembly Rooms…and it was very comprehensive so there's nothing to add to that…at all…' She finished the jumbled excuse for remaining silent about her family's disgrace.

'Nevertheless, I want you to tell me.'

So she did. Dispassionately, if disjointedly, she recounted to the passing pedestrians everything that had occurred to prompt her to flee to Matthew Cavendish in Bath.

When she had finished and sat with her lower lip caught between small white teeth, he said, 'And it was impossible to tell me that, honestly, days ago?'

'Yes,' she croaked, blinking.

'Why?'

Emma swung her head at the street scene. 'I don't know,' she whispered.

'Are you now planning to accept Dashwood?'

Sparkling fawn eyes met a heavy-lidded grey gaze. 'Yes.' She cleared her throat. 'Yes, I shall.'

Richard smiled tightly. 'Do you really think, Emma, I'll allow the possibility that a child of mine be reared by that vicious bastard?'

Emma's glossy topaz eyes widened in shock. Why had that not yet occurred to her? Stupidly, it had never once entered her head that she might have conceived following their bitter-sweet passion. 'It won't be,' she stated, with a desperate, shaky confidence.

Richard twisted a smile. 'You can't be sure of that, Emma.'

'The marriage will soon take place. Thus Dashwood would never suspect a child was not his,' she reasoned fervently.

'If he thinks he's purchased a virgin he'll expect her to be intact on her wedding night,' Richard pointed out quietly. 'Discovering she's duped him would be sure to set him thinking…and counting, after he'd shown her the full force of his displeasure. You've not exactly protected your reputation by your antics. You've been unchaperoned a good deal of the time. Even now, travelling alone with me casts doubt on your virtue. It's likely he'll deem the contract void. And that would be the best possible outcome.'

'He will marry me! The contract is sealed and everything will be fine. My papa will come home. The debts will be cleared. All will be fine!' throbbed out in a raw voice. 'Dashwood won't ever know of…of us!'

'It won't ever matter if he does,' Richard countered mildly. 'For you're not marrying him.'

Before Emma had a chance to reply, a dark hand and a dark, mocking expression indicated that they had arrived.

'Miss Emma…!' the elderly butler said in a croaky voice while goggling his astonishment at his young mistress.

'Hello, Rawlings.' Emma managed a wavering smile. 'Have you been well? Is my mother yet downstairs?' she immediately pressed on. Although it was mid-afternoon it had been her mother's habit when overwrought to lie abed moping for the best part of the day. With such tribulations as she now had to contend with, Emma wondered if she ever at all emerged from her chamber.

Rawlings nodded but his old eyes were warily observing the distinguished blond man who had entered the hallway and stood just behind her. 'She's in the parlour, Miss Emma,' he intoned in a flat underbreath, as if someone living perpetually in an atmosphere replete with tragedy.

Before the onset of this catastrophe, Margaret Worthington would have been enraptured by the vision of such an eligible bachelor in her home, Emma hysterically realised. Now she couldn't predict how her mother would react. Turning to Richard, she coolly said, 'Please excuse me, sir; Rawlings will find you some refreshment while, first, I speak to her alone. But, of course, she will want to thank you, as I do, for your trouble in bringing me home.'

'My pleasure…' was returned immediately, in a soft drawl that brought her eyes swerving to his, her cheeks slowly staining scarlet. She twisted away and walked further into the cold, silent house.

'Mama…?'

Margaret Worthington's greying ringlets rose from the scrolled arm of the chaise longue. She gawped. Her mouth worked slackly a few times as she tried to gain purchase among the folds of her kerseymere gown and push herself upright on spindly arms. They were extended towards her daughter as silent tears rolled down her sunken, wan cheeks.

Emma flew across the few feet that separated them and, falling to her knees, hugged her mother's bony body to her. Sharp shoulder blades dug into her palms and self-disgust drenched her on recalling how well she had eaten recently while in Richard's care.

'Hush,' Emma soothed as her mother's frame shuddered and she sensed her own hot tears drip to her lips and seep salt into her mouth. 'Hush…all will be well now. I am come home and all will be well. Papa will be fine…you'll see…'

Mention of her husband spurred resentment to rescind welcome. Mrs Worthington uttered a shriek of rage fit to wake the dead. 'You insufferably selfish girl…' she berated, beating at Emma's arm with a puny fist.

'I know, Mama. I know I have been selfish and I am come home to apologise and make amends,' Emma choked, knuckling wet from her cheeks as she rose and backed away. 'I shall contact Mr Dashwood, apologise to him, too. The contract is signed; he must honour it and pay the debts when we marry.'

That caused another screech and a handkerchief to be stuffed between bloodless lips. 'Come back to make amends?' Margaret spluttered past lace. 'Now it is too late you would make amends? Why abscond in the first place if now it is amends you want?' she snarled.

'I went to Bath to find Matthew Cavendish and persuade him to marry me. I wanted to marry someone I could love.'

'Matthew Cavendish? That drunken sot? You love him?'

Emma gave a weary shake of the head. 'No…but I believed I did when I left here and I do respect him, drunkard or no. I had no knowledge of his weakness. It seems you knew more of him than I…'

'I know a drunkard,' Margaret snapped. 'Oh, yes, I can spot a drunkard. Do you think I cannot after having lived half a lifetime with such?'

Emma sighed. 'Then you cannot decry me, Mama, for seeking a man to respect in marriage, having lived so long yourself in want…'

'And such duty and disappointment is not for you? Just for me?'

'No…it is for me, too, Mama. I am come home. I have said I shall contact Mr Dashwood. I shall beg his forgiveness if need be. Papa will surely then come home too…'

'I wish I could say that would make me rejoice,' Margaret said bitterly. 'But for appearances' sake no doubt I shall. Yes, I shall be glad to see him alive…for if he is turned up dead and we are forced to put him to rest as paupers when once he could have had a decent burial…' She found her feet with surprising agility, then froze, mouth agape, eyes riveted past Emma.

Emma turned and stared at Sir Richard and the butler stationed in the open doorway. Rawlings cleared his throat and intoned, 'Sir Richard Du Quesne, m'm…' before withdrawing and closing the door.

Emma smeared the heel of a palm across her damp cheeks. She was horrified at what he must have overheard, but she introduced him composedly. 'Sir Richard has been kind enough to break his journey to Mayfair to deliver me home. I expect you must want to thank him, Mama.' Noting she looked on the point of swooning from shock and embarrassment, Emma slid her small fingers in readiness beneath one of her mother's jagged elbows.

Richard executed a bow then, face inscrutable, walked closer.

'Sir Richard…' Margaret finally whimpered out with a watery smile. 'What a great, great honour this is…'

Emma slowly closed her eyes and turned away. So, disaster or no, it wouldn't prevent her mother fawning over this man, just as she had on the last occasion they had spoken, at her birthday celebration three years ago. Aware of her mother indeed thanking him profusely in a breathy, verbose way, in between plying offers of refreshment which were politely refused, Emma walked to the parlour window and gazed out sightlessly.

In her mind's eye she saw herself dressed in pastel apricot, velvet ribbon threaded into her hair…the belle of the ball on that particular occasion. Victoria had said she looked lovely and she'd even thought so herself, although she could recall her mother despairing over the unbecoming shade of orange she had chosen to wear.

The ridiculous expense of that ball had been borne in the hope she would finally net a husband. Even at twenty-four, the likelihood of her remaining an old maid was terrifying her mother, if not her liberal papa.

Richard Du Quesne had said he might then have been persuaded to offer for her with a little encouragement and she knew now that he meant it. He never lied. She might have had a husband to respect for three long years. In truth, there was never a man she respected more. Now it was too late, she realised it no longer mattered how many courtesans he'd kept, how many drunken brawls he'd participated in. She knew him now…knew intimately everything she needed to know. He was the most worthy man of her acquaintance. And even if he was not it wouldn't matter, because she loved him. And because of that she wanted him away from her in case she did or said something else that made him despise her even more than he must already. In all her life she'd never misled and mistreated anyone so often and so shamelessly.

Bitter regrets had her twisting about, interrupting huskily, 'Sir Richard will be wanting to get to his own home, Mama. It has been a long journey. I can tell you myself of how we came upon each other in Bath and so on…'

Richard's silver eyes rose from Margaret Worthington's thin, drawn features and met, mingled with melancholy amber.

'Thank you, once again, for your hospitality, sir, and for escorting me home. I'm sure you realise we have pressing matters…and must now bid you…bid you goodbye,' Emma quietly concluded.

'You must accompany Sir Richard to the door, Emma, as he has been so kind as to accompany you all the way home.' Margaret nodded meaningfully at her daughter, spots of excited colour in her cheeks.

Back in the cool hallway, Emma cast about in her numb mind for a little bland conversation to ease their parting. 'You…you will no doubt visit David and Victoria while close by. You must pass on my felicitations…'

He made no comment on that and Emma withdrew with a tiny farewell smile and backward steps.

'I meant what I said in the carriage, Emma,' splintered the solid silence. 'You're not marrying Dashwood. Don't contact him and don't defy me…you know how it affects me. I'll deal with Jarrett Dashwood. We've spent time in Jamaica together and understand each other very well.'

She so wanted someone she trusted to deny the terrifying gossip she'd heard of Jarrett Dashwood. Moistening her lips, she bravely asked, 'Is he as black as painted? A cruel and depraved man who ill-treated his plantation labour and…his women, too? I wondered whether you and he might be colleagues.'

'Similar perverted bastards, you mean?'

Emma coloured, winced, on recalling that particular insult outside the Assembly Rooms. 'No, I didn't mean that. I know you're not at all alike…'

Richard laughed mirthlessly. 'I'd like to think that's favourable on my account rather than his. Somehow I doubt it is.'

Before Emma could reassure him it was, he turned for the door, allowing idle words to flow back at her. 'Don't fret over any of it further…don't think of him. I'll deal with it.'

Margaret straightened her shawl about her scrawny neck and settled back into the sofa, wagging a bony finger. 'I will not have it that Sir Richard knows we are involved in a scandal. He has sent his card back already and visits us Wednesday. The *ton* will be dancing attendance on us once it gets out that we have Sir Richard's patronage. You must take a ride in Hyde Park with him and really crook some noses.'

Emma sighed. 'Papa's disappearance must have already stirred scurrilous whispers about us in London.'

'Oh, yes; but no one has proof,' Margaret smirked. 'For a while, I believe his cronies imagined he was in his cups and too foxed to rouse himself. Only his lawyer knows the truth and is luckily a loyal fellow. Petra and Daphne Blair cut me dead in Pall Mall, yesterday, while tattling behind their hands. Five minutes after *I* returned home, their calling card arrived. They were snooping to see if you were here! How I wish they would attend us this minute so you could verify the indisposition I gave you.' Margaret's thin lips puckered to a pleased pout. 'Sir Richard knows none of it. Do you think such an urbane aristocrat would associate with us had he an inkling of our woes?'

Emma closed her eyes in exasperation. Firmly she said, 'He does know, Mama. I told him.'

A shriek rent the air and Margaret flew to her feet. 'You have *what*? Oh…oh, this is the outside of *enough*! Dashwood and I have done our utmost to limit the scandal and you…you *broadcast* it?'

'You don't understand, Mama. Rumours are circulating in Bath, too. Sir Richard guessed of our involvement before I confirmed it. But he is an honourable man with no wish to gossipmonger or worsen our situation.'

Margaret eyed her daughter shrewdly, a little appeased. 'At one time, I recall he drew nothing but your censure. You were always so churlish, I was amazed he seemed so attentive to you…'

'It was all a long time ago, Mama,' Emma said, chilling miserably at such a wounding reminder. 'He is simply a kind gentleman who allowed me to travel home with him as he was to journey to Mayfair.'

'Pish…kind gentleman, indeed!' Margaret dropped back to the sofa. 'I am not blind. I can see how he looks at you…' she said slyly.

It was Emma's turn to fly to her feet. 'You are dreaming, Mama, and you know it,' she cried, walking distractedly about the room. 'The facts are thus: I am contracted to wed Jarrett Dashwood; Papa is absconded to avoid his duns and Dashwood's revenge; the house is cold and dark for we have no candles or fuel; there is scarce a morsel to eat; there are but three servants left now…and you imply it might all turn right because of how Sir Richard *looks* at me! Well, before you say anything very silly, please listen: I have it from his sister-in-law that he is to wed a duke's daughter. It is an alliance that will bring valuable mining rights in Devon which he is keen to have.'

Margaret looked crestfallen. 'A duke's daughter? Oh, well, I own that's hard to contest.' She glumly twirled her wedding band about on a bony finger and huffed a sigh. 'Leastways, we might be able to get some credit at the merchants, when it is known we are his friends…'

Emma shook her head at her mother in mild despair before approaching the window to gaze at the busy street scene. She didn't want to defy Richard's wishes but she knew she must contact Jarrett Dashwood. He was another gentleman she had treated badly. Her prejudices had been lively there too! She had no proof he would be a bad husband. Richard had not confirmed her fears about his evil ways. He had said he would deal with it, but what would he do? Dissuade Dashwood's suit because he wasn't sure whether *he* had impregnated her and he was unwilling to allow another man the rearing of his child? She had heard of instances of wealthy men being paternalistic towards their bastards, even when the child's mother no longer held their interest.

'Dashwood stipulated a woman of unimpeachable character.' Margaret cut astutely into her daughter's reflections. 'You have been negligent with your reputation and that won't mend.' She looked speculative. 'Perhaps Sir Richard might plead your case as you were chaperoned for a while by his mother.'

'I won't hear any more of Sir Richard, Mama!' Emma burst out, and swept to the door. 'He has his family around him at Silverdale and will soon be back there. We must sort out our own problems. I shall endeavour to start on it by writing to Mr Dashwood and you had best pray for a favourable reply.'

Chapter Thirteen

The young clerk craned his thin neck to peer over the top of a mountain of ledgers teetering on a wormy desk. His weak, adolescent jaw dropped. Such impressively imposing gentlemen never gave patronage to Critchley & Critchley. Quality fallen on hard times and middle-class merchants unable to afford more prestigious law firms to act on their behalf were the best they could hope for.

'The nature of your business, sir...if I might be so bold as to enquire?' he ventured in an unbroken squeak.

'Inform Donald Critchley that Sir Richard Du Quesne is here on a matter concerning a client of his: a Mr Worthington.'

Richard noted the youth's Adam's apple jiggle inside his loose collar and his artless eyes blink and swivel agitatedly. No doubt he imagined he was another creditor come to lay his account before Frederick's man of business.

The lad scurried away to another door and disappeared. A moment later both the apprentice and Donald Critchley were gaping at him.

'Sir Richard!' Critchley croaked, flustered by the astonishing appearance of one of the *haut ton's* fabled millionaires. 'Please do come into my office. Please do excuse the jumble.' He grabbed a bundle of papers from a chair. Dropping them to the floor, he dusted the seat with a sweaty palm before nervously extending it.

Richard graciously accepted a woolly handshake and a cracked leather seat.

'Some refreshment for Sir Richard—hurry… There is some port…'

'Nothing, thank you,' Richard cut over the man's panic. 'I have little time and this matter will soon be dealt with.'

Such appalling confidence had Donald flinching and frowning. A discreet look worked from the top of a gleaming head to expensively shod feet. Extreme power and wealth seemed to exude from this man like a bright white light that accentuated every crumbling corner of his littered office.

He cursed inwardly; Frederick had assured him he had provided a comprehensive listing of all his creditors. But then his friend was an arrant coward and apt to conveniently forget to mention one of such renown.

Donald knew of Sir Richard's business acumen and that of his friend Viscount Courtenay. Both men were engaged in commercial ventures jointly and severally that had made them very rich indeed. Both men shared the services of the finest firm of litigators. He blanched. In his mind's eye he saw a lifetime's endeavour snatched away…crippling lawsuits…

He should have refused to act for his spendthrift friend years ago. But Frederick had that hangdog way of looking at one with his mournful, bloodshot eyes that had the most hardhearted of men softening, believing his lies and promises. Unfortunately, it took only one creditor to lose patience and sue for the others to panic and pitch in too. This battered old desk had fair groaned beneath the weight of Worthington's promissory notes.

'Where is Frederick Worthington?' Richard genially interrogated.

'Er…I…er…I have no idea, Sir Richard,' Donald Critchley mumbled while his face ruddied and beads of sweat decorated his bushy eyebrows.

Richard grimaced in regret. 'Pity; I'd like to have contacted him. I'm aware he is embarrassed for funds at present and would welcome a contribution.'

Critchley's weary eyes popped wide, his drooping features lifted. 'You mean…you owe *him* an amount?' he spluttered in disbelief.

'I am lately returned from abroad and prepared to allocate funds to those with a stockholding in the plantation I sold.' Silver eyes steadily met those of the goggling, slack-jawed lawyer.

'I have no recollection of this. I am sure I must have certification, unless Frederick has kept it himself…' He leafed frantically through papers on his desk as though he might miraculously turn up the non-existent document.

'I should be able to provide certification…' Richard informed him idly.

'And…and how much would Mr Worthington receive from this investment?'

'How much do his debts total?' Richard rebuffed the question with one of his own.

Again the lawyer looked disconcerted. 'That is…er… confidential, Sir Richard… I'm sure you must…er… understand my delicate…er…my professional…'

'How much?' Richard insisted dulcetly.

'A little more than eighteen thousand pounds…or thereabouts.'

'What a happy coincidence. I believe his allocation should total that…or thereabouts,' Richard said drily. Taking a card from his pocket, he flicked it across the desk. 'So if by some fortuity you do see Worthington,' he added, with a cynical smile, 'give him that and tell him to contact me urgently, lest I soon recover my wits.'

At any other time the redolence of tobacco and alcohol and cheap musky perfume that clung to male clothes long after the woman was dislodged might have stirred a pleasant reminiscing. As it was, Richard simply stood on the threshold of the Palm House gambling den, his silver eyes sorting methodically through a seething mass of humanity and a haze of smoke to find a face.

He paced slowly forward, aware of astonished greetings as gentlemen looked up from baize and saw him. A few actually pushed back chairs, dropped their hands in order to come and shake his and chummily clap him on the back.

'Dickie!'

Richard pivoted on a heel at the bellow to spy Charles Mainwaring moving through the smog with Paul Wainwright hot on his heels. They shoved determinedly through the throng, and so pleased was Paul to see him, he actually proffered his newly replenished brandy balloon.

'Well, look what the cat dragged in,' Charles chortled affectionately. 'Courtenay with you?' he asked, glancing about. 'What's arranged for tonight, then? Something heavenly, I'll warrant,' he sighed enviously, dropping a wink at Wainwright. 'It's been deadly dull, don't you know, since Courtenay got himself leg-shackled and you took off abroad.' He ceased moaning to swig his cognac.

Richard strolled forward, still scanning tables, chatting amiably to his two old friends trailing in his wake. A languid hand was raised now and then in acknowledgement as acquaintances called out to him.

'*Is* Courtenay here?' Wainwright demanded, peering searchingly about.

'Not as far as I'm aware,' Richard replied, drawing on his cheroot then sipping from his glass.

'We'll have to go *en masse* to Hertfordshire. Abduct him if needs be,' Paul chuckled. 'It'll be like old times. We'll persuade him he can still function well enough without that pretty little wife of his.'

Richard laughed past the cheroot clamped at one corner of his mouth. 'You can try…until he persuades you you can still function well enough without your teeth.'

'You are staying, though, aren't you?' Wainwright wrinkled his beaky nose, shoving a hand through his springy dark hair. 'You *have* lined up a few pretty petticoats for later…and a few spare?' At Richard's preoccupied searching look past him, he queried, 'Well, what *are* you doing in this neck of the woods?'

Wasting time, by the look of things…ran responsively, self-mockingly through Richard's mind. Jarrett Dashwood wasn't here…neither had he been at any of the other seedy haunts he frequented with the thuggish little entourage he paid to accompany him. As did most friendless bullies, he liked to appear popular and to ensure that he had ample backing should a scuffle erupt. Mr Dashwood was in London, though, so he had been informed by a pinch-faced servant when he'd called at his home, and his message would be relayed as soon as possible.

Idly emptying the glass Wainwright had magnanimously relinquished, he returned it with a smile. 'Can't stop now…' He grimaced in mild apology and left them both squinting sorrowfully through smoke after him.

Back in his carriage and heading west towards Mayfair, he suddenly leaned forward and rapped out instructions for the driver to turn about and proceed east to Cheapside. Leaning his blond head back wearily into the cushioned squabs, he closed his eyes. He'd not seen Emma for three days—not since she'd politely dismissed him from Rosemary House—and it felt like three months…three damned years.

The longing was debilitating… Just to look at her would be enough: drown in her brandy eyes, watch the animation in her small expressive features as he said something that interested her, or she laughed at him, slapped at him, tossed insults at him. No, looking wouldn't be enough, he mocked himself. The yearning clenched his fingers as he fantasised about them plunging deep into a luxuriant mass of tawny hair.

A hand shot up and instead tugged irritably through his own lengthy locks as he tried to divert his mind from memories of her slender, supple body writhing beneath his, his fingers, his mouth teasing her scented, silky skin.

He swore viciously at the emerging crescent moon, wishing to God she'd wed some worthy young buck a year or so ago. That way he'd still be in blissful ignorance of this hellish emotion. No, he wouldn't, he again reasoned with infuriating efficiency. They had mutual friends: at some point their paths would have crossed. He would have seen her again and real-ised… And it would have been worse than this…so much worse. So he continued to curse less volubly at the night as the handsome matched greys pulling his splendid carriage made a cracking good pace through quiet streets towards Rose-mary House.

Emma glanced, frowning, away from Dashwood's terse, un-compromising instructions to meet him later as she heard the vehicle in the street below. She twitched the curtain to see who alighted. Her stomach somersaulted and her heart thumped crazily as a street lamp pooled a mercury sheen on his hair.

After a dazed moment, there followed a few frantic seconds when she actually twirled about on the spot, crumpling Dash-wood's letter in her fingers while scouring her mind for truth-ful excuses to avoid seeing him.

Deceitfulness drew its humbling, just rewards as she had learned to her cost, and she wanted no more of those. Truth was all she would now deal in. If she went downstairs, Richard was sure to ask if she had contacted Dashwood and she would not lie. Thus he would know she had deliberately gone against his wishes and have further reason to despise her…and she desperately didn't want that.

She stilled her agitated dance and forced her mind to work. She did have an honest reason to give to her mother why she must stay in her room even if it no longer seriously confined her. It was an indisposition that would release Richard from caring whether or not she contacted, or even married, her spurned fiancé. There was no longer any need for him to fret over a child of his being reared by Jarrett Dashwood.

The very evening of her return to Rosemary House a familiar cramping in her abdomen had heralded the start of her menses. She had not conceived. The initial draining relief had been replaced by a sense of dreadful loss that had had her weeping and her mother anxiously pressing a hot brick to her aching stomach, while muttering about the cursed regularity of women's trials.

'How kind of you to call, Sir Richard,' Margaret beamed at him. 'I trust you are not here to tell us you will be unable to take tea tomorrow?'

Richard smiled. 'No. I was just passing and thought to call in and see how you do.' He prowled the room's perimeter, stuffed his hands in his pockets and looked at the door. 'Is your daughter at home?'

'Oh, yes, sir,' Margaret confirmed, settling comfortably into the sofa. 'But she is ailing.' She coloured a little in embarrassment despite having no intention of imparting the nature of the malaise. Besides, the excuse she would use was perfectably valid. 'She frets so much over her papa, it has fair set her head athumping.' She flicked a glance at Richard from beneath her sparse lashes. 'Emma has said she confided to you our very great troubles.'

Richard approached and looked down at the small woman huddled into an array of shawls to ward off the chill of the fireless room. 'Yes, she has told me, and I find it hard to believe that any parents would insist their daughter marry someone so repulsive that she was forced to flee from home.'

Margaret flushed scarlet. 'Well, of course, had there been another way,' she gruffly murmured. 'Had Emma striven to attract a husband in her prime—that is to say…a gentleman of her own choosing…' Bony fingers clasped together on her lap. 'Naturally we only ever wanted what was best for her…'

'Naturally, I should very much like to think so,' Richard mellifluously concurred.

'Mr Dashwood offered us all a settled future free of debt. But now it is all gone awry. As parents we have been further scandalised by our own flesh and blood when all we intended was to give our dear girl security. The longer Frederick is away, the more I fret he might be tempted to take his own life to avoid further opprobrium.'

'Well, proof, then, madam, that every cloud has a silver lining,' Richard drawled. 'Should he do the decent thing, I shall be spared a task.'

Margaret simpered up stupidly at a stern, handsome face, while, vacant-eyed, her mind struggled on.

Richard executed a curt bow. 'My regards to your daughter for a speedy recovery,' was bitten out over his shoulder as he strode to the door, oblivious to the woman abruptly flopping back into the cushions in a swoon.

'You have a visitor, Sir Richard,' Thomas Webb informed his master as Richard discarded his gloves and silver-topped cane onto the stately Heppelwhite table in the flagged hallway of his Mayfair mansion.

Richard appeared not to have heard as he savagely flung off his coat and left it where it landed.

He was still seething that she had refused to see him. He knew Emma well enough: a headache would never lay her low. This was the girl who could uncomplainingly exist for days with little to eat; who could fight like a vixen, dash through undergrowth like a fawn, who had the courage to purloin a horse she couldn't even ride properly. It was the woman who would lash out at him with her tongue and her fists even as she trembled imagining how he might retaliate. A headache would never have prevented her coming downstairs. She had chosen not to see him. She was punishing him for seducing her. And what rankled most was that he knew he deserved it. Aware that his butler had spoken, he frowned at him.

'You have a visitor, sir,' Thomas Webb repeated with a circumspect peer at his master's tense, tic-ridden jawline. 'I have shown him into your study. He refused to offer up his name but says you are expecting him.'

Richard paced along the wide, spacious hallway, aglitter with chandeliers and crystal wall sconces, and as he walked he suddenly recalled how dark and dismal it had seemed at Rosemary House. He threw back his head with a curse. It had slipped his mind that the Worthingtons probably had little or no credit available to them at the merchants'. Now he'd have to go back and see the accursed woman again to ensure they weren't about to starve or freeze.

He irritably shoved open his study door, hoping viciously that Dashwood was within for he was never likely to more enjoy dealing with him.

He slowed his pace into the room as the stumpy, balding man twisted away from the fire where he had been warming himself. He hadn't changed in the three years since last he'd clapped eyes on him, Richard realised. He still resembled a glassy-eyed little weasel.

Richard glared at Frederick Worthington and then ignored him. He strode to his desk, selected a cheroot, stuck it in his mouth, lit it, poured himself a brandy, then sent his chair skidding back with a jab of a foot, and dropped into it. He drew deeply on his cigar, raised his booted feet to the edge of his desk, crossed them at the ankles and then gave Frederick his attention.

'Sit down.'

Frederick shambled a few steps closer. 'I heard you wanted to see me about a matter of business.' Sandy lashes shielded pale, wary eyes. His unexpected benefactor's barely restrained temper was making him exceedingly apprehensive.

'*Sit down,*' Richard growled with such mean ferocity that Frederick scuttled to the desk and bounced into the chair opposite.

Richard withdrew his cigar and studied its glowing tip. 'I've just been to see your wife and daughter... Well, I saw your wife, not your daughter.'

Frederick gawped at him nervously. He gulped a breath. 'Ah, yes. My daughter is away from home visiting...er... no...she might be indisposed...'

'That's what I heard,' Richard said with a dry laugh as he watched a smoke ring drift towards the ceiling. 'She says she's indisposed but I think she's lying and won't see me.'

Frederick goggled at him anxiously, wondering if he was a madman and all the talk of thousands of pounds available to clear his debts was merely a fantasy. Well, in truth he knew it was. This man owed him nothing and they both knew that. But, unless he'd been afflicted by a recent full moon, Sir Richard Du Quesne wasn't a lunatic. Far from it. He was an ac-. credited businessman and very influential...very affluent. So there had to be some point to all this. And now that he had mentioned his daughter it jogged his memory that Margaret had once imagined this fellow held a certain interest in Emma. Not that Frederick could recall any such attention, but then he rarely noticed anything other than the amount of spending cash in his pocket, or the time of the day, and whether it merited him wending his way towards Brook's or White's.

Richard removed his feet from his desk and sat back in his chair, stubbing out his cigar while he watched his grinding fingers with frowning thoughtfulness. 'There's just one reason why I'm contemplating clearing your debts and saving your miserable hide from gaol. She's the same reason I shall no doubt swallow a burning desire to kill you or even maim you a little for neglecting her so appallingly. She's also the reason I shall be persuaded to provide for you and your lady wife till you shuffle off this mortal coil in your own sweet time rather than mine. In short,' he said through lips strained thin against his teeth, 'whatever I do, I do for Emma, and you had best make very sure you show her daily gratitude for it, in the manner of a fond papa, and never allow her to know that this conversation took place.' Flint eyes suddenly speared the man to his seat. 'Is that quite clear?' he asked softly.

Frederick wobbled his jowls up and down in assent, his pale eyes blinking ceaselessly. He licked dry lips. 'May I...?' He looked forlornly at Richard's brandy decanter. It was shoved across the desk at him together with a glass. Once Frederick had poured with an unsteady hand, sunk the tot and wiped his wet mouth with the backs of hairy fingers, he said with a foxy look, 'You're not jesting? You really will pay my debts?'

At Richard's sardonic, silent agreement, Frederick laughed and poured himself another. 'That's damned amazing,' he chortled. 'Who'd have thought it? My little Emma's got two blades after her now! Astonishing, I tell you...'

'I'll tell you what's astonishing,' Richard sneered, standing up and tersely indicating that Frederick follow. 'The fact that a jewel was got from such base metal. Oh, I'll tell you something else, too; Dashwood doesn't count.' He then offered quite cordially, 'Come, I'll have the carriage brought round and we can reunite you with your family. Perhaps your daughter will feel happy enough to see me this time.'

Emma walked confidently forward, but kept on the perimeter of the crowds of people posing in their finery. Strains of a serenade could be heard and people were increasing their pace towards the gaily lit boxes and the orchestra podium situated towards the centre of Vauxhall Gardens. The groves and grottoes, waterfalls and pavilions that comprised these pleasure gardens drew visitors from all social classes, but tonight it was a special concert to mark thirty years since Mozart's demise that made available these delights on this Indian summer evening.

Promenading young ladies, laughingly at ease with their beaus or their parents, only served to emphasise to Emma just how terrifyingly foolhardy was her solitary excursion.

Despite Jarrett Dashwood's specific instructions that their tryst should be confidential and that she must see him alone, she had decided at the last moment to follow her own instinct, and persuade her mother to accompany her.

In the event it had proved impossible. By seven-thirty that evening, when her firm decision was made, her mother had been snoring in the cold parlour on the chaise longue, covered with a blanket. A Madeira decanter was on the table at her side with little left in it: apparently her father's comfort was, in his absence, consoling her mother. When the clock had chimed eight, and Margaret Worthington had refused to relinquish her comfortable oblivion, even with Emma's pleading and shaking, Emma had retrieved her cloak from the hallway and slipped quietly from the house to hail a hackney cab.

She was unsure whether to be glad or perturbed that Jarrett Dashwood had settled on such a public place for them to meet. On the one hand she felt some reassurance that there were so many people around; on the other, she knew that it was scandalously unseemly for her to be there unaccompanied, and she was terrified that someone she knew might spot her.

Rallying her courage, she again drew her cloak tighter about her and allowed the hood to conceal more of her face. With a heavy sigh she conceded that most of the past two weeks had seen her behaving in a most scandalous and unseemly manner. No doubt Jarrett Dashwood was keen to drive home that point by summoning her here alone. As she had been prepared to risk all by escaping him unchaperoned, he was sure to gain quite deliberate satisfaction from making her return to apologise in the same manner.

She had gleaned from his curt, explicit note that he was extremely angry yet extremely eager for a meeting. That had seemed to her exactly the reaction she should expect and it had reassured her. He was certain to be voluble in his censure, yet he obviously deemed the agreement still viable.

With her face lowered and sunk in depressing thoughts, she didn't see the dandy until he grabbed at her arm and addressed her lewdly, enveloping her in alcoholic fumes. Emma reflexively wrenched herself free, aware of his male companions jeering and laughing at his bold antics. She understood why he looked angry at her rejection: lone women frequenting these dimly lit walkways were usually happy to attract such attention.

A shaking hand went up to retrieve her hood, which had been knocked back in the struggle. Concealing her frightened pallor, she quickly turned away and had taken two paces when she heard, 'Miss Worthington?' It was what she had dreaded: a familiar voice addressing her.

Ross Trelawney walked away from a group of stylish people. He was frowning at her and Emma read frank surprise in his dark features as she looked fully at him and confirmed his suspicions. Ross glanced from her to the young buck who was now glowering with increased indignation on seeing another man had successfully arrested her progress.

'Mr Trelawney…how are you?' Emma greeted with a smile, forcing lightness to her voice. 'I…I had no idea you were in London.'

'I am only lately arrived from Brighton where I was visiting my brother and sister-in-law,' Ross informed her with a gleaming smile but his dark eyes narrowed thoughtfully. He took her arm, manoeuvring her out of a crush. 'Is Richard with you?' he asked without preamble. 'I called at his town house earlier and learned he was abroad.'

'Why…no,' Emma quickly said. 'I am…I am just on my way to meet…an acquaintance. I had best be off, too. I am already late…' She gave an apologetic little smile and bobbed in readiness to go. She knew she had to go quickly for, in truth, she was so pleased to see Ross she might, in her feeble state of mind, be persuaded to stay safely with him. She had always liked him, right from the start when he had been prepared to act as her champion without having known her more than a few minutes.

Ross caught at her arm, charming smile still in evidence. 'You must allow me to accompany you to your friend. Who are you to meet? Perhaps I might be acquainted, too.' His shrewd, penetrating gaze forced nervous topaz eyes to swerve away.

Ross knew that this was an independent young lady. Apparently untrammelled by etiquette, she was not averse to travelling alone or keeping her own company. Nevertheless, she was tense with anxiety and her arm quivered beneath his light restraint. Something was amiss. Richard obviously had no idea the woman he loved was walking the grounds of Vauxhall Gardens, frightened and unchaperoned. How he would react to knowing she had just been mistaken for a soliciting harlot by a drunken cub roistering with his chums, Ross didn't want to contemplate.

His brooding was interrupted by a gloved hand gliding over his arm. 'We're waiting for you, Ross,' the dark-haired woman said, but her sharp black glance was on Emma's profile. 'Lord Grantham is to convey us to his supper box.'

It was the distraction Emma needed; with a murmured farewell, she slipped her arm free and was almost running along the path that led away from the concert area and towards the southerly grove.

'Ah, there you are, my dear! I had almost given up hope of you putting in an appearance and that would have made me so much angrier…'

Emma felt her arm gripped and she was whirled about, by a man who had emerged from the shadows. He urged her along a narrow path which terminated in a small clearing with a bench. Jarrett Dashwood released her, crossed his arms over his considerable chest, and eyed her contentedly through heavy lids.

Emma's attention, however, was immediately drawn to the seat. Slumped on it was an unidentifiable male figure and, standing at either side, were two huge, burly men. She took an unsteady pace forward, her breath wedged dizzily in her throat, as she tried to discern what was familiar about the hunched body barely illuminated by the globe lamps twinkling, with incongruous prettiness, in wavering tree branches.

'You said we were to meet privately,' she hoarsely snapped at Dashwood. 'I am courageous enough to come alone yet you bring accomplices.'

Olive eyes glittered like wet pebbles. 'They aren't accomplices, my dear. The two standing are my employees, the one sitting is in fact a friend of yours, I believe. So, there you are. You are not alone. I am a thoughtful soul who has brought along for you an accomplice. I thought it might be nice to reunite you tonight, while you explain to me what it is about him you find so appealing.'

Emma's fearful gaze lurched to the slouching figure on the bench and she slowly approached on wobbly legs, her chest afire with dread. Gently raising the lolling head, she looked into Matthew Cavendish's battered features, blood trailing from nose and lip. A shaking hand touched his cold cheek, and he roused enough to moan her name. The strong smell of liquor enveloped her, for once giving her a surge of comfort, for his insensibility was probably due as much to that as the beating he had sustained.

She felt rage smouldering, reigniting her courage. Straightening, she turned proudly towards the thick-set, raven-haired man who was watching her so malevolently. 'How did you find him? Why have you brought him here?'

'My investigators found him, my dear, and…persuaded him to accompany them to London. As to why he is here…I have just told you. An explanation is, I believe, due as to why my costly, chaste fiancée should see fit to abscond to a drunken pauper.'

'Is there some point to any of this, Mr Dashwood? Have you come here to discuss our marriage contract, or just to prove to me that every appalling whisper I have ever heard of you is in fact justified?'

A grin split his swarthy coutenance. 'Why, both, my dear. How astute you are.' He paced closer to her while a hand went to an inside pocket and with a flourish he withdrew a document. 'To wit…the marriage document,' he leered at her. 'Which stipulates my intention to wed a virtuous spinster.' He sighed. 'Alas, you no longer fit the bill.' Very slowly, very deliberately he also withdrew an elegant silver box, struck a match from it, and brought the two together. When the contract was burning well his fingers opened and he allowed it to drop to the ground.

'There…one matter promptly dealt with. But the loss of my two thousand pounds, and that of my credibility, still remains,' he ruefully jibed. 'And I must own the money to be of less moment. You have made of me a veritable pantaloon in this farce.' He marched away from her, hands clasped behind his broad back, then came again close, and as he raised fiendish dark eyes to her face Emma realised he was, in fact, insane with bitter fury. 'So I have decided that you must atone. You must be punished…'

The blow made Emma gasp, burst coloured lights behind her eyes as she stumbled back a few steps and steadied herself against the hedge. A shaking hand went to her split mouth, pressing at warm blood. But she valiantly raised her head and glared her loathing. 'You are an evil madman and you will pay dearly for this.'

Jarett Dashwood nodded with satanic enjoyment. 'I could sense spirit the first time we met. I knew there was fire beneath the ice. Well, I'll extinguish it…eventually.' He confided in a fervent whisper, 'You know, when every pleasure has been taken so often it has palled, there can be a most exquisite sport in pain. I'll teach you that…' he vowed excitedly, as one promising a gift. 'As you absconded for eleven days you should doubly make amends. Twenty days you will this time disappear while I discipline you…for lessons should never be rushed.'

'You obviously rushed yours, Dashwood,' came Ross's scoffing drawl as he burst into view. 'Twice eleven is twenty-two…' he sneered as his fist smashed efficiently against the side of the man's head, sending him reeling.

Ross grabbed at Emma's arm and shoved her behind him while facing the two thugs who had suddenly sprung from inanimate, disinterested statues into sinister life at his unexpected appearance.

'Get him, you fools,' Dashwood shrieked while a hand clutched at his gaping cheek. 'Where's that dolt Watts? Can't he keep a watch? Is it too much to expect him to keep his infernal eyes open?'

Ross swung about at the unwitting warning of unseen danger but his desperation to protect Emma rather than himself was his downfall. As he pushed her away from the looming figure behind, a club caught him behind an ear and he collapsed to the ground.

Emma dropped immediately to her knees, cradling Ross's dark head in her lap, her frantic fingers soothing his brow.

'Get up, you little whore,' Dashwood screamed, while his fingers trembled incessantly over his wound. 'Get up so I can finish the bastard off.'

Emma frantically shook her head, arching her upper body into a protective shell about Ross.

'So that's how it is!' Dashwood barked. 'Not only do you dally with a drunkard but with a marauding Cornishman, too. Oh, I know of the Trelawneys. You have a knack of entertaining dangerous men, my dear…this footling toper excepted, of course. I'll own that, had not Trelawney been surprised, we might have been a little in trouble. He is a renowned pugilist and swordsman. Rather like his good friend…your cousin.'

Dashwood balefully circled her, jabbing a foot towards Ross and chortling as she guarded him, taking kicks on her slender arms. 'You overnighted with your *cousin* at the Fallow Buck, did you not, my dear? My investigators revealed that too. How you ever managed to whore your way to Sir Richard Du Quesne's precious attention is beyond me. And who would have thought it? He even gallantly dumped you back on your own doorstep when he'd done. I really must find time to thank him for running my errands.'

Emma's head spontaneously bowed at that, and he saw it and scoffed, 'I trust you're not anticipating further gallantry from that quarter? A knight in shining armour? *A silver squire?*' He laughed loudly, looking about at his henchmen who obediently joined in. 'I should tell you, my dear, Du Quesne is not renowned for returning to lightskirts he discards.'

Despite an outward show of nonchalance, there was a shrillness to his spite. Inwardly he cursed that the little bitch had managed to secure Du Quesne's notice, even for a short while. He was a menacing, unpredictable man. In Jamaica they had been bitter enemies. Du Quesne's coddling of his labour disgusted him. Slaves were there to toil or quench a man's lust and uppity ones needed to be made an example of to bring the others into line. What was most astonishing was that Du Quesne had managed to get a ridiculous yield from his workforce and his crop with such leniency. Any other planter on such a run of luck would surely have stayed, milked all resources dry... Not him. Once the fraudster overseers had been ejected, and the business was in fine order, he had sold the estate for a phenomenal price to his neighbour and, most startlingly of all, disbanded his workforce with manumissions and cash!

Closer to home he was a man with a quite deadly reputation. Not only had he and Courtenay brawled their way through many a long night and stood to tell the tale—and repeat the exercise—but his war record was exemplary.

It was a little-known fact, and one that Du Quesne refused to speak of, that Courtenay owed him his life. Suicidal missions had for some reason seemed to lure the young David Hardinge, prompting many to whisper he had lost his wits. The fact that he survived to inherit his viscountcy at all was credited to Du Quesne's valour and vigilance finally bringing them both home.

As soon as he'd learned from the detectives he'd hired that Emma Worthington had spent time alone with Du Quesne he'd been enraged. The man was too dangerous to meddle with, yet he'd known the little spinster would never return intact. There was no such thing as an unwilling woman where Du Quesne was concerned. He'd had her, then dumped her, he just knew it, and his irritation made him prod at Emma again with his boot.

Ross grabbed at the foot, twisting and shoving, sending him off balance and crashing onto his back. Dragging himself to his feet with Emma's assistance, Ross deftly sidestepped Watts, who had clubbed him, and rammed him head-first into the hedge. Retrieving the man's dropped club and testing its weight in his hand, he commanded in a concussed slur, 'Go, Emma. Go home this minute!'

'I can't leave you! You're injured. There are too many of them. You'll be killed!'

Ross grunted a laugh then winced as it pained him. 'I'll be killed if you don't go,' he muttered hoarsely. 'Believe me, I'd rather face this motley crew than Richard if he discovers I let you stay. Go now!' roared out of him with such vehement authority that without further thought she turned and fled.

Chapter Fourteen

Handicapped by burning tears that trailed to sting her torn mouth, she ran clumsily, every step pounding her skull, rattling her teeth in their sockets until the ache in her face from the blow Dashwood had delivered was a throbbing agony.

The dim pathways seemed endless, maze-like, and it was only the strengthening serenade that guided her towards the exit to the gardens. *Eine Kleine Nachtmusik* wafted delicately, the globe lamps overhead seeming to sway in perfect, incongruous tempo as the tepid breeze caught them.

Moments ago, Emma had accosted a couple strolling the deserted pathways to pour out that a man was in peril and needed help. They had peered through the dusk at her dishevelled appearance and bloodied face with a mix of doubt and contempt. Barely listening to her garbled pleas, they were soon hurrying away, probably having decided she was a footpad's decoy.

Trying to enlist the aid of an elderly gentleman·sauntering jauntily had also been fruitless. He'd obviously suspected she was away from the concert and seeking less cultured diversion in the shrubbery as he was. Freedom was gained thanks to the staggering amount of alcohol he'd imbibed.

Reaching the exit to the grounds at last, Emma sped to the roadside, and began scouring the gloom for a charley on his beat or someone disposed to help. A hackney passed, and too late her befuddled brain told her to hail it.

She spun about at the kerb, trembling violently, searching for another as she instinctively wrapped herself into her cloak for warmth and protection from prying eyes.

'What in God's name are you about, Emma?' The despairing words accompanied a grip on her arm swinging her about.

The relief was overwhelming. A shuddering sob exploded as she fell against him, clutched hungrily at him, leaned her cheek against his shoulder. His familiar height and breadth, the hint of sandalwood, the tenor of his dear voice combined to ensure she would have recognised him had she been truly sightless rather than simply blinded by prickling brine. 'They'll kill.Ross. You must quickly help him, Richard, or they'll kill him…' she cried out.

Dark hands secured her slippery face, tilting it immediately up to his. About to interrogate her, questions died on his lips, his eyes freezing on her injured mouth, the blemish beneath her eye.

Emma felt his hands start to vibrate against her skin, sensed him try to gentle their reflexive clenching. Through tear-spiky black lashes she watched his despair: a soundless mouthing of her name, lids slowly screening glaring, dilating pupils. Within a moment he was again examining her with fanatical intensity. A thumb brushed, feather-light, across her swollen purple lip, collecting the blood there.

'Dashwood did this?'

'He's with Ross,' Emma forced through chattering teeth, answering him obliquely. 'Ross sent me away. He has been clubbed but he's again conscious and poor Matthew has been beaten too! It's all my fault, Richard!' she choked. 'If it weren't for my foolishness none of this would have happened. It's *me* he wants to punish, yet Ross has sent me away, and now he'll be killed!'

'Hush…' Richard soothed, pulling her close, his fingers spearing up through tangled, tawny hair to cradle her scalp, his lips ceaselessly caressing her. Then, without warning, he suddenly bellowed, 'Wainwright!'

Through straggly locks, Emma spied a man run from the other side of the road to greet Richard with a jovial, 'Dammit, Dickie, you've started on the muslin early. It's not yet ten…'

'I have a favour to ask, Paul.' Richard cut sharply across his friend's ribald observation. 'I want you to take Miss Worthington home to Rosemary House, Cheapside, without delay.'

Paul Wainwright blinked at Emma's ashen, damaged face and then at Richard. 'Of course…why, of course…' he murmured, grimacing apology for his inappropriate jest while a hand pressed down his coarse dark curls. But he asked for no explanation. Richard's forbidding, rigid countenance tacitly conveyed urgency and gravity and suppressed a natural inquisitiveness.

'Take my carriage…' Richard dictated, indicating the sleek conveyance close by. The door was still open from when he had alighted, on seeing her, before the vehicle had properly stopped. 'And Paul…you're on pain of death on this,' was quietly emphasised. He gently prised away Emma's clinging hands, touched his lips to them, and handed her over to his friend. With a last, lingering look at her forlorn face, Richard was running towards the gardens. 'Take her straight home and see her delivered safely within to her parents!' was yelled back at Wainwright.

'I think I know you,' Ross said, squinting through double vision at Richard. He had sustained another glancing blow to the head and yet remained on his feet thanks to doggedness and cunning learned over two decades of every conceivable form of combat. The club swung viciously in front of him, keeping the thugs at bay, while he spoke to his friend.

'You do know me,' Richard reassured him as he paced steadily closer.

'Dickie, how nice to see you,' Dashwood greeted, yet he

spontaneously backed away at the blond man's purposeful stalking.

The thugs were ignored as though they were of no real threat; Richard's only focus was the swarthy-countenanced man his eyes had targeted like silver bullets.

'I was saying to Miss Worthington just a short while since,' Dashwood drawled, 'I really must thank you for returning her to me. Unsullied would have been preferable, but not to quibble…' The sarcasm was smooth but the frantic fingers that were not fidgeting incessantly at his bleeding face were urgently beckoning forward his bodyguards.

They had ceased aiming blows at Ross to gawp at the nonchalant newcomer. This swell had made Dashwood increasingly uneasy. If he fought like the Cornish fiend they had trouble. Even concussed, Trelawney battled with awesome instinct, feinting and dodging, using his fists, feet, the club with a natural skill.

One of the brutes gathered what little wit he had, decided to earn his fee, and surged forward, fists ready. With spare savagery he was hit once in the face. As his legs wobbled, a knee jerked into his groin, then, as he sank, found his chin, before he found the ground. Richard tipped him disdainfully off the end of a polished boot where he sprawled, stunned, before looking enquiringly at his colleague. Eyes swivelled in a square skull as the henchman nervously sought his master's instruction. Dashwood managed a thin smile and put up a hand for him to wait.

Watts, who had been hanging limply in the hedge where Ross had left him, started to stir, squirming to free his shoulders. Ross idly shoved him further into the bush with a booted foot. 'Ah, now I recall,' he said, with a grin at Richard, as he battled with waves of amnesia. 'Was it Devil's Cove in eleven? A consignment of tea and geneva? You must be Revenue.'

'No,' Richard said easily, 'but I am here to exact payment.'

'Don't be a fool, Dickie,' Dashwood whined, understanding

exactly what was meant and why. 'I have every right to be angry with the little trollop. She deserves more chastisement than she got. She and her conniving parents have fleeced me. What's it to you, in any case? It's my credibility at stake, my two thousand pounds, my fiancée…'

'She's mine,' Richard contradicted him coolly. 'She's always been mine…'

Dashwood peered speculatively at him from beneath heavy lids. 'Well, have her, then. I'll never take the little slut to wife now you're done with her.' He shrugged and coaxed chummily, 'Come, we can both make use of her. We oughtn't let petty rivalry worry us unduly. It's nothing to me if you still bed her. In some ways, we're very much alike, you and I…'

'We're nothing alike and if you say it again I'll kill you just for that.'

'A skinny chit with cat's eyes isn't worth this, Du Quesne! We'll call it quits. Take Trelawney and this worthless sot she's in love with and go.'

Richard turned to Ross. 'Are you ready to go?'

Ross deliberately lowered the club. 'Whenever you are.'

Ross felt in the inside pocket of Matthew Cavendish's coat and eventually located what he sought. He drew out the pewter flask and up-ended it, allowing a stream of whisky to fill his mouth. He swilled it round, wincing as it seared raw flesh. Anointing himself with a little of the liquor, he swore and shook himself as it found the contusion behind his ear.

'God, don't waste it,' Richard growled, and relieved him of the flask. He took a swig then lowered Matthew Cavendish from his shoulder to the ground, one hand keeping him upright.

The flask was waved at the carriage and it immediately pulled forward. 'Thank God Wainwright was about here tonight,' he sighed to himself.

Paul Wainwright jumped from the carriage and grinned at the three men, two swaying on their feet, their marked faces, their torn clothes, indisputable evidence of a vicious brawl. The other man was seemingly unconscious and reeking of alcohol. Before he could utter a jovial word a bloodied hand grabbed him by the lapels.

'Is Miss Worthington safely home?'

Paul nodded. 'Delivered to her mother and safely within Rosemary House, Dickie.' He chuckled and nodded to himself with intense satisfaction. 'I knew it… I just *knew* it. It *is* going to be like old times, isn't it?' With a flourish he ushered them forward, waving away the groom so he could hold the door himself for them as a sign of respect. 'Come on, gentlemen…get in. How many of them, Dickie? Five? Six? Weapons?'

'Shut up,' Richard directed mildly as he loaded Matthew Cavendish into his carriage, ignored the censorious gawping of his driver and groom, and got in himself. Ross clambered in after him and, as one, they fell back into the squabs, exhausted.

'I'm getting too old for this, Dickie,' Ross eventually said, flexing his strained shoulders. 'You know, I barely saw that first blow coming. It took me out for a while and left Emma at that bastard's mercy. He might have hurt her again.'

'Shut up, dammit!' Richard gritted as his blond head fell forward into massaging hands. He dropped one away and studied the bloody mess opened up across his knuckles again. Then he gazed sightlessly out into the gloaming for a while. Eventually he said quietly, 'Thanks, Ross. I owe you so much…I don't know how I can ever repay you… I daren't think what might have happened if you hadn't found Emma when you did… I just can't talk about it…' At his comrade's silence he turned his head. Ross was propped in the corner, arms crossed over his chest, head lolling, sound asleep, oblivious to his gruff gratitude. Richard smiled wryly, glancing at the carriage's other occupants: Wainwright, still grinning and shaking his head happily to himself as his imagination entertained him; Matthew Cavendish snoring quite peacefully. He turned back to brood, alone, at the night.

'But she's abed, Sir Richard!' Margaret Worthington exclaimed agitatedly. 'Even if I wanted to wake her, which I do not, it would prove impossible. I dosed her with laudanum to ease her hurt and get her a good night's sleep.'

Richard looked from Frederick Worthington to his wife and then slowly nodded. 'Yes...good...she needs to sleep,' he echoed while in his mind he raged, *Well, let me go to her. I must see her. I need her.*

Having delivered Ross, Matthew and Wainwright to his Mayfair town house, he had immediately journeyed on to Cheapside. The fact that Emma was now in peaceful oblivion was comforting, yet he desperately wanted to be close to her again, lie down beside her, take her in his arms and hold her lest another danger menace her before the dawn.

Frederick Worthington shuffled on the spot, a shaking hand wiping about his bristly chin. He blinked at Sir Richard's haggard profile, for the first time in the twenty-seven years of his daughter's life, tearfully distraught on her account.

Earlier that evening, when Sir Richard had brought him home to be reunited with his family he'd been feeling exceedingly content. Having woken his wife from her tipsy snooze, to be simultaneously nagged and hugged, he'd found that within five minutes all the gladness was gone.

Emma was missing. She *had* written to Dashwood, Margaret had nervously replied to Sir Richard's abrupt enquiry as to whether the two had been in contact, and a reply from Dashwood *had* been received. The fact that Emma had made no attempt to conceal Dashwood's letter, and it was easily located on her writing desk, had made the reason for her unexpected absence from home that evening ominously apparent. The time of eight-thirty and the venue of the south grove at Vauxhall Gardens was all Sir Richard had waited to learn before hurtling from Rosemary House.

Frederick glanced again at Sir Richard's dishevelled appearance: his fine tail-coat torn and dirty, his boots scuffed and dusty. Blood was caked thickly on his knuckles and was just visible on his temple, beneath a fall of fair hair. And the damage told its own story: Sir Richard had fought Dashwood and emerged victorious.

Frederick knew himself for an abject coward and he knew this man for an intrepid warrior. Sir Richard's military record alone was proof of his prowess; his youthful hellraising added another shocking dimension to his skill. Never before had he felt so thankful for anything or anyone. He prayed to God the deed was already done as he choked, 'I shall kill Dashwood for this. He has abused my little Emma!'

Richard swung back to face him, lips tight against his teeth. 'What the hell did you think he intended doing over the next twenty or more years? You're not deaf. You've heard talk. Yet you were prepared to sell a beautiful, spirited woman into what would have been a life of unremitting misery.' He stepped close to the man and glared, livid-faced, down at him. 'The worst of it is, she would have eventually welcomed a split lip over other atrocities.'

Frederick dropped his face to his hands, grazed his palms with his stubbly countenance. 'Does the bastard still live?'

'Yes…just…'

'I'll get Dashwood his two thousand pounds in pennies and feed him each coin. I'll swing from a gibbet myself to see him buried!' Frederick's shrieking voice caused Margaret to flee to an armchair and huddle into it.

'Dashwood is no longer a problem,' Richard bit out, but calmingly. 'And he has obligingly destroyed the marriage contract himself. Do likewise with your document.'

Margaret fidgeted in the chair, wringing her hands. 'Still Emma must be married,' she gabbled hysterically. 'Dashwood would never again dare meddle with her if she were wed. Frederick, we must find our daughter a husband.'

'Perhaps you'd best leave that to me, too…' Richard drawled witheringly, and with a curt bow he was gone.

'I don't believe Sir Richard would have said that, Mama,' Emma quavered.

'Well, of course he said it! Am I a liar? Is that what you mean?' her mother demanded. 'You may ask your papa.' She flicked a finger at Frederick who was pacing the room, head bowed, lost in his own thoughts.

'Sir Richard said quite clearly that he would assist us in finding for you a husband. And it must be done. You need the protection only a husband can give you. Dashwood obviously has no fear of your father.' A whip of a glance scorned her husband. 'But he will perhaps not harass a man's wife.'

Margaret inspected her daughter's white face, a shading of blue beneath her transluscent skin, extending from cheekbone to jaw, branding her with Dashwood's malice. 'Come closer to the fire; you look cold.' Margaret anxiously patted the seat beside her as her daughter's pallor increased.

Emma obediently took her place by the hearth and stared, sightlessly, into the blaze. Richard would never cold-bloodedly conspire in marrying her off! She wouldn't believe it! He had held her tenderly by Vauxhall Gardens; his concern for her injury had been palpable. Every soothing, gentle touch at her bruised face had shown he cared… But now he had offered his services as marriage broker? He would see her wed for convenience?

'Sir Richard has promised us lasting provision,' Frederick suddenly mumbled. 'Why would the man do that if he were intending finding for us a son-in-law? I don't understand it. He said he would do all for our Emma. He must mean to marry…'

'He is to marry a duke's daughter,' Margaret hissed into his speech with an emphatic, silencing nod. 'Emma has that news from his own relations!'

Emma's soulful golden eyes raised to her drop-jawed father

and suddenly *she* understood. She understood very well. Richard's concern, his generosity to her parents were born out of the desire he felt for her. He had shown her so very explicitly how ardently he wanted her. That lust was still unassuaged. He still intended her as his paramour despite her defying him ever again to touch her. The interdict was empty bravado, and they both knew it. But, thinking sensibly of it now, he would never have installed her in that town house so close to his home. She had been introduced to his mother, his other relations. She had met his neighbours. They shared mutual friends and similar social standing. To flout convention and decency and house a genteel spinster locally for such an obvious purpose would never have been his intention. More discretion was called for to prevent embarrassing those he cared about.

If Richard found for her a puppet husband it need not interfere with his plans at all. She would gain acceptability and status through marriage, and he would gain a mistress and copper-mining rights when he wed his heiress. Heaven only knew that such alliances were forged time and again throughout polite society: marriages brokered for money and pedigree that allowed men freedom to seek diversion elsewhere. It gave him access to any children of their union, too. If he appointed their nominal father, it would set his mind at rest that they would remain well cared for should he later distance himself.

'He must be lying about lasting provision! He has tricked me from hiding and will never settle my duns. I shall still face the Fleet.'

'No, Papa,' Emma reassured him huskily. 'He does not lie. If he has said he will discharge your debts and provide for you, then he will. He had already offered me lasting provision…weeks ago when first we met in Bath.' Emma felt blood seeping into her cold complexion as her parents' eyes swivelled to her.

'Why would he do that?' Frederick asked, frowning.

'Why do you think, you fool?' Margaret snapped. She

looked at her daughter and moistened her lips. 'And how did you respond to that, Emma?'

'I said, no,' Emma flung back immediately.

Margaret straightened the lap of her gown, smoothed it. 'If an agreeable gentleman could be found who would marry you and welcome Sir Richard's discreet…arrangement,' she stated matter-of-factly, with a shrewd peer at her daughter's flushing complexion, 'what would you say then?'

Emma sprang to her feet, whirled to face her mother, and then found no rebuke could be forced past the throb of anger and sorrow in her throat. 'I don't know what to say anymore,' she finally whispered back at them, before quitting the parlour to seek the peace of her chamber.

'There is a gentleman below to see you, Miss Emma,' Polly informed her softly, with a peek about her bedroom door.

Emma raised her head away from the pillow to blink at her mother's maid. Since her parents had quit the house for an afternoon stroll, in the hope of being confused with any other happy and harmonious couple, Emma had been fitfully snoozing fully clothed on top of her bed's counterpane.

Her heart leaped to her mouth at this unexpected visitor. Had Richard finally come? It was two days since the fracas at Vauxhall Gardens. She had not seen him since he had sent her home with his friend, although she knew he had returned to see her that night while she slept.

'Who is it, Polly?'

'A Mr Trelawney, Miss Emma.' The young girl chuckled saucily. 'A very handsome, charming gentleman, Miss Emma.'

'Oh, yes…' Emma agreed wryly, with an indulgent look as Polly coloured to her hair-roots for having so boldly voiced her opinion. It wasn't the gentleman she was hoping for, Emma realised. Nonetheless, her spirits lifted as she swung her legs to the floor then tidied her thick glossy hair and her crumpled gown.

'Mr Trelawney, how nice to see you,' she greeted a few

minutes later. 'I am so glad you are come so I can thank you
for the great service you did me.'

Ross took her hands as they were extended and raised them
to his lips. 'Think nothing of it, Miss Worthington,' he said
affably. More gravely he continued, 'My only regret is that I
didn't happen upon you a few moments sooner and save you
this.' A dark finger just touched the fading bruising on her
cheek. 'Now we're well acquainted, perhaps we should be a
little less formal. I'd like it if you called me Ross.'

'Thank you, Ross. Please call me Emma,' Emma agreed,
with a little dip of her burnished tawny head. She anxiously
looked him over. He seemed virtually unscathed apart from a
light swelling beneath one eye. 'Are you recovered? You took
such a nasty blow…'

Ross raised fingers to press at the back of his skull as though
testing his fitness himself. 'I'm fine,' he said, with a laugh.
'My mother says I must have stone for bone, judging from the
amount of times I've limped home and frightened her witless,
then been up bright and early demanding breakfast.'

'Your poor mama…' Emma murmured, not wholly in jest.

Ross grimaced his chagrin. 'You are looking very fine, if I
might say so. Are you feeling better?'

'I am much better…much wiser too.' A bashful look accompanied, 'I must own to behaving with idiotic recklessness
over the past weeks. I feel very ashamed at having put your
life at risk because of it.'

'I've risked my life lots of times, Emma,' she was gently
reassured. 'And for far less worthy reasons.'

'Thank you for your chivalry, sir,' Emma said. Then, to
ease the solemnity, she asked, 'May I get you some tea? Or a
little wine? I believe we have some cognac now our deliveries
have been made…'

'No…nothing, thank you.' Ross soothed her agitated need
to supply him with refreshment. 'I have just come to bid you
farewell…until we again meet. And I'm certain we will. I am
journeying west. I shall take your friend, Matthew, home to

Bath now he is recuperated— Oh, I am bid to convey his warmest regards— After that, I promised to call in again on my brother, Luke, and his family at Brighton; then on home to Cornwall.'

'Please return my good wishes to Matthew and say I shall soon write to him.' He was another gentleman who was owed apologies, Emma sorrowfully realised. He had been abducted and ill-treated simply because she had unwittingly drawn him into Dashwood's web of malice and revenge.

'Are you wondering where Richard is?' Ross shrewdly interpreted her melancholy mien.

Emma flushed and forced a vague smile at his unexpectedly direct question. 'Yes...no...' she flustered. 'That is...I'm aware he is a businessman and has things he must do. He is no doubt occupied...'

'Yes, he is. He's away from London for a few days but he will shortly be back. I know he intends coming to see you as soon as he is able.' Ross knew very well that his friend couldn't return from finishing matters with Dashwood soon enough. He also knew that not finishing the blackguard off permanently would prove a constant trial for Richard.

When Ross had taken his leave Emma felt oddly restless as though already missing his company. She returned, sighing, to her room and paced it aimlessly. Her head dropped despairingly back and she frowned at a blurry, fragmented ceiling, wishing that this awful feeling that she no longer controlled her life would go away.

Only a month ago she had been so confident and decisive. Any problem was logically scrutinised for a fitting solution. Now she felt incapable of analysing the gains and losses of being paired off with a stranger so the man she loved could dally with her. Yet in her soul whispered the truth: the gentlemen might remain blasé, but she was no sophisticate; it would finish for her in heartache. So her conscious thoughts simply skimmed the surface of it all, while she wished for someone she trusted to tell her what to do...to help her balance what she could reasonably expect with what she yearned for. And there was only one such confidante.

With a sigh she found her carpet bag and the few things she wanted to take with her and then sat at her writing desk to try and find words to explain to her parents why she must again be gone for a while.

An unsteady brown hand rasped over a shady, angular jaw. 'Something must have prompted her to leave today. What was it this time?'

Margaret shrugged. 'Who is to know, Sir Richard?' was sighed out in a martyred tone. 'It seems each time I tender sensible advice she sulks or runs away. I am done with trying to help…'

'That sounds very sensible,' Richard concurred exceedingly softly. 'What wise counsel were you offering?'

Margaret looked warily at his hard, sardonic face. 'Why, I simply promoted what you endorsed yourself, sir. You said you would assist in finding for her a respectable husband, did you not?'

A metallic glare was turned on her and then his eyes closed and he smothered a groaning blasphemy. With a defeated sigh and weary shake of his head he made for the door, Margaret close to his heels.

'My maid tells me a Mr Trelawney visited while I was out. Perhaps she has gone with him. He might be the person she alludes to in her note.'

'No, he is not.' Richard felt his insides twisting. Emma's distress and confusion had been apparent in each neatly scripted word in her note yet her mother didn't even know her well enough to realise that 'seeking advice from a good friend' meant she was travelling into Hertfordshire.

'What will you do, Sir Richard? Will you search for her? If you find her, what will you say?'

Richard barked a laugh. 'I've no idea, Mrs Worthington.

What would Mr Darcy say, do you think?' he savagely mocked himself. 'Would that I knew.'

'Mr Darcy? He of the novel she reads, you mean? Of what importance is he?'

'None, I hope…' Richard said.

She decided against purchasing a drink in the tavern. The mail coach driver had said it would be but a short wait for the large bay to be reshod and then they would be back on the road to Hertford. They had been travelling for four hours and had so far made very good time. Emma hoped to reach her destination a little after seven this evening. To occupy herself she walked towards the stables, reminiscing on the last time she had peered over a stall and caught sight of Star's golden flanks gleaming in the shadows. She ambled the ramshackle building idly observing horses being groomed or munching at their feed. She gained the last stall, about to glance in, but her attention was diverted to a racing curricle just turning in in a spray of gravelly dust…and then she flew backwards, heart pumping.

She must be mistaken, she impressed upon herself as she steadied her breathing. Just because she'd momentarily glimpsed a flash of very blond hair and an expensive equipage, it didn't mean… She surreptitiously peeked about the side of the stables again. The dusty curricle was by the tavern entrance; only the tiger was with it; the driver was nowhere to be seen. He had gone within, Emma realised, expelling some breath, and she was being ridiculous. And then he came without and she stared at him.

His impressive height and broad shoulders, the elegant cut of his dark clothes, the pearly sheen on his long hair as he abruptly swung his head to say something to someone standing behind tightened a knot of bitter-sweet melancholy. And she was suddenly aware she had travelled into Hertfordshire for no real reason.

She needed no advice. As she indulged in hungrily watching

him, unseen, she knew there was only one sensible conclusion to be drawn: for once he touched her again she would want him for ever. She would want that tender loving he had promised her, would want it until she died. She would want him there in the mornings, to talk of his family, to talk of their family…of their children and how they did with their lessons…how tall they were getting. She would want him to proudly listen to their daughter sing or play the piano. She would want to see him soothe their son's scraped knees as she had seen him tend to his nephew… She would want it all and have none of it. Perhaps not even keep him very long at all. And when that time came she might shatter into pieces and beg and weep, then watch him from shadows as he and a duke's daughter reared heirs.

Earlier that day Ross had told her that Richard was away from London for a while and foolishly she had given little thought to where. Naturally, he would visit his close friend, Viscount Courtenay, as soon as he was able. He was probably now returning to London having spent time with Victoria and David. And in her haste to escape him and seek her dear friend's counsel she had unwittingly followed him to the very same place. A hand covered her face and she laughed, shook with soundless hysteria at the awful farce of it.

'If you loiter about the stables someone might take you for a horse thief.'

'If you loiter about lone women someone might take you for a philanderer.' She composed her features, abruptly dropping her hands from her face, and looked up at him, wishing she'd been aware of his approach.

He gave her a slow, devastating smile. 'Well, we both know we're reformed characters, Emma…so what matter what anyone else thinks?'

Emma busied herself tidying her hair, straightening her cloak. 'What an odd coincidence,' she brightly remarked. 'I am just on my way to see Victoria. I expect you must be just returning from visiting David. I intended to write you a brief note thanking you for all your assistance with… Dashwood…and my papa and…Matthew. I expect I still shall once I am home. But for now, thank you very much, sir. And it was nice to see Ross earlier, before he left for Cornwall… Oh, and now I must go, too…the coach is about to leave, I see.' She made to sweep past him but he took a step sideways so she careered into him.

'Damn the coach! If you once more travel alone on public conveyances…!'

Emma backed away. 'I have to go!' she cried with the anger of desperation.

'Very well, go! Go away! I give up!' He flung his hands into the air in sheer exasperation as he spun away from her. Turning back almost immediately, he withdrew from his pocket a silver clip of bank notes. Taking a hand, he placed the cash on her palm then closed her fingers over it. 'Take some money for incidentals. Go and visit Victoria then go home. I've not recently seen David but I know he will insist on you being accompanied back to Cheapside. I promise I won't trouble you while you stay with them…I won't trouble you ever again.'

With that he abruptly left her and strode towards the tavern.

Stunned, Emma watched his broad, black-jacketed back for a moment and then rushed after him. 'I can't possibly…I can't accept your money. It's not…not right…'

'No one but us will know,' he replied coolly without slowing his pace. 'You're under no obligation; treat it as a loan, if you prefer. Go. I swear I will never trouble you again.'

Emma looked glassily at the notes in her hand then at the door closing as Richard entered the tavern. The coachman was waving and beckoning, indicating that they were ready to leave. She dithered on the spot, swinging her gaze between the tavern and the vehicle. The horses stamped restlessly and she saw one of the coach passengers poke her head through the window to glare in irritation at her.

Emma shook her head at the driver and he carelessly shrugged his caped shoulders and shouted something to the groom.

Emma watched her carpet bag hit the ground.

Chapter Fifteen

The savoury aroma inside the tavern reminded Emma of Mrs Keene's boarding-house 'specials' and that prompted a less pleasant memory: her mean abuse of Richard's generosity under the prim guise of altruism. She squirmed anew with remorse, his cash suddenly singeing her hand. It was hastily shoved into her cloak pocket as she peeked into a room. Two dour-faced peasants swivelled their heads, aiming clay pipes at her. She withdrew and moved on, the scent of more mellow tobacco leading her to a small sitting-room and drawing her hesitantly within.

He was sitting close to the hearth, his blond head turned towards the fire. One hand had dropped over the chair arm and between long fingers a smoke-curling cigar was slanted at the floor. His other hand propped a bronzed jaw. She sensed he was aware of her presence but chose to dismiss it.

'I…I thought you must be travelling back from visiting David…but you said you've not seen him.' Emma ventured a little conciliatory conversation.

Richard's hand rose from the oak boards and he drew on the cheroot until it glowed red but he didn't turn his head.

'Please don't ignore me. I want you to talk to me…' she said, voice quavering, hating trying so hard to make him look at her.

'Are you going to reciprocate and talk to me?' he asked levelly, watching the flickering flames. 'Or are you going to ignore questions you don't like?'

'Why are you here?' she asked, immediately avoiding answering him.

An acknowledging smile twisted his lips. 'You know why, Emma,' he mildly reproved. 'The first time we met in Bath, you fled. You've not stopped running since and I've not stopped chasing you from place to place.' He drew deeply on the cigar again then pitched it towards the grate. 'But no more.'

Oddly disturbed by that gruff, determined vow, she bristled defensively. '*I* never wanted you to follow me. I didn't expect to see you at Mrs Keene's or at the Fallow Buck...or even at Vauxhall Gardens. I certainly never expected to see you here.'

Richard laughed wryly at the ceiling. 'Of course you did. That note you left made more sense to me than your mother. But, as I said, I'm no longer playing games. I give up. I'm a thirty-three-year-old baronet with, I hope, a certain dignity and status to uphold. And you're an intelligent woman of advanced years, as you're wont to constantly remind me. It's time to act with a little more maturity.' A hand was extended sideways; his long fingers beckoned.

Emma slowly approached. She withdrew the silver note clip from her pocket and placed the money lightly on his palm.

Richard looked at it, and then at her. 'Thank you, Emma,' he said with studied politeness. He pocketed it, then determinedly drew her down to kneel by his chair. 'Let's reminisce,' he urged in a voice as thick and sweet as honey. 'I believe you omitted to mention the most vital stage of the chase. By my recollection, I followed you to the Fallow Buck...then you stole my horse and I trailed you to Abbey Wood where you ran away again...'

'How...how did you know I was travelling into Hertfordshire?' Emma hastily gabbled into his disturbingly comprehensive recollection.

'Your mother showed me the note you'd written. What about your future worries you?'

Emma blinked, seeking some way to prevaricate, and she was aware of him watching her, expecting her to do just that. So she settled on candour. 'My parents told me you would assist in finding me a husband to provide security and so on,' she stiffly explained. 'I must thank you for your trouble in that, too. I know it to be a very sensible course of action. Just as I have come to realise it was foolish wanting to seek advice from Victoria. At my age, I should be able to decide my own future...and now I have.'

Glossy amber eyes rose to his impassive dark face. He was waiting for her to elaborate, so, with a brisk lightness, she did. 'I have always been independent, and keen to travel. I have seen little of anywhere outside London. It is time I broadened my horizons,' she informed him, with a small, firm smile. 'I should like to visit some of the north of England. I have read of moors and rugged landscape which is spectacular...quite wild. So I shall, after all, be travelling to Derbyshire via London...taking the scenic route, I believe you said. And, of course, as I am judged to be a lady of educated pursuits, I will manage to earn a living of some sort, while I do a little exploring...' Her voice wobbled but her little smile was unwavering.

'That's what you think you should do, is it?' Richard said quietly. 'Tell me, what do you think I should do? Just let you go?'

A golden gaze bathed his unshaven jaw, his long-lashed, low-lidded eyes, silver barely discernible. He looked very tired and drawn. A pang of inexorable affection made her fingers tremble; they wanted to graze over his skin, touch the wound just visible beneath a fringe of silky silver hair: she wanted to soothe him. Then she realised what must be worrying him.

Drawing on her new, constrained maturity, she quickly explained, 'Oh, you need not fret that I... I am certain now that I...I am not with child. I wanted to let you know that I would never have met with Dashwood had the possibility still existed,' she finished, with a warm blush.

'I wish the possibility did still exist.'

There was such husky sincerity in the statement that she shot a searching glance his way. Why had he said that? Because she would be unbruised had she still been unsure of her condition?

'You've not answered me, Emma. What is there for me if you go away?' Desire harshened his face, burned coal in his eyes. Long fingers stirred in her hair, moved to caress her neck.

Oh, he wanted her still! But what loss was he rueing? she indignantly wondered. A mistress he'd not quite done with? Would that lust endure once he found another young courtesan to occupy his town house? Or would he then be happy enough for her to play the loyal wife to the husband he allocated?

'What is there for you, sir?' she echoed, with ungovernable shrill bitterness. 'I hear there is a duke's daughter and copper-mining rights and a small fortune to add to what you already have. I trust that is an acceptably adult understanding of your prospects…' She snapped back her tawny head, and sparking feline eyes raked his face.

Richard stared at her then tipped back his head and barked a laugh. 'Thank God for that! You're jealous,' he muttered in obvious relief. 'For a moment I really believed you intended going to Derbyshire to search for Darcy and Pemberley.'

He abruptly stood up, lifting her with him. 'It seems to me, Miss Worthington, we might fare better if we ignore gossip. Who told you about a duke's daughter? Amelia?'

Emma nodded, confused by his mild amusement.

'I never seriously considered marrying her, Emma, even for that copper lode,' he softly reassured her. 'How could I? I don't love her. Now David and Stephen have set this damnable precedent of love matches…immature as it may seem…it's all that will do. I know that's all you want.'

She swallowed painfully, her eyes magnetised by his, her mind in limbo…waiting.

A dark finger reached out, touched her face gently. 'That's why I'm hoping you'll accept the husband I've found for you, for he really does love you so much. And he's sure, when you've forgiven him for that callous seduction, you'll tell him that you love him, too.'

Emma forced herself back from him. 'Don't say that…it's not true…it's cruel…' she choked. The palm of a small hand cupped her swimming eyes.

A silence, solid with tension, finally fissured as he said coolly, 'I could have told you ages ago. From the moment I saw you sitting in the hallway at South Parade, I knew I'd never again let you go. Do you know why I said nothing? I was frightened you'd spurn me like this. I knew you'd think me an unprincipled liar plotting to lure you into my decadent clutches…just for a short while, of course, until I found someone new and ejected you into the gutter. That's accurate, isn't it?'

Emma turned sideways, arms crossed over her middle, head back as she fought for composure.

'Come, admit it. It's how you read my character three years ago and how you see me now. I'm a selfish rake, so how could I possibly love you…or any woman? The truth is, Emma, I can't love any woman…just you, it seems. And the truth is, I've treated all those women to consideration and generosity if not to much time or affection. And the truth is, if I could change all of it, boast a history of dignified abstinence in the wilds of Derbyshire, I would do it for you. But I can't. And I won't lie. I regret some of my past; that's all I can say. You're my future. I love you. And I know you love me.'

'How do you know?' whispered out of her.

'You could have run the other way,' he said, with a quirk of a smile. 'But you didn't. You ran at me because you trusted me…because you loved me.'

Their eyes locked timelessly, then, because she knew it was

all truth, because he never lied, the tears finally spilled and her joy frothed into an explosive sob that squeezed tight her eyes.

Richard approached her slowly, stopped inches away. 'Say you love me or I won't hold you,' he threatened softly.

She leaned into him, crying.

'Say it!' erupted in a pleading growl.

'I love you…' she wailed, and was lifted off the ground and crushed to a broad, muscular torso. Fair and tawny hair mingled as he bent close, soothing her, whilst spinning them slowly about in sheer thankful happiness.

'We were reminiscing…where were we?' he said as she quietened and clung to him. 'Ah, yes, Abbey Wood where you ran away again and I caught you…and proved to us both, without a shadow of a doubt, that you were absolutely right. I am a novice.'

Emma's limpid golden eyes lifted to smoky grey, identifying pain behind his rueful humour. She shook her head. 'I didn't think that, Richard. I didn't think that at all.'

'I did,' he said huskily. 'The one time in my life when I needed it to be right and it all went so wrong. The one time, too, I merited being slapped but you were too anguished to do it and that terrified me. I thought I'd cowed you. The shame wasn't yours, sweetheart. It was mine. I swear I'll never again hurt you…'

'You didn't hurt me much,' Emma whispered, shielding her pink face with a hard shoulder. 'Not in the way you mean… It was a different hurt…more in my heart. And I don't blame you: I'd made you think I was unchaste and I wanted you…I said so…'

'I never gave you a chance to deny me. I only asked for consent when positive the seduction was done.' He sighed in remorse. 'I was furious with you, Emma,' he rawly admitted. 'When Stephen told me of the gossip circulating that evening in the Assembly Rooms, I knew it referred to you: you'd absconded from London and Dashwood, and I knew him for a sadistic fornicator. It all seemed to fall so logically into place. I was sure he must have violated you. And the galling thought of perhaps rearing his male child as my heir was racking me as I tracked Shah… Yet by the time I caught up with you I had become reconciled even to that: I loved you and would marry you no matter what. Then you seemed to defend him, which made me angrier… When I discovered you'd deceived me all along about being any man's lover…that I'd agonised needlessly over rearing any man's bastard as my own…I was too mad with relief and frustration to know what I was doing. It was impossible to decide whether to reward or punish you. So I veered between the two, I suppose, like a demented fool.' He laughed against her soft, thick hair. 'I told you you'd render me insane, Miss Worthington. And so it proved.'

'That's how it seemed, Richard,' Emma whispered with bashful wonderment. 'Exactly like that. As though you were both rewarding and punishing me. It was really quite…'

'Tell me, Emma, please. I need to know.'

'It was really quite…thrilling…unique, perhaps, for I've nothing to compare…' She glanced at him, horrified by what they were discussing, and her face flamed. 'I must be a terrible wanton to speak so…'

Long fingers threaded into her amber hair. 'No, you're not. Not yet…but with all that passion in you I'm optimistic…' As a small fist thumped his arm he grunted a laugh. 'It was thrilling and unique and unbearably erotic…just like you. But I swear it will be sweeter next time.'

Richard studied her beatific face, watched curiosity and shyness flit across her beautifully expressive features. He touched his mouth to the small, healing cut on her lower lip. 'Say you'll marry me—Emma, please. Put me out of my misery. I don't want to resort to blackmail and threaten your father with the Fleet.'

'That's not blackmail, sir, it's almost an inducement.' She sighed. 'I can't believe any sensible man would want my parents as his in-laws…'

'But I'm not sensible, sweetheart. I'm completely mad about you.'

She snuggled against him. 'I suppose I'll marry you, then,' she teased. 'Might we journey on the little way further to David and Victoria and let them be the first to know?'

At his smiling agreement, she queried brightly, 'If I'd boarded the coach would you have followed? Or had you really decided to give up?'

'I never expected you to leave. I was quite confident you'd never accept my money. Failing that, gentleman that I am, I would have given you a ten-minute head start.'

Dusky-fringed topaz eyes narrowed at him. 'You're very crafty…'

A smile impenitently acknowledged it. 'Are you grateful I don't give up?'

Emma nodded, blushing as his eyes became sultry.

'Show me,' he whispered huskily against her full, soft lips.

And with diligent inexpertise she did exactly that.

Shining amber and ebony tresses fluttered and tangled as Emma and Victoria whirled about joyfully then warmly embraced. Victoria spun Emma about again. Coming to a breathless halt, she blurted, 'Oh, it's so wonderful to see you, Em. Why did you not write and say you were coming? This is such a wonderful surprise! Oh, I just can't believe it. David!' she abruptly called. She peered past Emma along the Italian marble and mahogany hallway of her opulent home at the blond man smiling indulgently at them. 'And Dickie is with you! Why? How intriguing…David…*David*!' she squealed excitedly.

'What is it, Vicky?' A man's fond, firm baritone was heard as a door opened. David Hardinge, Viscount Courtenay emerged into the hallway in his shirt-sleeves, a black Labrador at each heel, looking for all the world like a contented country gentleman.

'Emma is here,' his lovely wife squeaked, with a double-handed indication. 'And Dickie, too!'

David stared, frowning, then a slow grin spread over his handsome features and he paced into the hallway. He stooped to embrace and kiss Emma on both cheeks then carried on walking.

He circled Richard, looking him up and down, then blue eyes targeted his friend's face. 'You look like a heathen with that ungodly colour. I told you you'd stay there too long. You should have come back last year, when you said you would.'

'Hello, David, it's good to see you, too,' Richard returned drily. He extended a hand as David did, gripped and embraced him in perfect unison, felt no embarrassment at the surge of emotion that tightened his chest, blocked his throat, clamped shut his eyes, for he was aware that David felt it equally. When finally they broke apart, David slid a hand to his shoulder, shook him with profound affection and croaked, 'It's been too long, Dickie. You're a bastard! You promised you'd be back last year.'

'I'm back now,' Richard said. 'I'm back for good.'

David smiled in understanding. 'I told you she liked you. I told you that three years ago.'

'I remember; I just wish you'd told me how much,' Richard laughed, as his grey eyes strayed past to linger lovingly on Emma.

'Ah, but that was for you to find out, my friend,' David said softly. 'Bit of a battle, was it?' he asked, with an elevation of his dark brows indicating he'd noticed the wound on Richard's head and his general air of fatigue. 'Come, let's find somewhere comfortable to sit and something ancient and alcoholic with which to celebrate. You can tell me all about it while the girls gossip. You're going to be a godfather again…' David added brightly.

Richard looked at him, then at Victoria, and he shook his head emotionally. 'That's marvellous!'

* * *

Richard lifted his feet to rest them on the small table close to David's. They were seated outdoors on the flare-lit, flagged terrace that ran the length of the southerly wing overlooking magnificent formal gardens that marched off into shadows. He sank back in the comfortable chair, threw back his pale head and studied the night sky.

The breathtaking beauty of it struck him anew as he pondered the many times that he and this man had sat beneath it together: in amicable contentment, as they did now, when no words were necessary; in appalling anguish as they had on battlefields a decade and more ago, when no words were possible. Then there were the numerous occasions between those polar instances when wenching, drinking, brawling in their youth. He lifted his glass to his lips, drew on his cheroot, then asked David, 'What are you thinking?'

There was a pause before David replied, 'I'm thinking if it wasn't for you I'd have nothing. No life… I owe everything I've got to you…'

A dark hand came out and comfortingly gripped his friend's forearm resting on the chair beside him. 'It was a long time ago and I would have expected the same from you…you know that.' With sublime disparity he added, 'Besides, you taught me about investing in stocks and shares.'

After a little undisturbed drinking and smoking, David asked, 'What are *you* thinking?'

Richard turned his head and smiled crookedly. 'I'm thinking, if I'm perfectly honest, you drove me to such distraction with your antics, I came close to killing you myself on occasion.'

'What are you really thinking?' David asked mildly.

'I'm thinking I've never felt so bloody done up.'

'I remember that…' David said with a huge grin. 'Courting can be hellish hard work.'

Richard smiled at the stars. 'I'm also thinking you must have a few interconnecting chambers in this damned great place of yours.'

'Victoria allocates guest rooms, Dickie,' his friend solemnly teased. 'Nothing to do with me which room you get.'

'Make it to do with you,' Richard mock-threatened, 'or I might remind you you owe me everything.'

'You sound desperate…'

Richard sat forward abruptly and shoved vibrating fingers under his friend's face. 'Look at that!'

David obligingly inspected his friend's shaking hand. 'Nasty graze,' he observed. 'I hope Dashwood's looking a worse mess.'

'Dashwood's looking a corpse; and that's what he should be…' was gritted out in response.

'No,' David said gently. 'Trelawney was right. I wouldn't have let you kill him either. If you had, it would have ruined everything. It would have tainted your future with Emma. You've done the right thing.'

Closely watching Richard's rigid profile, David asked quietly, 'You're happy enough, though?'

Richard stared into his glass, stared at a velvet blue, diamantéd horizon. 'Happier than I've ever been. It's like finally finding peace…it's hard to explain…'

David nodded. 'I know,' he said huskily. 'That's exactly it. And in a moment that peace will take us inside. We'll retire before midnight, whereas once we'd have set out about now and returned watching the dawn come up, trailing empty bottles.'

Richard sank back into his chair, shaking with cathartic hilarity that bordered on hysteria, and the infectious sound soon had David guffawing too. The tension of the past torturous, hectic weeks finally released, Richard gasped, wiping at his eyes, 'Perhaps it's just our age, Davey…we're not getting any younger.'

David shook his head, smiling nostalgically. 'We had some good times,' he stressed slowly. 'Some damn good times…'

'Yes…' Richard agreed, with a far-away smile. 'Definitely plenty to tell the grandchildren…'

'Well…grandsons, perhaps.…' David corrected him with a wry grimace.

And with that they shoved back their chairs and strolled into the grand house, two black dogs padding after them.

'And then what happened?' Victoria whispered, agog, her eyes fixed on her friend's lightly bruised face as Emma came close to concluding her narrative of the action that had buffeted her between heartache and heaven over the past weeks.

'My papa says that Dashwood still lives but has been dealt with. I've not had a chance to ask Richard exactly how. On the way here we barely spoke two words…' She shot an expressive glance at Victoria. 'It's possible to drive a curricle and pair one-handed, you know; or get the tiger to take the reins.'

'I do know,' Victoria said, with a shrewd little smile. 'It's amazing how very ingenious an amorous man can be. Oh, not that he's ever had any practice whatsoever, you understand, in kissing and cuddling while keeping a straight path on the road,' was added ironically.

Emma gave a little laughing scowl. 'They are so very alike, aren't they?'

'Indeed; that's why you have nothing to fret over. They do reform, you know. David is perfect in every way: a wonderful husband and a doting papa.'

As the last pitcher of steaming water filled the porcelain tub, Victoria dismissed the servants then helped her friend disrobe.

Emma sank into the luxury of warm, perfumed water, sighing as it lapped at her weary body. 'But I'm so glad Richard did not kill Dashwood,' she murmured sleepily. 'It would have overshadowed all this bliss.'

Victoria rhythmically soaped Emma's creamy, slender back with scented soap. 'Well, I'm sure Richard has taught him a good lesson! David says Dickie can be a vicious fighter. The vile man will never again dare bother you.'

As Emma dipped her head, Victoria gently poured a stream of warm water over her long, amber hair. She leaned forward and whispered, 'You sly thing! Why did you never let on that you liked Dickie? You never had a good word for him. You always said you thought him a disgraceful libertine.'

Emma shook back dripping tan tresses, making Victoria squeal as the droplets scattered over her face and gown. 'And so he is!' Emma endorsed fiercely. Then she sighed, 'But I love him anyway. I expect I'd love him even if he didn't reform…and that's quite worrying.'

'He *is* a fine gentleman, Emma,' Victoria quietly reassured her. 'I love him myself for he brought David home from the war alive when he wanted to die on foreign soil. I've never made much of it to you before because you seemed to hold Dickie in such disfavour. Besides, Dickie never willingly speaks of it and it's almost like breaking a confidence. He is not one to brag so I shall tell you what sort of heroic man your future husband is. When I wed my first husband—in David's absence abroad, and in ignorance of him still loving and wanting to marry me—David was so mad with grief he returned to the battlefields. He deliberately sought out peril and Richard followed, shielding him until he could bring them both back safely…to a heroes' welcome. I owe Dickie so much—all my happiness—and I'm so glad my best friend is to have him. I couldn't wish for more. You make such an excellent couple and I'm so happy for you I feel I could burst.'

Emma closed hot, wet eyes. 'I'm not surprised at his courage,' she gasped. 'I know he is a worthy man. In truth, he always attracted me far too much. I understand that now. But I never believed he would sincerely notice me and I couldn't bear being just another conquest. I feel…felt so vulnerable when with him. So I would never allow him close. I think part of me always knew, once we touched, he could shatter all my defences and make me do anything he asked.'

Victoria put a hand to her dewy eyes. Laughing and sniffing, she said, 'Neither of us must say anything else likely to make the other blub.' Briskly she added, 'Now let me tell you happy news: David is to again be a papa.'

Emma touched Victoria's arm with a damp hand. 'I'm so pleased for you, Vicky. I'm so pleased for me, too. Despite everything, it has all turned out so right for us both.'

'Begging pardon, your ladyship,' one of the young maids meekly interrupted. 'His lordship wants to speak to you downstairs,' she informed Victoria with a deferential little bob.

'David probably wants to show Lucy to her godfather. If she is awake I shall bring her in to you, too, before you retire.'

With a huge, warm towel draping her slender curves, Emma dismissed the young maid with a smile and murmur of thanks. She sat on the high feather mattress dabbing at her damp hair and body. She shook out the nightclothes Vicky had found for her, thinking of Richard, and the need to see him once more before she slept had her sinking slowly backwards onto the bed, eyes closed. She turned onto her side, peeping through drowsy lids at a star-studded night. Nestling her head into the pillow, she smiled softly, privately, realising she had never felt more languidly tranquil.

As she heard the door click, she murmured, 'Is Richard yet retired, Vicky? I'd really like to wish him goodnight.'

'Good. He really wants to let you do so,' came back softly.

Emma shot upright on the bed, damp towel clutched tightly.

She moistened her lips as he walked slowly into the candlelit room. He had never before seemed so tall, so blond, so handsome…or so devastatingly predatory.

'Richard…I…I just wanted to say goodnight and…'

As he passed the tub he dipped his hand into the water, testing it.

'Good, it's still warm.'

Emma stared at him as he began to loosen his cravat then dropped it to the floor. His jacket soon followed and she realised what he intended. 'Richard…!' she squealed in a gulp. 'I don't think you should. You shouldn't be here! It's not seemly... You can't! The servants might gossip. David and Victoria might be embarrassed...'

Naked to the waist, he reached her and stooped to lightly brush his brandy-scented mouth over hers. 'Hush. I just want to hold you, that's all. I want to sleep with you in my arms. As far as the servants are concerned, we're married; it's only a few days before the event. And don't fret over David,' he added with a crooked smile. 'Nothing embarrasses him.'

Within a moment more he was blithely lowering his awesomely powerful physique into the tub, with a long exhalation of sheer ease.

Emma watched him with a mingling of horror and fascination. She knew he had been naked in the woods when he'd made love to her—in retrospect she had wondered how on earth he had managed to shed even his shirt when she couldn't clearly recall him releasing her long enough to undo one button—but she had seen little of him, her eyes had been closed so much. Now, as he began soaping himself, she let the towels clutched to her drop, and hastily pulled the embroidered lawn nightgown over her head. Once decently attired, she approached the tub and sank down behind him.

Richard continued bathing, almost as though he was unaware of her proximity, so, retrieving the soap from the dish, she lathered an expanse of tanned torso, her fingertips exploring little dips and nicks here and there on his back. She noticed the large muscles in his broad shoulders flex as she began her ministrations.

'Do you like it when I touch you like this?' she asked curiously.

His silver head dipped at the water and he smiled. 'I love it when you touch me in any way, Emma.'

Emma dropped the soap to the dish and ran two slippery palms up the smooth, firm contours at either side of his spine. Large hands covered her fingers as they strayed playfully over his shoulders to splay on the satin-sheathed steel of his chest.

Emma frowned at the nasty lacerations across four knuckles. 'Your poor hand,' she sighed sorrowfully. 'It will never heal.'

He sank back into the tub and ebony-pupilled grey eyes caressed her. 'That's nothing, sweetheart. I've had far worse injuries than that.' He took her hand resting on the side of the bath and ran it over a faint, proud scar on a forearm. 'A piece of a Frenchman's bayonet is in there somewhere.' Raising her fingers, he pressed them to the base of his skull and she sensed the dip. 'A bullet in the Peninsular...'

He continued teaching her about his body via the wounds he'd sustained over the years. Finally, he slid her hand below the water and to his hip and moved her small fingers over a ragged cicatrice. She looked enquiringly at him. 'Another shrapnel wound?' she guessed.

'A broken bottle. I rolled on it while brawling in Cheapside. Close to your home as I recall. About fifteen years ago. The dolt of a physician who stitched it was more drunk than me. It never knitted properly.'

'I was twelve then. You were fighting outside my home when I was twelve...' Emma murmured.

'Shall I show you how much I want you, Emma?' he softly asked as his slate gaze roved over lambent amber eyes, the fluffy halo of damp fawn hair lightly curling and framing her pointed, pixie face.

At her almost imperceptible nod, she felt his fingers mesh with hers underwater, then he moved her hand so the back of it slowly skimmed the silky fever of erect manhood on its way back to the surface. She watched his reaction with awe. His eyes closed, his breathing ceased for that infinite moment and the planes of his lean, handsome face seemed equally stiff.

'Is this what a mistress does?' she whispered. 'Washes you and...touches you? I am your mistress now, aren't I?'

Eyes still closed, one side of his sensual mouth relaxed into a smile. 'You're my fiancée now. And I can't recall,' he mentioned with convenient amnesia, 'any mistress helping me bathe.'

Raising their clasped fingers, he kissed the back of her wet hand before letting it go and abruptly standing up. Emma averted her eyes hurriedly and handed him a towel. As he dried himself she wandered back to the bed and perched upon it, watching from beneath lowered lids…and thinking… thinking.

'It…it might be best if you return to your own chamber, Richard, now you have bathed… Please…'

He tucked a towel about his waist and proceeded to dry his hair as though he'd not heard her.

'There are still some things we should talk of before we again… That is…'

'What things?' flew out from beneath the towel over his head.

'I don't believe…I find it hard to believe that you truly love me,' she whispered raggedly.

As the towel was whipped from his hair and hurled towards a chair, Emma sprang to her feet, then sank back to shift uneasily on the mattress again.

'Why is that?' he enquired, dead calm.

'I've…I've treated you so badly,' she croaked. 'I've lied constantly, been deceitful, hit you and insulted you. I even swindled your money for those dinners at Mrs Keene's. Why would someone as worthy and generous as you love a person as mean as me?' she cried in anguish. 'And I'm not young or pretty…'

With a curse he crossed the room in two strides, so fast, she shot backwards to the centre of the enormous bed. With tender obstinacy, he pulled her to the edge. Lifting her, he carried her towards the pier-glass then spun her about to face it. A muscular brown arm banded her tight to his hard, hot body, her toes barely touching the floor, her nightdress askew and displaying the perfection of one long, lissom leg. 'What do you see?' he demanded.

When she tried to avoid looking at her reflection, a hand

went to her face, tilting it up. 'Look, Emma,' he instructed hoarsely. 'Tell me what you see.'

Hesitantly she looked into the glass. Wide, dusky-fringed oval eyes stared back at her with the liquid profundity of precious stones. Her hair crumpled over the snowy cambric of her nightgown like amber satin and her complexion was tinged with a peachy blush.

Richard's hand framed her jaw, his thumb following the curve of her full lower lip. 'I'll tell you what I see, shall I? I see a woman who three years ago fascinated me because she, alone, shunned my company. She hinted that I was a shameless hedonist and she wanted nothing to do with me. And I knew then that she was special to me. Not just because she had the courage to tell me the truth but because she was beautiful. Not conventionally pretty, but uniquely beautiful. When I saw you dressed like this at Mrs Keene's boarding house that first evening in Bath, and you threatened to accuse me of rape, it was dangerously close to prophecy, Emma. I thought I'd never seen anything quite so tempting in my life. That's how you affect me. I've been fighting to keep my hands off you most of the time. Not touching you has been a constant ordeal. And you've known that. Deep down, in here…' he slid a possessive hand over a breast to rest on the quivering ribs beneath it '…you've known that very well. That's why you've insulted me and hit me and been deceitful; it's the only defence you've had and I've never once blamed you for using it.'

Emma's eyes rose to his in the glass and clung, adored him. 'I see a lovely, lucky woman and the wonderful man she loves…her Silver Squire.'

He smiled and dipped his head to rest a bronze cheek atop her tawny hair. She twisted immediately to face him, sliding her arms up around him and hugging him close, closer still as though she would fuse their bodies.

'I love you. Don't ever say again that I don't or that you're undeserving, or plain. Whatever rubbish your mother's drummed into you over your looks, is just that. Utter rubbish! You're the most beautiful thing I've ever seen,' he vowed huskily as he swung her up in his arms and carried her to the bed.

Chapter Sixteen

'What were you and Richard talking about?' Viscountess Courtenay asked her husband as he lounged, naked to the waist, on the edge of the bed, watching her brush her glossy jet hair.

'Business ventures we're contemplating, our misspent youth, women…that we love…' he tacked on with a teasing smile as he saw her eyes narrow and glide to his reflection in the dressing-table glass. 'And how inquisitive they become at entirely the wrong time. Your hair looks perfect, sweetheart. Come to bed,' he ordered huskily. When she still gazed dreamily into space he added, 'Oh, Dickie also told me that Wainwright and Mainwaring are coming to Hertfordshire to kidnap me and take me back to Mayfair and a life of vice.'

'Don't tell stories, David! I'm not prying…I'm just interested in your reunion with your best friend.'

'I never lie to you, Vicky,' he reminded her, with a smile.

Victoria rose from her stool, contentedly aware, as always, of her husband's deceptively sleepy blue gaze on her. 'Perhaps you manipulate the truth a little. I think they make an excellent couple.' She happily reverted to her original train of thought. 'I've never said so, because I thought Emma truly disliked him, and thus it would never be, but I've always hoped they would fall in love. I'm so happy tonight.'

'Me too. I'll be happier still when you come here.'

In obeisance, she gracefully swayed up the three steps to their decadently large four-poster. David lithely came upright; his hands shot out, were placed firmly on her hips, and directed her between his spaced feet. Her idle fingers combed through lengthy strands of dark hair while she smiled serenely into space. 'I could tell three years ago that Dickie was interested in getting to know her better. But then I couldn't be sure what was designed, so I said nothing to Emma. After all,' she remarked archly, 'the most honourable intentions sometimes, confusingly, masquerade as lechery...so *I've* found...so Emma, *also*, has found...' She squealed as a warm hand deftly breached her diaphanous nightgown. It ran possessively up a smooth, shapely leg on its way to cup and caress a pert derrière.

'But we're alike in other ways, too,' David purred. 'So you need not fret your friend might be seduced by my friend beneath our roof, then abandoned.'

'Richard does love her so very much, doesn't he? Oh...the deed is already done,' Victoria insouciantly added, with a flick of a slender white hand.

'Yes, he loves her utterly, and... Has he, indeed?' David grunted an approving, male laugh. 'He didn't tell me that.'

Victoria sighed with pleasure, her eyes drowsy, as a tender mouth steamed kisses against her lace-covered midriff and reverent fingers stroked her baby-rounded abdomen. 'Tell me what he did say,' she persevered.

'He wants to give her everything she's never had: beautiful clothes, fabulous jewels, whatever her heart desires.' Her doting husband truthfully indulged her curiosity.

Victoria smiled contentedly down at him. 'He *is* so like you. And Emma *is* like me. All she wants is Richard. She'd take him as a pauper.'

'I know. So does he. But it won't stop him wanting to give her the sun...the moon...the stars...'

Victoria placed her hands on her husband's broad, naked

shoulders. They slid over his cool, solid flesh, then she pushed him down onto the bed and flopped on top of him. 'Oh, that's impossible, David!' she giggled as she enveloped him in silky, rose-scented skin and hair. 'You already gave those to me…'

'Will your mother be disappointed?'

'Disappointed? Why should she be?'

'I imagine she hoped you'd marry well,' Emma quietly mentioned. 'A duke's daughter would have been preferable to…' The rest was muffled by his body as he urged her closer, dropped a kiss on a crown of burnished coppery-gold hair resting against his shoulder.

'She's a little like your own dear mama in one respect: she's keen to see me wed; to whom matters little. She's seen David reform and, damn him,' he chuckled, 'ever since he renounced bachelorhood, I've been treated to veiled lectures on the redeeming effect of a good woman.'

At Emma's solemn silence he reassured her, 'She'll be delighted with her new daughter-in-law. She's often said how much she likes you. She realised straight away I cherished you but imagined it was a platonic love. Amelia let slip to her that you were in Bath because of a romantic attachment. Had she not, it would by now have occurred to my mother to put you in my way.'

'Do you really think so?' Emma asked doubtfully.

'Oh, yes,' he said drily. 'She said you'd make someone an excellent wife and that your beau would be a fool not to propose. She also said that with a little embellishment you'd be stunning.'

'What did you say?' Emma asked, unsure if she was pleased or mortified.

'I said I was confident you would soon be wed, and that it was pointless primping perfection.'

In thanks for the compliment, Emma languorously grazed her cheek against the masculine skin beneath it. 'I think our mothers mingling will result in a volatile reception. Might we wed quietly, Richard…and soon, and present them all with a *fait accompli*? Please?'

'Oh, yes,' he agreed, with a grunting laugh. 'Very quietly and very, very soon. Before we journey back to London or Silverdale. Perhaps in the chapel at Hartfield…as David and Vicky did. It would take but a few days to arrange, if you don't mind wearing a gown purchased locally. Vicky can attend you and David act as my groomsman.'

Emma closed her eyes, sighed her quiet rapture. 'I'm so happy, Richard.'

'Good,' he said huskily. 'Then I am, too.'

'Truly?'

'Truly.'

She shifted against him, her legs nudging his, almost accidentally. They had been lying wrapped together for so many long, blissful minutes while they talked, yet he'd made no attempt to kiss her properly or touch her. Had he meant what he said about simply wanting to hold her? Sleep with her in his arms? Part of her wanted that to be true…wanted to admire his noble restraint…and part of her wanted to demand he kiss her into insensibility. Now acknowledged, the longing niggled, making her fidget.

'Richard?'

'Mmm?'

'I'd like it if you kissed me goodnight.'

'I can't do that, sweetheart. Go to sleep.'

Stung into silence for a moment, she then gasped, 'Why not?' anxiously wondering whether she was ignorant of a physical reason preventing it.

'I can't lie in bed with you and kiss you…then stop. Just holding you so close is torture. You know how much I want you, Emma…I showed you,' he reminded her huskily.

After a throbbing quiet, Emma ventured demurely, 'Will you still cuddle me till I sleep?'

'You could have given my hard predicament a little more sympathetic thought, sweet.'

His low, velvety reproof, thick with need, made a delicious shiver ripple through her. And she *was* giving it thought…too much. She could scent rich earth, balmy night air; hear woodland musically sighing, while guttural noises rasped her throat. She could sense soft lips, hard fingers flowing over her, branding, tantalising… 'What have you done with Dashwood?' she distractingly burst out, reflexively clinging to him as her heart hammered with stimulation.

Mistaking her agitation for fright, strong arms and legs bound her to him, as though he would calm and protect her by merging their flesh. 'Don't worry about him, sweetheart. He's finished with.'

'But what have you done with him?'

'Sent him back to Jamaica. I'm sure there'll be a welcoming committee: newly freed slaves with memories of their own or their kins' dealings with him over two decades. They'll be anxious for a quick reunion.'

Thick sable lashes brushed up. She stared at the unaltered rhythmic rising and falling of bronze skin beneath her cheek, his warmth wafting a light herb scent of the water they had both bathed in. 'Will they kill him?'

'First chance they get.'

She pushed back from him and looked down into silver eyes, smoky in the muted glow of the candlelit chamber. He raised a hand, threaded it into her long amber hair, savouring the sensation of it streaming through the forks of his fingers. Smoothing it away from her face, he anchored its sheeny weight by winding it about a broad palm so her delicate, elfin features were revealed. 'Does that worry you? That people he has tormented and abused for years might finally settle scores?'

'I don't think so,' Emma whispered. 'I know now he is a very evil man. Had he managed to abduct me, he would have shown me no mercy…'

'Hush. Don't speak of it,' Richard groaned, drawing her down into the security of his arms. 'I can't bear to think of it.

You asked me to verify his devilry and I stupidly said nothing. And it wasn't simply to avoid frightening you. If I'm truthful, resentment played a part. I was sure you believed me equally despicable. I should have told you that no gossip did justice to his depravity. It might have stopped you meeting him. Arrogantly, I trusted forbidding it would be adequate.'

'Don't blame yourself, Richard!' Emma cried, distraught on seeing his eyes glaze. 'I might not have heeded your warning, in any case: I so wanted to atone for my escapades that I acted with little sense or caution.' After a short pause, she quizzed, 'But how did you persuade him to go?'

'I gave him a choice: a little sojourn abroad while he licked his wounds and pondered the error of his ways or a magistrate and all the attendant ignominy of a prosecution for having Cavendish kidnapped and beaten, and for assaulting and plotting to abduct my fiancée. Once he'd obligingly burned that marriage contract he had no hard proof of being defrauded or that you were ever betrothed. He has always deluded himself he has some reputation and standing. He hates ridicule and would want none of this broadcast.

'His henchmen are probably gone to ground but with a little incentive they'd betray Dashwood and he knows it. He also knows my capacity for retribution is enduring and far outstrips his. That worries him the most: that I'll hound him to the grave. When I told him I intended soon marrying you, he was very keen to put distance between us.'

'I feel terribly guilty that Matthew was embroiled in this...'

'I'll make it up to him. Financially, he and his family will never want.'

Emma looked at his taut jaw, his eyes fixed on the pleated damask canopy above. As she wriggled closer, her silky tawny hair trailed his torso; tender lips touched a lean, brown cheek. 'I never really loved him, Richard. But he was a good friend. There's never been anyone else in all my life I've liked in that way. Except you, of course. But then that's so different...so much more...' She watched the tension in his face relax as she struggled to voice her devotion to him. 'Even three years ago you set my heart racing,' she shyly confided. 'Although I would have died rather than let you know, of course. I was sure you would never really be interested in me…and it hurt.'

'How interested did you want me to be, sweetheart?' he laughed. 'I almost proposed. David realised…probably before I did myself…that I'd fallen in love at first sight. I was captivated by everything about you: your looks, your wit… everything about you. What I should have done,' he said, with a thoughtful smile, 'was drag you over to your mother at that tedious soirée and offer for you there and then. I'm sure I would have got her approval.'

'*Approval?*' Emma choked. 'Oh, I *daren't* think! She might have dropped to the floor and kissed your feet…she *still* might!' she cried in genuine dread.

'If I'd asked you to marry me three years ago, would you have accepted?'

'Oh, yes; I would never have let you go. Had you reconsidered when sober, I would have sued you for breach of promise. I would have hounded *you*…chased *you* from place to place.'

'Sounds like heaven… If only I'd known…' he growled ruefully. 'So, in fact, Cavendish didn't figure too seriously even then,' he mused with an amount of masculine satisfaction.

'It was always just an infatuation. Have you never been enamoured, Richard?'

'I'm totally enamoured now.'

'You know I mean when you were younger.'

'In my impressionable youth I suppose I was regularly besotted with pretty opera dancers or opera singers…or their like…'

'How do you know you didn't love them all?' Emma asked, a trifle waspishly now she'd prised the revelation from him.

'Because it happened so regularly, sweetheart,' he said, with a wry laugh. 'After six months or so with a blonde I'd fancy a brunette, or they'd feel inclined towards someone richer, or someone offering commitment. It was all just a trade of basic needs. By the time I reached my late twenties it would never have occurred to me to still fool myself over motives.'

As Emma started to withdraw, his hands curved about the tops of her arms. He slid her on top of him, locking her slender, satiny legs under the hair-roughened, brawny length of his. 'Do you know what makes it all so insignificant, Emma?' he asked gently. 'In your dignified innocence you're more erotic than any of them…all of them.'

Emma dipped her face, then lambent doe eyes rose, met his, hoping to learn more.

– 'If I had no money at all, you'd stay. You love me touching you. You respond because you can't help it. You respond even when you'd rather not…and never because there might be clothes or cash or trinkets in it for you. You haven't the artifice to deny me until the price is right. Do you know how wonderful that makes me feel? How powerful? The money I gave you at the tavern kept you with me. But not as a bribe or as a payment. I knew you'd stay long enough to return it. With any other woman I've wanted they'd stay long enough to spend it. If I was dispossessed tomorrow I know I'd still have you in my bed, loving me. There's never been anyone else I could trust to stay in those circumstances. But, in truth, I've avoided those who might. I've chosen to keep company with venal women. I've never felt guilty about putting any off or refusing to fight to lure back any tempted away. I'd die for you. Give you everything I have. That's how powerful you are.'

Emma whispered his name, traced feather-light fingers over his hard, angular jaw. She relaxed down onto him, nestling her head into the cosy cleft on his shoulder.

'What happens in the end?'

'What?' she whispered, frowning against his face.

'I didn't finish the novel. Does Darcy marry Elizabeth? I imagine so.'

She giggled, with sheer silly joy, her body bumping against his, causing the proof of his noble restraint to burn, like a hot, hard log, into her belly. 'Of course! He's an honourable gentleman who acknowledges the error of his arrogant ways. He kindly pays debts incurred by a wastrel relation of Elizabeth's and wins her love and respect.'

'Sounds like a fantasy…'

She recognised the wry laughter in his voice. 'That's why I liked it so. I liked fantasising that one day I would happily marry such a worthy man.'

From the edge of an eye, she watched the corners of his mouth lift, his long, lush lashes fall. He rolled over slowly, holding her close until she was turned completely onto her back. Idly he braced himself over her.

A trusting golden gaze merged with silver gleaming down at her as a knuckle brushed slowly, rhythmically against her cheek. 'Do you fantasise a lot?' he asked, something in his honeyed, husky tone sending those thrilling tremors hurtling through her again.

'I…I used to daydream about the characters in novels…pretend them real. I used to like to go elsewhere in my head,' she self-consciously revealed.

'Well, next time you go…every time…take me with you?' The request was accompanied by an appealing smile. 'Shall we now fantasise that you're happily to marry a worthy man?'

Pearly lids veiled topaz eyes and a sultry smile curved her soft mouth. 'I thought you were too mature to still play games.'

'Oh, some games improve with maturity.'

'Who sets the rules?' she asked in a tiny, breathy voice.

'You do.'

'Always?'

'Always.'

'But…my rules are that I'd only happily marry a worthy man I adore, a man who will give me sweet, tender loving, for so I've been promised.'

'And so it shall be...I solemnly swear...until you want more.'

At her quick, startled look, a soundless laugh preceded gentle reassurance. 'You'll know when... Shall I tell you my favourite fantasy?' he offered casually. He could see a confusion of innocent curiosity and suspicion in her beautifully limpid eyes, but, after an indecisive moment, she nodded. 'On each wedding anniversary I should like it if you stole Shah and fled to the woods...'

'Will you be angry when you chase me?' she asked with sweet solemnity.

'Only if you want me to be... You make the rules.'

Emma slid a small hand up into fine ivory hair, gently touched the wound beneath his fringe, grazed the backs of her fingers along the stubble on his shady jaw, feeling utterly at peace in her love and trust and loyalty.

'Whatever happened to my wicked silver squire?' she teased.

'Whatever happened to my fiery wildcat?'

She drew his head down slowly until their mouths nearly touched, wanting to prove her adoration his way. 'Take me back now to find them, Richard...'

*   *   *   *   *

Don't miss the conclusion to Mary Brendan's Regency duet in Volume 6 of the *The Regency Lords & Ladies Collection,* available in December 2005.

Celebrate the charm of Christmases past in three new heartwarming holiday tales!

COMFORT AND JOY by Margaret Moore
1860 Llanwyllan, Wales

After a terrible accident, Griffin Branwynne gives up on the joys of Christmas—until the indomitable Gwendolyn Davies arrives on his doorstep and turns his world upside-down. Can the earl resist a woman who won't take no for an answer?

LOVE AT FIRST STEP by Terri Brisbin
1199 England

While visiting friends in England for the holidays, Lord Gavin MacLeod casts his eye upon the mysterious Elizabeth. She is more noble beauty than serving wench, and Gavin vows to uncover her past—at any cost!

A CHRISTMAS SECRET by Gail Ranstrom
1819 Oxfordshire, England

Miss Charity Wardlow expects a marriage proposal from her intended while attending a Christmas wedding. But when Sir Andrew MacGregor arrives at the manor, Charity realises that she prefers this Scotsman with the sensual smile...

On sale 2nd December 2005

MILLS & BOON

Live the emotion

*H*istorical
romance™

THE SLEEPING BEAUTY
by Jacqueline Navin

Lady Helena Rathford is a coveted matrimonial prize
– one adventurous Adam Mannion is determined to
win. He'll wed her, bed her – then hasten to London,
his prospects and his future secure. But then he meets
Helena – and rather than becoming his prize, she
becomes his whole world…

THE OUTRAGEOUS DEBUTANTE
by Anne O'Brien

Theodora Wooton-Devereux and Lord Nicholas
Faringdon are not enthusiastic participants in the game
of love – until a chance meeting sets them on a different
course. Soon the handsome gentleman and the beautiful
– though unconventional – débutante are the talk of the
town, but fate is not on their side. A shocking scandal
rears its head and forbids that they may be united…

On sale 2nd December 2005

*Available at most branches of WHSmith, Tesco, ASDA,
Borders, Eason, Sainsbury's and most bookshops*

Visit www.millsandboon.co.uk